MIDNIGHT
OBSESSION

ALSO BY MELINDA LEIGH

Scarlet Falls Novels

Hour of Need
Minutes to Kill
Seconds to Live

She Can Series

She Can Run
She Can Tell
She Can Scream
She Can Hide
He Can Fall (A Short Story)
She Can Kill

Midnight Novels

Midnight Exposure
Midnight Sacrifice
Midnight Betrayal

Rogue River Novellas

Gone to Her Grave
Walking on Her Grave

Rogue Winter Novellas

Tracks of Her Tears

Rogue Vows Novellas

Burned by Her Devotion

MELINDA LEIGH

MIDNIGHT OBSESSION

Montlake
Romance

Text copyright © 2017 Melinda Leigh
All rights reserved.

Published by Montlake Romance, Seattle

www.apub.com

Amazon, the Amazon logo, and Montlake Romance are trademarks of Amazon.com, Inc., or its affiliates.

ISBN-13: 9781503939257
ISBN-10: 1503939251

Cover design by Jason Blackburn

Printed in the United States of America

For my kids.
I'm so proud of the adults you've become.

CHAPTER
1

Come inside or you'll catch your death!

Words from Nicole's childhood rolled through her head as she clip-clopped around a patch of ice on the cracked sidewalk.

Stupidest saying ever. Who the hell would chase their own death? It should end with *death will catch you.* Since she'd been orphaned and homeless at fourteen, it was only a matter of time until Nicole and Death stopped playing tag.

Her micro skirt and stilettos left her legs exposed to a February that had gone from cold to brutal. A gust whipped around the corner and under the hem of her Goodwill coat, rattling her bones like ice cubes in a glass.

She should go inside, but she didn't do lots of things she should.

Chewing on a fingernail, she thought about ditching this last client. Deon would get real mad. When he sent her out, he expected her to return with money. She weighed her options. Go home, get a beating. Stay here, freeze her ass off. She shivered hard. But Deon knew how to beat a girl. Probably because he liked it. Plus, her greedy need for a high was almost as relentless as Deon's demands for cash. She'd finish what she'd started.

But Nicole glanced up the street and saw nothing but icy black-top shining under the streetlight and steam fogging from the storm drains. Her client was late, and the emptiness of the night bumped her anxiety to high. The quiet wasn't natural, not in this neighborhood. West Philadelphia hadn't improved since the Fresh Prince left town.

Come on.

A dark blue van rolled to a stop in front of her. *Finally.* Nicole trotted out to the curb on tiptoes, her feet numb, her legs shaky and frozen.

The vehicle's window lowered, but the driver's face was shadowed. "Get in."

She opened the passenger door and slid into the seat. The inside of the vehicle smelled funny—metallic, almost sweet. He drove away from the curb. Teeth chattering, she looked behind her, but a curtain separated the front of the vehicle from the cargo area in the back.

The driver flipped a switch on the dash. Heat blasted from the vents.

"Thanks." She brought her face around to the windshield and raised her hands to the warm air as the vehicle climbed an on-ramp. *Wait.* "Why are we on the expressway?"

Usually, customers wanted to get on with it.

"You'll see." A few minutes later, he exited toward the waterfront and drove past the marine terminal. Lights moved in the darkness as they rolled by the rail yard and its sky-high stacks of storage containers.

"Where are we going?" she asked.

"You'll see when we get there." Impatience sharpened his voice.

"You only booked an hour." How far was he going to drive?

"Don't worry. We'll be done well before then."

Nicole glanced over her shoulder, alarm prickling her neck. As the interior warmed, the smell from the cargo area intensified. She envisioned a stained mattress and bedding that hadn't been washed in years.

Get over it!

She'd done worse. Much worse.

A dirty mattress wouldn't kill her. At least she'd be out of the cold and wind. But he had a van. Why hadn't he just pulled into an alley? He didn't need to drive this far for a little privacy. The cold snap had driven most bodies off the street. Cops had been rounding up the homeless and forcing them into shelters all week. Frozen bums weren't good for the City of Brotherly Love's image.

At least it was warm in the van, and he couldn't be *that* bad. He'd been considerate enough to crank the heat for her, right? She should be grateful.

Then what was setting off her creeper alarm?

She glanced to her left. An overhead light passed over the vehicle, casting his profile in shadow. His focus was on the road, not on her. Most men who hired her were already thinking about sex, looking, touching, making sure they were getting what they paid for. But this guy didn't even seem all that interested in her.

She opened her coat as the interior warmed. Might as well give him a look at what he was paying for. She shifted, crossing her legs and flashing the merchandise. But he continued to stare through the windshield, distracted by whatever was going down in his own head.

Weird.

He slowed as they neared a construction site on Columbus Boulevard. Mounds of dirt shrouded with black tarps surrounded a cleared area. Snow and ice topped the mounds like whipped frosting on devil's food cupcakes.

He parked, and she scanned the area. The site was empty. She couldn't see anything beyond the piles of dirt except the skyline, where the lights of the Walt Whitman Bridge glowed.

"Wait here." He climbed out of the van.

She heard the rear door open, then lots of scraping sounds as he took something out of the back. Making room?

He opened her door and extended a gloved hand. "Come here."

"Outside?" Her voice squeaked like a dog toy. Her first thought was that he had to be kidding, but one look at his eyes told her he was dead serious. Her belly went queasy. She'd been on the street for years, working just about every day. Sheryl had come home beaten multiple times. Once Nicole had had to take her to the emergency room. Until tonight, Nicole had been fortunate.

But her luck had run out.

She took his hand. His fingers closed around hers in a solid grip. Strong. Very strong. Too strong for her to do anything but what she was told. She couldn't run in her heels, and she wouldn't get fifty feet barefoot on the icy ground.

There wasn't anyone around to hear her scream.

Her knees wobbled as she climbed out of the van. The cold punched through her coat and shook her to the marrow.

He handed her a flask. "Drink."

Taking it, she tilted it to her lips and sipped. Whiskey burned a fiery path through the center of her body but didn't manage to warm her.

"I have a script for you to read."

Great. He wanted to role-play in the middle of an Arctic front. What was up with him? Her creep meter kept waving back and forth between *He's OK* and *He's going to kill me.*

"Can't I read this inside the van?" She shivered, her teeth clacking like castanets.

"No. It has to be here. But I promise it won't take long. Afterward, I'll make sure you get home."

She took the sheet of paper. The wind kicked up, fluttering the corners of the page. Cold tears blurred her vision. The man shined a flashlight on the page.

"Read it," he demanded in a voice that sparked a hot prick of renewed fear in the pit of her belly.

This was wrong. All wrong. Without lifting her head, she surveyed the area again, but the piles of dirt all around the site blocked the view. There was no one around. She was on her own.

Her gaze dropped to the page. The three short, strange sentences sealed her fate.

This was it then. The end, and she'd meet it alone and cold. Made perfect sense. That was how she'd spent most of her life.

Her voice trembled. "I see my master in paradise. He calls to me. Take me to him."

His next moves were smooth and sure. He stepped around her. One hand grabbed her hair and pulled her head back, exposing her throat. Her scalp stung. A flash of metal shone in the corner of her eye. She knew what it was and what was about to happen.

Her instincts told her to run, but resignation and terror held her feet in place, like hands gripping her ankles. Panic raced through her veins, her heart beating so fast and hard it felt as if it would crack through her ribs, burst from her body, and fly away. Tears slid down her cheeks.

The slice was mercifully quick. She barely felt the cut of the blade or the gush of her blood onto the white snow at her feet. The liquid flooded her body with warmth.

But with every beat of her pulse, her heart squeezed more life from her body. Every beat of her heart brought her closer to death. Weaker. More distant. Distress slid away as her body drained.

She fell to her knees. Dropping to the ground behind her, he grasped her shoulders. He pulled her back to his chest, supporting her against his body. His hand stroked her hair away from her face, his touch loving.

Reverent.

As her vision dimmed, she sagged sideways. He cradled her in his arms. Leaning over her, he pressed his forehead to her temple and whispered, "You are home."

CHAPTER

2

Dr. Louisa Hancock had built a career out of studying instruments of violent death. Humans began hunting with stone-tipped spears hundreds of thousands of years ago, and she often wondered about the first man who had turned weapons against his own kind.

In the artifact storage room of the Livingston Museum of Archaeology, she examined her latest acquisition for the *Celtic Warrior* exhibit: an iron spearhead purchased from the estate of a recently deceased private collector. Artifacts required careful maintenance. Temperature, humidity, light, and pollution all caused artifacts to deteriorate. Pieces in the collection needed to be rotated in and out of the exhibit to preserve them. She was always looking for new additions.

The spear wasn't a particularly valuable piece, at least not in monetary terms. She examined countless relics, yet each one generated a stir of awe in her belly that had nothing to do with its dollar value.

Once a geek, always a geek.

Despite the terrifying events of last October, relocating to Philadelphia the previous summer for a fresh start had been the best decision she'd ever made. She loved her job as assistant curator, and her personal life had taken an astonishing turn. Sports bar owner Conor Sullivan had moved into her apartment and her heart. The whirlwind hadn't yet settled on that momentous event, and the sheer power of what she felt for Conor stunned her.

Without him in her bed the last few months, nightmares would have finished off what a serial killer had started. But she wasn't going to tell Conor that. He already worried about her.

Her gloved fingertip brushed the spear tip. The ancient weapon had developed a lovely oxide patina. The leaf-shaped blade tapered to a conical socketed shaft. More than two thousand years ago, the iron spike would have been mounted on a long wooden pole and either thrown or thrust at its target. The ancient point was dull from corrosion, but when it had been fashioned, it would have been sharp enough to run a man through. She made a note to have a replica made to show museum visitors what the weapon had looked like when it was new and deadly.

The exhibit she'd designed brought the past to life. Life-size models of warriors fought in front of an epic battle scene mural. The dramatic display portrayed a Celtic warrior with more accuracy than a pitted length of metal in a glass case.

Louisa wanted museum visitors to see the past the way she viewed it, by imagining events as they'd unfolded. History was anything but boring. Civilizations were built on foundations of drama and death.

She shook thoughts of death out of her head. No small task after what had happened to her just a few months before when a serial killer had targeted—and murdered—museum interns. Louisa had been abducted, held prisoner, and had nearly died. The darkness still brought back terrifying memories, but she was determined to be a survivor rather than a victim.

At the stainless steel table that bisected the room, Louisa photographed and measured the spear then carefully repacked it. Transferring the paperwork to the computer workstation, she generated a new acquisition file. She scanned the original receipt, completed the provenance, and entered a detailed description for the collection catalogue. Then she stored the spear with other objects waiting transfer to the public exhibit.

As she left the climate-controlled artifact storage room, her phone beeped. Conor.

She answered the call. "Hi."

"Hey, gorgeous."

Would there ever come a time when the sound of his deep voice didn't make her toes curl? She hoped not.

"Will you be at my dad's house for dinner?" she asked.

"Yes, but I have to stop by the bar first. Pat wants me to read something. Though selfishly, I'd rather have you to myself tonight." Distant thuds and grunts told her he was at the boxing gym.

For a second, she wished she were there with him. He'd been teaching her to box, both for fitness and self-defense, and she was surprised how much she enjoyed it. Hitting things was shockingly cathartic, and she was developing actual biceps. Of course, watching Conor in action was always a treat. All those rippling muscles and sweat . . .

She glanced around to make sure no one was within earshot and whispered, "We know where that would end up."

"Exactly."

Louisa's father had lived with them for several months, but he'd closed on a historic town house last week. Since her dad had moved out, Conor had been making enthusiastic and frequent use of their privacy.

She glanced at her watch. It was almost five o'clock, and Conor had scheduled time at the gym to coach the teen he mentored. "Shouldn't you be working with Jordan right now?"

Conor's disappointed sigh reached through the connection. "He didn't show."

"Oh no. Again?" Louisa turned down the corridor toward the administrative offices, her heels clicking on the tile. "I hope he's all right."

"Me too. He's been having a really hard time since Shawn took off."

Louisa volunteered at Haven, an after-school program for at-risk teenagers started by her best friend, local attorney Damian Grant. The Haven Project's goal was to keep kids off the street and out of gangs. Louisa had been tutoring Jordan for months, and Conor had been teaching the teen to box in an attempt to focus his frustration in a constructive way. Jordan's grades had improved. With continued hard work he could catch up to his peers, if he stayed out of trouble . . .

Big *if.*

Jordan's older brother, Shawn, had been with the program too, until he'd quit school and left home six weeks ago. Would they lose Jordan as well? Both boys had been devastated when their father had died in prison a few months ago.

"I'll give him a little more time in case he missed a train," Conor said. His tone shifted from serious to playful. "What are you wearing?"

"You know what I'm wearing. You saw me this morning. My gray suit."

His low chuckle sent a tingle across her skin. "What are you wearing *under* the suit?"

"Oh!" Louisa couldn't control the happy grin that spread across her face. "Sorry. Now I get it." She lowered her voice. "I'm not in my office."

She glanced around. The hallway was empty.

"Even better." Conor might be across town, but Louisa pictured the wicked gleam in his eyes.

"You'll just have to wait until we get home to find out," she whispered.

"I'll see you in an hour." He laughed, then his tone dropped. "I love you."

She paused. Though he said it often, the words and the sincerity that shone through them still caught her by surprise. "I love you too."

Ending her call, she stopped at her administrative assistant's desk.

April looked up from her end-of-the-day cleanup. "From the flush on your face, I assume that was Conor?"

Louisa's face heated. "Yes."

"Don't be embarrassed." April fanned herself. "Enjoy it. That man of yours is hot enough to reverse menopause."

"Yes, he is." Louisa laughed.

There was no denying the truth to that outrageous comment. Conor Sullivan was six feet two inches of lean, sexy man. His black hair always needed a trim, he habitually neglected to shave, and his turquoise eyes were capable of lowering Louisa's IQ twenty points just by focusing on her. But the best thing about him was that, although he rocked the bad-boy look, he was the sweetest man she'd ever met.

"And since you're disgustingly happy for a Monday, I assume the new acquisition met your expectations?" April gave her short red hair a sassy shake.

"It's perfect."

April shut down her computer. "Are you still going to see your father tonight?"

"I am. It'll be his first dinner party in his new town house."

"He can cook?" April asked with a flutter of her eyelids, not bothering to hide her interest in Louisa's widowed father. Unfortunately, Ward Hancock, world-renowned expert in Viking burial customs, was oblivious to anything that wasn't a thousand years old.

"Yes. He's no gourmet, but he's getting better." Louisa glanced at the clock. "It's five o'clock already? I'd better get moving."

"Would you give this to your father?" April turned to the credenza behind her desk and picked up a long cardboard box. "It came for him this afternoon."

"Sure." Louisa glanced at the overnight shipping label. It was addressed to Ward, care of her. The return address was local. "It's strange that he got a package here."

Her father often spent time at the museum, but his involvement was voluntary and unofficial.

"Someone must have met you both at one of the special events we threw in January. They probably sent it to you because you're on the museum website, and he's not." April took her purse from the bottom drawer in her desk. "I'm off too. Unless you want me to deliver that package to your father for you . . ." She waggled her dyed red eyebrows.

Louisa laughed. She was tempted to say yes, just to shake her dad out of his absentminded professor stereotype. But she wasn't sure he was ready for April-level excitement yet. "No. Thank you. I'll see you tomorrow."

"Have a good night then." April lifted her knee-length parka off a peg by the door. "Is Conor picking you up?"

"No."

Zipping her coat, April gave her a look.

"It's time to get back to normal." Louisa needed to return to her routine. Besides, sunset had moved back far enough that she could walk home before the daylight faded.

"I'm not the one you have to convince."

"I know."

After the attack, Conor's protective instincts had shifted into overdrive.

April flipped the end of an orange scarf over her shoulder. "Good luck. There's more snow forecast for the end of the week. Stay warm."

"You too." Louisa retrieved her coat and locked her office. Carrying the box to the lobby, she paused at the exit to dig gloves from her pockets. Then she pushed through the glass door and stepped into a breath-robbing wind. Even for a Maine native, the cold front hanging over Philadelphia felt bitter.

She hunched against a gust that ripped down 19th Street. The ten-minute walk left her cheeks frozen and her feet numb in her pumps. She stopped at her building and took the elevator up to her apartment. Inside, her rescue pit bull, Kirra, greeted her, a round ball of furry enthusiasm. With her docked tail, cropped ears, and scarred body, the dog looked scary but was actually a big baby.

Kirra was her first pet, but Louisa couldn't imagine living without her furry friend. Conor had used the dog to soften her up by asking her to dogsit the stray. *Smart man.* However she'd come to adopt Kirra, she was grateful. She'd never thought it was possible to love an animal this much.

Louisa tossed her coat over a stool in the kitchen and rubbed the dark blue-gray fur. "You probably have to go out. Let me change. I'll be quick." Louisa changed into warmer clothes, added a knit hat to her winter gear, and then suited Kirra up in her red doggy coat before taking the elevator to the first floor. Carrying the box, she leaned into the wind as she and Kirra left the white-tiled lobby. They crossed the street and entered the park. Rittenhouse Square was a planned green space the size of a city block. Diagonal walkways met at a central plaza.

The dog nosed through the snow, looking for the perfect spot to pee. Louisa felt a gaze on her back. She turned in a circle. At nearly five thirty, the sun had disappeared behind the surrounding high-rises, leaving parts of the square smothered in shadows. The walkways had been shoveled clear, but a thin layer of snow and ice coated the statues and shrubs. Pedestrians hurried by, hands in pockets, shoulders rounded against the cold, intent on reaching their destinations. All seemed normal.

Louisa glanced down at the dog. Kirra sensed it too. Her attention was riveted at the darkness beyond the reflecting pool. Maybe there was another dog nearby. Conor suspected Kirra had been used as a bait dog. She grew nervous when near unknown canines.

There isn't anything to worry about. It's your imagination.

But her abduction had left a mark, and the hair on the back of her neck continued to shiver.

She quickened her steps and exited the park on the opposite side.

Putting the shadows of Rittenhouse Square behind her, she headed toward her father's street of brick town houses that dated back to 1800. By the time she hurried up the marble steps to his glossy black front door and rang the bell, she was shivering and her cheeks burned from the cold.

The door opened, and Ward smiled wide as he took the box from her and let her into the foyer.

"Come in. I started a fire in the study. Let's get you two warmed up." He leaned down to the dog, unsnapped her coat, and handed it to Louisa. Kirra's entire body wagged as he rubbed behind her ears. "How's my best granddog?"

The happy snorts Kirra emitted sounded more pig than dog.

Louisa hung their coats on the tree by the door then kissed her father on the cheek. More than two decades of heavy drinking were embedded in the lines of his face and the dull gray of his hair, but his green eyes were bright and clear.

"Here." Ward handed her a key. "I made you a key to the house."

"Thanks." Louisa tucked it into her pocket.

"Where's Conor?"

"He'll be here around six. He's supposed to be working with Jordan today."

"Supposed to be?"

Static crackled from her sweater, and Louisa smoothed it away. "As of five o'clock, Jordan was a no-show."

"Damn. He has midterms next week. This isn't a good time for him to slack off if he wants to graduate in June. I hope we don't lose him like we lost Shawn." Ward also volunteered at Haven. Helping the kids seemed to give him purpose, and even though he'd only been working with Shawn for a short time, the loss weighed on him.

"I know, but there isn't much we can do that we're not already doing." Louisa followed her father down the hallway. In one of Philadelphia's most expensive neighborhoods, the five-bedroom town house was a glory of twelve-foot ceilings, gleaming wood floors, and detailed molding.

"No. At some point, he has to want it for himself, but there's a lot of temptation out there," he said. With his own sobriety still new and fragile, he empathized with the kids he tutored. Many of them struggled with substance abuse and appreciated his candor.

They passed through an arched doorway into the study.

"What's in the box?" He set it on his desk.

Louisa crossed the room and opened her hands to the fire. "I don't know. It came for you at the museum."

Ward set it on his desk, moving aside a pile of research papers and books to make room. "Pleasure before business is my new motto."

"It suits you." Blessed heat—and happiness—soaked into Louisa's skin. "April wanted to bring it."

Ward paused. "Did she?"

"Uh huh."

"Perhaps I should have invited her to dinner." He slit the packing tape with a letter opener.

Maybe he was *ready for April-level excitement.*

Turning to warm her back, Louisa watched him open the box.

He dug through a pile of packing peanuts, then unfolded a square of felt. "A scramseax!"

Louisa walked to the desk. "It's in exquisite condition."

Designed for close-quarters fighting, the Viking short sword was about fourteen inches in length and only mildly corroded considering its age. The blade was wedge-shaped, narrower at the back and fuller at the sides. Though the grip had long since rotted away, it would have been made of wood, bone, or antler. A warrior would have preferred a broadsword on the battlefield. But this shorter weapon would have been useful in close-quartered house raids.

Switching on a banker's lamp, Louisa's father found reading glasses and a pair of vinyl gloves in his desk drawer, and spent the next fifteen minutes examining the sword. She knew, though he'd handled hundreds of similar artifacts, like her, he was enamored with each and every one.

Ward pointed to the narrow, tapered base that would have been inserted into the handle. "Whittle tang, nicely preserved. Likely ninth or tenth century."

Louisa tugged at the baggy elbow of his wool sweater. "What are you going to do with it?"

"Of course I'll donate it to the museum," he said.

As an archeologist and scholar, her father didn't believe in private collecting. Artifacts were part of humanity's shared history and should be accessible to everyone.

"There's more." He lifted a yellow envelope from the box. After slitting the flap with the letter opener, he withdrew a folded piece of stationery and a thin, eight-by-ten book. "It's a photo album."

He opened the note. Louisa read over his shoulder.

Thank you. I couldn't have done it without you.

He turned it over. "It isn't signed."

"Maybe the photo album will tell you who it's from."

Laying the book on the desk so Louisa could see, he opened to the first page. She leaned over the desk.

"No. Don't look." With a hiss, Ward tried to close the book, but it was too late. Some things, once seen, could never be unseen.

"Oh my God." Louisa's eyes locked onto the color picture before the cover fell. She felt the blood drain from her head, leaving her instantly dizzy.

He took her by the arms and steered her toward the door. "Let's go into the kitchen. I need to call the police."

Numbness spread through her body as her father guided her from the room. In those few seconds, the image had seared itself into her brain: a flash photograph of two dead bodies.

CHAPTER
3

The metallic slam of barbells landing on mats and the thuds of fists on pads echoed in the always-packed boxing gym. Conor cast another glance at the door, then sent a right cross into the heavy bag. The punch was solid, rattling the chains that suspended the bag from the ceiling. Shaking his stinging bare knuckles, Conor checked the clock on the wall. Five thirty.

Still no Jordan.

Conor reached deep for patience. Jordan Franklin's imprisoned father had recently ODed, his mother worked two jobs, and the neighborhood gang was actively recruiting. Attorney Damian Grant's skill had saved Jordan's ass from an assault charge six months ago. The legal near miss seemed to have shaken him. Jordan had been making steady progress before his brother's vanishing act, but now he was clearly struggling. There was only so much that anyone could do if the teen was determined to self-destruct.

In the center ring, Tito worked one of his young fighters through a series of combinations. Jab, cross, hook, uppercut. The kid had nice snap but kept dropping his left hand.

Tito thwacked him in the head with a mitt. "Keep your guard up."

The white-haired trainer still had fast hands and a quick eye for talent. Conor was hoping if he coached Jordan in the basics that Tito might take him on. Of all the trainers that worked at Southpaw Boxing, Tito was the one who had a soft spot for troubled kids.

Jordan needed something positive in his life, but he'd missed their last two workouts. And the fact that he'd left Conor hanging without even a courtesy call was a bad sign.

Unfortunately, Conor knew firsthand how much aggravation an angry, frustrated teen could be. When Conor was twenty, his parents had died in an accident. He'd left college so he and his older brother, Pat, could raise their two younger siblings and keep the family bar in business. Danny and Jayne had both been in middle school. Neither had coped well with losing their parents. They'd been in constant trouble, especially Danny, but he'd turned out just fine in the end, knock on wood. Despite the happily-ever-after with Danny, Conor wondered if he really had the energy for another angry young man.

He checked his phone. No message from Jordan.

Conor detoured into the locker room to change into his street clothes. A few minutes later, he stepped back into the gym just as the metal exterior door opened and a blast of cold air swept inside. A beefy young man in a dark gray hoodie strode onto the mat, his hands shoved into the front pocket of his sweatshirt, his movements stiff. Though the hood shadowed his face, Conor recognized Jordan.

"Sorry I'm late, man," Jordan said, head down.

Setting down his duffel bag, Conor crossed his arms over his chest. "Where have you been?"

"Had to stay after school." The lift of Jordan's shoulders was casual, but tension in his muscles contradicted the gesture. Jordan was up to something.

"That's funny because your mother called. She said the school reported you absent. Again." Conor's hand darted out, and he yanked the hoodie back. He still had fast hands too.

"Hey!" The young man raised a hand as if to shield his face. Jordan's eye was bruised and swollen. His lip had been split, and a cut on his cheek had scabbed over. His knuckles were as battered as his face.

"Fighting again?"

Obstinate eyes met Conor's for a split second before focusing on a point over his shoulder. The kid had a quick temper and issues with authority.

"It was nothing." Jordan's tone turned sullen. "Somebody got in my face is all."

Conor yanked at the kid's shirt, and he winced as he surveyed the bruises on the young man's torso. He walked a circle around him. On the back of Jordan's shoulder, a DIY tattoo of three sixes looked fresh and raw. "You call this nothing?"

Jordan was silent, but the shame in his eyes spoke clearly.

"We talked about the Sixes, and you promised to stay clear of the gang." Conor rubbed a hand down his face and channeled the composure he'd needed with his siblings all those years ago. Yelling and criticism wouldn't work. Jordan didn't mean to act out any more than Danny had. Jordan missed his brother and father. Teens weren't known for making good decisions under the best circumstances.

"Believe me. I'm trying." Anger and humiliation tightened Jordan's mouth.

And Conor got it. The tattoo hadn't been Jordan's idea. For a split second, Conor pictured Jordan struggling while the triple sixes were needled into his flesh.

"I'm sorry. I shouldn't have made assumptions," Conor said. He didn't bother suggesting that Jordan press charges. Ratting out the Sixes could prove fatal, not just to Jordan, but to his family as well.

Gangs were ruining the city.

"Where were you all night?" Conor asked.

"Around."

Frustrated, Conor picked up his duffel bag. "You're in no shape to work out today. I'll drive you over to Haven, and you can concentrate on your history. You need a B on that exam next week."

"Never had a B in my life."

"Louisa says you can do it."

Jordan frowned, obviously doubtful, as he put his sweatshirt back on.

Conor herded him toward the door. "She's always right. She's scary smart."

Jordan snorted his agreement.

"You shouldn't have stayed out all night. Your mother was frantic."

Jordan shoved his hands into his front pocket. "I didn't want her to see me."

"She would have handled it."

Jordan just shook his head. "Not after Shawn."

"What do you mean by that?"

The lift of Jordan's shoulders was quick and not very convincing. "Just that she thinks the Sixes had something to do with why he took off."

But Conor wondered if Jordan knew more than he was saying about his brother. "Call her on the way to Haven. She doesn't need any more to worry about."

"I know," Jordan said with true regret.

They stepped outside. A gust of wind blew snow from the overhang into their faces. Conor zipped his jacket. Jordan raised his hood. The teen either didn't own or wouldn't wear a winter coat. Conor had given up asking.

"I can take the train back," Jordan said. The SEPTA station was only six blocks from the gym.

First of all, it would be multiple trains. Secondly, Conor was not sending the kid off on his own again after he'd been missing all night and day. God only knew what he'd been up to. "I'm heading home anyway."

Jordan nodded, but he still wouldn't look directly at Conor.

What had he done?

Conor prayed it had only been a fight. "Call your mom. Now."

Jordan had a brief, uncomfortable conversation with his mother, full of *I knows, I'm sorries,* and *I won't do it agains.* The voice on the other side of the connection was all angry mother.

Jordan ended the call in silence, his shoulders caving in a miserable, sullen slouch. Conor let him marinate in his guilt. This was not the time for a pep talk. Sometimes teens needed a pat on the back. Other times, a kick in the rear was more appropriate. This was one of the latter situations.

They turned down a side street toward the lot where Conor rented a parking spot near the bar he owned with his siblings.

Conor saw the movement in his peripheral vision. A black Escalade screeched to a stop at the curb, and three bodies rushed out. Metal flashed as one of the attackers swung an object at Conor's head.

A knife!

Adrenaline shot into his bloodstream.

He reacted on instinct, ducking under the arc. The point swept toward his face. Air whooshed overhead as the blade missed his scalp by a scant inch. Conor leaped backward, giving him a few seconds to assess his opponent.

Dressed in saggy jeans and an oversize black jacket, he was tall and young-man lean. The orange bandana over his face proclaimed him a member of a West Philly gang, the Sixes. A set of mean brown eyes peered over the top of the bandana.

The man lunged, leading with the knife, this time coming in with an upward stab to Conor's gut. Conor shuffled back with his feet, sucking his belly out of the way. Leading with his shoulders, he blocked the knife's trajectory with a hard left forearm and delivered a simultaneous punch to the attacker's face with his right hand.

Knowing his assailant would continue to try and stab him, Conor closed the distance between their bodies. He looped his left hand under and around the man's arm, trapping the forearm. Conor used his right hand to grab the man behind the neck. A knee to the ribs bent him double. Conor drove three more knee strikes into his attacker's belly. Then he pushed the man's arm behind his back until he felt the shoulder pop out of joint.

Taking the knife, Conor let him drop to the ground.

Where was Jordan?

Twenty feet away, two men in Sixes attire were struggling to shove a hooded Jordan into the back of the Escalade. Conor sprinted toward the vehicle. He caught the first gangbanger by surprise, taking him to the concrete with a full body tackle. They hit the pavement hard, sliding along the asphalt. Luckily, Conor was on top, and the gangbanger was getting the brunt of the scraping action.

They came to a stop, rolling off the curb and into the street. Conor ended up on the bottom with two hands around his throat. Conor grabbed both thick wrists. The man's sleeves rode up, revealing matching 666 tattoos on his forearms. The pressure on Conor's windpipe closed off his air. He gasped, his lungs crying for oxygen.

The gangsta reached into his pocket. Not waiting to find out what kind of weapon was on its way, Conor tucked one foot behind his opponent's leg and bridged over his shoulder, flipping them over. His opponent landed on his back with Conor on top. He drove a downward elbow into the man's groin.

And that was the end of his fighting spirit. The gangsta rolled onto his side and puked in the gutter.

Panting, Conor levered up on one knee.

Jordan!

One-on-one, Jordan was going toe to toe with the third man. They traded a few punches. Jordan was holding his own. But number one had recovered and was moving in to help his pal. Conor gave number two a quick kick to the head to make sure he stayed down.

Scanning the street, he spotted a length of rusty wrought iron. Grabbing it, he lunged toward the Escalade. The man struggling with

Jordan saw him coming. He shoved Jordan toward Conor, jumped into the Escalade, and took off. Jordan hit the sidewalk and rolled.

Number one stopped to drag number two to his feet. Then the two assailants limped after the SUV. It stopped at the next block to let them in. Tires squealed on pavement, and the vehicle sped off.

With the danger hightailing it away, Conor's lungs and legs gave out, and he ass-planted on the cement. His chest burned, his ribs no doubt bruised from their impact with the concrete. He fought to slow his breathing. Ten feet away, on the ground, Jordan was busy sucking wind.

"Why are they after you?" Conor asked between painful breaths.

Jordan just shook his head.

Conor had always known his habit of picking up strays was going to get him into serious trouble.

Oh wait. It already had.

The business back in October *should* have taught him a lesson in how to mind his own business. Apparently, his weakness for helping troubled kids was an untreatable personality disorder. But he absolutely, positively drew the line at gang involvement. He'd risk his own neck, but nothing was worth bringing that kind of violence to his family or Louisa.

"I didn't join. I swear." Jordan rolled onto his hands and knees and got to his feet. The kid's legs looked as rubbery as Conor's felt. But he took the cue from the kid and heaved to his feet. Leaning on his thighs, he coughed and spit some blood into the street. Rubbing his sore ribs, he tried to remember taking a shot to the face but couldn't.

Lights swirled as a patrol car pulled to the curb. Conor's friend, Officer Terry Moran, climbed out of the vehicle. "What happened?"

"Got jumped." Conor pointed him down the street in the direction the gang had disappeared. "Shiny black Escalade." He panted. "Three guys in Sixes orange bandanas. The license plate was covered."

With one hand on Conor's shoulder, Terry relayed the description over his personal radio.

"Are you all right?" Terry asked.

"We're fine."

"We?" Terry gave him a doubtful look. "You're sure you're OK?"

"Yes." Conor glanced around.

Jordan was gone.

CHAPTER
4

"Brings new meaning to the word *stiff*, doesn't it?" Detective Anthony Ianelli watched the forensic investigators and uniforms crawl over a patch of snow-covered ground. Situated between the railroad tracks and South Christopher Columbus Boulevard, the cleared construction area was the size of a parking lot. Over the mounds of dirt that surrounded the site, he could see the stacked shipping containers of the rail yard and the towers and cables of the Walt Whitman Bridge in the distance. Two news crews gave reports from just outside the yellow-taped crime scene perimeter.

His partner, Detective Emmanuel Jackson, tugged a black knit cap over his bald, black head. Jackson's black wool overcoat sagged on his stooped shoulders and fit the rest of his tall, thin body like a lawn and leaf bag.

They walked toward the activity, stepping carefully. A week-old blanket of snow had melted and refrozen, covering the ground with a crusty layer of white. They both knew the snowpack over a vacant construction site could conceal nastier things than weeds and litter. No one wanted to step on a used condom or needle.

"No one was here over the weekend?" Jackson asked. "Doesn't look like there's any security."

"Nothing to guard yet. Just frozen mud. Ground was excavated a few weeks ago. Nothing's happened since. Union issues." Ianelli blew into his cupped fists, his warm breath puffing into the frigid February air. "I heard it's a weird one."

"I hate weird shit."

"Me too." Ianelli gave his paunch a Buddha rub. They'd skipped lunch. Usually, he hated to miss a meal, but today he was glad his stomach was empty.

"Who's the ME?" Jackson asked, shoving his hands into his coat pockets.

A generator hummed, and a crime scene tech flipped the switch on the portable floodlights, simulating daytime. Chunks of ice shone like glass in the artificial light.

Ianelli searched the figures moving around the scene. Despite the bulky shapes of PPE coveralls donned over parkas, he had no difficulty recognizing the tall and formidable-looking medical examiner. "Sorry. Looks like Gonzalez."

Dr. Renee Gonzalez was one of the many, many people Jackson had managed to offend in his time in South Philadelphia.

Jackson's annoyed grunt puffed out in front of his face like his own personal cloud. Ianelli had no doubt his partner's annual performance review included the HR equivalent of "does not work and play well with others."

"What did you do to piss her off?"

"Doesn't take much." Jackson sniffed.

Ianelli should have expected the evasion of his question, but it still irritated him. They'd only been partners for two years. He and Jackson had a good working relationship, but no one would ever call Jackson a *sharer*. In fact, he was the definite outsider in the department. He'd been transferred from another precinct after an investigation of cops beating confessions out of suspects. Two detectives had been indicted, and several others reprimanded. Had Jackson been involved? If they'd been able to charge him, he'd have been fired. The fact that he'd been transferred indicated it was more likely that internal affairs had simply not had enough evidence against him, but they wanted to break up any possible collusion within the precinct.

They stopped to sign the crime scene log. The patrol officer handed a clipboard to Ianelli, who signed and passed it to his partner.

Jackson scribbled on the next line. "Who found the bodies?"

"Homeless guy." The officer nodded toward a running patrol vehicle. "We locked him in the back, but he doesn't seem to mind. Probably the warmest he's been all week."

Jackson and Ianelli moved on. Fifty feet from the road, the medical examiner and forensic technicians gathered around a muddy clearing in the snow. Ianelli and Jackson approached, ice crunching under their shoes. As Ianelli joined the group, Jackson walked a few feet away and studied the scene from a distance.

In the center of the muddy area, two corpses, a man and a woman, lay side by side on narrow slats of wood. Their arms were crossed over their abdomens coffin-style. A folding knife protruded from the man's frozen grip. Four icicles were arranged on the woman's abdomen into a rough letter *R*. The outer edges of the wood pieces were charred, and the scent of gasoline sharpened the frigid air. Two pizza boxes, some Tastykakes, and two six-packs of Rolling Rock sat next to the victims' heads.

"Dr. Gonzalez." Ianelli's greeting froze on his lips as he stared at the remains. "What are they laying on?"

Crouching next to a plastic kit, the ME squinted up at him. "It looks like an industrial pallet."

The ends were trimmed off into points so the wooden platform was shaped like an elongated hexagon.

"Are those pizza boxes empty or full?" Jackson asked.

A forensic tech glanced up. "Full. One plain pie. One with pepperoni."

The dead man was young, maybe eighteen or twenty years old. His features and skin tone suggested Hispanic descent. He was dressed only in athletic shorts, sneakers, and some gold bling hanging around his neck, and he was beat to hell. The woman was older, a hard thirty. Her throat had been slit, and blood had soaked the front of her threadbare coat. She'd been standing when she was killed or the blood would have pooled under her body instead of pouring down the front of her.

"Any thoughts so far?" Ianelli asked.

"What we have is two dead bodies and an unsuccessful attempt to set them on fire." Dr. Gonzalez raised a gloved hand to block the floodlight.

Ianelli's gut did a queasy roll. It wasn't the gore that bothered him but the strange setting of the scene.

Nodding, Gonzalez straightened. "As you can see, the man was severely beaten. His body is well nourished, and his overall muscular development suggests he's an athlete." She pointed to the side of the man's head, where blood matted a wound. "While some of these contusions seem to be left by fists, many others, like this one, were clearly caused by an object."

"Any idea what sort of object was used?" Ianelli asked.

Gonzalez studied the wound. "Something long and thin. There's a pattern to the marks. We'll try to match it at the morgue. Internal injuries and/or the head trauma are the most likely possibilities for cause of death." Gonzalez pointed to the man's hands. "His knuckles are bruised and torn."

"He definitely fought back," Ianelli said.

Gonzalez nodded. "There are some smudges of blood on that medallion around his neck that could possibly contain ridge marks."

Fingerprints were a detective's dream, and a bloody print would give the prosecutor a hard-on. Juries loved that shit.

"Fingers crossed the print doesn't belong to either of the victims." Ianelli's gaze shifted to the woman. Except for the gaping wound across her throat, she appeared uninjured.

Gonzalez consulted her clipboard. "The female victim's throat is cut, but I see no evidence that she was beaten. Her teeth are decayed, and she's malnourished."

"Tweaker," Ianelli said. Rotten teeth screamed meth addiction.

The wind kicked a cloud of snow dust across the scene.

"Possibly," Gonzalez agreed. "The neck wound is deep, bisecting the jugular vein and carotid artery and extending to the posterior wall of the trachea." She pointed to a yellow evidence marker twenty feet away, where the snow was stained deep red. "She was likely killed over there."

Ianelli studied the ground. No clear footprints. The snowpack was too frozen. Ianelli could feel the cold seeping through the soles of his shoes. "Any IDs on the victims?"

"No." She shook her head. "But the male has a gang tat on his shoulder."

"In that case, his fingerprints should be in the database." Ianelli focused on the blue ink, a set of triple sixes. "Looks like the Sixes. They've been trying to expand their territory lately. If the woman is a crackhead, her fingerprints might turn up in the system too. Any idea how long they've been dead?"

Holding her gloved hands in front of her body, Gonzalez tilted her head and used her shoulder to scratch her chin. "The internal organs have not yet reached ambient temperature. Under normal conditions, a corpse loses approximately one point five degrees of body heat per hour." Dr. Gonzalez paused, her lips pursed in concentration. "These bodies cooled much faster." She consulted a clipboard on top of her kit. "Taking variables into account, I estimate they were dumped here between ten o'clock last night and four o'clock this morning."

Ianelli nodded, although he thought *dumped* was the wrong word. These bodies had been placed with care.

Dr. Gonzalez removed her vinyl gloves and tucked them into an evidence bag. "The autopsy will have to wait until they thaw, probably a day or two. But we'll try to get fingerprints tonight."

Ianelli glanced at Jackson, who stood a few feet away, eyes scanning the scene and taking in all the details. He might not talk much, but his partner noticed everything.

Dr. Gonzalez packed up her equipment and turned toward her van. She shot Jackson a death glare as she passed him. She definitely hated him, but why?

Jackson stared at his scuffed shoes until she'd passed. Then he shoved a stick of gum in his mouth.

Ianelli rubbed his hands together. "Dragging two bodies out here and arranging all this." He waved an arm toward the scene. "Took some time. He'd want it to be dark, and even then, why bother? Why not just dump them and run?"

"Because all of this was important to him. Every painstaking detail." Lines gathered around Jackson's eyes as he stared. "Knowing the blaze would attract attention, he set the fire and took off. He didn't hang out to watch them burn.

"Then the snow melted and put the fire out. If our killer was a fire bug, he would have stayed and tried to get the blaze going again." Jackson waited for the ME to leave, then pulled a pair of nitrile gloves from his pocket, approached the bodies, and squatted. "So the fire wasn't the key element to him."

Ianelli followed him, peering over his shoulder. "This guy looks pretty fit to me. Our killer must be a strong son of a bitch to beat him this badly."

"Maybe. Maybe not. He needed a weapon to do it." Jackson waved a hand over the beer and takeout. "What do you think all this is?"

"Freaky shit gives me heartburn." Ianelli surveyed the surrounding area. He could hear rush-hour traffic, but the road was out of sight. Given the cold, this area would have been empty and dark the night before. Any members of the homeless population who had evaded official roundups would have sought shelter beneath overpasses and in abandoned buildings. "That pallet wouldn't fit in a trunk. You'd need a truck or a van to haul this crap out here."

Jackson turned in a circle. "No buildings in sight. No traffic cams either."

In this blank space of the city, there were no other businesses or homes to canvas, no surveillance cameras that might have captured footage of the killer. Ianelli and Jackson walked the perimeter of the crime scene, then spiraled inward to inspect the bloodstain.

Jackson pointed to the ground. "Let's get a cast of these tire tracks."

Ianelli squatted. "The ground is too frozen to see footprints, but . . ." He gestured toward scrapes in the snowpack that led from the tire tracks to the bodies. "He dragged the pallet from his vehicle. To leave marks in this ice, it had to be carrying some weight."

"The girl was killed here." Jackson's gaze traveled the length of the marks. "Maybe the man was already dead."

"Be easier to subdue one victim at a time." With a creak in his knees, Ianelli stood. He really needed to lose some weight.

Jackson pointed toward the blackened, pointed end of the pallet. "What's this?"

Ianelli leaned closer. "Scratches?"

"No, not scratches. Something's carved into the wood." Jackson pulled a Maglite from his pocket and focused it on the wood.

"I see it now," Ianelli said as an image took shape. "Can't tell what it is, though. The wood is charred."

"Maybe forensics can clean it up for us." Jackson called a forensic tech over to mark the carving.

The bodies were taken away in black bags. They talked to the homeless guy, who didn't know jack, including his own name or what year it was. A patrol officer hauled him, protesting the violation of his personal liberty, off to a shelter. Shortly after that, the news crews packed up and left to cover a vehicle pileup on I-95. Ianelli and Jackson took another look at the scene sans victims.

"We can check with the Gang Task Force. See if anyone knows the dead guy." Jackson turned toward their vehicle.

"Be tough to recognize him the way his face is beat to shit." Ianelli followed, anxious to be in the car with the heat running. His hands were so cold they felt blistered. Ice crystals crunched under Ianelli's shoe. "The woman's too old to be the girlfriend."

"Hooker?"

"Why would a young guy like that need a hooker? He'd have his pick of young *thangs*."

"Maybe she got in the way. Wrong place wrong time."

Ianelli's phone went off. With a glance at the screen, he recognized the number of a new confidential informant and ignored the call.

"Not important?" Jackson asked.

"Just a CI I'd rather not deal with right now." Or ever. Ianelli shoved the phone back in his pocket. He'd only met with the scumbag once, and he already regretted getting involved with another piece of shit. But in his line of work, he didn't get to spend his days with the cream of the societal crop. No, a homicide cop was stuck with the dregs. He glanced over his shoulder at the bizarre scene. But this . . .

This went beyond the normal selfish, callous, and brutal violence he dealt with on a day-to-day basis. This was disturbing in a way that made all the hairs on the back of his neck stand up and suggest he run like hell for the nearest church.

Jackson's phone rang. Getting into the car, he pulled it from his pocket to answer it. The conversation was brief. "We're on the way."

"What?" Ianelli asked.

"Patrol answered a call in Rittenhouse Square. The responding officer suspects it might be related to this." Word of the bizarre corpses had spread rapidly. Jackson nodded toward the crime scene. "Guess whose house?"

"No idea." Ianelli turned the key in the ignition. The car wheezed to life. He pulled away from the curb and headed north.

"Ward Hancock."

"No shit." Ianelli thought back to the strange carving they'd found at the scene. Louisa Hancock had helped them identify symbols in the past. If forensics could clean up the image . . . "Ward Hancock or his daughter might have an interesting take on the weirder aspects of this scene."

Jackson shot him a *seriously?* look. "Do you really think Dr. Hancock would help us after all the grief we gave her? We tried to pin a murder charge on her boyfriend."

"We thought he was guilty. Our bad." Ianelli swatted at the guilt crawling up his shoulder. He'd almost put an innocent man in prison, but he'd been focused on trying to stop a killer and hadn't had time to baby a suspect. He tapped a thumb on the steering wheel. "If we convince her she'll be helping others, she'll do it. She's classy that way."

"Classy? Or rich and beautiful?"

"You're talking about the woman of my dreams." Ianelli pressed his hand to the center of his chest. "But Louisa Hancock and I come from different worlds. And she can't cook, so it was never meant to be. My wife's cooking will keep me loyal. I have my priorities straight. Looks fade, but a good lasagna recipe is forever."

"That food baby of yours is growing."

Ianelli grinned. "We had gnocchi last night. Mm mm mm."

Jackson frowned. "Sullivan will have a stroke if we involve his lady."

"You still don't like Sullivan? He was innocent, remember."

"Whether or not I *like* him has nothing to do with it. He turned out to be OK." Jackson snorted. "But I still think Conor Sullivan is too good to be true. He has to have a dark side."

"Aren't we jaded?"

"Just experienced."

"You are one suspicious bastard." Personally, Ianelli thought that the more guilt a man carried, the more suspicious his nature. Jackson thought everyone was up to something, which made Ianelli wonder what his partner could be hiding.

"Besides, if Ward Hancock called the police and the beat cop thinks it's related to our crime scene," Ianelli turned left on Washington Avenue and drove toward Rittenhouse Square, "then Dr. Hancock is already involved."

CHAPTER
5

Conor wasted thirty minutes with Terry giving him a statement and descriptions of his assailants, but realistically, the cops weren't going to catch any of them. Conor hadn't seen their faces, and although he knew damned well they were part of the Sixes, Terry couldn't arrest anyone for having an orange bandana, and the Escalade's license plate had been obscured.

Jordan's vanishing act shouldn't have surprised him, but it had, and Conor was as disappointed in himself as he was in the kid. Didn't he ever learn? But damn it, before his brother had gone, Jordan had been turning the corner. He hadn't been in trouble for months, he'd applied himself to boxing and his schoolwork with diligence, and Conor had thought he'd sensed the first stirrings of pride in him.

Still irritated and worried, Conor sent Louisa a quick text to let her know he'd be late. Then he stopped at the bar to change his shirt and check in with Pat. He parked in a mostly illegal spot in the alley and went in through the back door. He glanced in the main room. Bartenders Beck and Ernie were handling the happy hour crowd.

Conor headed for the office. Pat sat behind the scarred old desk in the squeaky chair that had belonged to their father. At six-four, Pat was a bear of a man, grizzly on the outside, teddy on the inside.

"What do you need me to review?" Conor asked as he grabbed a clean *Sullivan's* T-shirt from a pile on the filing cabinet. He took off his jacket and changed his shirt, tossing the torn one in the trash can.

Pat pointed to his own mouth. "Looks like you need more sparring practice."

Rather than worry Pat, Conor let his brother think he'd taken a hit at the gym.

Pat handed him a thick envelope over the desk. "Insurance renewal docs. I marked my notes with Post-its. We should consider making some capital improvements to knock the premiums down."

"I'll read through it tonight." Conor tucked the envelope under his arm. "Has Jayne read them?"

"I made her a copy. We can review them together in a couple of days."

"Danny?"

"He said he'll go along with whatever we want to do."

The four Sullivan siblings each owned a quarter of the bar. Pat, Conor, and Jayne ran the business. The youngest, Danny, had moved to Maine to live with his fiancée.

Pat checked his watch. "Why aren't you picking up Louisa at work?"

"She walked to her father's new house."

"Alone?"

"Yes. Alone. She's trying to get back to normal. The last thing she needs is my paranoia. It was still daylight and—"

"You don't have to convince me that she's safe." Pat held up his hands.

No, Conor had to convince himself. He'd almost lost her, and every time he closed his eyes, he remembered that night in vivid and horrifying detail. The constant rewind made him want to play bodyguard 24/7. But that wasn't fair to her.

Louisa wasn't just tall, blonde, and beautiful. She was also brilliant and sensible. She didn't take foolish risks. He knew that. Just as he knew the ten-minute walk from the museum near Logan Square to the condo in the Rittenhouse was perfectly safe, especially in the early evening when the after-work crowd would be heavy.

But as he'd learned, love wasn't rational.

"When are you going to marry that woman?" Pat asked. "If you want to have a couple of kids, you're not getting any younger."

"Wow. Thanks." Conor noted that Pat's once bright-red hair had faded over the years. He was blonder now, with some white hairs around his temples. But Pat had already done the wife and kid thing. He and Leena were the happiest of couples, with three rambunctious little Sullivans underfoot.

"Well, ask her already." Pat rolled his eyes. "We'll have a party. I might have stashed a twenty-year-old bottle of Macallan for the special occasion."

"Remember the last time you *celebrated* with scotch, after Jayne told us she was pregnant?"

Pat grinned. "Not really."

"I practically had to hand-truck you home."

Pat might be six-four, but he had the alcohol tolerance of a kitten. And scotch made him particularly emotional. Pat going all sentimental-Irishman was the last thing Conor needed right now. He made a mental note to find—and hide—that bottle.

"You're getting ahead of things."

Pat crossed his arms over his chest and gave Conor a smug look. "Then what's in the velvet box in the safe?"

Conor had buried the small box under copies of insurance policies and legal documents that they typically ignored until renewal time rolled around.

Oh shit.

It *was* insurance renewal time. How could he have not remembered?

Pat's stare remained expectant. Since their parents had died, he and Pat were about as close as two brothers could be. Pat wasn't going to let this go.

Conor dropped into the chair next to the desk. "I saw it in a window on Samson Street, and it just looked like her."

Jewelers' Row was a gauntlet for a man in love. One glance at the vintage-style diamond and emerald ring had reeled him into the shop.

Pat leaned back, a satisfied smile spreading over his face. "When are you going to ask her?"

"Is it too clichéd to do it on Valentine's Day?"

"Why are you so worried about this?" Pat shifted forward. The poor old chair protested with a metallic squeal. "You love her. She loves you. It's simple."

"We've only been together for a short time," Conor said. "I'm not sure she's ready."

"But you know she's the one." Pat's tone went matter-of-fact.

"I do." Looking back, Conor had known the moment he'd met her.

"Then do it."

But it still took her by surprise every time he said *I love you*.

"I want it to be right. She deserves a perfect proposal." Conor knew damned well no one had taken care with her feelings in the past, a fact that still angered him.

"She loves you, Conor."

"I know she does." He didn't doubt it for a second. "But I don't think she's comfortable with our relationship yet. She doesn't have much experience with people putting her first."

After Louisa's mother had died, her father ran off to Europe and did his best to drink himself to death. She'd forgiven him his sin, but Conor hadn't. In his world, family took care of family.

Pat's face fell into an angry frown, then he brightened. "No worries. We'll have her unused to being alone in no time."

"Don't get all pushy with her."

Pat waved off Conor's concern. "That reminds me. Danny wants to FaceTime with the whole family on Sunday."

"Maybe he and Mandy set the date?"

"That would be my guess." Pat pointed at Conor's chest. "You're the last holdout. Ask that girl to marry you already and start a family."

Conor turned up a palm. "What are you, a barkeep or a matchmaker?"

"Both." Pat grinned back at him.

Conor sighed, reaching for the words to describe his hesitation. "I won't rush her. Too many people in her life have pushed her into things. I won't be one of them."

"In my humble opinion—"

Conor laughed. "Your opinions are anything but humble."

"Because I'm usually right." Pat's face broke into a know-it-all smile then went serious. "She'll say yes, Conor."

"Like I said before, I want everything to be perfect for her." Conor stood and straightened his jacket.

"Don't wait too long. Life is short, and perfection is boring," Pat warned. "You have to enjoy life when it's good. There's no guarantee it'll stay that way."

With Pat's not-so-cheery prophesy in his head, Conor headed toward Rittenhouse Square. Traffic was its usual rush-hour nightmare, and his restored Porsche crawled up Broad Street. He could run the two and a half miles home faster.

Conor reached for the radio. Making a left on Fitzwater Street, he blasted The Black Keys. By the time he reached Center City, it was after seven.

In Rittenhouse Square, Conor parked in the garage structure, then walked the remaining couple of blocks to Ward's new town house. With Louisa on his mind, he barely noticed the cold. Turning onto Ward's street, Conor tripped at the sight of two police cars parked out front. An unmarked car sat behind a patrol vehicle.

Panic punched through his sore ribs, and he bolted up the brick sidewalk.

Something had happened to Louisa.

He took the five steps to the front stoop in two strides. His knock was answered in a few seconds. A uniformed cop opened the door. Over the cop's shoulder, Conor could see Louisa in the foyer, pale-faced but whole and apparently uninjured.

"You're all right?" he asked her, ignoring the cop.

She nodded. "Yes."

He exhaled. Relieved, even as the fresh anguish in her eyes twisted his gut. Sensitive to her mistress's moods, Kirra leaned against her shins.

Conor focused on the cop. "I'm Conor Sullivan."

"Please let him in," Louisa said. "He's expected."

Stepping into the foyer, Conor bypassed the uniform and wrapped his arms around her. "What happened? Is your dad OK?"

She rested her forehead on his chest for a few seconds, then lifted her face to look up at him. "Dad's all right. But—I don't know how to explain it. You'd better come back to the study."

"You should have called me."

"You were already on your way."

He reached down to greet the dog with a stroke to her head. Then Louisa led him down the hall. "Detectives Ianelli and Jackson are here."

The detectives who had handled the museum murders didn't work in Rittenhouse Square. They were from Conor's neighborhood, South Philly. Why would they be at Ward's house?

"Why?" he asked as they approached the arched doorway.

"It's not what you're thinking. It doesn't seem to be related to what happened in October." But her voice didn't sound convinced. "What happened to your mouth?"

"Long story. I'll tell you later."

They went into the study. Ward's desk occupied one half of the space. The other half held a sofa and two chairs arranged in front of the hearth. Flames flickered in the fireplace, and Conor unzipped his jacket.

The two cops were on the sofa, while Ward sat in a wing chair, his elbows resting on his knees, his face in his hands. All three men stood when Conor approached.

About forty years old, Detective Ianelli was Italian enough to pass for a Soprano. His gut had swelled since Conor had last seen him, and the cop looked more pregnant than Conor's sister, who was due in June. Detective Jackson was a tall, thin black man with a shaved head the same color and sheen as the polished wood floors. Unlike his partner, he appeared thinner. With Ianelli's weight gain, they were an updated version of Laurel and Hardy, minus the fun factor.

Back in October, both detectives had given Conor and Louisa a hard time, but the cops had helped in the end. Ianelli, with his army medic background, had saved Louisa's life. Conor didn't hold a grudge, though he didn't entirely trust them either. He shook the men's hands without bothering with social niceties. "What's going on?"

Jackson gestured toward the empty chair. Conor guided Louisa into it. Taking her freezing hand in his, he perched on the arm. Kirra leaned on her mistress's legs again.

"What happened to your mouth?" Ianelli asked, pointing at Conor's lip.

"Long story," Conor said. "What happened?"

"A package arrived at the museum today, addressed to Dr. Ward Hancock, care of Dr. Louisa Hancock." Jackson gestured to Ward. "Inside was an artifact."

"A ninth-century Viking short sword," Ward clarified. "And you'd better call me Ward or this is going to get confusing."

Jackson nodded. "Ward also received photos of a crime scene."

"A crime scene?" Conor searched their expressions, but the cops wore their usual game faces. Ward, on the other hand, looked devastated. Louisa's expression turned bleak. She closed her eyes for a few seconds. The elegant line of her throat moved as she swallowed. The way she hugged her waist was a fist to Conor's heart. She didn't deserve this. Whatever it was had traumatized her.

"I'll make some coffee." Ward got up and all but ran out of the room.

Conor pressed the cops. "What kind of crime?"

Ianelli elbowed his partner. "May as well show him."

Jackson glowered. Conor knew that the cop didn't like to share information.

Ianelli shrugged. "Dr. Hancock and her father have already seen it. They'll tell him about it as soon as we leave anyway."

"It's gruesome," Jackson warned.

"Show me," Conor said. He needed to know what images would be visiting Louisa in her nightmares, and he wanted details to assess any possible threat.

The ever-suspicious Jackson narrowed his eyes. "You have to promise not to tell anyone what I'm about to show you."

Conor could deal with Ianelli, but Jackson was an arrogant jackass through and through. This time, Conor had no patience for his attitude. "OK."

Jackson pulled on a set of gloves and opened a plastic bag on the coffee table. He removed a photo album, touching only the very edges. He opened the book to the first page.

Louisa jumped to her feet and moved to stand by the fireplace.

Conor leaned over the table, the air whooshing from his lungs as he stared at the picture. The photo had been taken at night, with the aid of a flash. On a wooden pallet, the bodies of a man and a woman lay side by side. Conor took in the gruesome, bizarre details. "Jesus."

"Yeah," Ianelli agreed. "This is some sick shit."

"What's with the pizza and beer? Did he have a party while he killed them?" Conor's stomach flipped over at the thought.

"The food was not consumed." Jackson took another photo from the back of the file. This one was a daytime shot of the same scene. There were no bodies in the picture, but the other objects were in place.

Ianelli pointed to the picture. "When we arrived at the scene, the bodies were positioned exactly the same as in the photo sent to Ward. But after the killer took the pictures, he tried to set the bodies on fire. Fortunately, he's no Boy Scout. The fire went out before it did any real damage."

Conor pointed to the pizza, beer, and Tastykakes. "You're sure this isn't just litter."

Jackson nodded. "We think it has meaning."

"When were the bodies discovered?" Conor asked.

"Earlier today," Jackson said.

Conor stared at the gruesome photo. "Where?"

Jackson hesitated, as if deciding how much information to divulge.

"I'm sure there's a news report." Conor was already tired of the verbal sparring with Detective Jackson. "If you don't tell me, I'll look it up on the Internet. Or I'll call Channel Six and ask them directly."

Jackson frowned. He clearly didn't like being backed against a wall. *Tough.* Their previous, single-minded pursuit of a killer had almost put Conor in prison. "A vacant construction site off South Christopher Columbus Boulevard. Past the rail yard."

"Neither Dr. Hancock nor her father recognized the victims," Ianelli added.

They'd made her look that closely? *Bastards.* Anger simmered in Conor's chest as he glanced over at her. She was staring into the fire, her arms still wrapped around her body. Both of these detectives knew what she'd been through. Ianelli was somewhat sensitive, but the abrasive Jackson was only interested in his case.

Conor studied the picture. The way the beer and food were arranged next to the bodies looked like the impromptu shrines that popped up all over the city when someone died in a violent or shocking way: teddy bears left on street corners where children were killed by stray bullets, flowers left on sidewalks where people died in auto accidents, white crosses to mark places cars collided with trees. Except this case was backward. The killer had left these gifts, not friends of the victims. "When were they killed?"

"We're waiting on the autopsy report," Jackson said.

"Have you identified the victims?" Conor focused on the man. Did he look familiar? The damage to his face made it hard to distinguish his features.

Jackson shook his head. "Not yet."

"Tattoos indicate the man was in a gang. The woman could be a meth addict." Ianelli leaned back and crossed his arms over his gut.

The cops knew more than they were saying, but that was all Conor was going to get out of them. Frankly, he was shocked they'd shared as much as they had.

They must want something.

"But why would he send the pictures to Ward?" *Care of Louisa.* Conor felt sick. A killer knew where she worked, and she'd carried his message to her father. "And how does the antique sword play into all this?"

"We don't know," Jackson said. "All we can assume is that the killer feels a connection with Ward."

Conor added, "But sending the package to Louisa suggests a link with her as well."

Footsteps in the hall silenced Jackson's response, but his mouth was grim. Ianelli closed the photo album.

Ward returned with a tray loaded with china cups and a thermal carafe. Bending over the table, he poured coffee and handed cups to Conor and the detectives, then he retreated to his chair.

"Thank you." Ianelli curled his hand around the cup, as if afraid the small handle was too delicate for his sausage-thick fingers. "The note says, *Thanks. I couldn't have done it without you.* Do you have any idea what that means, Ward?"

"No," Ward said, his voice tight.

"Have you gotten any strange e-mails lately?" Ianelli asked.

"I'm not good about answering e-mail. I haven't checked in a few weeks." Ward winced. "Probably more like a month. Maybe even two."

Ianelli's mouth thinned. "We'd like to take a look at your e-mail."

"Of course," Ward agreed and supplied his account login and password.

Jackson sat forward and considered his coffee. "Tell us about the sword. Do you have any idea where it might have come from?"

Ward considered the question. "It's a Viking short sword, probably from the ninth century, and it could've come from a number of places: a small museum, a private collector, the black market, et cetera."

Jackson added a teaspoon of sugar to his cup. "Can you place a value on the artifact?"

"The piece is in excellent condition, but the lack of provenance reduces the value." Ward ignored his coffee.

"What do you mean by provenance?" Jackson asked.

"Origin and history of ownership," Ward clarified. "With no paperwork, there's a good chance this piece was stolen or otherwise illegally acquired."

"How rare is it?" Jackson asked.

Ward leaned forward. "It's a beautiful piece in pristine condition, but it isn't one of a kind. This isn't the Ark of the Covenant. There are many examples of Viking swords sitting in museums and private collections. You could probably go on the Internet and buy one today. Without provenance, I'd have to estimate the value at a thousand dollars. With authentication, maybe twice that price."

Jackson steepled his fingers. "Can you give us a list of artifact dealers?"

"I can," Louisa said. "I acquire pieces regularly for the museum."

Ward clasped his hands. "But this might not have come from a legitimate dealer."

"And artifacts can be purchased online as well," Louisa said.

"We'd still like the list. We'd also like a copy of your calendar for the past month," Ianelli said. "And please think about the people you've met recently, especially at the museum or when you were with your daughter. If there's anyone who seemed odd or set off any alarms."

Ward scratched his chin. "Nothing comes to mind."

Ianelli turned to Louisa. "You too, Dr. Hancock. The package was addressed to you. Please review your contacts, appearances, colleagues, e-mail."

"My father and I have been in the newspaper a few times lately," she said. "He had a book signing at the Square Café, and Dad attended a few museum functions."

"Can you get us a guest list for the museum events? Or do you need us to get a warrant?"

She reached for the strand of pearls around her neck and rolled them between her fingers, a vulnerable gesture Conor hadn't seen in weeks.

"They were public events," she said. "The press was there. Pictures were posted online. I doubt any of the guests had any expectation of privacy. I'll have my assistant print out a list."

"What are *you* going to do, detectives?" Conor asked.

Ianelli shut down. "We're conducting a thorough murder investigation. We'll catch him."

"We'll probably get back to you with additional questions." Jackson stood.

"We'll have a car ride by the house during the night, Ward," Ianelli said, rising. "And be careful, both of you. The phrasing of the note feels personal. This killer either knows you or feels as if he does."

Which meant that Louisa was once again on a killer's radar.

CHAPTER
6

After the police left, Louisa cleared away the coffee cups. She tipped one over, spilling coffee across the counter. As she mopped up the mess, her movements felt simultaneously automatic and awkward.

Keeping busy was better than having time to think. If only she could learn to block her imagination while she slept. The photo had dragged her nightmares into the light. Had the dead couple been as frightened as she had been back in October?

Trying to force the images out of her head, she set the tray on the quartz counter in the surprisingly modern kitchen. The roasted chicken sat on the stovetop, having been removed from the oven and ignored. Doubting anyone was hungry, she covered it with tinfoil and transferred it to the refrigerator, then loaded the cups and saucers into the dishwasher.

A shoe scraped on the wood floor behind her. Conor. Every cell in her body recognized his footstep.

He wrapped his arms around her, pulling her back to his chest and holding her close. The solid feel of his body grounded her.

"Are you all right?" he asked into her ear.

"As all right as possible, considering the circumstances." But she knew the moment she closed her eyes to sleep, she would see that photo in vivid color. Her mind would spend the night imagining all the pain and terror the victims had experienced in their final hours.

"Well, I'm not."

Leaning against him, Louisa held up a delicate cup. "This china was my mother's. Dad had it shipped from the house in Maine. He says using it reminds him of her. She's been gone for decades, and he's finally ready to face her death."

Conor's arms tightened around her.

She set down the cup, shut off the faucet, and dried her hands on a dishtowel. "When I was younger, I didn't understand the level of his grief, but now I do." Turning, she looked up at him. "I don't want to lose him again. He doesn't need this additional stress."

"Neither do you." His turquoise eyes were turbulent. He tucked a strand of hair behind her ear. "I just wish I'd been here. I hate that you had to handle it without me."

"You can't always be with me." She needed to be able to function alone, right?

"I know." He brushed his knuckles across her cheek. "If I could take it all away, I would."

"You can't shield me from this, Conor." Louisa splayed her hand on the center of his chest. Under the soft cotton of his shirt, his heartbeat thudded against her palm. "I know you want to spare me any more trauma, but this is real and it's happening, and I need to deal with it. Closing my eyes will only make it worse."

Conor kissed her forehead.

"I'll never get those poor people out of my head," she said in a quiet voice. One quick glance was all it had taken. The image was branded onto her mind.

"I know." His sad tone reminded her that behind that Hollywood-handsome face was the kindness that made her fall in love with him. The need to take care of others was hardwired into him. He rescued stray dogs, mentored angry teens, and walked women to their cars in the dark. His white knight syndrome was an integral part of his personality.

Her fingers curled into the fabric. "Keep in mind that after what happened in that basement, reality just might be less scary than what my imagination can conjure."

"Now that I understand." His nod was solemn. "I'll have no trouble sleeping with the light on tonight."

"Now will you tell me what happened to your face?" She touched the corner of his mouth, where his lip was just a little swollen.

He took her hand and kissed it. "It's nothing. A couple of guys jumped me and Jordan on our way out of the gym."

"What?" She'd assumed his split lip had been a training mishap.

"They were members of the Sixes."

"But why would they attack you?"

His eyes darkened. "They weren't after me. They wanted Jordan."

"Where is he?"

Conor sighed. "I don't know. He disappeared while I was peeling my body off the concrete. I suspect he saw Terry coming before I did."

Jordan wouldn't want to be mixed up with the police, even as a victim. But Conor was clearly disappointed.

"I'm sorry."

"What if the Sixes are determined to initiate him and refusing to take no for an answer?"

"Is there anything we can do?"

"No." He took her hand and kissed the knuckles. "I love you for wanting to help, but the Sixes are where I draw the line. They kill for kicks, and I won't have them coming after you or my family. I told Jordan to stay away from them, but I can't make him."

"All right." Louisa knew that Conor was protective of his siblings. As an only child, she observed the close bond between the four Sullivans with awe.

She hadn't had anyone to trust since her mother had died. Not her father, who had run off to Europe to drown his grief, not the aunt who'd raised her solely to access her trust fund, and not the family friend who'd abused her vulnerability. Earning her PhD at nineteen hadn't done anything to expand her social circle.

She'd had more than a wall around her heart when she'd met Conor. There had been a moat and archers as well. But he'd breached all of her defenses.

Thank God.

After spending most of her years alone, she now had Conor, his family, and a few friends. She even had her very first dog. Her father had returned, clean and sober and wanting to have a relationship with her. She was grateful for everyone who was part of her new life, but the adjustment to caring and being cared about was more difficult than she'd expected. She'd learned young to lock her heart away to protect it. Until Conor had come along, she hadn't known what she was missing.

"Where's my dad?" she asked.

"In the study. He could stay with us tonight," Conor suggested.

"I'm right here." Ward carried the cream and sugar into the kitchen. "I'll be fine tonight, but thank you for the offer."

"We keep the guest room ready." She hated to leave him alone. He'd passed the six-month mark of sobriety, and the last thing she wanted was for a stressful situation to make him backslide.

"I've imposed on you two enough these last few months. I'm going to stay in my own house." He set the china on the counter. "I have a security system. Besides, if he knew where I lived, he would have sent the package here, not to the museum. I just moved into this house last week. I haven't even notified my colleagues of my new address, and considering what happened tonight, I'm going to hold off on that for a while. No one knows where I am."

But Louisa was worried about more than the direct threat.

Ward took her gently by the arms. "I know what you're thinking, but if I got through the attack on you without reaching for a bottle, I can handle some fan-boy attention from a criminal."

"But you'd still be safer with us." One of the main reasons Louisa had chosen an apartment at the Rittenhouse was its excellent security. The view and the amenities available through the attached hotel were all icing.

Pressure built in her chest at the thought of a threat to her father. That was the difficulty with letting people into her heart. Love always carried the risk of loss.

"If there is any possibility that I am in danger, then I certainly won't bring that risk to you," Ward said.

"But the condo is more secure."

"No buts." Ward shook his head. "I'm your father. I love you more than anything in the world. I'm sorry if it took me years to show you that. For a long, long time, I honestly thought you were better off without me. But I can do better now, and I absolutely will not put you in any further danger. This isn't negotiable. Now it's late, and you should get home."

Leaving her dad felt wrong, but she couldn't make him stay in the condo.

"I'll get our coats." Conor left the kitchen.

Louisa put her hand on her father's forearm. "I don't want anything to happen to you." She'd missed him for too many years to lose him now.

Ward covered her hand with his. "Nothing is going to happen. The detective said he'd have a car ride by overnight."

A few drive-bys hardly felt like enough. How quickly her life had taken another dark turn.

Conor returned and held her coat for her.

"Please be careful." Louisa slipped her arms into the sleeves. "This killer has already committed two murders, and that note was disturbing and personal. Very personal."

CHAPTER
7

In the window of the Square Café, he hunched over his steaming cardboard cup of coffee and pretended to browse the shelves of travel books. Through the glass, he could see down Delancey Street, right to the doorstep of Dr. Ward Hancock's town house.

Though he'd only met the esteemed Viking expert once, at a book signing in this very store the previous month, he'd felt the bond instantly, as if they'd known each other all their lives. They had so much in common. He'd been ready with a dozen questions as he approached the table. Then he'd seen *her* standing behind her father. His daughter. So regal and cool.

So perfect. Like a princess.

His thoughts had gone blank. All the questions he'd rolled around in his mind for weeks had suddenly disappeared. Unable to even look her in the eyes, he'd picked up the signed book and moved along the line after only a brief, muttered greeting. Basically, he'd blown the whole thing because of her.

And now she was inside that town house.

He'd followed her from the museum to the Rittenhouse Hotel, and then to this town house. He'd watched Ward Hancock let her in. Sending the package to her at the museum had been nothing short of genius. Of course she would take it to her father.

Why was he so fascinated by her? It was Ward Hancock he had to see. They needed to talk. There was so much to discuss. He didn't have time to fantasize about Ward's daughter, but something about her spoke to him.

What was he going to do about it? Maybe Louisa Hancock needed to play a part in his plan . . . But what was her destiny?

He'd have to think about Louisa's potential role. In the meantime, he had work to do.

Correction.

They had work to do. He and Ward. Together.

Ward had written the books, but *he* was bringing them to life. What he'd left near the rail yard was nothing short of a work of art. History brought to the present. Not unlike the *Celtic Warrior* exhibit designed by Ward's lovely daughter. He'd been to the museum to admire her work.

He owed the scholar so much. It was Ward who had shown him the way. Ward's book had explained how life—and death—were supposed to occur.

Only the scholar truly understood. He felt closer to Ward than anyone else on earth. No one else understood him. And he felt sure that once Ward knew the plan, he'd be on board. How could he not? It was all his idea.

How had Ward felt when he saw the pictures? He wished he could have been in the room to see the scholar's reaction.

The door to the town house opened and two people exited, Louisa and the tall man in jeans and black leather who had arrived later after the police. The ugly dog was once again wearing its coat. They strode down the sidewalk toward the square.

Toward him.

His sex responded with a surge of heat and need. Why did she affect him this way? Yes, she was the brilliant daughter of Ward Hancock, but he had no time for a woman. He had to focus on his work.

On death.

He began stepping backward then stopped. They had no idea who he was and no reason to suspect him of anything. He could watch them all he wanted.

They approached a patch of ice, shining in the light of the street lamp. The man took Louisa's elbow. The gesture seemed protective. Intimate. He must be her boyfriend.

A small surge of jealousy fired through his veins. The boyfriend was not good enough for her.

As they passed the bookstore, the dog bristled, turning and staring straight through the plate glass window, as if it knew he was there.

As if it knew he was thinking about its mistress.

Even in the silly red coat, the creature was formidable. Its body was compact and muscular, the head broad to accommodate the wide and powerful jaws. Its ears had been cut, and it bore other scars of a fighting animal.

The boyfriend paused, his head rising, his gaze sweeping his surroundings, as if he too could sense the unnatural scrutiny. Scanning the sidewalk in both directions, the boyfriend shifted Louisa to his opposite side.

Inside the coffee shop, he took an involuntary step back. The boyfriend looked as formidable as the dog. He was rough looking when compared to Louisa's elegance, the sort of man who would fight to protect what was his.

As if that would matter. If *he* truly wanted Louisa Hancock, nothing would stand in his way.

But did he want her?

A true warrior would simply take her. If anything, the boyfriend presented an enticing challenge and made him want Louisa even more.

The couple walked on. Stepping out of the cafe, he followed them toward the park.

He couldn't take his eyes off her.

She was lovely. Absolutely perfect. Tonight, she was wrapped in a thick wool coat, but when they'd met at the book signing, she'd been dressed in a well-tailored suit that highlighted her slim figure. Tall and elegant, she had long blond hair that gave her a Nordic appearance. She was also a scholar, and her mind was as appealing as her face.

Was there a more perfect woman?

No.

But his schedule allowed no time for frivolity. He had to focus on the scholar. He needed Ward's help to attain his goals. But he couldn't help himself. He was drawn to Louisa like a sailor to the sea.

He followed the couple at a discreet distance. They cut through the park, crossed the street, and entered the building. He waited, but the boyfriend didn't come out. He quelled a quick burst of temper at the thought of another man sharing her bed.

He retraced his steps back to Delancey Street and stood across from Ward's town house.

He simply had to convince Ward to join him. But how? For a moment he was tempted to knock on the glossy black door and introduce himself. Restraint was not his strong suit. But as close as he felt to Ward, that was no guarantee the connection went both ways. Ward might not even remember their meeting and would likely close the door in his face, if he opened it at all.

Tonight he'd pray for a vision, for guidance from the one who visited his dreams, the one who made everything clear. He reminded himself that his fate wasn't entirely in his control. The dreams would come at the will of the gods.

He realized with some regret that he might need to be more direct with Ward. Eventually the scholar would come around to his way of thinking and agree to be his mentor. They might not be related by blood, but their spirits were kindred. He'd known it the moment they'd met.

That day had been the start of everything, the moment when he'd realized what he had to do.

When he'd realized that mankind had gotten it all wrong. The world of the living was merely the beginning of an eternal existence that superseded anything on earth. It wasn't life that should be cherished and celebrated, but death.

And his was going to be glorious.

CHAPTER
8

Sullivan's was a South Philadelphia institution. The bar had occupied a busy corner a short walk from the sports complex for more than three decades.

Louisa sat in a booth permanently reserved for family at the back of Sullivan's Tavern. Kirra lay under the table, snoozing. Louisa's attention wavered between the Flyers game and watching Conor behind the bar. As much as she enjoyed hockey, the play of muscles under his snug black T-shirt was a fine sight.

Tuesday night Flyers fans packed the bar. They gathered in semi-circles around the wall-hung flat screen, rapt attention fixed on the hockey game. The night had been full of groaning, cheering, and drinking. At nine thirty, the score was tied. The game paused for a commercial and Louisa's gaze slipped back to Conor.

He opened three bottles of beer and loaded them on a tray while his older brother, Pat, filled glasses with amber liquid at the tap.

Conor turned as if he could sense her scrutiny. He crooked a finger toward her, beckoning her to come closer. Most of the crowd congregated on the opposite side of the bar, nearer to the TV screens. The sleeping dog didn't stir as Louisa crossed the bar. She slid onto a vacant stool at the quiet end and leaned her forearms on the scarred wood. Conor filled a glass, tossed a lime slice in, and set it in front of her.

"You're probably tired. I'm sorry the game's running so late. It was a bad night for Beck to call in sick."

Hockey games necessitated a full bartending crew, and neither one of them had wanted her to stay home alone, not after what had happened the night before, and the brutal nightmare that had woken her well before dawn.

"It's fine. I'm enjoying the game. The enthusiasm is contagious." Honestly, despite her building's tight security, sitting amidst the rowdy crowd was comforting.

"Following hockey now?"

She sipped the club soda he'd brought her. "It's an exciting game." Like many aspects of her new life, she enjoyed watching sports more than she'd expected.

The day had been uneventful. She'd worked until five, then stopped to change her clothes and collect the dog before taking a cab to the bar. Neither she nor her father had heard from the police or received any more strange packages or messages. But she felt as if something were going to happen.

As if someone were waiting to act.

The door opened and Conor's policeman friend, Terry, came in. In jeans and a sweatshirt, he was clearly off duty. He greeted Louisa with a quick hug and stepped up to the bar next to her.

Terry leaned an elbow on the bar. "You have a minute, Conor?"

"Give me a sec." Conor filled a pitcher of beer at the tap and passed it to a customer. Then he filled a tall glass with amber liquid and brought it to Terry.

"What can you tell me about that kid you were jumped with yesterday?" Terry plucked a peanut from a small dish and popped it into his mouth.

Conor leaned across the bar. "Jordan?"

Terry nodded.

"He's had a rough few years," Conor said. "But he's been making a good effort to get his grades up and stay out of trouble. Why? Did you find out otherwise?"

"No." Terry ate another peanut. "I have nothing on Jordan, but his brother is a different story."

Shawn was eighteen and there had been no sign of foul play when he'd run off, so the police had had no reason to look for him.

Terry sipped his beer. "Shawn is now wanted for questioning in a gang execution that took place about six weeks ago. A witness just came forward and put him at the scene."

"No." Louisa sagged on her stool. "Shawn's a good kid."

"Who was killed?" Conor asked.

"A member of the Big K." Terry offered Louisa the peanut bowl. "There's a hot turf rivalry between the Sixes and the Big K. The assumption is that if Shawn was at the scene, he either did the killing or he saw it. Either way, the gang task force wants to talk to him."

Louisa passed on the peanuts. The news about Shawn had squashed her appetite. "What do you think happened?"

Terry picked up a laminated bar menu. "We don't know, but it doesn't look good for Shawn. Killing a rival is often a membership requirement for a gang."

Conor shook his head. "Shawn doesn't seem like the type of kid who would get involved with a gang. He's smart. His grades were good."

"I just thought you'd want to know." Terry dropped the menu.

"Thanks." Conor went back to filling orders. Terry took his beer and slid into the crowd around the TV.

Louisa digested the news about Shawn. Why were the Sixes after Jordan? Had Shawn killed the gang member? Conor's assessment of Shawn was accurate. He was a smart kid, but he also had a temper. Like his brother Jordan, frustration simmered just under his skin and could surface as a violent outburst at any time.

Conor's sister, Jayne, walked by, hefting a tray to her shoulder and weaving her way through the tables to the kitchen. A minute later, she reemerged, one hand pressed to the small of her back, the arch in her posture emphasizing her rounded, pregnant belly.

Conor returned. "Do you want food?"

"No." Louisa slid off the stool. "I'm going to put my things in your office and help Jayne."

"Are you sure?" he said, doubt heavy in his voice. "Have you ever waited tables?"

"No." Louisa had never needed to work in a restaurant or retail establishment, and she hadn't spent much time in bars either. But Jayne looked tired and clearly needed a break. The second waitress on duty would not be able to handle the whole crowd. Besides, Conor's family treated Louisa with kindness and warmth. The least she could do was carry some drinks. "But I want to help. Do you have another apron?"

"Sure. There should be extras hanging in the kitchen." Conor leaned over the bar to give her a quick kiss on the lips. "Thank you."

"You're welcome." Pleased, Louisa found an apron hanging on a hook in the kitchen. Tying it around her waist, she returned to the main room.

Pat and Conor were filling drink orders behind the bar. A bell clanged, an excited roar erupted, and fans exchanged high fives.

"What can I do?" Louisa asked Jayne.

"Table three needs a fresh pitcher." Wincing, Jayne pointed to the table, then rubbed her pregnant belly.

"Why don't you sit down for a while?" Louisa asked, concerned. "I can carry trays."

"I'm all right." But Jayne's face was pale enough to highlight every freckle on her nose.

Conor came out from behind the bar. "What's wrong?"

"It's nothing. I've been getting these little twinges all week."

"Sit," Conor ordered. "Does Reed know about these *twinges?*"

"I'm not sick. I'm pregnant," Jayne protested. "Reed is away visiting Scott at college. I'm bored."

"I'll bet you didn't tell Reed you weren't feeling well," Conor said. "There's no way he would have left you if he'd known."

"He worries more than Pat." Jayne slid into a booth. "He's terrified that I'm going to fall every time I step out the door in the snow. You wouldn't believe the emergency equipment we own. I keep telling him we don't live in Maine. Can you believe he bought me traction cleats?"

"He loves you." Louisa smiled.

Jayne rubbed her belly. "He does."

Louisa delivered a few drinks. A buzzer sounded, and a disgusted roar erupted. The energy in the bar deflated faster than a tire that had backed over a spike strip. Disappointed fans drained glasses and settled tabs. Louisa helped clear tables as the crowd thinned. By the time the chaos had settled, it was eleven o'clock, her feet were sore, and she was exhausted in a good way.

"I'll close up if you drive Jaynie home," Pat said to Conor behind the bar. Emerging, Pat kissed Louisa on the cheek. "Thanks for helping tonight."

"You're welcome," she answered, satisfied that she'd been able to help the Sullivans instead of the other way around.

Thirty minutes later, Jayne had been safely delivered to her doorstep, and Louisa and Conor were home. They stripped off their coats in the foyer and went into the bedroom.

"I'll be out in a minute." Conor left his phone on the nightstand and ducked into the adjoining bathroom. She heard the shower turn on as she opened a text from her father.

Can you come over before work? I need to show you something.

Sure, she answered.

Tossing her cell phone on the dresser, Louisa sat on a chair and tugged off her boots. The shower turned off, and she called out, "My dad wants me to stop by before work tomorrow."

"I'll go with you." Conor's voice echoed on the tile.

"You don't have to."

"I want to."

"All right." As much as she hated the loss of independence, the reality of having a connection to a killer couldn't be denied. It brought back memories of another murderer and filled Louisa with terror. Her throat tightened, and her voice broke. "But I hate that we have to do this all over again."

"I know."

She turned her head as Conor emerged from the bathroom. Naked. She watched him cross the room, rubbing a towel over his wet hair.

He tossed the towel over his shoulder. "See something you like?"

"Maybe," she teased, grateful for the distraction.

His smile said he wanted to eat her alive, but then he probably did. Heat rose into her cheeks and spread through the rest of her body. One look from him, that's all it took to quicken her pulse and warm her skin.

And he knew it.

He returned to the bathroom. Water rushed in the sink, then turned off. His phone beeped on the dresser.

"Would you get that?" he called out from the doorway, toothbrush in hand. "It might be Jaynie."

"Yes." She looked over at the display. "It is."

She entered Conor's passcode and read the message. "She feels much better."

"Thank God."

"She says she'll call you in the morning."

Conor had acted calm tonight, but he'd been worried about his sister. He was already a fabulous uncle to Pat's kids. Conor should definitely have his own children. Louisa had few pleasant memories from her own lonely childhood. She had no idea how to be a good parent. Could she learn? Would she ever be ready to find out?

Shivering, she opened a dresser drawer and took out flannel pajamas.

Conor came out of the bathroom. "You don't need those."

"I'm freezing." But she had a feeling he had a cure.

"I can fix that." Conor stalked closer, clutched her shoulders, and pressed his body against her back. In the mirror over the dresser, his eyes turned serious. "I won't let anything happen to you."

"I know." She always felt safer when she was with him. "But you can't always be with me."

"This time I will be." His voice turned hoarse.

"It wasn't your fault."

"If I had been with you, it wouldn't have happened." His grip tightened on her shoulders. "I won't take a single chance this time."

This time . . .

The words made it seem as if this was just the beginning of a whole new horror. Conor's eyes went dark, as if he too was thinking of evil revisiting them. She swallowed the raw helplessness creeping into her throat. *Stop it!* There was no point in letting her imagination run loose. Instead, she steered it to Conor and the intimacy between them that always kept the darkness at bay.

She put her hand over his. "It wasn't your fault."

He nodded, but he didn't look convinced.

"Is it weak if I just don't want to think about it tonight?" Her current train of thought was going to lead her directly into another nightmare.

"No," he whispered, his breath warm on her neck. "There's nothing we can do for now except be careful, and we're already doing that."

And the fact that the entire situation was out of their control made it worse.

She leaned back, letting him support her weight. Needing him to block out all her senses, she turned her head and inhaled him. He smelled delicious, and she wished she'd showered with him. "I'm still freezing."

"Let me remedy that." His hands stroked from her fingertips to her shoulders and back. "First, these clothes will have to come off." He slid his hand under the hem of her sweater and drew it over her head. He tossed it over his shoulder. She watched, mesmerized, as his strong fingers splayed across her belly.

"Are you trying to seduce me?" Louisa protested, but at the same time, she tilted her head to give him better access to the sensitive skin along the underside of her jaw.

"Of course I am. Is it working?"

"Yes." *Always.* "You know I can't resist."

"But you are an incredible woman. Brilliant." He swept her hair aside and kissed the base of her neck. "Beautiful." His lips cruised along her collarbone. "Compassionate." His teeth grazed her shoulder. "And you deserve to be seduced."

The hardness pressed against her back and the sight of his big hand sliding up her belly transfixed her.

"Do you like watching me touch you?"

Her face flushed.

"I love making you blush." The gravel in his voice told her how much he wanted her.

Had she been cold?

His eyes held hers in the mirror. His eyebrows waggled. "Do you want to play hot librarian and rock star?"

"That's not necessary." She laughed, her tension easing. Conor had taught her that sex didn't need to be serious to be intense, and that humor was a great outlet for stress.

"Necessary? Laundry is necessary. This is pure pleasure." He chuckled. "But maybe you're right. Let's skip the costumes and get you naked. I need my hands on your skin and my mouth—"

Louisa's phone vibrated on the dresser. Expecting another text from her father, surprise filled her when she read the screen. "It's Damian."

"What's wrong?" Conor frowned as she answered the call.

For a casual interaction, Damian always texted, and he would never call her at this late hour.

"Is Conor there too?" Damian asked.

"He is. I'll put you on speaker." She lowered the phone so Conor could hear Damian's voice.

"The police showed up at Jordan's house. They took him to the station. I'm on my way there now. Would you go to his apartment? Yvonne is hysterical, and she needs someone to stay with Tyler so she can go to the police station."

Conor moved to the closet, pulled out a pair of jeans, and stepped into them commando.

"What are they charging him with?" Louisa sat down and shoved a foot into a boot. *Please let this be a misunderstanding.* Yvonne and her family had been through enough.

"Nothing yet," Damian said. "Yvonne said they claim he's just being brought in for questioning, but they were talking about alibis and murder."

CHAPTER
9

Conor leaned against the wall, feeling useless. On the sofa, Louisa sat next to Jordan's mother, Yvonne, rubbing her shoulder as the woman wept into her hands.

This wasn't Conor's first visit to the West Philadelphia apartment. The unit was a tight fit for the family, but Yvonne kept it ruthlessly clean. After her husband had gone to prison, she and the boys had left their row house and moved into the one-bedroom. Conor knew her budget was tight. The boys shared the bedroom. Yvonne slept on the pull-out sofa in the living room. The neighborhood wasn't the sort where kids could go outside to play after school.

Conor shoved his hands into his pockets. The room was freezing. He checked the thermostat. Fifty-five degrees. Louisa wore her coat, and three sweaters dwarfed Yvonne's thin frame.

She lifted her head, took a quivering breath, and hiccupped. Though her skin was light, she had slightly exotic features that suggested mixed-race descent. Her dark hair was home-trimmed short. She was five years younger than Conor. But her thirty-three-year-old face looked fifty, and she was the desperate kind of thin that came from malnutrition rather than a diet.

Yvonne hadn't composed herself enough to speak since she and Damian had returned from the police station a few moments before.

"Well?" Conor asked Damian.

From his Ferragamos to his gelled blond hair, Damian Grant looked every inch the successful attorney. The glow from the single lamp emphasized the worry lines on his face.

"They're questioning him about two murders," Damian said. "The bodies of a man and a woman were found on Monday. There was a thumbprint on a medallion that the man was wearing—a medallion that belongs to Jordan. The cops ran the print and Jordan's name popped up. They haven't charged him with anything yet, but they are holding him in juvenile detention."

"Why?" Conor asked.

Damian's chest rose and fell. "They gave several reasons. The Sixes jumped you and him on Monday, so he could be in danger. Plus, they know he didn't go to school on Monday, and that Yvonne's work hours don't allow her to provide adequate supervision. He denies being involved with the Sixes, but the cops don't believe him. The fact that his brother is missing and wanted for questioning in a gang-related murder investigation doesn't help."

"Did Jordan say where he was on Sunday?" Conor asked.

Yvonne straightened and wiped her eyes with her fingertips. "No. He was supposed to be here watchin' Tyler. I got a double shift at the restaurant. When I got home it was after midnight. The boys' door was shut. I didn't want to wake them. Tyler is a bear if he doesn't get enough sleep. I took a shower and went to bed. When I went in to wake them for school, Jordan wasn't there." She dragged in some air. "I couldn't believe he left Tyler. He's only twelve. I've never been so mad—or so scared. Until now. If I could go back to Sunday night and open their door, maybe I could have found him and brought him home." Guilt slumped her shoulders. "I wouldn't have known where to look for him anyway. So I guess it doesn't matter."

But Conor imagined she was used to feeling guilty.

Yvonne covered her face with her hands for a few seconds, as if she just couldn't face any more bad news. She lifted her head, a spark of certainty in her eyes. "Jordan would not murder a woman. And he wouldn't join the Sixes, not after he promised me he wouldn't."

"They may not have given him a choice," Conor said quietly, thinking about the fresh tattoo on Jordan's shoulder. But he couldn't imagine Jordan hurting a woman either.

Louisa wrapped an arm around the crying woman.

Conor jerked his head toward the door. He and Damian stepped out into the stairwell. Dampness seeped from the cement and made it seem even colder than outside. Light from a dim, dusty bulb shadowed the steps that led down to the basement.

"Who do they think he killed?" Conor shoved his hands into the pockets of his bomber jacket.

"A local boxer named Mario Avana and a prostitute named Nicole Evans." Damian's mouth tightened. "They were particularly nasty murders, Conor. The man was beaten and the woman's—"

"Throat was cut." Conor finished as seemingly random facts came together. The timing, the dead couple, the battered male victim, Jordan's bruises and odd behavior on Monday.

Damian's head snapped around until he faced Conor. "How did you know?"

Conor told him about the sword and note that were sent to Ward on Monday.

"The murders happened between Sunday at ten p.m. and four a.m. on Monday." Damian turned and paced the tiny stoop. "When did you see Jordan last?"

"Monday, about five thirty in the evening," Conor said. "He was late for our workout, and when he showed up, he'd clearly been in a fight."

Damian shuddered. "I have to tell you, Conor, this is really bad. I don't want to believe Jordan is guilty, but the evidence is pretty damning."

"What do they have?"

"Besides the fingerprint, they also found hair that clearly didn't belong to Mario or the hooker. Jordan had to provide DNA when he was arrested for assault last summer. Even though he wasn't charged, they kept the sample. They're running tests to see if there's a match, but the hair is dark brown and the right length. They're expediting the test and expect the results to be in late tomorrow or Thursday. As if that wasn't bad enough, he took a swing at one of the cops, and he's sporting a brand-new Sixes tattoo."

Conor rubbed his temple. "What does Jordan say?"

"Mario and two pals beat him down in the street a few blocks from his apartment and gave him the tattoo."

"Did Jordan say where he spent the night?" Conor asked.

"Jordan said he was in bad shape, it was late, and he didn't want to wake his mother, so he stayed with a friend, but he won't ID the friend. He also won't name the guys who were with Mario. I assume he's more afraid of the Sixes than going to prison."

"Rightfully so."

"The cops don't believe him. Or don't care. I'm not sure which." Damian's breath fogged in the air. "I can't get a read on Detective Jackson, but I remember how hard he pursued you as a suspect."

"Me too." And Conor hated to think of Jordan being railroaded into a murder charge. "How does the hooker play in?"

"I have no idea. The cops aren't saying much about her. They kept asking Jordan if he knew her, and he kept saying no." Damian crossed his arms and tucked his hands in his armpits. "I don't think they know how she's related yet."

"The kid's a hothead, but I can't see him killing a woman like that." Conor couldn't believe Jordan could be so cold-blooded. "Were there any witnesses to the fight?"

"The police said they went door-to-door, but no one admitted to seeing anything."

"Not a surprise," Conor said. "People around here don't trust the police, and they don't get involved in their neighbors' problems. I'd hate to see him go to jail."

"The chances of that are very high. They're holding him for resisting arrest and assaulting an officer. The cops found his bloody fingerprint on the victim, and he admits to fighting with Mario. We'd be hard-pressed to find twelve people who'd sympathize with him. He has a history of violence, his father was in prison, and he won't provide an alibi for Sunday night. If that DNA comes back as a match . . ."

Jordan would be in deep.

"But if Mario and his boys won the fight with Jordan, then how did Mario end up dead? The body I saw in the picture was badly beaten. Much worse than Jordan."

"Maybe Jordan was angry and went after Mario later. Maybe he didn't go alone." Damian scuffed a toe on the concrete. "There isn't much I can do, Conor. The cops will only tell me what they have to, and Jordan won't talk, even to me."

Conor scrambled for an explanation. "None of this makes any sense. How is that package sent to Ward related to all of this? Why would Jordan send Ward a Viking sword, and where would he get one? And how the hell would he have gotten two bodies and a wooden pallet out to that construction site? He doesn't even have a driver's license or own a car."

"I don't know, Conor. The Sixes could have helped him. They could have stolen a van. But without those questions, they would have filed charges. One thing we both agree on is that Jordan has a violent temper."

Conor knew Jordan was all hot temper. He was the exact opposite of cool and calculating. "But Jordan doesn't *plan* anything. That's his big problem."

They went back into the apartment. Damian promised Yvonne he'd keep her informed and that he'd follow up with the police.

The police could hold Jordan for forty-eight hours without pressing charges. Conor had been in a Philadelphia holding cell. He couldn't imagine being locked in one for two days. Jordan might be impulsive and irrational, but he was still a kid, even at eighteen. He wasn't even out of high school yet. There'd be no possibility of getting him out on bail or visiting him until he was charged. Right now, he was at the mercy of the system.

Unfortunately, Conor had little difficulty imagining Jordan fighting until someone ended up dead.

Less than five minutes later, a knock sounded on the door. They exchanged worried glances, and Conor looked through the peephole. Ianelli and Jackson stood on the other side, with a couple of uniforms behind them.

Jackson held up a folded paper. "Open the door. We have a search warrant."

CHAPTER
10

Freshly showered, Louisa emerged from the bedroom in her bathrobe. She squinted at the early morning light streaming through the apartment windows. Lack of sleep had left her head aching and her eyes gritty.

Her gaze swept the kitchen. Where was Conor?

As if on cue, the front door opened, and he led Kirra into the foyer.

"We went for coffee." He set a bag on the kitchen counter and held a cardboard cup toward her.

"Thank you." Louisa accepted the coffee and took a long swallow. "When was the last time I told you that you were the best boyfriend ever?"

"Not today." Conor set his own cup on the kitchen counter, along with a bakery bag.

"Well, you are. You walk the dog *and* bring me coffee. Are those donuts?"

"Specifically, Federal Donuts." He reached down to unsnap the dog's leash. "Two hours of sleep calls for quality sugar."

Louisa and Conor hadn't left Yvonne's apartment until four. They'd stayed until the police had finished hauling boxes of personal items from the boys' bedroom. Then they'd driven home and slept barely two hours before her alarm had woken them.

"I love you." Louisa drank more coffee.

"I'm glad to be of service." He removed two donuts from the bag and handed her an old-fashioned glazed donut. Leaning close, he kissed her on the mouth.

Smiling, she kissed him back then ate the donut in a few bites. Caffeine and sugar tingled in her bloodstream. "You don't have to take off your coat. I'll be ready in one minute."

"We'll be here." Conor drained his coffee.

Louisa returned to the bedroom to tug on a sweater, jeans, and boots. When she emerged, Conor and Kirra were waiting by the door. The black watch cap he wore brought out the turquoise of his eyes and made him look dangerous and devastatingly handsome, hot enough to melt ice. Louisa chuckled. April was rubbing off on her.

He eyed her casual outfit. "You're not dressed for work."

"I'm taking a personal day. Dad needs me this morning, and I want to check on Yvonne and Tyler later." Plus she didn't think she could focus, and as much as she loved her job, she was learning to put the people in her life before work. If her father's new motto was *pleasure before business*, hers was *family and friends come first*.

Conor held her coat open for her. She slid her arms in, wound a scarf around her throat, and pulled on gloves and a hat. Grabbing her coffee, she led the way out of the apartment.

Ten minutes later, they arrived at Ward's town house. Louisa knocked on the door, but her father didn't respond. She pressed the doorbell. "What time is it?"

Conor checked his phone. "Seven thirty."

She waited a few more minutes, then gave the bell a second ring. "Where is he?" She dug in her purse for her phone. She called her father's number. "He's not answering."

"He gave you a key, right?"

"Yes." She fished it from her bag.

Conor handed her the leash and took the key. "Let me go first."

Anxiety built behind Louisa's sternum, and she and Kirra followed him inside and waited in the foyer.

"The alarm isn't beeping," Louisa said.

Conor went down the hall, looking through doorways. "He's not in the kitchen." He continued toward the study.

"Dad?" she called up the stairs, the pitch of her voice rising with her apprehension.

Conor returned, his steps quickening as he moved down the hall. "Wait here."

He jogged up the steps. She heard him opening doors and calling for Ward. Conor's boots sounded on the staircase to the third floor.

Conor reappeared and descended, his face grim. "He's not up there, and the lamp that was on the nightstand is broken."

"The garage?" *Please. Let him be in there.*

The town house was narrow and deep, and the garage exited onto a narrow alley behind the house. Leading Kirra, Louisa followed Conor down a short flight of stairs. A hall led to the wine cellar and utility room, which were both empty. At the end of the corridor, they froze. Kirra raised her head and whined. She put her muzzle to the floor and sniffed. As her nose lifted, a low growl rumbled in her chest.

The security system was wired with two control panels. One was mounted in the coat closet near the front door. The second, located next to the interior door that led to the garage, was broken and hanging askew on its bracket.

"Oh no." Disbelief washed over Louisa in a freezing wave. Someone had broken into her father's house, and he was missing.

Conor turned and they moved back toward the steps.

"I'll call Detective Ianelli." With shaking hands, Louisa took out her phone. She scrolled through her contacts for his number as they hit the landing.

"No need." Conor looked out the front window. "He and Jackson are here."

Louisa's thumb froze over her phone screen. "Why would the police be here?"

"Maybe they have more questions for your dad." Conor opened the front door and let the detectives in. Kirra emitted a low growl as Detective Jackson stepped into the foyer. Was the dog on edge? Kirra had never liked Jackson. Maybe she was just a good judge of character.

The cop took a quick step back, one wary eye on the dog.

Ianelli scanned their faces. "What's wrong?"

"I was just going to call you," Louisa said. "My father isn't here, and his alarm has been destroyed. Why are you here?"

"Your father left me a message late last night. He asked us to stop by this morning." Ianelli frowned. "Why are *you* here?"

"Same reason," Louisa said.

Ianelli faced Conor. "The alarm was destroyed?"

"Smashed, actually," Conor said.

"Where?" Jackson asked.

"Garage." Conor nodded toward the doorway that led downstairs. Jackson headed down the steps.

"I'll check the master. Stay right there, and don't touch anything." Ianelli went upstairs.

The detectives were gone for less than five minutes. Conor wrapped an arm around Louisa and drew her close. But she was numb. Shock fell over her like a blanket of ice. How could this happen? After the strange gift, her father would have been careful.

The detectives returned, their faces grim. They conferred in whispers for a few minutes before addressing Conor and Louisa.

"Ward's car is in the garage," Jackson said. "It appears that the intruder came in through the overhead garage door. He left a coat hanger lying on the cement."

"There's a broken lamp upstairs," Ianelli paused. "And a little blood. The sheets have been pulled off the bed."

Conor hadn't mentioned the blood.

"I don't understand." But deep inside, she did. Too well, and fear blossomed into the first stirrings of panic as she pictured the bodies in the photo. The man beaten to death. The woman with the gaping wound in her throat. Her stomach went queasy.

Jackson walked away, his cell phone pressed to his ear.

"I suspect there was a struggle in the master bedroom." Ianelli guided Louisa and Conor into the kitchen. "It's easy to open a garage door from the outside. You slip a wire coat hanger through the opening at the top of the door and use it to pull the emergency release. Then the door can be raised manually. The interior door isn't even a deadbolt. A child could have opened it with a credit card."

"But my father has a security system." Louisa eased into a chair. Kirra retreated under the table and rested her muzzle on Louisa's foot.

"The system is old and could use some updating," Ianelli said. "What the intruder did is called a 'crash and smash.' A thief breaks in through the entry door. The security system can't tell the difference between the homeowner unlocking his door and the intruder breaking in. The system gives the homeowner thirty to sixty seconds to deactivate the alarm. In that time, the intruder locates the panel and smashes it before the delay runs out. The alarm is in pieces, no longer hard-wired to the phone line. The system never had a chance to call the police or sound an audible alarm. Most newer systems have fail-safes with wireless or cellular communications specifically designed to prevent this kind of break-in."

Louisa had no response. *How could it be that easy?*

Ianelli said, "I want you both to sit right here while we go through the entire house more thoroughly. Which rooms were you in?"

Conor sat next to Louisa and took her hand. "I walked through the whole house looking for Ward. I touched doorknobs as necessary but nothing else."

The detectives walked through the first floor then went up the stairs. Louisa heard the squeaking of floorboards as they searched the rooms.

Conor rubbed her shoulder. "I'm sorry."

Her lungs tightened, and she felt lightheaded. "I should have insisted he come home with us. I shouldn't have taken no for an answer."

"Look at me." Conor turned her chin to face him. "This is not your fault. Your dad is a grown man. You can't make him do anything."

Louisa brushed a tear from her cheek. "He stayed here because he didn't want to endanger me."

"That was his choice, but I wouldn't expect any parent to act differently. You are his number one priority. That's the way it's supposed to be. And he didn't think he was in danger. Neither did the police. No one saw this coming." Conor slid his chair closer and took her hands in his. "But don't give up on him yet. Your dad's smart. He's not going to give up easily."

"He just got his life back together." But inside, all Louisa could think was that she'd just gotten him back in her life. For the first time in decades, she had family. "It isn't fair."

As she sat in the quiet kitchen, she remembered a Christmas, before her mother had gotten sick, before childhood had come to a crashing halt the moment Louisa had heard the first whisper of "cancer." Though Dad had always worked much of the time, he had always cleared his schedule for the weeks around the holidays when the university closed for winter break. Her mother had insisted. There'd been three trees to decorate in the big house in Maine. Lights had sparkled from greenery on the bannister and mantel. Her father seemed to spend much of the day trying to catch her mother under the mistletoe hanging from the foyer chandelier. And every night, a pajama-clad Louisa would curl up in his lap and they would read from his ancient dog-eared copy of *A Christmas Carol*. If she closed her eyes right now, she could conjure the slightly musty scent of that old book in her imagination.

Once her mother was diagnosed, all of that had ended almost as if it hadn't ever been real, as if Louisa's entire life before the age of ten had been a dream. Her father had taken leave from the university to care for her mother. He'd barely left her side. The month her mother had been admitted into hospice care, he'd gone with her. His sister had moved in to care for Louisa. After her mother had died, he'd returned a shell of who he had been.

And then he'd left.

Louisa shook the memory off. She and her father had spent the last few months building a new relationship, trying to leave the sorrow of their past behind. Conor always said that the past couldn't be changed, but the future was wide open.

But maybe Fate had a different philosophy.

Conor squeezed her fingers as the detectives reentered the kitchen. Staying far away from the dog, Jackson leaned on the counter and crossed his arms over his chest.

Ianelli turned a chair to face Louisa. "Does your father usually make his bed?"

"I don't know." Louisa didn't poke around in her father's bedroom, even during the time he'd lived in her condo.

"The sheets were hanging off the bed, a few dresser drawers were open, and we found his wallet on the floor," Ianelli said.

As if someone had dragged her father from his bed.

"No sign of his cell phone," Jackson added. "We'll try and trace it."

"I can do that." Louisa took out her own cell. "He keeps losing his phone, so he made me download an app to find it for him."

She opened the app and waited. "It isn't working."

Nor did they hear a ring when she called her father's number.

"Maybe the battery is dead." Regret crossed the detective's saggy face. "Did he say anything about why he wanted us all here this morning?"

"No." Louisa opened her phone and showed him the texts. "But I assume it was about the package he received on Monday."

"I want you to walk around with me and see if you notice anything out of place or missing." Ianelli stood.

"All right. But he just moved in last week. He still has boxes in the garage." Pressing her palms on the table, Louisa got up. "I don't have a good feel for where everything is supposed to be. Dad is still moving things around to suit him."

"Did you help him move?"

"I spent most of last Saturday and Sunday helping him, yes." Louisa followed the detective into the hall. Conor stayed close behind her.

"I assume he used a moving service?" Ianelli asked.

Louisa nodded. "He hadn't been in Philadelphia long. Many of his household items had to be shipped from Maine."

Her father had closed up the house Louisa had grown up in and put it up for sale. Letting go of the past, he'd said, and embracing the future. Her lungs constricted again. Would he have a future?

"We'll need the name of the moving company." Ianelli paused, looking back through the doorway into the kitchen. "Everything looked normal in there?"

Louisa surveyed the room. "I think so."

"I already have your father's e-mail accounts. He doesn't employ an assistant?"

"No." Louisa sighed. "Except for writing, he hasn't actually worked since last summer when the Swedish university let him go."

"Why did they fire him?"

"His alcoholism interfered with his job," Louisa admitted. While she hated that her father had hit an emotional wall, she'd been grateful that the crisis had turned him around and brought him back to her. "He's been sober for six months." She almost smiled with pride, then remembered he was gone.

They walked through the first-floor rooms and ended up in the study. Moving and having purpose helped.

"This is where he spends most of his time." Louisa crossed to the desk, searching for a clue as to what had happened to him. Why had her father wanted to see her this morning? His laptop sat on the corner of his desk, the top closed, as she would expect. The books he'd written on Viking history and burials covered his desk. *Odd.* If he were going to do research, he wouldn't be reading his own books. In fact, he rarely opened them unless he needed a specific reference. He knew the material inside and out. She scanned a notepad covered with his usual indecipherable scribbling.

"Don't touch anything," Ianelli said. "There's a forensic tech on the way. He's going to dust for fingerprints."

Louisa bent over the desk. Someone had made a sketch on the blotter paper. She pointed to the drawing. "Did you see this?"

The detective nodded. "I was hoping you'd know something about it."

Conor peered over her shoulder. "It looks like a drawing of the crime scene photo I saw in that album."

"Looks pretty accurate too," Ianelli added.

Louisa studied the picture. "There is some dispute in the scientific community about whether eidetic memory really exists, but my father has extraordinary recall." She gestured toward a page tucked in one of the books. "He marked a page. Can we open the book?"

"Let me." Ianelli snapped a pair of nitrile gloves on his hands. Then he opened the book by only touching the edges of the pages. The volume opened to an illustration of an excavated Viking gravesite.

Louisa studied the drawing, looked back at her father's sketch, and she knew.

"Since I saw the photograph on Monday, I haven't been able to get it out of my head." No matter how hard she'd tried. "It looked strangely familiar. I kept wondering if I somehow knew one of the victims. But looking at this, I realize it wasn't the victims that I recognized, it was the positioning of the bodies and the objects arranged around them that seemed familiar. I think my father drew the same conclusion."

"Is that your father's book?" Ianelli asked.

"Yes. It was just published in January." She pointed to the drawing. "This is a sketch depicting the Viking gravesite as my father believes it originally appeared."

Louisa had seen the illustration in the book many times. She stepped away so Ianelli could get closer. In a color-washed sketch, a man and a woman dressed in period clothing lay side by side in a wooden boat surrounded by food, drink, and some household goods. A sword lay at the man's side.

Ianelli and Conor shared a glance. They saw it too.

"There are a lot of similarities in these two pictures. What am I looking at here?" Ianelli pointed at the book's illustration.

"A dead Viking warrior, probably a chieftain. The woman was likely a slave," Louisa explained with a sick feeling in her belly. Conor moved closer, taking her hand.

"Was she some kind of human sacrifice?" Ianelli leaned over the page.

"Not quite, although the Vikings did sacrifice humans to their gods," Louisa continued. "When a Norseman died, he was often buried with goods for him to use in the next world. For a poor man, that might mean a single knife was put in the grave with him. But for a high-ranking chieftain, the ritual would have been much more elaborate. The body would have been finely dressed and perhaps placed in a boat or ship if the man was wealthy. He would have been surrounded by grave goods: weapons, animals, slaves. A warrior who'd been valiant on the battlefield expected to go to Valhalla after death. Food and drink would have been provided for his journey. It was considered an honor to die with one's master. They would ask for volunteers among the female slaves—"

"Who would volunteer?" Ianelli looked up.

Louisa hugged her arms. "The *volunteering* might not have been optional. In any case, the girl would then have sexual intercourse with the men in the village. When the funeral day arrived, she'd be killed by an old woman in charge of such things, then laid to rest beside her master."

Ianelli looked disgusted. "She was gang-raped, then murdered and buried with her master."

"My father insists that we can't impose current-day values and mind-sets on people who lived this far in the past. He says death wasn't the anomaly it is today. Few people survived past the age of forty. Their world was harsh and brutal, and they had no expectations of a long, happy life." Louisa paused. "But I imagine your explanation is fairly accurate."

"Did the sex have a purpose?" Jackson asked from behind his partner, and Louisa wondered when he'd come into the room. She hadn't heard him enter.

"Supposedly to make sure she would serve the master properly." And they all knew what the word *serve* meant, Louisa thought. "A prostitute could be a reasonable modern substitution."

The slave girl and the prostitute were both killed to serve men's needs. The prostitute's death was more recent, but the slave had no doubt suffered an equally violent and appalling end.

Jackson's frown lines crawled down to his chin. "So you think the murder scene was set up in an attempt to copy a Viking send-off, and the woman was killed to accompany the man into Valhalla?"

"I won't speculate on motive, but the parallels are there," Louisa said. "The pizza and beer are food. He was left with a weapon and a woman." She closed her eyes. "Wasn't the wooden pallet under the victims pointed at both ends?"

"Yes," Jackson's eyes narrowed.

"Making it boat-shaped." Conor finished her thought.

Jackson rocked back. "You said these are burial rituals. What about fire?"

Louisa nodded. "Yes. Burial was more common, but remains were also cremated."

Ianelli glanced at his partner, then focused on Louisa again. "Tell me about Valhalla."

"The Vikings believed that if a worthy warrior was felled on the battlefield, a Valkyrie would lead him to Valhalla, the hall of the slain, which was presided over by the god Odin. The Valkyries were supernatural female beings who helped Odin by selecting warriors worthy of Valhalla. There, warriors would fight all day and return to the hall at night to feast. For the Vikings, this was the best outcome for the afterlife and the desire to go to Valhalla was one of the reasons they were such fierce fighters. They walked into battle completely unafraid. They believed if a man lived to be old and died in his bed, he would be stuck in *Helheim*, which was cold and dreary, certainly nothing like the Christian version of heaven."

The connection to Vikings and Valhalla seemed too bizarre to be true, and even as terror formed a cold ball in her belly, Louisa couldn't process the link made by her mind.

Or maybe she didn't want to.

Her father was gone, taken by the person or people who'd killed the two people in the photograph. Would he meet the same fate? Had he already?

She shut that idea down before it consumed her.

Ianelli sat back in his chair, apparently digesting the new information.

A delusional killer ran loose in Philadelphia.

Remembering her close encounter with another unstable murderer, Louisa shivered and reached for the strand of pearls she usually wore, but in her casual state of dress, she hadn't put them on. Conor's hand caught hers, his strong fingers wrapping her in warmth that made her want to climb into his lap.

"What can you tell us about the package Ward received?" Conor asked.

"A lot, actually." At the desk, Ianelli straightened. "The return address on the package is bogus. It's a vacant home in the northeast part of the city. The package was shipped same-day delivery early Monday morning from a Pak 'N Mail on Torresdale Avenue in the same neighborhood. The surveillance camera in the store is broken, and the owner doesn't remember who sent the package. The other businesses in the strip are boarded up. The Pak 'N Mail looks like it's next."

"If the store is failing, then business must be slow. How could he not remember a customer from just a few days ago?" Louisa asked.

Ianelli lifted a disbelieving eyebrow. "That's what he said."

"So the package is a dead end." Frustration—and fear—filled Louisa.

Where was her father? Was he even still alive?

She had to believe he was.

She thought back to the note that had come with the short sword. *Thanks. I couldn't have done it without you.* "The note credited Dad with helping the killer. Maybe he needs more assistance."

"With what?" Ianelli asked.

"I don't know. Information? Dad is an expert on Vikings," Louisa said. "The killer seems obsessed with them too."

"Let's hope you're right," Ianelli said. "If he needs your dad, he'll keep him alive."

"We're still working on that list of artifact dealers you e-mailed to us," Jackson said. "But so far no one remembers seeing a piece like that sword recently. No one knows who might have owned it or where they might have purchased it."

Conor squeezed Louisa's hand. "How about the pizza boxes? Any way to trace those?"

"No," Jackson said. "They're generic, and you know how many pizzas are sold on any given night in this city."

"Did you find any fingerprints on the package or its contents?" Louisa asked.

Ianelli nodded. "Sure. Plenty of them. Yours, your father's, your assistant's, a guy in the museum mailroom, and a few others. But none have popped in our criminal fingerprint database."

For elimination purposes, an officer had taken fingerprints from Louisa, Ward, and everyone at the museum who had touched the package.

"So you have no leads," Louisa said.

Neither detective responded.

"About Jordan Franklin. You still have him in custody?" As usual, it was Conor who threw the curveball, right at the detectives' heads. "There's no way in hell that kid could have conceived or followed through on those murders, and since he's sitting in your holding cell, he sure as hell didn't kidnap Ward." Conor waved his hand over the open book and the photo of the carving. "Do you have any real suspects? Any at all?"

Jackson's gaze flattened. "We're still investigating. But you shouldn't be so quick to discount Jordan Franklin. He's violent, and we've tied him to the male victim with physical evidence. If he has any information that might help us find Ward, I'd think you'd want us to get it."

Ianelli shot his partner a look, then turned his dark, solemn eyes back to Louisa. "We know you're upset. I don't blame you. We'll have autopsy results of the two victims from the construction site today, and we have some leads to follow. I can't be any more specific, but you need to know that we're doing everything we can to find the person responsible. We already have your father's e-mails, contacts, and calendar. We're working on background checks on the people that have interacted with him recently. Although there aren't many, and most of those seem to be in Sweden."

"That's where he spent the majority of his time over the last few decades," Louisa said.

Mentally, Louisa amended her previous assumption. The police had no additional leads that they were willing to share. While she understood that they couldn't divulge all the details of their investigation, she couldn't sit back and wait for them to find her father. They had to follow policies and procedures, which would slow them down. Even if the police refused to admit it, they all knew Ward had been taken by the killer.

CHAPTER
11

Conor fumed as the cops spewed useless information. He didn't want to hear about the leads that *didn't* pan out or the parts of their investigation they hadn't finished.

"There is some indication that this might be a gang-related killing," Ianelli added. "The male victim was involved with the Sixes, a gang that runs out of West Philly. There's a chance this is part of a larger turf war or initiation rite."

Conor glanced at the drawings. "I can't see a gang imitating a Viking burial."

Gangs in Philly tended to utilize drive-by shootings as their main mode of communication.

"Sometimes pending members are required to kill as part of their initiation," Ianelli said. "We can't ignore the fact that Jordan's brother Shawn is hiding and wanted for questioning in the murder of a rival gang member."

Ianelli was the friendlier of the pair, but neither of the cops gave away any emotion in their expressions. Ianelli just stonewalled with a smile rather than a scowl. In a way, Conor almost respected Jackson's brutal honesty more than Ianelli's more diplomatic bedside manner.

"Maybe Dr. Hancock is seeing parallels that don't exist." If only Jackson wasn't such a prick.

"Then why would the killer send the picture and sword to Ward or kidnap him?" Conor asked. He swallowed his temper as he waited for the cops to respond.

And he heard nothing but fucking *crickets*.

"Jordan didn't kill those people." Conor couldn't believe it.

Neither cop so much as blinked.

"Two people have been brutally murdered, and now my father is missing." Louisa's face was drawn and pale, and his heart broke for her. She didn't deserve this, not after everything she'd been through. And he didn't even want to imagine what was happening to her father right now.

Ward might have done a poor job of parenting until the last few months, but late was better than never, and he certainly didn't deserve to die. Louisa had been thrilled to have her father back in her life. God, Conor hoped the cops knew more than they were saying. They'd been working this case since Monday night. If they didn't have any leads by now, then they weren't going to find Ward anytime soon.

"Detectives?" a uniform called from the doorway. The detectives had sent uniformed officers to the other houses on the street to question the neighbors. Ianelli and Jackson stepped out.

"Babe, I am so sorry this is happening." Conor squeezed her hand. He didn't tell her that everything was going to be fine. He respected her too much for empty promises. Besides, she was too smart.

The cops returned in a few minutes.

"One of your neighbors was up feeding her baby and saw a dark cargo van drive into Ward's garage around two a.m.," Ianelli said. "Have either of you seen a vehicle like that in the neighborhood?"

"Not that I remember." Conor glanced at Louisa. She shook her head.

But how would they notice a single vehicle considering the volume of traffic that drove around Rittenhouse Square every day?

"Call me if you do." Ianelli looked toward the hall, where a uniform had appeared.

"Forensics is done," the uniform said. "They bagged the sheets and took a sample of the blood in the bedroom."

"We'll call you if we have any new information." Jackson headed for the door.

Following his partner, Ianelli paused, his gaze on Louisa. "I want you to know that finding your father is our number one priority."

After the cops left, she wandered down the hall into her father's study.

Conor followed her. "Are you all right?"

"I can't just sit here and wait. I want to talk to the neighbor." She pulled her keys from her coat pocket and headed for the foyer.

"We'll be back in a few minutes," she said to the dog.

They went out onto the front stoop, and Conor pulled the door closed.

"It feels ridiculous to lock the house now." But she did it anyway.

Louisa and Conor stood on the sidewalk and scanned the surrounding homes.

He turned to face the house. "If she saw the garage entrance out back, she must live on the same side of the street."

Narrow and deep, the town houses backed to a cobblestone service alley, where the garage entrances were located.

He searched the windows. A curtain moved in the window of the house next door. Through the glass, he saw a woman holding a baby over her shoulder. "There she is."

They went up the steps. The door opened before they rang the bell.

The woman was about thirty, with dark hair fastened on top of her head in a messy bun. She balanced the baby on a bib-draped shoulder. "Can I help you?"

"I'm Louisa Hancock and this is Conor Sullivan. My father lives next door."

"Oh, I'm so sorry. The police said there was a break-in." The baby fussed and the woman started rocking from side to side. "I'm Katrina Walsh. Please come in."

They stepped into a foyer about the same size as Ward's, then followed Katrina down the hall to the kitchen. "I was just trying to have some breakfast. Can I offer you something? Coffee?" Her mouth turned in a wry twist. "It's decaf, I'm afraid. It feels like such a cruel irony that I can't have a drop of caffeine when he's up all night."

Dishes filled the oversize sink, and the fancy granite island was cluttered with plates of half-eaten, congealing food.

"I'd apologize, but I'm totally over the mess." She walked to the island, where a bagel waited on a plate. The second her hip perched on the edge of a stool, the baby began to squirm. She stepped away and rocked.

"You saw someone go into my father's house last night?" Louisa prompted, but the new mother was distracted.

Stroking the baby's head, Katrina jiggled him. "It was about two a.m. We're still waiting for junior here," she nodded toward the baby in her arms, "to sleep through the night." She blew her frizzy bangs out of her eyes. The baby squirmed and started to make mewling sounds. "I'd be happy for four consecutive hours of sleep no matter when they happened."

She swayed with the baby, but he wasn't having any of it. "This is crazy. I just fed him. He cries. All. The. Time. My husband and I are debating whether it's colic or demon possession."

"Let me take him for a few minutes." Conor tossed his jacket over a stool and held out his arms. "What's his name?"

"William. At this point, I'd pass him off to just about anyone." She handed him over with relief. "You're an angel." Katrina nuked a cup of water and tossed in a tea bag. "I haven't sat down for a meal since my husband left for Japan two days ago."

The baby's cries amplified. Conor shifted the baby over his shoulder and rubbed the tiny back. The new position seemed to soothe him, and he quieted. Now maybe the new mom could focus on what she'd seen the night before.

Louisa sat across from Katrina. "My dad is missing."

"Oh no!" Katrina froze for a few seconds, and the shock seemed to sharpen her attention. "I'm so sorry."

"Thank you," Louisa said. "Could you tell me more about the van you saw?"

Nodding, Katrina stayed on point. "The van looked beat up. No windows. I thought it was odd to be arriving at such a late hour. But I haven't even met your father yet. I don't know what kind of vehicle he drives or when he comes and goes."

"Could you see what color it was?" Louisa rested her palms against the island counter.

"No." Katrina wrapped her hands around her mug. "It was dark. I was sitting in the rocking chair in the nursery, half dozing, while my insatiable spawn nursed for the fourth time since midnight. The street-light doesn't quite reach your father's garage door. It was a dark color. Maybe black, dark gray, navy blue. Something like that."

"Did you see the driver?" Conor asked.

"No, the way the view is angled, I could only see the back three-quarters of the van."

"Did you notice when the van left again?"

"No. Shortly after I saw it go inside, I got William down in his crib and went straight to bed."

"Would you show me the nursery?" Conor rested his hand on the baby's back. He couldn't see the infant's face, but William felt heavy and limp, as if he were sleeping.

"Of course." Katrina led them to the hallway and up the stairs. She opened a door at the end of the corridor and stepped aside.

Conor walked into the room. The rocking chair was angled toward the window. He crossed the room and peered down through the glass. From this angle, she would have seen the side and top of the van, maybe even some of the rear.

"Can you think of any distinguishing marks on the van? Patches of rust. Holes. Bumper stickers—"

"There was a dent in the rear bumper," Katrina said.

"Which side?" Louisa asked.

Katrina closed her eyes for a minute. A thinking line appeared between her brows. "The van was facing the house, so that would make it the right side. Oh! I just remembered the van had those rails on the top that you could attach a ladder to, the kind a contractor might drive. William was crying so hard when the police were here I didn't remember the dent or the rails. I should call them."

Conor led the way back downstairs. "Yes. They need all the information they can get."

"I'll do that right away." In the foyer, Katrina tilted her head at the baby. "You have the magic touch. Can I rent you?"

Conor moved his fingertips in a circle on the baby's back. "Under ordinary circumstances, I'd be happy to help out. I love babies. But we really need to go." He turned to Louisa, who looked a bit intimidated. Had he ever seen her with a baby? No. He hadn't.

"He's so fragile. You're much more comfortable with him than I would be." Louisa reached up and hesitantly touched the back of the baby's head. A wistful smile lifted the corner of her mouth. So she wasn't used to babies, but maybe she'd like to be. Someday. When this was all over.

Katrina reached for her baby. Despite her obvious exhaustion, love shone from her eyes.

Cradling the downy head, Conor shifted him from his shoulder to his mother's arms. "You should call someone to help out."

"My mother is coming tonight." Katrina smiled at her baby. "The minute she gets here, I'm crawling into bed. Or I'm taking a shower. Maybe a shower then bed."

"That sounds like a good plan." Conor grabbed his jacket from the kitchen.

Katrina showed them to the door. "Good luck. I hope you find your father."

"Thank you," Louisa said.

"Lock up, and keep your alarm set." Conor closed the door softly behind them.

They collected Kirra and headed back to the Rittenhouse, walking in silence until they reached the condo.

Inside, they stripped off their outerwear, then Louisa paced the floor of the living room. "I can't just sit here and wait."

Conor stopped her with two hands on her biceps. The intense desperation in her eyes warned him that she wanted to take action. "You are not a cop."

"I know I'm not. But I hate feeling so useless." She slumped for a moment, and then her spine snapped straight. "Wait. I have an idea."

"I don't like the sound of that."

"It's nothing dangerous." She pulled her phone from her pocket and made a call. "Hello, Xander? This is Louisa Hancock. I need to ask you a favor. Are you free today?" She paused, listening, then frowned. Her gaze shifted to the clock on the cable box. "When will you be back? I'll see you at three then."

"Who was that?" Conor asked, suspicious.

"The dealer who sold the museum the last acquisition for the *Celtic Warrior* collection. He specializes in antique arms and armor, both as a dealer and manufacturer of re-creations." Louisa resumed her pacing. "If anyone knows about Viking pieces in this area, it's Xander. His shop is about forty minutes away. We have a few hours until Xander returns to his shop. I wish I could think of some other lead to check out."

Conor faced her again and gave her arms a quick shake. "Getting involved in this investigation is dangerous."

The idea terrified him, and her nightmares said it scared the hell out of her too. But he knew she would never let fear stop her.

"I know, but I have to do something." Louisa's mouth tightened. "This is my father. He's gone. The police are checking backgrounds and interviewing artifact dealers, but I *know* Xander. He won't just look through his transactions for me. He'll talk to me. Whoever sent Dad that sword kidnapped him."

"Jackson and Ianelli know that too," Conor argued. "They're on this. We both know from the last investigation that they don't like to share information with us."

Yet he understood her point exactly. When she'd been in danger, Conor had gotten the runaround from the cops. He hadn't been satisfied with sitting back and letting the police handle the case. The cops had come around in the end, but Louisa might not be alive if Conor hadn't followed his hunch.

"I'm going to call Reed," Conor said. Jayne's husband, a former homicide detective, was in Denver visiting his son at college. Jayne and Reed had married in December. "Maybe he can help."

Reed didn't answer his phone. Conor left a message. Now what? They had hours to wait to see her artifact dealer contact.

"We don't even know if Dad's still alive." Her voice broke.

As much as he wanted to find her father, Conor's heart clenched at the thought of her being anywhere near this case. He wanted to lock her in a secure room and guard the door with a machine gun until the culprit was in prison. But despite her elite upbringing, Louisa wasn't the ivory-tower type of girl. Money truly did not buy love, and growing up, she'd learned the hard way to depend only on herself. The people in her life had continuously let her down.

He would not.

"I can't let anything happen to you." He cupped her jaw.

"The police aren't perfect. Their last investigation almost got us killed. Everything they do is slowed by red tape and procedure. The autopsies haven't even been done yet. How long will it take them to process the evidence and get the results from their laboratory tests?" She didn't wait for him to answer. "More time than my father has." Her gaze met his. Tears shone in her green eyes.

"OK. But we leave the gangs alone. I can't risk them coming anywhere near you or my family."

She tilted her head into his hand. "Agreed. I would never do anything to put them in jeopardy. We'll talk to Xander and go from there."

Conor brushed her cheek with his thumb. "You don't know how much I don't want you near any of this. I love you more than I can possibly express with words."

"I know. I'm sorry. I seem to be nothing but trouble."

"Don't ever think that." Emotions roiled in his chest as he thought back to October, to Louisa almost dying. He pulled her close and held her.

"I don't know what I'm going to do if . . ." Her voice trailed off, as if she couldn't bear to finish her thought.

"Shh. We don't need to go there yet." He stroked her back. Her body trembled in his arms, and he remembered the frustration, the anger, the terrifying helplessness he'd felt when she'd been taken. The sheer desperation of that night came flooding back to him.

"Conor." Her hands gripped his shoulders. Desire and despair warred in her eyes. "I'm scared, and I'm numb. Make me feel. Please."

Her plea stripped him raw.

He lowered his head, the need to connect with her overruling all else. His mouth claimed hers, and heat flared between them. Coming up for air, he slid her sweater up and over her head. He unhooked her bra, letting it fall to the floor. His palms brushed over her breasts and need throbbed through him like a pulse, as if his heart beat for both of them. His hands skimmed up the sides of her ribs. His fingers paused on the bullet scar, and his heart skipped a beat.

In a very short period of time, this woman had become his everything.

Her hands found the hem of his shirt. He ducked his head as she ripped it from his body, her hands seeking his skin with the same desperation as his.

"I can't lose you." A primal need to be part of her roared through his veins like a subway train. The sheer volume of it blocked out all his other thoughts.

"You won't." Her hands slipped down his abs and unsnapped his jeans.

But he couldn't wait, and though he felt like an animal, he had to be in control. Of this.

Of her.

He slid his hand into the front of her jeans. As he worked her toward a quick release, her head fell back. A deep groan built in her throat. Her hands gripped his arms, as if she needed him for balance.

But it wasn't enough. His every sense demanded he be steeped in her.

He lifted her to the counter and yanked the jeans from her ankles. He tossed them on the floor. "I need all of you. Don't hold back."

"I couldn't if I wanted to," she panted.

He dropped to one knee, draped her legs over his shoulders, and put his mouth to her center. Her taste filled him, and he drove her up and over another peak. Her body went taut.

She cried out, "Conor."

The sound of his name from her lips pulled him to his feet. He wriggled out of his jeans and stepped between her legs. No barriers. There was nothing between them. They were both stripped bare. Equally exposed. Vulnerable.

Never had a woman reduced him to this state.

Conor's desire grew. Physical sensation wasn't enough and never would be with her. There was so much more to the bond between them.

He wrapped her legs around his waist and carried her to the bedroom. Lowering her onto the mattress, he eased on top of her. Hooking one of her legs over his arm, he slid inside her. Her head fell back and she moaned, the sound low and deep and primitive.

"Open your eyes." Conor slowed. His movements were careful and deliberate as he withdrew and thrust into her again. "I want to see you come for me."

Her eyes fluttered open. He kept his rhythm deliberate. He loved her with his body, but now his heart was in control.

As much as he wanted the act to last forever, pleasure and passion and love built until he couldn't hold back anymore.

In the end, he wasn't in control at all.

He released into her with a final roar and collapsed on her. His heart pounded as if he'd just finished three rounds of sparring.

What had just happened?

It wasn't like him to need to dominate. Louisa was his partner, not his conquest, and he was as much in love with her mind and her heart as he was with her body.

He lifted his head. "I'm sorry if I was too rough. I didn't hurt you, did I?"

"You would never do that." Her fingers played with his hair, and she seemed calmer than before.

"I don't know what got into me. I should have been focused on you." But his lack of control over the situation had taken over.

"No one has ever made me feel what you do." She stroked his jaw. "I can't hold anything back with you. There's no part of me that you don't possess. My body and my heart belong to you."

But it was she who owned him, body and soul.

He rolled onto his back, pulling her with him. She rested her head on his chest. A few minutes later, his heart rate and breathing slowed to normal.

He glanced up at the clock. "I'm going to grab a shower before we drive out to your artifact dealer."

"You're coming with me?" she asked.

"I'm sure as hell not letting you go alone." He would do anything she asked, except let her out of his sight.

"I wouldn't go see a complete stranger alone, but I know Xander. I've been dealing with him for years, even before I moved to Philadelphia."

"I'm still going with you." As much as Conor believed she was his partner and equal, this was not up for debate. He would never allow her to compromise her safety. He levered up on one elbow and traced the scar on her ribs. "I will help you find your father, but I need a promise from you."

Her head tilted.

"I want to be with you every moment from now until this is over." He stroked her cheek. "We do this together."

"Deal, though I hate to put you at risk. Your family needs you."

Conor kissed her mouth. He wanted to find Ward, but not at the expense of Louisa. He took her hand, kissed it, and held it to the center of his chest. "If anything ever happened to you, my heart would shatter."

Louisa's eyes teared. "What did I do to deserve you?"

The dog interrupted the moment with a telltale whine at the door.

"I'll take her out." Conor rolled off of her, took a quick detour into the bathroom, then pulled on a pair of jeans and a T-shirt. He stepped into his running shoes, leaned over, and gave Louisa a soft kiss. "Be right back."

He stopped in the hall for the dog's leash and his jacket. In the elevator, he said to the dog, "Be quick. We were in the middle of something important."

Kirra wagged her stump, but being a couch potato, she did her business quickly. Conor walked her back into the building and stopped to collect the mail. Back upstairs, he gave the dog a treat and sorted the mail. Bills went into a pile, and he tossed the junk mail into the recycling. Taking an envelope addressed to Louisa with him, he went back into the bedroom. The empty bed and rush of water directed him to the bathroom. Leaning on the counter, he took a minute to enjoy the sight of Louisa's nude silhouette through the steamy glass.

Then he stripped and joined her. She'd twisted her hair on top of her head to keep it dry.

"We don't have time." But as she said it, her eyes drifted down his body.

Nice.

He resisted the urge to flex a bicep. "I know. You need to eat. Doesn't mean I can't enjoy the view."

Smiling, she got out and dried herself while Conor took a two-minute shower. Then, with a towel around his hips, he joined her in front of the vanity to brush his teeth. Already dressed in jeans and a sweater, she picked up the yellow envelope and opened the flap. "What's this?"

"Probably junk." Conor finished up and went toward the bedroom for clean clothes.

He was fastening the button on his jeans when her gasp stopped him. He rushed back into the bathroom. She'd dropped the envelope and was staring at something in the palm of her hand.

"What is it?" He stepped closer.

It was a heavily corroded ring. Louisa's face, so pleasantly flushed just a minute before, had drained to white. Conor picked up the envelope, shook out a slip of paper, and read the note: "For my beloved."

CHAPTER
12

Ianelli couldn't believe Dr. Hancock was once again linked to a weird-ass case of murder and kidnapping. This lady couldn't get a break. He stared at the ring on her granite countertop. "What is it?"

She looked rattled. Again. And he felt all sorts of shitty for not being able to find her father. Lately, he'd felt shitty about all kinds of things.

"I know it's a bronze ring. I can't say more for certain without documentation, but I can make an educated guess. Based on the short sword my father received, I'd bet this is a Viking marriage ring."

Jackson leaned over and studied it. "It's awfully small."

"It was meant to be worn on the smallest finger." Dr. Hancock reached for the bottle of ibuprofen and then the glass of water that Sullivan had put down at her elbow.

"Are these rare?" Ianelli asked.

She swallowed two tablets and washed them down with a gulp of water. "No. Farmers find small items like this all over Britain and Europe, much like New Englanders are always uncovering arrowheads."

They all knew it wasn't the cost, but the meaning of the ring that had significance.

Ianelli bagged the envelope, ring, and note. The message freaked him out the most. *For my beloved* sounded way too personal for his comfort. "Do I need to tell you to be extra careful?"

"No." She closed the lid on the bottle with shaky hands.

"She won't be out of my sight." Sullivan looked like he meant it.

"We'll see what we can find out from the packaging and postmark, and there's always the possibility of finding fingerprints." Ianelli stood and followed Jackson to the door.

Sullivan let them out, his face grim. "Find this guy before he comes after her."

Jackson went out the door.

Ianelli paused. "We're doing our best."

Sullivan shoved a hand through his hair. "Right."

"Seriously." Ianelli glanced back as he stepped into the hall. "We don't want anything to happen to her either. She's a class act. Look after her. Call me if you see anything suspicious."

With a nod, Sullivan closed the door.

Ianelli and Jackson rode the elevator downstairs and walked outside, where their unmarked car waited by the fountain, drained dry for winter. They got into the car. Ianelli poured the bottom quarter of his coffee down his throat and tucked the empty in the cup holder. There wasn't enough caffeine to get his brain running on all cylinders today. Two hours of sleep after questioning Jordan Franklin and searching his mother's apartment couldn't have prepared him for Ward's disappearance. Lunchtime had arrived, they hadn't eaten, and his energy was lagging. "Do you think Ward is still alive?"

"This guy beat a trained boxer," Jackson said. "A fifty-nine-year-old scholar wouldn't be able to put up much of a fight."

"No," Ianelli agreed in a depressed voice.

Damn it. Ianelli liked Ward and his daughter. And she didn't need any more heartache. He scratched his scalp, as if the motion would activate his brain cells. "Assuming he's not dead yet, where is he?"

"Our best bet is to focus on the murders." Jackson scrolled on his phone. "This killer didn't hold onto his first victims very long. If you weren't hung up on the pretty doctor, you'd admit that the chances of finding Ward alive are slim."

Ianelli shot his partner an irritated glare. Jackson was exceptionally smart, but he could also be a complete dick, and not the kind that was a flattering noir nickname for a whiz detective. But Ianelli elected not to point out his partner's personality flaws.

"I'm not counting Ward out yet. If Dr. Hancock's theory is right that this killer wants Ward's expert opinion, he'll need to keep him alive to provide it." Ianelli didn't address the jibe at his inability to remain objective. Every cop had certain victims and cases that slid under his skin. But maybe nothing got under Jackson's rhino hide.

What mattered now was finding the killer—and Ward Hancock.

Plus, telling Jackson he was an ass was like telling a fish it could swim.

So Ianelli circled back to the case. "Dr. Gonzalez was going to do the autopsies this morning. It's after one. Let's swing by her office and forensics before the meeting with the gang task force guys. We can drop this ring off while we're there."

"Tell you what, you go see Dr. Gonzalez and check on forensics." Jackson looked up from his phone screen, his forehead crinkling in thought. "That FBI art crime expert just e-mailed me back. I'll meet with him while you're with the ME."

"You're just avoiding Gonzalez."

Jackson shook his head. "We have a lot of ground to cover. It'll be faster if we split up. Avoiding Gonzalez is just a side bennie. Besides, my presence will only make her mad. You'll do better without me."

"Still not going to tell me why she hates you?"

"It's personal." Jackson clamped his mouth shut and shifted his gaze to the passenger window.

Ianelli felt his eyebrows shoot up. "I didn't know you had a personal life."

Jackson sighed. "It's not much, I promise."

Nope. Jackson wasn't going to own up to anything. *Not a shock.*

"I know this case is a priority, but we haven't experienced this kind of speed with forensics . . ." Driving toward the medical examiner's office, Ianelli considered their past cases. "Ever."

Jackson gnawed on a piece of gum. "The mayor is still hypersensitive about the media backlash on the Museum Murders, and the captain has concerns about the unusual aspects of this case."

"So do I."

The Philadelphia Forensic Sciences Bureau had been struggling with a massive backlog of evidence for years. Recently, outsourcing had reduced the delays, but having your case sent to the front of the line was a nice break.

Ianelli parked in front of the square brick building that housed the medical examiner's offices and the forensics department. He got out, leaving the engine running.

Jackson rounded the vehicle and talked over the roof. "You want me to swing back here and pick you up?"

"Nah." Ianelli stepped up onto the sidewalk. "I'll get a ride back to the station. Meet you there."

Jackson waved, slid behind the wheel, and pulled away from the curb.

Inside the block structure, Ianelli signed in and made his way to the medical examiner's office, where the receptionist told him Dr. Gonzalez was in the autopsy suite. Ianelli hesitated. Many detectives were compelled to attend the autopsies of their cases, but watching the ME slice through dead bodies wasn't Ianelli's cuppa. But he was short on time, so he suited up and went in.

Dr. Gonzalez was stepping away from a stainless steel table. She stripped off her gloves and lifted her face shield. "Good timing. I've just finished."

Timing is everything.

He waited in silence as she removed her blood-spattered outer gown and tossed it into a bin, then stopped at the sink to scrub her hands. Dr. Gonzalez intimidated the hell out of him, but not because she was taller and a thousand times more athletic. It was the sheer and utter capableness that exuded from her every atom. Dr. Renee Gonzalez got shit done.

She dried her hands and turned back to him. "First of all, my time of death estimates stand. With the variables in temperature, there's no way to accurately narrow that window. Now let's start with the male victim. Cause of death was blunt force trauma to the head." She moved to a computer against the wall and clicked on a file. On the table next to the computer lay a cane, a length of pipe, and a piece of rebar. Close-up photographs of wounds were lined up on the screen.

"We found traces of rust in some of the wounds on the male. The object used to inflict that damage was metal with a diameter of approximately one inch." She pointed to an image. "This is the head wound. When we parted the hair, we could clearly see there's a texture to the contusion." She used the mouse to hover over two other pictures. "We see it here and here as well."

Ianelli's gaze flicked to the ribbed steel reinforcing bar on the table. "Rebar."

"Yes." Gonzalez nodded. "The texture or ribbing is a good match for the pattern on the contusions. Also, rebar is intentionally left to rust a bit before it's used. The combination of the ribbing and rust help grip the concrete and make it stronger."

"Rebar is all over the city." Ianelli grimaced.

"That is unfortunate, but the ridges and rust would hold onto DNA evidence the same way it grips concrete."

"If we can find it, there'll be DNA on it."

"I would bet on it." Gonzalez moved to a second set of photos. "Moving on to the female. This victim was not in the exemplary condition of the male. Her teeth and internal organs show damage consistent with heavy meth use, so you were right about her addiction. The blade of the knife that was in the male victim's hands matches the wound on the female's throat. Fingerprints from the handle are being matched. You can check with Michael to see if those comparisons are complete."

"Thank you, Doctor." Ianelli tossed his gown and booties in the bin on the way out and made his way to the lab where forensics tech Michael White worked.

At a stainless steel table, Michael hunched over a microscope. He looked up as Ianelli walked in. In his mid-thirties, Michael looked like the geek he was: skinny body, wire-framed glasses, and the Elmer's Glue pasty skin of a man who spent all his time in the lab.

"We're still processing the evidence, but I have a few interesting finds that I thought you might want to know about immediately." The tech slid off his stool and moved to another long table against the wall.

"The only fingerprints on the knife were Mario's. We only found one set of prints, and they line up with the position of his fingertips on the knife at the scene."

"So the knife was wiped and then placed in Mario's grip," Ianelli said.

"Seems that way," Michael said. "Normally, we don't see one clear set of fingerprints on anything. We get partials and smudges and consider ourselves lucky to get one or two usable prints."

"Anything special about the knife?" Ianelli asked.

"Unfortunately not. It's a very common, inexpensive utility knife. Mass-produced and sold at thousands of retailers across the country."

So Ianelli would try to trace it, but he wouldn't hold his breath. "Did you come up with anything else?"

"Yes. I managed to brush away some of the charred wood and get a clearer image of that carving on the front of the pallet. I made you a copy of the picture." He handed a photo to Ianelli.

"What the hell is that?" Ianelli squinted at the image. It was an animal. "A horse maybe."

Michael shook his head. "Too many legs for a horse."

Ianelli counted eight. This case just got weirder and weirder.

"Thanks, Michael." Ianelli went downstairs and caught a ride back to the station with a patrol car. En route, he tried to call Jackson but got flipped to voice mail. He sent him a quick text: Where are you?

Jackson wasn't at the station either. Ianelli hit his desk. He booted up his computer, went through his e-mails, checked his inbox, and reviewed the statements from Ward's neighbors taken by the uniforms. Ianelli's query in ViCAP, the FBI's database of violent and sexual crimes, hadn't turned up any real matches.

"Excuse me, Detective Ianelli?"

He looked up to see a twelve-year-old in a patrol uniform standing next to his desk. OK, the guy was probably at least twenty-five, but had been cursed with big blue eyes and a freckled baby face no criminal would ever take seriously.

"Yeah."

"You had us review the surveillance videos from Rittenhouse Square. I found footage of a dark cargo van turning into the alley behind Ward Hancock's town house at two-oh-five a.m." The kid handed him a USB flash drive. "I thought you'd want to see it for yourself."

"Thanks." Ianelli inserted the drive into his computer and clicked on the video. The camera's range didn't include Ward Hancock's garage door, but the van turning into the alley matched the neighbor's description: dark gray or blue, roof rails, dented rear bumper.

"Unfortunately, the camera is focused on the storefront." The kid peered over his shoulder. "The alley entrance is in the periphery, and the image of the van is blurry. We can't see the license plate number or the driver."

"See if the tech guys can clean it up." Ianelli made a copy of the file and handed the drive back to the patrolman.

"Yes, sir."

Jackson hadn't returned when it was time to meet Pete Giles from the gang task force. After leaving his partner another message, Ianelli gathered his files and headed for the conference room alone.

The meeting left him with a folder full of information on the key members of the Sixes but few answers. He already knew the gang task force was looking for Shawn Franklin because a witness had seen him running from the scene of a gang execution six weeks ago, and the bodies at the construction site had been left with too much care to be typical violent-and-messy gang murders.

Ianelli swept the files into a pile and went back toward his desk. Then he fielded a call from a Reed Kimball. Wonderful. Conor Sullivan's brother-in-law was a former homicide detective. Despite his slight irritation at the intrusion, Ianelli gave Kimball a brief rundown of the case so far. He omitted the forensic details they would hold back from the public, though. Professional courtesy was no justification to jeopardize the case.

Ianelli ended the call as Jackson came down the hall, which was just as well. Jackson wouldn't have approved of the professional-courtesy share.

"Did I miss the meeting?"

"You did." Ianelli dropped the files on his partner's desk, which faced his. "Where've you been?"

"The FBI agent liked to talk." Jackson draped his coat over the back of his chair and dropped into the seat. "Agent Murray's assessment of the sword matches Dr. Hancock's. It's a nice piece but nothing extraordinary, certainly not worth stealing for its monetary value. However, he made a few calls and found out that a Viking battle-axe of questionable provenance appeared at an auction house a few weeks ago. He'll try to find out where it came from. Hopefully, we'll hear from him later today. No one else reported any recent interest in Viking artifacts or a ninth-century short sword."

"One possible lead, even a remote one, is better than nothing."

"I suppose." Jackson stretched his neck. "How was your day, dear?"

With a snort, Ianelli summed up the autopsy and forensic findings.

Jackson nodded, absorbing the information. "What did Giles with the gang task force have to say?"

"Not much we didn't already know. Our male victim, Mario Avana, was a solid Sixes member. He'd had some moderate success in a few local boxing tournaments." Ianelli skimmed another report. "They have nothing on Jordan, but they want to talk to Shawn about that murder of the Big K member."

"Face it, we have more loose ends than anything else." Jackson got up and put on his coat.

"Where are we going?"

"To talk to the hooker's roommate," Jackson said. "We've been chasing Mario's killer all day. Let's see if we can figure out how the killer found her."

Ianelli grabbed his coat, and they went outside to the car. He held out his hand.

"I can drive the car." Jackson propped a hand on his hip.

"You know I hate to be driven."

With a shrug, Jackson tossed him the keys.

Ianelli slid behind the wheel. "I have control issues."

"No kidding." In the passenger seat, Jackson fastened his seat belt.

Ianelli started the car. Had his partner really been with the FBI agent that long? Or had he been doing something else? Something he didn't want to explain? And once again, Ianelli wondered what had initiated Jackson's last transfer. Had Jackson beaten confessions out of suspects?

All questions there was no point in asking. Jackson wouldn't give him a straight answer.

Ianelli pulled away from the curb. "So what do we do with Jordan Franklin? Do you really think he's guilty?"

"We continue to hold him in detention as long as we can. I'm sure he's guilty of something," Jackson said. "Besides, if we let him out, chances are he'll either disappear or end up dead."

"Too much about this case doesn't make sense." Ianelli bit back his frustration. "According to Jordan's statement, the fight with Mario took place around eight p.m. and Mario kicked his ass. Say Jordan went after Mario later when Mario wasn't with his pals. But if Jordan killed Mario, why wouldn't he take his medallion back?"

"Maybe he killed Mario by accident and freaked out afterward."

"Then when and why did he kill the prostitute?" Ianelli merged into traffic.

"Maybe she saw him kill Mario. Maybe his missing brother helped. According to everyone we've interviewed so far, Shawn is a very smart kid."

"So we could be looking at Jordan *and* Shawn, rather than Jordan *or* Shawn," Ianelli admitted. "It fits with that notebook full of Viking letters and their meanings that we found in the boys' bedroom."

At least one of the Franklin boys had been studying the Viking alphabet. There had been other notes inside as well, and enough general information on Vikings to disturb Ianelli, considering the killer had an identical obsession.

"Which Jordan claims not to know anything about." Jackson snorted. "Too bad his prints were on the outside cover."

"But not on the inside." Which Ianelli thought was odd.

Jackson shrugged it off. "Maybe Shawn is the better artist or he kept the written records."

"We don't know that the notebook belonged to Shawn. He's never been arrested. His prints aren't on file."

Jackson rolled his eyes. "Who else's fingerprints would be on a notebook found in *Shawn's* backpack in the bedroom he shared with his brothers?"

They'd eliminated Yvonne and Tyler as possibilities the night of the search.

Jackson tapped a hand on his thigh. "Let's say Shawn and Jordan went after Mario hoping to find him alone. They killed Mario. Either the hooker got in the way or she saw them off Mario. So they had to kill her."

"That fits the kid's personality better," Ianelli said. "Jordan is a hot mess."

The kid had punched a cop when they'd brought him in, and he'd exploded multiple times during the interview.

But the theory still felt off to Ianelli. "Something about these murders just doesn't feel like the sort of random violence gangbangers commit."

Jackson turned to stare out the window. "I'm never surprised by the violent acts people are capable of committing."

Ianelli's phone beeped. He glanced at the display. "It's Michael in forensics."

He answered the call. "Michael. Ianelli and Jackson here. You're on speaker."

"Just got the DNA report back." Michael's voice sounded faint through the tiny speaker. "The hair sample found on Mario Avana's body belongs to Jordan Franklin."

CHAPTER
13

He gazed through the doorway at his guest. Dr. Ward Hancock was awake. Dressed in flannel pajamas, the scholar sat on the edge of the cot. His elbows were propped on his knees, and he cradled his head in his palms as if it hurt. A metal shackle and heavy chain connected his ankle to a water pipe that ran below the concrete foundation.

"I'm sorry the accommodations are so rough." He felt terrible not being able to provide more appropriate lodgings for his esteemed guest. The heat was unreliable, but blankets were plentiful. "I'm sure you've slept in worse places. You're an archeologist. Don't you camp at excavation sites?"

Ward lifted his head but ignored the question. He rubbed his bruised and swollen jaw. His resistance proved he wasn't yet on board with the grand plan.

"I'm sorry I had to hit you, but you didn't give me any choice." A couple of jabs to the jaw had knocked the scholar out cold. Then he'd had to carry him down to the van, which he'd brought into the garage after he'd broken in. "Do you need an aspirin or perhaps an ice pack? I wish you would have come along without an altercation."

"Did you really expect me to?" Ward shifted his jaw back and forth, as if he were trying to determine if it was broken.

"I suppose not."

The scholar hadn't cooperated, but then how do you react to finding a man at your bedside in the middle of the night? Breaking into the town house had been ridiculously easy. He'd found how-to videos online. Hello, YouTube. Luck—or the gods—had been with him as well. If the security system had been newer, his crude method of disabling it wouldn't have worked.

"I took the liberty of bringing some of your clothes from your house." He pointed toward a stack at the foot of the cot. "Jeans, sweaters, socks." He didn't want Ward to catch pneumonia. "Try to think of yourself as a guest."

"What are you doing?" Ward looked around his quarters. The bathroom was just steps away from his cot. The door had been removed, of course, but he would still have a measure of privacy. A scholar deserved respect, at least as much as was possible under the circumstances.

"You must have a headache. Maybe we should discuss this tomorrow." He took a step back.

"Wait!" Ward called out. "Why did you kidnap me?"

"To fulfill our dream."

"What are you talking about?" Ward stared, open-mouthed.

"This is our dream, Ward."

"You're the one who killed those people and sent me the short sword," Ward said.

"Yes. I thought the gift was appropriate. I didn't realize until later that you needed to play a more pivotal role in my quest."

"You're crazy."

"Don't be so judgmental," he snapped. "This was all your idea."

Relax.

Ward was an intelligent man. He'd come around. After all, his own plan was still evolving. While he'd been fascinated by the Vikings as long as he could remember, it wasn't until recently that the voice had made his destiny clear. The scholar needed time to process his new role.

Forcing himself to calm down, he leaned on the doorframe. The night's adventure had been stressful, but now that it was over, he was exhilarated. Dr. Ward Hancock was here. The plan was underway.

"I don't even know you." Ward stood and walked the length of his chain, stopping six feet before the doorway. The links rattled as they scraped across the concrete.

"That hurts. I can't believe you don't remember me." He supposed a single, brief meeting wouldn't have been so monumental from the scholar's perspective, but deep inside, he'd hoped he'd made an impression on Ward. He should have known better. Hope did not make people love. He'd learned that the hard way.

All his life, he'd known he was different, that he didn't quite fit in with his peers, that he was meant for something greater. But it was only after enduring great loss and reading Ward's books that his dreams had revealed his true fate.

"Well, I don't." Ward stopped. "Why am I here?"

"Because I need your help. You *are* the expert."

"In what?"

"Valhalla." The sound of the word rolling off his lips gave him goose bumps. There he would find others like him. Valhalla was filled with warriors who were not content to allow misfortune to bulldoze over them. Those who would fight until their dying breaths despite overwhelming odds.

"What do you need to know about Valhalla?"

"Everything. I've read all your books. You describe the Hall of the Slain perfectly. But how do I get there?"

"You want to go to Valhalla?" Ward asked. "Hand me a knife. I'll send you there right now."

"Come now. Of all people, you know it isn't as simple as that." Frustration stoked the embers of anger in his belly. He mustn't fail. The voice in his dreams was adamant. "A warrior must prove his worth in battle, and even then, the selection is made by a Valkyrie. No man can send another to Valhalla. The reward must be earned, and the warrior chosen. Things that are easy to obtain are worthless."

"So what do you need me for?"

"For professional guidance." Excitement filled him. "How do I prove my worth? How many opponents must I kill?"

Ward looked horrified. "I'm not helping you kill anyone."

"You needn't worry about that. I'll do all the killing. I just want your advice on who and how. For instance, is it best to use bare hands or weapons? The voice is always so cryptic when what I need is concrete instructions."

"What voice?"

"The one that comes to me in my dreams." The voice that delivered his prophesy.

Ward paled. "Who were those people you killed?"

"Mario was a promising fighter. Frankly, I thought he would have been more of a challenge." The fight had been a disappointment, but perhaps taking Mario directly after he'd fought another young man had been the mistake. Mario had already been tired when their match had begun. But excitement had gotten the better of him. He hadn't been able to wait, and Mario had been easily manipulated. At the mention of a possible sponsorship, the fighter had gotten into the car without another question.

"And the woman?" Ward swallowed, his eyes closing for a second.

"I don't remember her name. She was a prostitute I arranged to meet online. Any hooker would have filled the need. Mario was the important one. He fought well until the bitter end. He never gave up but went down swinging. He deserved to be properly accompanied on his journey, don't you think?"

Ward didn't respond.

"Let me ask you this. Mario didn't have a weapon, but I did. Do you think that matters? Do I need to fight with brutal disregard or do the Valkyries value honor? Everything I've read about the Vikings— and I've read each of your books multiple times—indicates they killed with single-minded brutality. They showed no mercy. They slaughtered priests and women and children. What's your opinion? Is it ruthlessness on the battlefield or courage? What are the Valkyries looking for?"

Ward backed up and dropped weakly to the cot. "I can't believe this is happening."

Clearly the man hadn't recovered from the blow to his jaw. A scholar wasn't a fighter. He wouldn't be used to being struck.

"I'll tell you what. We'll talk again later, after you've recovered and come to terms with our arrangement. I've left you food and drink." He gestured to a gallon of water, beef jerky, and a sack of apples piled by the door. "Get some rest, Ward. We have a lot of work to do." He backed out of the room, closing the heavy door and fastening the padlock. Even if Ward somehow managed to free his leg—the man *was* brilliant—the room had no windows and the padlock was heavy-duty.

"I'm not helping you with anything!" The door muffled Ward's shout.

He paced in front of his guest's quarters. Ward would come around to his way of thinking. Until then, the room was secure. The warehouse was well insulated and isolated. No one would hear Ward if he called out. Eventually the scholar would help him achieve his goal. He had to.

A new idea occurred to him.

Louisa.

She wasn't an expert on Vikings, but her knowledge had to be fairly extensive. He couldn't get her out of his head anyway. Every time he rethought his plans through, she played a larger role in them. She was the perfect woman. Perfect for him.

Maybe even perfect forever . . .

But that was a decision he didn't have to make yet. Until then, it was time to select the next challenge. He walked past the cargo van and over some red streaks on the concrete. Mario had fought well indeed. Doubt welled in his chest. Would Mario have lost if the fight had been more fair? If that blow to the head hadn't taken him down in the first moments?

Had the victory been valid?

But he couldn't afford to lose, not yet, not before he'd proven his worth. If he died now, he'd miss his true calling. Valhalla only waited for the best.

CHAPTER
14

Louisa got out of the car. A frigid wind swept across the hilltop, and she wrapped her coat around her body. The cold matched the empty chill inside her.

Buch's Antique Arms and Armor perched on top of a rise in Holland, a Pennsylvania suburb forty minutes northeast of Philadelphia. Despite its proximity to the city, Holland held onto its rural roots. From the rise, snowy pastures rolled away on all sides. The farm next door looked vacant and sported a For Sale sign near the road.

Jayne and her husband had moved to the suburbs. Reed wanted a yard for their child. Would Conor want grass and trees some day?

There were so many things they'd never discussed. She'd been injured, then her father had lived with them for months. They'd barely been given a week on their own before all this happened.

Though she usually enjoyed the view, this morning she didn't pause for a deep breath of fresh air. Conor rounded the car and wrapped an arm around her. She leaned into him.

Did it make her less of an independent woman to appreciate the strength in him? Oh, who cared? She needed him, and he was there for her. As always. And she was over worrying about what others thought. The only opinions that mattered were those of the people who actually cared about her. She wished she'd learned this lesson earlier in life, but she couldn't go back. Nor did she want to. Every incident in her past, even the painful ones, had led her to Conor.

Xander had built his shop on what had once been a farm. A large barn and a detached garage sat behind the main building. During a previous visit, he'd given her a tour. The barn had been converted into a workshop for sword making, complete with drafting tables, computers, and the various machines he used to heat, mill, and grind the swords.

Louisa headed for the showroom. The bell on the glass door rang as Louisa led Conor inside. An impressive array of ancient swords, axes, and daggers sat in glass cases. Medieval armor hung on the walls. Usually, she had to restrain herself from perusing the stock, but today she barely gave it a glance.

She'd brought her father here to meet Xander just a few weeks ago. *Where was Dad? What was happening to him right now?*

He'd been missing for thirteen hours. She knew firsthand what it was like to be at the mercy of a killer. She inhaled deeply through her nose and forced the thoughts from her head. Conor was right. If she wanted to find her dad, she couldn't allow her personal nightmare to cripple her. But the very act of searching for her father brought her ever closer to a murderer.

A killer who had already professed his love for her with a wedding ring. *For my beloved.* Clammy sweat dampened her palms.

Conor touched her arm, as if he could sense she was struggling, and she moved forward.

"Xander?" she called out as they walked through the shop. But no one answered.

"Argh!" The sound of a man's grunts drew them to the back door. In the yard, between the store and the barn, a shirtless Xander wielded a broadsword. *Wasn't he cold?* Big muscles rippled as he slashed and spun. A leather-and-straw body dangled from what appeared to be an old deer-hanging station. He lunged, the point of the sword piercing the faux leather body like a hot blade sliding into butter.

He stood back. A satisfied grin split his face. Xander Buch was the size of a linebacker. With long red-blond hair and a matching beard, he could easily have passed for one of the Vikings he claimed as ancestors.

"Xander." Louisa called him again.

His head swiveled and his grin widened.

"Louisa!" Xander's voice boomed from the other side of the yard. Like a dog's bark reflected the size of the beast, the deep tones in his voice didn't lie. Xander came across the yard, grabbing a shirt and drawing it over his head on the way. Louisa was always surprised he wasn't wearing a kilt instead of threadbare jeans and scuffed cowboy boots. A blue bandana held his hair away from his face.

He grasped her hand in both of his, and his hearty shake rattled her joints. "Were you pleased with the spear head?"

"Yes." Louisa extracted her hand and gave her fingers a quick shake to restore the blood flow. "It's perfect. Thank you."

"Then what can I do for you? You know if I'd found anything I think would interest you, I'd call."

She gestured toward Conor. "This is Conor Sullivan."

"Good to meet you, Conor." Xander gave Conor an equally enthusiastic handshake then turned back to Louisa, his eyes questioning.

"I was hoping you might give me some information," she said.

"I'm at your service." Xander led them back into the shop. They went through a door marked Office. Workbenches lined three walls of the back room. He hung the sword on a wall rack. A full set of recreated leather body armor lay on the closest bench. Xander lifted the metal helmet and put it on his head. Four hammered plates of metal were riveted together into a bowl shape. A thin guard extended down over his forehead and nose.

"What do you think? I belong to a group that reenacts Viking battles and raids. It's great fun. We erect a mock village and plunder all day long." Xander replaced the helmet and turned back to Louisa. His eyes narrowed. "What's wrong?"

Louisa inhaled. "My father is missing.

"Missing?" Xander opened a bottle of whiskey on his desk, splashed amber liquid into three tumblers, and handed them out. "You look like you could use this."

Louisa nodded and lifted the whiskey to her mouth. She rarely drank alcohol, but her nerves could use some blunting. The scents of wood and smoke that rose into her sinuses reminded her of the weeks immediately after her mother's death, when her father had sat in his office and poured scotch until he'd passed out. Upon waking, he'd repeated the process. The study had reeked for a month after he'd left.

But that hadn't kept Louisa from sleeping in his chair in an attempt to find some small measure of comfort in the familiar wrap of the leather cushion around her small body.

She set the glass down. "Have you heard about a Viking scramseax changing hands lately? Excellent condition. Ninth or tenth century."

Xander went quiet. "That's the same question the police detective asked me when he called earlier."

"Did he say why?" Louisa asked. Both the double murder and Ward's home invasion had been on the news. Media attention was inevitable in a city the size of Philadelphia. But the police were trying to keep the link between the cases quiet.

Xander shook his head, a silver ring in his earlobe catching the light. "No. The detective who called simply said a Viking short sword was involved in a case he was working on."

"Yes," Louisa said. "Someone sent my father this sword the day before he disappeared."

Xander poured himself another shot. He offered the bottle to Conor, who shook his head. Glass in hand, Xander froze, his gaze locking on Louisa's face. "Holy shit. The home invasion near Rittenhouse Square that was on the news. That was him, right?"

Louisa nodded, her eyes hot with unshed tears.

"I'm sorry," Xander said. "I lost my dad last summer. I miss him every day. I hope Ward is OK."

Louisa fought for composure. "Thanks."

Moving closer, Conor put his still-full glass on the table and placed his hand on the small of her back. "As you can imagine, Louisa is very worried about her father."

"I wish I could help." Xander perched on a stool. "But as I told the detective, I don't know of a short sword that meets that description."

"That doesn't rule out a private or black market acquisition. Do you know any local private collectors?" Louisa asked. The postmark on the package had been local.

Xander pulled his beard. "I'll dig through my records. More sales have shifted to the Internet over the past few years. I don't remember every client." Xander swiveled on his stool and opened a laptop on the workshop table behind him.

Louisa put a hand on Xander's tree-limb-size forearm. "I don't want to get you involved. This could be dangerous."

Xander gave her hand an amused pat. "I can handle myself."

But she couldn't live with herself if Xander were hurt because of something she'd dragged him into. "I mean it, Xander." She lowered her voice. "This could be tied to a murder case."

"In that case, we'd better find your father ASAP, don't you think?" Xander turned back to the laptop and reached for a pair of glasses. "Do you want me to call you at the museum if I get lucky?"

"No. Please call my cell." Louisa fished a business card from her purse, crossed off her office number, and wrote her personal cell phone number on the back. "I'd like to keep this between us. And thank you, Xander."

Outside, the icy wind was a slap in the face. She folded her unbuttoned coat across her body for the brief walk to the car. Conor opened the passenger door for her.

Louisa's phone vibrated just as she slid into the passenger seat of her sedan. "It's Damian."

She answered the phone as Conor rounded the front of the vehicle and got into the driver's seat.

"Do you have good news or bad?" she asked Damian.

"Bad, I'm afraid. The police are going to charge Jordan."

CHAPTER
15

Conor watched Louisa clench and unclench her hands in her lap. The news about Jordan had upset her, as if the lack of progress on her father's case hadn't been enough strain.

He turned Louisa's Beemer toward West Philly. "I know you want to keep searching for leads to find your father, but Yvonne has to be scared out of her mind."

"This is all connected somehow," Louisa said. "If we find the killer, we find my father."

Finding a killer was the last thing Conor wanted her to do. The ring that had come in the mail made him want to go back on his promise. If it were entirely up to him, Louisa wouldn't leave her apartment until this was all over. But he knew that wasn't an option, and he couldn't blame her. What would he do if someone in his family disappeared? Actually, he knew. When Jayne had run into trouble in Maine, he, Pat, and Danny had gone after her. The Sullivans stuck together. Their bond had gotten them through their parents' deaths, Danny's PTSD, and the deranged killer who'd gone after Danny's fiancée and Jayne.

"We need to find the connection between Jordan, Mario, and the killer. Besides, Yvonne needs all the support she can get." Her voice sounded calm, but the hands in her lap were clenched tightly enough to blanch the color from her knuckles. Her grip tightened and loosened in a rhythmic pattern.

"Of course." Conor took the ramp onto I-95 South and merged into the left lane.

His cell rang, and he answered the call on the car's speakerphone.

"Conor, it's Reed. I spoke to Detective Ianelli."

"And?"

"I can't think of anything the Philadelphia police could be doing that they aren't. They've even pulled the gang task force and FBI into the investigation." Reed sighed. "I wish I could be of more help. I'm checking out and heading for the airport. There's bad weather here. No flights out tonight, but I'm on standby. I'll be there as soon as I can."

"I appreciate it, Reed." Conor ended the call and reached for Louisa's hand. He rubbed her cold fingers. "At least we know the cops *are* doing everything possible."

"But my father is still missing."

At three thirty, rush hour hadn't yet clogged the interstate. Threading his way through traffic, Conor shaved five minutes off the drive back into town. He found a spot at the curb a half block from Yvonne's apartment building. Parking the car, he hoped it would still be here when they came back.

Yvonne's neighborhood was decorated in urban blight. Graffiti, broken glass, and bullet holes were the mediums of choice. The apartment building was four town houses wide and three stories high, with a central door leading into the concrete stairwell.

He scanned the street. Down the block, a group of boys hunched against the cold. Conor felt their scrutiny as he got out of the car. Without staring, he sized them up over the roof of the Beemer. Eight teens, all male, all wearing saggy jeans and heavy hoodies, were studying him with the same deliberate effort to look casual that Conor was working. Curiosity, or more? His paranoia tapped him on the shoulder.

More. Definitely more.

Conor picked out the leader by his posture and the body language of the others around him. A hood shadowed his face, so why did he seem familiar? Conor kept an eye on the group as he escorted Louisa to the door. Broad daylight didn't guarantee safety on this block.

They went inside. The building had no security, the exterior lock and intercom system having been long since disabled. Two doors on each side of the corridor led to the four individual units on each floor, with a flight of steps running up the center. Yvonne's apartment was the first on the right.

Louisa knocked softly. Footsteps sounded, and Conor could hear someone moving toward the door. Yvonne was no doubt looking through the peephole. A chain lock scraped and she opened the door, her eyes swollen and red-rimmed.

They stepped into the combination living room and kitchen. To the right, light poured into the living room through the double window that overlooked the street.

"We wanted to see how you were doing." Louisa greeted Yvonne with a quick hug.

"I don't know." Yvonne backed up to the sofa and dropped onto it. "I didn't go to work, and I kept Tyler home from school today. I'm afraid to let him out of my sight."

Conor didn't blame her one bit. One of her sons was missing and another was headed to jail.

She brushed her bangs out of her face. "I thought having my husband die in prison was bad, but it doesn't compare to seeing your child put in handcuffs." She sniffed. "Or finding out he is being charged with murder."

Louisa sat down next to her. "What did Damian say?"

Yvonne shook her head. "He said the DNA test came back positive. Now they have Jordan's fingerprints and his DNA on the body and his statement that he'd fought with one of the victims." She inhaled a sob, pressing her hand to her mouth as if trying to contain the sound. "Jordan has made some big mistakes, but he's not a cold-blooded killer. He did not kill that woman."

"We don't think so either." Louisa wrapped an arm around her shoulders. "Damian is the best. You have to have faith."

"Conor!" Tyler rushed from the bedroom. He was scrawny and the home buzz cut made his face appear gaunt. "I didn't know you were here." His gaze darted to his mom, and his smile dimmed.

Conor greeted the boy with a fist bump, pulled him into a gentle headlock, and rubbed his knuckles lightly on his scalp. Growing up with his own brothers, he knew nothing spelled out *everything is OK* like a noogie.

"Hey, let me go," Tyler giggled.

Conor released him, and he bounced around like the room like a puppy just let out of its crate.

"Do you want to play Madden NFL?" Tyler asked.

Conor and Louisa had bought Jordan and Tyler the Xbox for Christmas. Yvonne had argued that the gift was too expensive—and too frivolous, but Conor had convinced her that the boys needed something to do. They couldn't go outside to play, and being trapped in the apartment was depressing.

"You only want to play with me because you always win," Conor said.

Tyler grinned. "You're getting better."

"Compared to what?" Conor laughed. "Maybe we can squeeze in one accelerated game."

Tyler's eyes pleaded. They landed on his mother and welled up with tears. A sniff and swipe with his sleeve wiped them away.

Poor kid.

He'd had an awful night and was no doubt terrified that Jordan wasn't coming back. The least Conor could do was give him a short distraction.

"Do you mind?" Conor asked Louisa. "It'll be quick."

"Of course not." Louisa gave him an understanding smile.

"Awesome!" Tyler did a touchdown dance. "You are going down."

"Watch the trash talk, little man. I've been practicing. Someday, I'm bound to beat you." Conor was halfway down the hall when the sound of glass breaking stopped him. He whirled. An object had been hurled through the living room window. A bottle? It landed on the carpet, shattered, and burst into flames. Whatever flammable liquid had been inside splashed toward the hallway. Fire rushed toward Conor, blocking his path back into the living room.

"Get down!"

Louisa and Yvonne were on the other side of the fire. Both women huddled on the floor. Louisa was on her phone. Conor could hear her giving the address to the 911 operator.

He smelled gasoline. He glanced around for something to put out the blaze. No fire extinguisher in sight, and the sprinklers overhead did not turn on.

Hell, the smoke alarm wasn't even sounding.

Conor cursed the landlord and his firetrap of an apartment building.

Smoke filled the room as the fire crawled across the floor, reaching for the window curtains and the chair that Louisa had been sitting on a minute before.

"Tyler!" Yvonne waved smoke away from her face.

"Conor will take care of him." Louisa herded Yvonne toward the door.

But was whoever had thrown the Molotov cocktail still outside?

No matter who was outside, they had no choice. The fire had engulfed the carpet and was licking at the curtains.

"Get out!" Conor shouted over the crackling fire. "We'll meet you outside."

Louisa shoved her phone into her pocket. Her eyes met Conor's over the blaze, and panic gripped him. He wanted to be at her side.

"Mama!" Tyler raced from his room.

"Tyler!" Yvonne screamed, lurching toward her son.

"I've got him," Conor yelled over the crackling of flames.

123

He mouthed *I love you* to Louisa then grabbed the boy around the waist and dragged him down the hallway.

Tyler resisted, his thin body flailing in Conor's grasp. "No! I have to make sure my mom gets out."

"They're going out the front. They'll be fine," Conor said with a quick prayer that he was right. "We'll meet them outside."

The boy stopped fighting. In the bedroom, Conor closed the door behind them to block the smoke and went to the window. He unlocked the window and tried to open it, but it was stuck. He checked the lock again but still couldn't budge the sash. Nailed or painted shut?

"What are we going to do?" Tyler gripped the back of Conor's jacket.

"Put on shoes and a jacket." Conor picked up a chair and swung it at the window baseball-bat style and broke the glass. He gave the remaining pieces a few more good hits to knock out the biggest shards. Then he grabbed a blanket from the bed and tossed it over the sill so they wouldn't disembowel themselves on the way out.

Thank God they were on the first floor.

Turning back, he held his hand out to Tyler. The boy took it and Conor boosted him through the opening, keeping the boy's body clear of any sharp edges. As soon as the kid was out, Conor followed him. The second his feet touched concrete, he tucked Tyler behind him and searched the sidewalk for Louisa.

There. She stood on the sidewalk with Yvonne. Conor took one second to draw fresh air into his lungs, his brain acknowledging that Louisa was fine. Then he checked the street in both directions as he herded Tyler toward his mother. People were pouring out of their apartments and from the row houses across the street. Sirens wailed. Two police cars preceded a fire truck.

But Conor didn't see anyone suspicious. The doorway down the street was empty. Yvonne ran to meet them, wrapping her son in a fierce embrace.

A peal of bells sounded from the building. The fire alarm. Finally.

"Stay alert. Whoever did this might be out here," Conor said. Then he moved back toward the apartment building. He went in through the main entrance. People rushed down the stairs toward him. A man passed, carrying a young child on his hip. Next to him, a young mother clutched a screaming baby to her chest. The alarm echoed on concrete and bricks in a deafening clang.

"There's an old woman on the third floor who needs help," the man called to Conor as he took the mother and children outside.

Conor rushed up the stairs. In the middle of the second flight, an elderly black woman came down at an agonizingly slow pace. Both hands held the railing as she placed each foot carefully, feeling for the next step as if she couldn't see her feet.

"Let me help you." Conor took her arm.

"My eyes aren't what they used to be." He towered over the cotton-ball bun on the top of her head.

Smoke billowed up the stairwell. She coughed. He had to get her out of here now.

"How about I carry you." Without waiting for an answer, Conor scooped her up.

"Heavens." She clutched at the lapels of his jacket.

On the bottom landing, firemen pushed past them.

Conor carried the old woman outside and left her with a paramedic. Bowing out, Conor found Louisa across the street. He reached for Louisa's hands. She returned his grip with a squeeze.

Thank God she was all right.

Looking down at their joined hands, she frowned. "You're bleeding."

"Where?" Conor felt nothing.

She turned his hand over. "Here."

There was a small cut across the back of his wrist. "Just a nick. Probably did that going out the window."

"I'm just grateful everyone is all right." She touched his jaw, brought his face to hers, and kissed him on the lips.

The four of them huddled on the sidewalk watching the firemen drag hoses into the building. Thanks to the quick response, the fire was under control quickly.

He surveyed the growing crowd. His gaze landed on a tall man in a dark blue hoodie. The wind shifted, blowing the hoodie back and giving Conor the first clear view of his face. Recognition was shock.

Instinctively, Conor pulled away from Louisa and moved toward him, but the crowd closed between them. By the time he pushed through, the young man was gone.

But Conor knew who he was and how to find him. The leader of the Sixes was the fighter Tito had been training on Monday.

Had the Sixes burned Yvonne's apartment? Why?

CHAPTER
16

Death was on the way.

He could sense its approach, but adrenaline flooded his brain, short-circuiting all thoughts, reducing him to his primitive nature. He couldn't stop his arm from swinging down one more time. The bar in his grip connected with bone and blood and flesh. His opponent's skull crunched under the force of the blow. Blood spattered. His body was numb, his hearing muffled by the pulse of his heart in his temples. His vision tunneled to see only his opponent, lying still on the stained concrete.

Straddling his opponent's belly, he froze. His chest heaved as he watched.

The man's first reaction was panic, eyes widening until rimmed entirely with white. Fascinated, he watched as the man struggled to draw just one more breath, one more pump of blood from heart to veins, a final small jolt of oxygen for the brain.

He was learning that people would do anything to experience one additional second of life. They will hang on to this world, not knowing what lies ahead, until acceptance is their only option. But by that time, it wasn't really a choice, was it?

If only this man knew the truth. Then this final moment wouldn't be filled with terror but excitement at the opportunity to advance into the next stage of existence. The voice in his dream the night before had reiterated this message. Life was full of pain. Death would bring him eternal glory.

His opponent emitted a final wet rattle and went still.

He felt the life force ebb. The man's soul flickered, like a candle in a draft, and he knew the very second the light was extinguished. Eyes went blank, and the body underneath him deflated into an empty shell, with no more animation than a piece of meat.

His surroundings returned with an overwhelming rush of sight and sound and sensation. His breath fogged in the bitter February night. The cold damp rushed over the bare skin of his torso, but the sensation wasn't unpleasant.

No. It was exhilarating.

Adrenaline buzzed through his body. Oxygen rushed to his brain. His heart beat with renewed vigor, almost as if he were absorbing the dead man's life force.

This opponent had been more worthy and had actually landed a few blows before going down. The greater challenge made the thrill of victory all that much sweeter.

He drew a forearm across his face. His arm came away smeared with blood. It trickled from a small cut on his scalp, coated his chest, and slicked over his skin like oil. Some was his. Most was his opponent's. To the naked eye, there was no difference. But that dark red, homogeneous liquid was the very essence of existence. Without the steady flow of it through a man's veins, he was nothing.

He looked over at his audience. Ward sat on a wooden chair, his ankle manacle attached by a short chain to a support post, his face nearly as bloodless as the dead man's.

He called out to the scholar, "He fought well. Do you think the Valkyrie will come for him?"

But Ward didn't answer. Looking ill, the scholar bent at the waist and rested his face in his hands. Ward obviously needed a minute to compose himself. After all, studying warriors and their bloody deaths at a millennium's distance was a completely different experience than seeing it happen in front of his eyes. Before this night, Ward's professional career had been clinical. Now the scholar was participating in history as it unfolded.

He reached for his opponent's face, intent on closing the eyes. But then he hesitated. When his time came, he wanted to go forth open-eyed, looking forward to what lay ahead.

This man had fought well and deserved the same opportunity to be one of the chosen. He was prepared to send the worthy warrior off with honor. From the beginning this had been a fight to the death. He'd only planned for one of them to leave the warehouse upright. Everything was ready for the journey.

He wiped the worst of the blood off with a towel, then went to the wall and retrieved the specially made, narrow pallet. Taking the handle of the pallet jack, he wheeled it into position and rolled and lifted the man onto the wooden slats.

His pulse slowed as he worked, and the cold air chilled his sweaty skin. Reaching for a sweatshirt, he pulled it over his head then wheeled the pallet to the back of his van and opened the rear doors. Inside, the warrior's companion for the journey lay on a black tarp, hands and ankles bound, shivering. Above the duct tape across her mouth, her eyes were wild with fright.

This time, he'd made his capture in advance. This time, he was more organized.

She was not as brave as the man had been, but that was to be expected. She didn't need courage.

Muffled screams sounded behind the silver tape.

"You can't kill her," Ward shouted.

Pausing, he blinked at the scholar. "What choice do I have?"

"You can let her go."

"You of all people know that I can't do that." He gestured toward the dead warrior. "He deserves better. He deserves the appropriate servant for his journey."

"He can get to Valhalla alone," Ward said, his voice calmer. "The Valkyrie will be with him."

He walked to the back of the van and stared at the scholar for a few seconds. "You know damned well that isn't the way it has to happen. Frankly, I'm disappointed in you." He motioned toward the dead man. "This is what all of your books are about: how warriors lived and how they were honored in death. I'm not sure what you don't understand about this situation. I included you in my project because I wanted your advice, but you refuse to cooperate. I've been asking for your expertise since I brought you here. You won't give a serious answer to a single question. All I get are bullshit responses because you can't stomach the very violence you've been studying for decades. Why should I keep you alive if you're not going to help?"

He expected Ward to flinch at the threat, but the scholar's gaze didn't waver. Ward was tougher than he'd expected. Not sure how he felt about that, he went back to work.

Shifting the woman to the side, he made room then maneuvered the ramp into place. Wheels squeaked as he rolled the pallet into the van. The woman protested with more muffled cries as she tried to squirm away from the dead body. He shut her up with a flash of his knife.

With his cargo secured, he returned to contemplate the scholar. "Originally I was going to take you with me. I wanted you to see your research put into action. But I can see you need some time to think about your role in my plan."

He reached for the padlock that held Ward's ankle chain to the post and unlocked it with a key.

Ward's fist swung out. Shocked, he blocked the older man's pathetic blow, swatting it away as if it were a mosquito. He squeezed the scholar's fist in his own until Ward crumbled, defeated, to his knees. Ward clutched his hand to his middle.

"I should have expected some resistance from a man who spends his entire life studying warriors. I almost respect your resilience." Almost. He swallowed a lump of fury. "I don't want to kill you, but I will if you're more hindrance than help."

He unlatched the chain and dragged the scholar back to his room. After fastening him to the pipe, he retreated to the kitchenette, which had once been a break room. He filled a bag with ice and took it to Ward. The scholar sat on the edge of his cot, his hand cradled in his lap. A broken bone should teach him a lesson.

"Put this on your hand." He tossed the ice onto the cot.

Ward lifted his head. The look in his eyes was bleak.

"You shouldn't be sad. This is a glorious event. The warrior has moved on to a better place. He will spend the rest of his days fighting and feasting with Odin in the great hall. Valhalla is the best afterlife that any true fighter could hope to attain." His smile felt beatific. "The dream came to me last night. A woman with long blond hair, like your daughter's. She said that all will be well if I follow the plan." She'd been perfect. "I wonder if she is the Valkyrie. If so, I must do exactly as she says. Only she can take me to Valhalla."

But the scholar's stare didn't change. Why didn't he understand?

"I'll be back in a few hours." Frustrated, he turned away from the scholar.

"Why are you doing this?"

"The answer is simple. I *will* go to Valhalla, and you will help me get there."

Angry, he closed and locked the door, then made his way back to the van. He drove it outside, then lowered the overhead door. He couldn't leave the dead warrior in the same location, so he'd found another. Humming, he drove toward Fairmont Park and what would be the fighter's resting place. He'd chosen a superior location, peaceful, with trees and snow-covered ground and a view worthy of a Viking.

He glanced back into the cargo area. The woman huddled as far from the warrior as possible. The dead man looked peaceful and battle worn.

Would the Valkyrie find him worthy? Would she take him by the hand? He hoped so. The Vikings didn't honor their opponents because the men they killed were truly their enemies. The men he killed were more like training partners, and he wished them no ill will.

Eventually, he would wear the same satisfied death mask as he waited for the Valkyrie and the glory that he had earned. He drove to his destination. The icy hillside with its view of the river suited a Viking. He dragged the woman from the back. She shivered as he guided her through the ceremony. Her end was merciful and quick, the blood that flowed onto the snow symbolic of her sacrifice. Though her profession had aged her beyond her years, she was almost lovely in death, a sight he took as an affirmation.

Despite the bitter cold, satisfaction churned through him as he laid the warrior to rest. A thin slice of frigid air hit the side of his face as he selected four icicles and spelled out his prophesy in the same way that a Viking seer would have done a millennium ago. When the scene was set, he stood back and admired his work for a moment before lighting the pyre. Once the fire was set, he made a swift exit. He had too much work to do to risk being caught.

An hour ago, he'd felt like a regular man. Ordinary. He and his opponent had been the same. Now the world had been irrevocably altered. He couldn't help but consider the irony.

The only time he felt truly alive was when he killed.

CHAPTER
17

Showered and dressed, Louisa crossed the master bedroom before seven a.m. Kirra, sensing something was amiss, stuck close. Louisa eased to her knees and hugged the dog. Kirra never minded tears in her fur, and there was something about the dog's presence that always brought her comfort.

Rising, she left the room. The door to the guest suite was closed, and she hoped Yvonne and Tyler were still sleeping. They'd all been stuck at the fire scene giving statements and waiting to see if and when Yvonne might be able to get into her apartment to collect anything that was salvageable.

Unfortunately, what the fire hadn't consumed, the firemen had destroyed with their axes and hoses. From what Louisa had seen from the street, Yvonne and Tyler had nothing. They hadn't made it back to the condo until nearly midnight.

She went into the kitchen and found Conor assessing the contents of the refrigerator. He removed a carton of eggs.

"I'm not really hungry." She stood next to him and rested her head on his shoulder. Kirra leaned on her shins.

"When was the last time you ate?"

"Good point." Yesterday was a blur.

"I made coffee." He nodded toward a mug on the counter. "You tossed and turned a lot. Did you get any rest?"

"A little." A disturbing mix of dreams and nightmares had invaded her sleep. "I dreamed of a vacation we took when I was in grade school. I don't even remember where we were, somewhere tropical. It was just the three of us. We'd taken a small sailboat out to watch the sunset. There wasn't much wind, but no one minded." Louisa closed her eyes for a few seconds, reliving the damp warmth of a tropical breeze across her face, the restricting bulk of the life vest they'd always made her wear, the scents of Coppertone, insect repellent, and the sea mingling in her nose. "We saw dolphins and sailed until the sun went down. I remember the lights along the shoreline dancing on the water."

"It sounds all right so far," he said.

"The first part was." She paused, a shudder rippling through her. "The dream ended with the boat sinking and my parents being sucked into the sea while I watched, bobbing helplessly in my life vest on the surface."

Conor turned to press a kiss to her temple. "I'm sorry."

"I don't know why I dreamed about that night. It was a quiet sail. Nothing special happened." Despite its nightmare finale, the dream soothed her.

"Maybe you just needed to remember that they loved you before it all went to hell."

"I don't think I ever forgot, but I definitely let bad memories crowd out the good ones."

"You were awfully young. Children can't control how they react. Your happiness was ripped out from under you. The adults in your life left you to fend for yourself. I don't think it takes a psychologist to make the parallel between that dream and the way your future spun out of your control."

"Probably not." Louisa set the dream aside and reached for the coffee mug. "I hope Yvonne got some sleep. I still can't believe her boss fired her for missing a second day of work under these circumstances. What is she going to do?"

The anger that fired in her belly felt a heck of a lot better than the cold horror she'd been harboring since her father had received the sword.

"You've given them a safe place to hide from the gang. For now, that's about all you can do." Leaning over, Conor kissed her temple. He lit a burner under a frying pan, cracked eggs into a glass bowl, and began to whip them with a wire whisk. "We'll stop and buy them some clothes. I can offer her a job."

Best. Man. Ever.

Even in her current state of despair, she held onto gratefulness for having him in her life.

"I love that you help everyone," she said.

"Yvonne's a waitress. I need a waitress. Seems logical." Conor poured the beaten eggs into a frying pan. The embarrassed flush on his face made her smile. Chivalry wasn't dead. He was in her kitchen making sure she didn't face another terrible day with an empty stomach.

How did she get so lucky?

But the scent of comfort food, fresh coffee, and Conor's goodness could only do so much to ease the tension inside her. "How are we going to find my father?" Louisa tamped down the bigger question: Was he still alive?

She couldn't face the possibility that the answer could be no.

"Unfortunately *we* can't. The police are going to have to do that." Conor scooped the scrambled eggs onto a plate and turned off the stove.

The phone in the kitchen rang. Nerves reignited in Louisa's belly. Only Rittenhouse staff used her landline. Everyone else called on her cell phone. Not wanting the phone to disturb Yvonne and Tyler, Louisa crossed the tile in two quick steps and picked up the receiver. "Yes."

"This is Gerome," the doorman said. "The police are on their way up to see you, Dr. Hancock."

Louisa thanked him and hung up. She turned to Conor. "It's the police."

She couldn't imagine they had more information about Jordan. According to Damian's last text, an arraignment hearing was being scheduled. So were they here about her father? Or did they have more information about the ring and note she'd received from the killer? Or maybe they had an update on the fire.

Bracing herself, she turned and leaned back against the counter, her hands wrapping over the edge on either side of her hips.

Conor answered the door. She heard the voices of Detectives Ianelli and Jackson, then Conor led them into the kitchen. Kirra gave their shoes a few suspicious sniffs. Jackson moved away, and the dog retreated to her bed.

"Did you find my father?" Waiting for the answer, Louisa tightened her grip on the stone. Conor moved to stand next to her.

Ianelli's gaze met hers. "No."

Louisa didn't know whether to be relieved or not. As long as his body hadn't been found, there was hope. But hope could be a dangerous thing; the more she clung to it, the harder she would crash if it were ripped away.

"We heard Yvonne and Tyler were here," Jackson said.

Conor stiffened. "Didn't you grill Yvonne enough last night?"

"Actually, we're not here to see her, and we're not the bad guys." Ianelli perched on a stool.

"You don't always act like the good guys either," Conor said.

"This is a complicated case," Ianelli snapped in an uncharacteristic show of temper. Both detectives wore wrinkled suits and exhaustion lined their faces. "We want to catch a killer. We don't always have time to tiptoe around people's feelings. Mrs. Franklin and Tyler won't be safe until this case is solved." He focused on Louisa. "You either. And we won't find your father until we find the killer."

"Jordan isn't guilty." Conor crossed his arms over his chest.

Jackson propped a fist on his hip. "How can we possibly know that? Jordan won't tell us what we need to know."

"Are you going to offer his family protection?" Louisa asked, trying to focus the conversation on being proactive rather than on the contest of wills Conor and Ianelli seemed to be locked in.

Jackson shook his head. "Unless Jordan talks, we have no reason."

"What do you think he knows?" Conor pressed his bicep against hers in a shoulder-to-shoulder, we're-in-this-together stance.

"We need to know where he was all night Sunday. And if he's been in contact with his brother. We also need the names of the men who were with Mario when they attacked Jordan on Sunday." Jackson swept a hand over his shaved head. Stubble rasped.

"Yvonne and her son Tyler are staying with us for as long as necessary," Louisa said.

"They're moving in with you?" Ianelli glanced around the sleek kitchen.

"Just temporarily." Louisa looked him straight in the eyes. "They had nowhere to go, and they're obviously in danger."

Had he expected her to turn her back on a family in need?

Obviously, that's exactly what Jackson had expected. "What if they're taking advantage of you?"

"First of all, I don't see how they could be." The idea seemed ridiculous to Louisa. "Secondly, I could live with that, but I couldn't live with myself if something bad happened to them that I could have prevented."

Ianelli's face softened with the slightest trace of guilt. "That's nice of you. Not many people would step up."

"We couldn't just leave them on the street." Louisa folded her arms across her waist.

Conor slid an arm around her shoulders in silent support.

"I saw the Sixes gathered on the corner outside Yvonne's apartment last night," he said, his voice clipped as if he were losing patience. "I was pretty sure I recognized their leader, so I made a few calls. His name is Orion Turner."

"We know who he is." Jackson's lips snapped shut.

Conor kept his attention on Ianelli. "What do you know about him?"

"You're right about him being the leader of the Sixes." Ianelli rubbed the back of his neck.

"Did you know that Orion Turner trains at Southpaw Gym? Is it too much of a coincidence that Orion and Mario and Jordan all box?" Conor shifted his gaze back and forth between the cops.

Had they known? Louisa couldn't tell.

Conor's jaw sawed back and forth as if he was grinding his teeth to dust. "You were holding Jordan when Ward disappeared, so you know Jordan wasn't part of his abduction."

Neither cop responded.

"We all know why he won't give up any information. They'll kill him and his whole family. Tonight's fire was just a warning." Conor's voice rose.

"Then I guess it's a good thing they're here," Ianelli said. "The sooner we solve this case, the better for everyone."

Louisa's patience thinned. "Why are *you* here?"

Ianelli straightened. "A private collector of ancient weapons recently died. His widow has sold off some of the pieces. One, a Viking battle-axe, recently appeared at an auction house. The axe's legitimacy was questionable, so the item was pulled from the sale."

Finally, a real lead!

"The widow lives here in the city. Our FBI liaison has arranged for us to meet with her this morning to see the collection." Ianelli grimaced, as if what he was going to say next was painful. "Agent Murray said if he needed an expert on ancient weaponry, he'd consult you. We'd like you to come with us. You'll be able to match the pieces and paperwork much faster than we would and tell us if the short sword sent to your father was part of the collection. As much as we don't want to involve you further, we don't feel like we have a choice. We need to work fast."

"I agree." Louisa didn't want to waste another second. The clock was ticking. She couldn't stand to think of her father spending another day with a killer. Or worse, not making it through another day.

"We've arranged to meet with her at eight thirty," Ianelli said.

"All right." Louisa checked the time. It was almost seven thirty.

"Here's the address." Ianelli handed Conor a piece of paper. "Don't go early, and don't go to the door without us."

Conor showed the police out. Returning to the kitchen, he nudged a plate of eggs toward Louisa, but the detectives' visit had stirred her anxiety.

They had the first real clue to her father's disappearance.

She pushed the plate away. Following this lead could take them closer to finding him and the killer with whom she already shared a frightening bond, at least in his personal delusion.

CHAPTER
18

Driving into Society Hill, Conor said a quick prayer that this lead played out and the cops found Ward.

Alive.

The widow, Vivian Banks, lived in a big-ass mansion. The Banks house was a three-story brick monstrosity, with dozens of black shutters, a neat row of dormers, and a chimney the size of a smokestack. A narrow alley led to what had originally been a carriage house out back but had likely been converted into a modern garage.

Conor parked in the alley entrance.

In the passenger seat, Louisa placed a hand at the base of her throat. "The detectives are late."

"By a minute." He captured her hand in his. Seeing her in such obvious distress was killing him.

"What if they never find him? What if my father is already . . . ?"

"Don't go there yet." Conor rubbed her fingers. "The cops will be here any second. I know you're crazy worried, but take a deep breath."

The radio station announced an update on the weather report, and Conor turned up the volume. Friday's forecast had shifted from snow to ice. He made a mental note to call Pat and make sure they were prepared. An ice storm could cripple the city for days. Sullivan's had a generator, and they tried to stay open if at all possible. Many people didn't have heat during a power outage.

The detectives' sedan turned into the driveway and parked behind the Beemer.

Conor opened his car door. "Ready?"

Louisa was already getting out of the car. A thousand-needle wind hit them as they followed the cops to the front stoop. The woman who opened the door was in her mid-fifties and slim to the point of frailty.

"Come in." She leaned heavily on a four-pronged cane as they entered the high-ceilinged foyer. In the center of the gleaming hardwood, a chandelier hung over a glass pedestal table. With shaky steps, she led the way into a modern parlor. In front of a roaring fire, two low-slung white leather couches faced each other across a narrow glass coffee table. Two funky metal and gray fabric chairs made up the third side of the furniture U.

"Mrs. Banks, this is Dr. Hancock and Mr. Sullivan." Ianelli motioned between them. "Dr. Hancock is the museum curator we asked to consult on the case."

"Call me Vivian, please." Vivian carefully eased down onto a couch and set her cane to the side. Pain compressed the corners of her mouth. Her left hand trembled, and she quickly covered it with her right.

"I'm sorry, ma'am." A gray-haired maid in a pale blue uniform hurried into the room and collected their coats. "I was in the kitchen and didn't hear the doorbell."

"It's all right, Bethany." Vivian scanned her guests. "Would you care for tea or coffee?"

Louisa shook her head. "Nothing for me, thank you."

The three men also declined, and Vivian sent the maid away with a quiet, "Thank you, Bethany. I'll call you if I need you."

Conor handed the maid his jacket and took a seat on the leather couch next to Louisa, facing Vivian Banks.

Louisa had dressed for the meeting in a slim cream-colored suit and pale-blue silk blouse. On the other side of the glass coffee table, Vivian wore slim dress slacks and what appeared to be a cashmere sweater. The two women belonged to the same exclusive club.

"Thank you for seeing us this morning." Ianelli eased onto the edge of a chair as if he were afraid his weight would snap one of its pencil-thin chrome legs.

Jackson wandered to the fireplace, rested an elbow on the mantel, and watched.

"I'm so sorry for your loss." Louisa leaned forward, her hands clasped on her closed knees.

"Thank you. I miss Doug. We were cheated out of our golden years." Vivian's eyes teared, and her gaze drifted to a photo on the end table. She was younger, and healthy in the picture. The man hugging her close had been older by about twenty years but looked robust. Behind the couple was a large sail set against a huge expanse of clear blue sky. "Doug was diagnosed with throat cancer before our fifth anniversary. By the time he finished his chemo and the disease went into its first remission, I was diagnosed with Parkinson's disease. We spent the last ten years fighting illnesses. His cancer came back, and as you can see, my Parkinson's is winning." Her mouth upturned in a wistful smile as she glanced back and forth between Conor and Louisa. "Don't waste a moment of your time together. You never know what the future has in store."

Sounds like Pat.

Vivian sank back into the cushions, her energy clearly flagging. "I'm sorry to hear about your father, Louisa. Forgive me for being forward. It was on the news. There's been no sign of him?"

"No." Louisa clenched her fingers. "We're hoping any information you can give us about your husband's artifact collection might help find my father."

"I'll do whatever I can," Vivian said.

The sound of the front door opening and closing echoed down the hall.

Vivian straightened. "I hope you don't mind. I invited my son to join us this morning. He's more familiar with Doug's collection than I am."

A thirtyish man swept into the room, tugging off an expensive-looking parka and tossing it over a chair, revealing his khaki and cashmere rich-boy duds.

"Good morning. I'm Rowan Banks." He approached the group, shaking hands with the detectives as Vivian made the introductions. Tall with light brown hair, Mr. Preppy had the perfect teeth of a man who'd been raised with plenty of money.

The cops introduced themselves and Louisa and Conor. Rowan took a seat next to Vivian, and he gave Louisa a too-interested smile. Such was the problem with having a gorgeous girlfriend. Everywhere they went, men noticed her. Conor couldn't even take her to the gym without the guys falling all over her.

Conor did the math. Rowan was too old to be a product of Vivian and Douglas's union. A previous marriage maybe?

"How much do you know about your husband's artifact collection?" Louisa asked.

"Not very much, I'm afraid," Vivian said.

Louisa frowned. "Have you ever seen a short sword or a ring in the collection?"

"Not that I recall. Sorry." With a glance at Rowan, Vivian grimaced. "Doug would get so excited every time he purchased a new piece, I assumed they were expensive. But when I went to sell a few items, I was shocked at the low valuation the dealer gave me."

"You should have waited for me," Rowan admonished. "I could have told you the collection had more sentimental than monetary value for Dad. It's not worth selling."

"I'm moving to a smaller house. I can't take the collection with me." Vivian turned questioning eyes toward Ianelli. "Now we've learned that some of the pieces might not have been legitimate, and you think there could be a connection to Dr. Hancock's father's disappearance?"

"That's why Dr. Hancock is here," the detective said. "Why don't we let her get to work?"

"Of course." Vivian gestured to Rowan. "If you don't mind, I'll let Rowan show you my husband's collection. I'm afraid my energy isn't what it used to be."

Rowan stood and gestured toward the doorway. "I had no idea some of Dad's purchases weren't on the up and up." A wry grin twisted his mouth. "It doesn't surprise me, though. Dad wasn't much of a rule-follower. He wanted what he wanted, and he was accustomed to having his way."

Rowan led them down a hallway and into the library. Bookcases and glass-cased weapons lined three walls. An antique desk the size of a Buick spanned the wall between two casement windows. Outside the window, a bare tree limb bowed to the wind, scratching at the glass.

"My father's books are here." Louisa stopped in front of a bookcase. "But so are those of many of his peers'."

Rowan waved a hand over dozens of file folders fanned across the desktop. He gestured toward the high-backed leather chair behind the desk. "I've sorted the paperwork as best I could. No doubt you'll get through it faster than I did."

Louisa spent the next few hours reviewing the collection paperwork and the items in the display cases. "There's no reference to either a short sword or a ring, but I did find some pieces likely purchased through questionable sources. There are several empty spots in the display as well. Rowan, do you remember what was here?" Louisa asked, pointing to a display case.

He paused next to her. "No, I'm sorry. Vivian sold a few items. You could check with the auction house."

"I already accounted for those pieces," Louisa said.

"She didn't sell a sword at auction," Ianelli said. "We already checked."

"So where does that leave us?" Jackson asked.

Louisa dropped into the chair and rubbed her forehead. "There's no one else who has access to the collection or might know if a piece was missing?"

Rowan shook his head. "Vivian and I have the only keys to the house."

"None of the staff has a key?" Jackson asked.

"No," Rowan said firmly. "We had the locks changed recently. Vivian felt insecure living here alone. She wanted to make sure no one could wander in."

"I'd like to take copies of these documents with me and review the paperwork again in case I missed something." Louisa stacked the folders. "If Mrs. Banks is still interested in selling, I could also give her estimated values. I might even be able to arrange some acquisitions either by the Livingston Museum or others."

"Thank you. I'm sure she would appreciate any help you could give her." He scanned the stacks of files on the desktop. "I could drop the copies by your office later today," Rowan offered. "This is going to take a while."

Perfect. Conor needed a reason to take an unapproved house tour. He caught Louisa's eye and, behind the cover of a chair back, he made a *drag-it-out* gesture with both hands.

With a single blink of understanding, she smiled at Rowan. "That's not necessary. I can wait."

He gathered the paperwork and went into an adjoining room. Conor heard a machine humming. Louisa began to photograph every artifact in the room, which wasn't necessary but would definitely kill some time.

The police detectives hovered while she worked and Rowan ran the copier in the next room.

Conor ducked his head through the doorway. "May I use the restroom?"

"Of course." Rowan added paper to the copier. "Make a left. It's just down the hall."

"Thanks." Conor slipped out of the room.

He checked the parlor, but Mrs. Banks wasn't there. He stopped in the powder room, flushed the toilet, and ran the water for a few seconds. Then he wandered—OK, he sneaked—around the first floor for a few minutes, without finding anything exciting. A noise drew him back to the kitchen. The maid was scrubbing a pot in the farmhouse sink.

He cleared his throat and coughed into his fist. "Excuse me. It's Bethany, right? Could I get a glass of water?"

Bethany smiled. "Of course."

She dried her hands on her apron. Opening the refrigerator, she pulled out a glass pitcher filled with water and cucumber slices. Then she took a tumbler from the cabinet, poured, and handed it to him.

"Thank you." As he drank, he wandered around the big, sunny room. Framed family photos covered one wall above the wainscoting. He spotted a college-age Rowan in riding clothes. He sat on a shiny black horse with a blue ribbon pinned to its bridle. Next to that photo was a tropical beach snapshot of Vivian and Doug with teenage Rowan and another young man who looked to be a few years older. The same young man showed up in a picture aboard a sleek yacht. *Who was that?* "What a shame the house has to be sold. Will you be out of work?"

"I don't think so." The maid returned to the sink. "Mrs. Banks will need help wherever she goes."

"Well, that's good."

The maid didn't answer. Wasn't she happy working for the widow? Conor's inquiring mind wanted to know.

Acting casual-like, he sipped his water. "How long have you worked here?"

She blew a stray gray hair from her forehead. "I was with Mr. Banks for thirty years."

"Before he married Vivian?" And therefore, she knew everything, Conor thought.

"Yes." She lifted a wet hand from the sink and used the back of it to scratch her forehead.

"So you knew Rowan's mother?" Conor fished for information.

She rinsed the pot. "Marla was a sweet soul. People talked when they married, of course. They called her a gold digger because she was so much younger. But Mr. Banks wasn't one to care about what people thought."

"Who is this?" Conor pointed to the sailboat picture.

After setting the pot on a drying rack, the maid dried her hands and walked toward him. She pointed to the photo of a young man standing on a sleek sailboat. "That's Asher. Rowan's brother. He's quite the sailor."

Her words praised him, but her tone was reserved. Sensing a sad turn to the story, Conor drank his water and kept quiet.

She turned toward the window over the sink, which looked out over the courtyard and carriage house. "Marla died in a car accident."

"How tragic."

"Yes." The maid sniffed. "As much as Mr. Banks doted on those boys, he wasn't the sort of man who could be alone." The maid's lips flattened tighter than elevator doors. Whatever came next, it was clear that Bethany disapproved. "He remarried within the year."

"The boys must have been upset."

"They were. In time, Rowan came around all right, but not Asher. He was always . . ." She hesitated, and he had the feeling she was being careful about her choice of words. "More emotional."

Why hadn't Vivian or Rowan mentioned Asher? "When was the last time you saw him?"

"He's only been here a few times since the funeral." She frowned. "Poor Rowan has been left to care for Vivian all by himself."

"Does Asher live far away?"

"No. He lives right here in Philadelphia. In Bala Cynwyd." The maid picked up a cloth and dried her pot. She squinted out the window. "Now that's odd."

Conor followed her gaze. "What?"

"The door to the carriage house is open." She crossed the tile floor and lifted a gray wool coat from a wall hook. "Excuse me. I'll go and shut it."

"I can take care of that for you," Conor offered.

Crow's-feet crinkled the corners of the older woman's face as she smiled. "That would be very kind of you. The older I get, the less I can stand the cold."

She opened the back door for him. Conor stepped out into the cold. Pushing his hands into his pockets, he crossed the icy bricks to the carriage house. He went inside. He'd assumed the building had been converted into a garage, as was normal, but it seemed to be used for storage. Dust and mold scented the stale air. He looked down and spied fresh footprints in the dirt-covered concrete aisle.

Someone had been in here recently.

Patio furniture crowded one corner. Other odds and ends were piled in another: two Weedwackers, and a leaf blower. He peered around a wood divider and saw a pile of blankets and a flashlight tucked behind bags of mulch.

Was someone sleeping in the carriage house?

How recently?

On his way out, he secured the door latch. The hair on the back of his neck lifted. Something scraped behind him. He whirled just in time to see a shovel flying toward his head.

CHAPTER
19

Using her cell phone camera, Louisa photographed the last piece in the collection. She didn't fully trust all the information in the files and wanted to have her own pictures as references. In case another artifact showed up in a package, she'd know if it came from the Banks collection.

Memories flooded her as she worked, Douglas Banks's oversize desk and leather chair reminding her of her father's study in the Maine house.

Even when he wasn't at the university, her father always seemed to be working. But he never minded her company. She'd wander into his office, and he'd let her read whatever he was working on, no matter how gruesome the subject matter. And with Viking history and legends, the subject matter could be barbaric. Her mother was often appalled at the gory topics of dinner conversation between father and daughter, but her father had reasoned that Viking legends weren't any grimmer than fairy tales.

Louisa distinctly remembered enjoying her mother's exasperation. It made her feel as if she and her father shared a common interest, that they had a special bond that was theirs and theirs alone. She'd held onto that bond long after he'd left, wishing it would bring him back to her.

More than two decades later, it had, but was it too late?

Rowan was still making copies. Ianelli had offered to help and was in the next room with him. Detective Jackson stood in the corner, his phone pressed to one ear. None of them were paying any attention to her.

So while they were all busy, Louisa searched Douglas Banks's desk. She went through the contents of each drawer. Then she slid out each drawer and checked the underside. Nothing. She circled the room and scanned the shelving units again. Her gaze landed on her father's books. His latest volume was missing, but Douglas Banks had died before the book had been released. She moved books and looked behind them. Spotting the corner of a piece of paper protruding from the top of one, she picked it up and flipped through the pages. A folded piece of paper had been inserted in the middle. She unfolded it. Handwritten in blue ink was a brief description of an artifact: one Viking short sword, ninth century, whittled tang, fourteen inches long, excellent condition, one thousand dollars. There was no date, no signature, no seller, and no origin. She slipped her phone from her pocket and took a snapshot of the paper.

"What are you doing?"

Louisa startled. Rowan had come out of the adjoining room.

He stared at her, his eyes accusing.

She forced herself to relax. "I was just looking at my father's books. I noticed Mr. Banks had copies of all but the latest."

"Did he?" Rowan asked in a flat voice.

Louisa straightened. She had no time for Rowan Banks's games. "Yes. And look what I found inside. It's a handwritten description that matches the sword sent to my father. Does it look familiar?"

"No," Rowan said, shifting closer to look at the paper. "Just looks like random notes to me."

"Let me see that." Ianelli pushed past Rowan. He pulled a pair of purple nitrile gloves from his pocket. Taking the paper by the corners, he read it. "It's not signed, and it doesn't list a seller."

"No. But that is a fair description of the short sword."

Ianelli looked doubtful.

Detective Jackson leaned close to her ear. "Where's Sullivan?"

Louisa glanced around the room. Conor wasn't in sight.

"He went to use the restroom." Louisa tried to smile. Damn it, she'd never been good at lying. She'd better learn—and fast.

"That was a long time ago." Jackson's face settled into a deep frown. Behind him, Ianelli lifted a disbelieving brow.

What was Conor doing all this time?

Afraid her expression would give her away, Louisa turned back to scanning the shelves. She saw photos of Doug, wearing dusty clothes and a huge grin, at what appeared to be an archeological site. She squinted at the lush green background but found no clues to identify the location. Another photo showed Doug and Vivian dressed as Vikings at a charity event. Vivian's gown and Doug's warrior garb were impressively accurate. Most Viking costumes inaccurately showed warriors wearing horned helmets, which would have been totally impractical in battle. Doug clearly took all things Viking very seriously.

Louisa's eyes moved on to a snapshot of Doug holding a shiny new sword. The background caught her attention. It looked familiar. She barely stifled a gasp as she realized the landscape behind Douglas Banks looked like the view from Xander's hilltop workshop.

Xander knew Douglas Banks.

She took a quick picture of the photo, then pointed it out to Ianelli. "You might want to check out an artifact dealer named Xander Buch. He's local and I saw his name on multiple documents. And I'm pretty sure this picture was taken outside Xander's workshop."

"Will do." The cop took the photo with gloved hands. "Can I have this?" he asked Rowan.

"Of course." Rowan slid the pile of copies into a thick accordion file, secured the string closure, and handed it to Louisa. "Thank you for helping Vivian."

"You're welcome." Louisa tucked the folder under her arm.

Rowan looked past her at the detectives. "Conor isn't back?"

"I'm sure he'll be along in a minute. Do you remember where you were Sunday night?" Ianelli deflected Rowan's question by asking his own.

Rowan looked miffed. "I was here."

"All night?" Ianelli asked. "I thought you had a condo on the waterfront."

"Vivian almost fell down the stairs recently, and she's been having difficulty sleeping." Rowan looked tired. "I believe either the stress of my father's death triggered some more severe symptoms with her Parkinson's or she wasn't being careful about her meds right after he died. I've been staying here rather than my own place for the last six weeks."

"Why don't you hire a nurse?" Ianelli asked.

"Until Dad died, she was managing all right. I've already made inquiries about hiring one, at least for the night shift. I don't mind helping her out, but . . ." He looked away, guilt lowering his brow.

"But you'd like to have a life of your own," Louisa finished.

Rowan led the way back into the hall. "Selfishly, that's part of it. But also, given the recent progression of her disease, I suspect it won't be long before she's going to need assistance with bathing and dressing. She'll be more comfortable having a nurse help her with those tasks."

A scream ripped from the back of the house.

Louisa's heart jolted. *Where was Conor?*

The detectives ran for the doorway and raced down the corridor. Louisa and Rowan followed close behind. Louisa skidded into the kitchen. The maid stood next to the open door, one hand covering her mouth. Though the opening, Louisa could see Conor kneeling on an older man's back in the courtyard. The older man was short and square. White hair topped a weather-beaten face.

Conor's leather jacket and jeans were smeared with dust and ice, but Louisa focused on the thin rivulet of blood trickling down his forehead. *How badly was he hurt?*

"He went outside to close the carriage house door for me," the maid cried. "Next thing I knew, they were fighting."

Conor looked up. "He swung a shovel at my head. Luckily, he didn't have much strength behind the blow. I'm OK."

Ianelli went outside and handcuffed the man while Jackson made a call on his phone. Conor stood and dusted off his jeans. Ianelli hauled the other man to his feet.

"That's Dennis O'Donnell," Rowan said. "He used to work here."

Conor walked into the kitchen. Worried, Louisa steered him to a chair.

"Let me have a look at that." Louisa tipped Conor's face. Relief swept through her like a wave as she examined the shallow wound. *He really is all right.* "It's still bleeding."

"Cuts on the head always do. It'll stop in a few minutes," Conor said. "I can't believe I was attacked by a senior citizen."

Glancing over her shoulder, she asked Rowan, "Do you have a first aid kit?"

"Of course." He walked out of the room. Rowan returned and handed Louisa a small, white box. "Here it is."

She opened it. The cut on Conor's forehead was about a half-inch long. She opened an antiseptic wipe and cleaned the gash. After tearing open the paper on a gauze pad, she pressed it to the cut. She knew his injury wasn't serious, but adrenaline buzzed in her veins. He could have been killed. Selfishly, all she could think was that she couldn't bear to lose him. She'd already lost her mother. Her father was missing. And in the months that she and Conor had been together, he'd filled all the cracks in her soul. If he were gone, she would be empty.

Louisa lifted the gauze. The cut had stopped bleeding. Digging through the kit, she found two butterfly bandages and an instant cold pack. She lifted Conor's chin. "You're going to have quite a bruise."

"Won't be the first time." He wasn't a stranger to blood and bruises. He'd been an amateur boxer, but that was long before she knew him, thank goodness. She didn't think she'd like seeing him come home bloodied and bruised on a regular basis.

She massaged the ice pack until it chilled, then handed it to him.

He pressed it to his head. "Thanks."

Jackson left his partner with the suspect and came back into the kitchen. Turning to Rowan, Jackson rubbed his hands together. "It appears Mr. O'Donnell was sleeping in the carriage house. He's made a little nest of blankets and he had filled a bag with small items, possibly to sell."

"Nothing out there has much value," Rowan said. "But this is why we changed the locks and security codes on the house when we fired the staff."

"Is there any possibility he took the short sword before you changed the locks?" Jackson asked.

"I suppose it's possible," Rowan admitted.

Vivian came into the room, the rubber feet of her cane squeaking. "What happened?"

Rowan explained.

"Oh," she exclaimed. "I hope you're all right, Mr. Sullivan."

"I'm fine," Conor assured her.

Rowan pulled a chair out for Vivian. "I'll make sure the carriage house gets proper locks."

"Why did you fire Mr. O'Donnell?" Jackson asked.

Vivian's sigh was a defeat.

"Because I can't pay him," she admitted. "Doug's estate is tied up in the family trust. He received a nice allowance, but now that he's dead, those payments stopped. I feel terrible, though. Who is going to hire poor Dennis at his age?"

Rowan put a hand on her shoulder. "I offered you money. You don't have to sell the house."

"It's all right, Rowan. This is why your father insisted we buy this house, even though it's much bigger than we needed. Your grandfather was paranoid about money leaking outside the Banks bloodline, and he tied up his money in as many legal knots as possible. But Doug found a loophole allowing withdrawals for primary residences. Then he put the house in both our names so it would be a marital asset. It's worth four million dollars. Once I sell it and the boat, I'll be set." She patted Rowan's hand. "I really can't manage the stairs anyway. This will work out nicely."

Rowan's frown aged him ten years. "There would have been more money if Dad hadn't given it all to those charlatans who promised to cure his cancer."

"He needed the hope," Vivian said. "He wasn't a man who could sit back and accept his life was over."

"Are you pressing charges against Mr. O'Donnell?" Jackson asked around.

"No," Conor said. "I feel bad for the old guy."

"He hit you with a shovel," Jackson said.

"He's probably pretty desperate." Conor shrugged. "And didn't want to be caught trespassing or with stolen goods."

Jackson looked to Vivian.

She shook her head. "No. I feel bad enough. He's been our landscaper and maintenance man for ten years."

"Then I guess we'll let him go." Jackson went out back.

An uncomfortable silence fell over the room for a few seconds.

"When was the last time you saw Asher?" Conor asked Vivian.

She exchanged a guarded look with Rowan.

Louisa wondered who Asher was, how Conor had found out about him, and why Vivian and Rowan didn't want to talk about him.

"I've only seen my other stepson twice since the funeral." Vivian stared at her hands. "Even when you know someone is dying, you're never quite prepared for when it actually happens. Asher took Doug's death hard. I've tried to call him, but he won't return my messages. I'm trying to give him space and time to grieve."

"He's supposed to be getting the sailboat ready for sale, but I don't know what progress he's made. He won't return my calls either. I even went to his house," Rowan said. "He either wasn't there or wouldn't answer the door. I have some trust documents that need his signature too."

"Can the trust be amended?" Louisa asked. Some aspects of her mother's trust were concrete, but others could be changed for certain life events: marriage, divorce, death, the birth of a child.

"No." Rowan shook his head. "Asher and I can manage the investments, but the structure is unalterable."

A few minutes later, both cops came back into the house and announced they were leaving. Conor and Louisa followed them to the foyer.

"Thank you." Rowan showed them to the door, and the maid brought all four coats. Buttoning up, they went outside.

Jackson strode toward the police vehicle, his phone pressed to his ear.

After the door closed behind them, Conor leaned close to Ianelli. "Do you know about Asher?"

"Yes," Ianelli said.

Conor nodded. "You might want to look at him harder. I got the feeling from the maid that he was having some emotional issues."

"Will do," Ianelli said and got into his car.

Conor pulled the keys from his pocket, but Louisa took them from him. "I'll drive."

"I'm fine."

"The man with the head injury is strictly a passenger." She slid behind the wheel and started the engine. "How did you find out about the other stepson?"

"I have my ways."

He charmed the maid, Louisa thought. He could charm any female with a pulse. It was his superpower. She started the engine.

"It's just a cut. I can drive," Conor grumbled.

She eyed his head. "You're getting a bruise."

"I'm fine. Think of it this way, if old Dennis hadn't bashed me in the head, we wouldn't have learned about the issues with the Banks's trust," Conor said. "I'd like to know more about their financial situation. Money is always a motivator. Why did you want copies of all the papers?"

"I only gave them a cursory read. I'd like to research Mr. Banks's sources in more detail. There were other dealers besides Xander."

"What did you find on him?"

"Six of the pieces in Mr. Banks's collection came from Xander." She told him about the picture taken outside Xander's place.

"So he lied to you yesterday." Conor rolled his shoulder, and she made a note to check him for injuries later. He wouldn't bring them to her attention.

"He knew Douglas Banks, and he clearly wasn't an Internet-only client." Louisa shivered. "So Xander definitely omitted some information."

"Lying by omission is still lying in my book." Conor turned her seat heater to high. "Was he protecting his clients or himself?"

"Good question." Giving the engine a moment to warm, she pulled her phone from her purse, opened the photo app, and showed Conor the picture of the sword description. "I found this on the bookshelf, tucked inside one of my father's books."

"Any idea who wrote this?"

"No, but there are examples of Douglas Banks's and Rowan's handwriting in all this paperwork. I'll try and compare when we get home. Maybe we'll get some information from Xander."

"Do you think he's up to something?" Conor asked.

"Like?"

"I don't know, but ass-covering is never a good sign."

Louisa considered Conor's suggestion as she put the car into drive. "Before today, I would have said no." Louisa steered the car out of the driveway. "But now I feel like I can't trust anyone. Let's drop in on Xander."

"Are you sure that's a good idea? The police will be questioning him."

Anger warmed Louisa's blood. "Oh, I'm sure. He knew about Douglas Banks's collection and he said nothing. I need to see Xander again."

"Why don't you let the police handle that?"

"There isn't any solid evidence that he did anything illegal. I doubt the police can get a search warrant based on my intuition. My father could be there right now."

"OK, then." Conor pointed to the windshield. "Take 476 North."

Traffic clogged the interstate. An hour later, Louisa parked in front of Xander's shop. She'd spent the drive trying to calm down, but arrived even angrier. When she pushed open the glass door, she spotted his shaggy red head in the back of the store. Conor touched her arm as she surged forward.

"Easy."

Xander was talking on the phone and writing notes on a piece of paper. He looked up as they walked closer. His eyes grew concerned as he studied Louisa's face.

She waited until he hung up.

"What is it?" he asked in a cautious voice.

"You knew Douglas Banks." Louisa waited for an excuse.

Three heartbeats of dead silence followed as Xander obviously struggled to think of one. She wished his expression wasn't hidden behind the bushy beard, but his pale blue eyes gave him away. "I did."

"His collection is full of Viking artifacts—pieces you sold to him." Louisa lowered her voice. "And he's been to this shop. You sold him a replica sword."

"Yes," Xander admitted.

"Why didn't you tell me this yesterday?"

"Doug is dead." Xander feigned a casual shrug. "He's hardly a threat to anyone."

"But his collection is still at large." Louisa seethed, all her deep-seated distress about her father surfacing. She had the first real clue, and Xander could have given it to her a full day earlier, when Ward had been missing for hours instead of days. "What if this information meant the difference between life and death for my father?"

Xander blinked away. His face tightened, his eyes narrowing as if he was coming to an unpleasant decision. "I had to protect my clients," he finally said. "I don't give out personal information without checking with them first."

"As you pointed out, your client is dead," Louisa said.

"His family's privacy is protected by extension. It's a matter of personal integrity."

Louisa cut him off. "You actually weighed your personal integrity over my father's life?"

"I did what I had to do. I'm sorry if you can't understand." His words were full of moral superiority.

"I'm sorry too." Louisa punctuated her anger with a fist to her thigh. Below that thin layer of fury, fear simmered, whispering in the back of her mind that her father could be dead. "I can't believe you held back information because you didn't want your reputation to suffer."

Suddenly she knew. It wasn't just his reputation that concerned him.

"How long have you been selling black market artifacts?" she asked.

Xander shut down. "I'm not going to answer that."

Louisa wished she could withdraw the question. Pointing out Xander's illegal activity hadn't done her any service. She'd let her emotions get the better of her. She of all people shouldn't be surprised. This wasn't the first time she'd been betrayed by someone she'd trusted.

"But it wouldn't be wise to spread that rumor around." Xander moved forward, his posture threatening.

Louisa's empty belly went cold. She was tall, but Xander was twice her size. His frame was broad, and all the sword wielding had left him heavily muscled.

Conor edged in front of Louisa. "It wouldn't be wise for you to get any closer."

She'd almost forgotten he was there. He'd been quietly observing, waiting patiently in case he was needed. Xander was a few inches taller, and twenty or thirty pounds heavier, but Conor projected the kind of cool confidence that said he'd faced bigger men—and won. Xander's fighting experience was choreographed, while Conor's was one hundred percent genuine.

Xander backed off. "Get out of my shop."

Louisa didn't waste any time. Conor kept his eye on the dealer until they'd exited the shop. He took the keys and put her in the passenger seat, anger evident in the tension of his body.

"I'm sorry." Louisa snapped her seat belt. "I didn't intend to threaten him. I just—Oh hell, I don't know what I was doing."

And now she was angry at herself for losing her cool, and possibly a chance to gain more information about her father's whereabouts.

"You didn't do anything wrong. You needed information to find your father. Knowing what was at stake, Xander lied to you, and you're shocked. You have every right to be madder than hell."

"But I shouldn't have provoked him. He certainly won't cooperate now."

"He wasn't going to cooperate anyway. Don't worry about it." Conor reached over and rubbed her leg.

"But the visit wasn't a total waste." Louisa reached into her pocket and pulled out a small notepad. "While Xander was sizing you up, I stole the tablet he was writing on."

Conor gave her a surprised glance. "I'm impressed. I didn't think you had it in you."

"I didn't plan it. But when I saw his handwriting, I needed to be sure." Louisa opened her phone and compared Xander's handwriting to the sword description she'd found at the Banks's house. "I'm no expert, but it looks the same to me."

"Call Ianelli," Conor said.

The detective promised to interview Xander Buch that afternoon.

"But what could Xander have to do with my father's kidnapping or the murders?" Louisa asked.

"He's a Viking wannabe. So is the killer." Conor pointed out the connection she'd been denying.

And Louisa had introduced him to her dad.

"We should stop for food," Conor said. "You didn't eat breakfast, and now it's lunchtime."

"I'm not hungry." Louisa's stomach roiled with enough emotions to fill it. She leaned against the headrest, glad that Conor had taken over the driving. Her thoughts were scattered like confetti after the day's revelations. They had gone from zero suspects to three: Xander, Rowan, and Asher. The police would also include Shawn and Jordan, but Louisa couldn't believe the boys could be responsible. Granted, she was at the museum when her father worked with the boys after school, but they'd seemed to have a good rapport. "We should stop at the museum too. My boss might recognize some names. He's been in this area much longer than I have."

Conor merged into the fast lane. "If we keep digging, we're bound to turn something up."

"Every family has its secrets if you're willing to dig deep enough for skeletons."

CHAPTER
20

Ianelli directed a dashboard heat vent toward his face. He wasn't looking forward to examining another death scene during this frigging Arctic front.

Fairmont Park was one of the largest park systems in the country, with over nine thousand acres of green space. The Philadelphia Museum of Art sat at the head of the park. Jogging and bike paths lined the Schuylkill River and meandered through the acreage. Even in the bitter cold snap, die-hard runners hit the trails daily. Lemon Hill Drive wound upward away from the river. Ianelli drove past a Prius, three compact SUVs—and the medical examiner's van.

The brutal weather slamming Philadelphia wasn't keeping the killer indoors either.

"Odd place to dump a pair of bodies," Jackson said from the passenger seat.

"Isolated enough, dark and empty at night, especially in this weather." Ianelli parked on the side of the road just short of the mansion. Built in 1800 as a summer home for a Philadelphia merchant, the Federal-style mansion was now owned by the city and operated as a historical house museum. On the shoveled asphalt, a dozen joggers, clad in tight black pants, colorful coats, and snug hats, gathered next to a fluttering rectangle of crime-scene tape.

Jackson unlatched his seat belt. "Maybe the responding officer jumped the gun. Maybe these bodies aren't related to the others."

Ianelli didn't respond. While he wouldn't admit to leaping to a conclusion, the second he'd laid eyes on the bodies Monday night, his instincts had told him they were dealing with a serial killer.

They got out of the car and climbed the snow-covered hill. Ianelli took in the stunning view of the icy river, the Victorian-era Boathouse Row, and the cityscape beyond. A frigid blast of wind froze his eyeballs until they watered. At five thirty, daylight was in its death throes. Blue and red lights from emergency vehicles swirled on the dingy white landscape. City snow lost its pristine appeal soon after it fell, pollution and road grime staining it the dirty gray of white socks that needed a good bleaching.

A uniform herded the gawkers away from the scene. The detectives checked in with the officer in charge of the crime scene log.

"Who found them?" Ianelli's gut cramped as he surveyed the bodies. The wooden pallet was tucked into a tiny clearing in the foliage. The man was beaten, the woman's throat slit.

Shit.

He'd been right. Serial killer.

"A runner said he ducked into the trees to take a leak." The uniform pointed to his cruiser. "He was shaking so hard, I put him in the back to warm up."

"Thanks. Can you hold onto him for a few more minutes?" Ianelli asked.

"Sure." The uniform went back to crowd control. "OK, people. Move along."

Ianelli and Jackson approached the scene. Dr. Gonzalez was already at work. Her parka-and-boots-clad frame leaned over the bodies. Jackson walked closer and peered over her shoulder. She gave him one slightly irritated glance. He backed off to a respectful distance, and she went back to work without comment, the seriousness of a second set of ritual-type murders seemingly putting their feud on hold.

"They were killed overnight." Dr. Gonzalez wrote something on her clipboard, then set it down on top of her kit. "The setup is *almost* identical to the last."

"Almost?" Ianelli asked. His gaze absorbed similarities and sought discrepancies between the new and previous scenes.

Like the first victims, these bodies were stretched out on a trimmed wooden pallet and supplied with pizza, beer, and Tastykakes. The man was well muscled and dressed in athletic shorts. He clutched a knife in his hands, which were folded on his abdomen. The woman wore a spandex tube top micro dress. Four icicles in the shape of a crude letter R lay across her abdomen. The edges of the pallet were charred, but once again, melting snow had likely put out the fire the killer had set.

"Let's start with the female. I don't see any obvious indications of drug use." Dr. Gonzalez pointed a gloved finger at the female's wrist. "Also, these are new: ligature marks."

"She was restrained?" Ianelli asked. There had been no signs that the first female victim, Nicole Evans, had been tied up.

"Yes. From the depth and size of the wounds, I believe the killer used plastic zip ties." Gonzalez moved to the woman's head. "And there's some torn skin and adhesive residue around her mouth."

"Tape," Jackson said. "He needed her to be quiet."

"So he grabbed the woman and held onto her for a while this time," Ianelli suggested. "Does that mean he planned further ahead?"

Jackson blew out a foggy breath. "We don't know that he didn't do that the last time. Maybe this girl put up more resistance than Nicole Evans did."

Ianelli tucked his hands in his armpits. "According to Nicole's roommate, Nicole left their room sometime after midnight, and she died shortly after. If he held Nicole, it wasn't for long."

"Nicole's roommate is a tweaker," Jackson said. "Meth addicts aren't known for their reliability."

Ianelli considered the roommate's interview. She'd been twitchy and distracted, but she'd also been upset about her friend's death. "True, but her statement matched Nicole's time of death. If this woman was abducted earlier, it would show greater planning."

Jackson lowered his voice. "He's taking his time, enjoying the preparation."

"Finding more pleasure in his work," Ianelli added.

Shit.

Ianelli searched the snow surrounding the bodies. His gaze fell on a yellow evidence marker next to a large deep-red stain in the snow about fifteen feet from the victims. "Her throat was slit over there."

"With the same deep, sure slice," Dr. Gonzalez said, inspecting the wound in the female's neck.

"Was he beaten with a length of rebar?" Ianelli asked the ME.

The male victim had shoulder-length hair pulled back with a leather thong. She separated a spot of matted, frozen hair. "I think so. The wound looks very similar to the first male victim's, but I won't be able to confirm the same weapon was used until I do the autopsy. Here's another huge difference. All of the bruises I can see were delivered with the weapon."

Jackson leaned over her shoulder again, as if looking for himself. "No fists?"

"So far, all the bruises in sight have rebar marks," she said.

What the hell did that mean? Ianelli focused on the man's wrists. "The male wasn't restrained. So the killer forcibly abducted the woman, but not the men?"

Jackson's eyebrows drew together into a straight bushy line across his forehead. "The females were both slender. Physically overpowering them wouldn't have been that difficult. But both male victims were in professional athlete condition. Not so easy to manhandle a full-grown man in that kind of shape."

"So how did he get the men?" Ianelli turned to the ME. "When do you think you'll be able to do the autopsy?"

"They're as frozen as the last pair. Hopefully they'll thaw enough by late tomorrow afternoon, but I can't make that promise." Dr. Gonzalez packed up her supplies and stepped back while the bodies were black-bagged and rolled away. "We'll soak their fingertips as soon as we get them back to the morgue. That should thaw the skin enough to get prints." Her head tilted.

"How long?" Ianelli asked.

"An hour. Maybe two." Dr. Gonzalez would be working late tonight.

This was no longer an isolated case. Two sets of bodies changed the entire dynamic of the investigation. No more guessing as to whether there would be more deaths. Now it was only a matter of when. Everyone involved would be putting in overtime until they found the killer.

The detectives spent another twenty minutes inspecting the scene with the forensics team before heading toward the car.

A newswoman shoved a microphone in Jackson's face. "Detective Jackson, is it true that The Icicle Killer has struck again?"

Ianelli saw the angry glitter in his partner's eyes and stepped forward. No good could come of Jackson mouthing off to the press. Again. "You know we can't comment on an ongoing investigation." Ianelli gave her a grim, polite nod.

But she just wouldn't take the hint. "Can you confirm that you're handling The Icicle Killer case?"

Ianelli exhaled through his nose, his lips mashed tighter than a window seal. His face was so tense, when he opened his mouth, his jaw cracked. "You'll have to wait for the press conference."

"Have you found Dr. Ward Hancock?" she pressed.

"No comment." Ianelli gritted his teeth.

Eyeing a throng of reporters headed across the salt-dusted parking lot, he and Jackson slid past her and made for the car. Inside, Ianelli locked the doors and took a breath. "Don't they realize that giving killers fancy names feeds their egos?"

"More murders mean more stories." Jackson popped a stick of gum into his mouth and chewed it as if it deserved punishment.

"That's cold."

"That's media-thinking," Jackson said. "We held back the link between the murders and Ward Hancock's disappearance. The real question is, who leaked the information?"

"It always seems to happen." Ianelli started the engine. "Do we agree it was the same killer?"

"Yes." Jackson fastened his seat belt. "There are too many parallels between the two scenes that we didn't share with the media."

Ianelli steered the car toward the expressway. February in Philadelphia was like having his nuts frozen in an ice cube tray. How many more years until he could retire and move to Florida? "So what do we do with Jordan Franklin?"

"Jordan couldn't have killed this pair from jail. That's for sure." Jackson stared out the windshield, his breath sending vapor trails in the cold air. Their piece-of-shit police vehicle was slow to warm up. "But he could still have killed Mario. Maybe Shawn killed the new victims. We really need to find him."

"We've been looking for six weeks. We haven't found Orion Turner either. How the hell did he even get back on the street?" Jackson unbuttoned his coat. "I thought the task force had him cold on robbery charges."

"The DNA evidence went missing." Ianelli blew out a hard breath. "I thought the captain's head was going to explode when he found out."

"Unfortunately it isn't the first time evidence has disappeared. Probably not the last time either."

Every big police department had to deal with some dirt.

Ianelli considered the two sets of bodies. "Mario and his pals beat the crap out of Jordan, but someone else beat Mario to death with a piece of rebar. Maybe the killer didn't land any of the blows with his fists. Mario could have gotten those from Jordan. The killer is the one using the rebar."

"That would explain the differences between the bruises on the two male victims."

Ianelli reached for the takeout coffee in the cup holder. It was cold, but he finished it anyway for the hit of caffeine. Ten minutes later, he parked in the precinct lot. The pollution-black snow that banked the lot was just fucking depressing. He got out of the car and stared at the back of the ugly-ass, brown brick building. His phone beeped. He glanced at the display, recognized the number of the CI he'd been avoiding, then stepped away to answer the call. He couldn't put this guy off forever. "Ianelli here."

Jackson leaned on the car and waited.

"We need to meet," the CI said. "But don't bring your partner. I don't trust him."

Ianelli wasn't sure *he* fully trusted Jackson. Ianelli scratched his neck. The CI would have to wait. This was one meeting Ianelli couldn't take with his partner. In fact, it was a meeting he didn't want to take at all. The CI was the worst of the worst, the kind of person that made Ianelli need to shower after a meet. But he'd committed himself, and there was no way out of it now. Regret was a bitch.

There was way too much drama in his life.

"I'll call you A-sap." Ianelli ended the call and returned to his partner. "If we're entertaining non-gang suspects, how many do we have?"

"Too many, and not enough."

"Xander Buch. Strong possibility. Agreed?"

"Agreed," Jackson said. "He's big enough, he knew more than he said about Douglas Banks, and he doesn't have an alibi for either pair of murders."

After receiving Louisa's message, they'd driven out and interviewed the artifact dealer in person. They'd been in his shop when they'd gotten the call about the new bodies.

"And he likes to pillage pretend villages in his spare time." Ianelli liked Xander for the murders, but his personal opinion wasn't enough.

"Too bad we don't have enough evidence for a search warrant." The fact that Xander had done business with Douglas Banks and that Banks had a collection of Viking artifacts wasn't enough. They had no proof that the sword delivered to Ward Hancock came from Banks's collection. That said, they had asked the local police to keep a watch on Xander Buch. At this moment, a plain-clothes detective was following the artifact dealer. If Xander was the killer, they were hoping he'd lead them to Ward Hancock.

"Do you think Ward's still alive?" Jackson asked.

"Until I see a body, that's the assumption I'm working on." But Ianelli didn't think it looked good for Ward. He'd been missing for a day and a half. The longer he was gone, the lesser the chances of finding him alive. "What now?"

"I got nothing." Jackson brushed at a streak of road grime on his overcoat. "I don't like the fact that we haven't been able to find Asher Banks. Did you hear from Rowan?"

"Yeah. He e-mailed me a list of the businesses owned by the family trust. I have a uniform running down the list, looking for local addresses. So far, nothing has turned up. I put a geek on getting more info about the trust too, but we have to be careful about legal issues. The Bankses haven't done anything wrong, and they can afford very good lawyers."

But they solved a lot of crimes by following the money trail.

Ianelli rubbed his face. He was so tired his skin hurt. They'd been running down leads at balls-to-the-wall speed for three solid days. They'd interviewed dozens of people, reviewed phone records and background checks until their eyes crossed. They'd recruited uniforms to watch hours and hours of surveillance tapes. They'd put out BOLO alerts on Orion Turner and Shawn Franklin, and they'd attempted to contact Asher Banks multiple times with no luck. A neighbor thought he might be out of town, but he wasn't answering his cell phone. So far, nothing was panning out on this case.

Since then, he'd stopped home only twice. Cravings for fifteen minutes of ordinary life nearly overwhelmed him. If he wanted a clear head, he needed to take a break. Sometimes, a new idea popped into his head when he wasn't thinking about the case.

"I need to stop home and take a shower." He lifted an arm and sniffed. "I've been wearing this same shirt since yesterday, and I haven't said more than two sentences to my wife."

"Everything all right there?"

"Fine. She's pregnant. We just found out." Sharing an intimate personal detail with his partner of two years shouldn't have been uncomfortable. He spent more time with Jackson than his wife. And yet . . .

"Congrats, man." Jackson's face split into a rare smile, which frankly looked alien on his perpetually cranky face.

"Thanks." Ianelli was trying to act appropriately excited, but as usual, fate had crap timing. "But this wasn't a good week to catch a soul-sucking case like The Icicle Killer. Shit, now the media has me using that attention-whore nickname. Is it too early for a scotch?"

Jackson squinted at him. "How long you been married?"

"Ten years." And trying to have a kid for nine of them, but no one knew that. Just as no one knew what they'd gone through to make it finally happen. And still, he felt like he wouldn't be able to take a deep breath until the first few months of the pregnancy were over. Or maybe until the kid was born.

Or graduated from college.

He opened the console, took out a roll of antacids, and chewed two. How had his life become this complicated?

"You should take her flowers."

Ianelli barked out a surprised laugh.

"What?" Jackson raised a *what-the-fuck* palm.

"Sorry." Feeling punchy, Ianelli shook his head. "I just didn't expect the romantic suggestion from you. You're the least sentimental guy I know."

"Yeah, well, I'm beat. I'm getting sappy." Jackson rubbed his eye with a knuckle. "My eyelids feel like sandpaper."

"Let's take an hour." Barely enough time for a shower but better than nothing. He needed to look at something that didn't remind him of death for a while.

"By that time we might have prints to work from," Jackson agreed. "Don't forget the flowers."

"Yes, Oprah," Ianelli smart-assed.

Hopefully, the quick dinner break would jump-start their brain cells. Without identifications of the bodies and some fresh forensic evidence, their case was going nowhere.

Another message chirped to Jackson's phone. "Our break just got cancelled. The captain is putting a task force together. He wants us at the precinct now. Let's look on the bright side—more cops to chase down leads might give us the break we need."

"Amen to that." Ianelli rubbed at the ache in his temple.

For now, The Icicle Killer was free to abduct and kill more people.

Ianelli thought about the media's nickname for the killer. "What do you think the icicle *R* means?"

"No idea."

"Maybe we should ask Dr. Hancock."

"Can't hurt." Jackson lifted his phone.

Ianelli held up a hand. "I'll call her. Your bedside manner sucks."

Jackson shrugged. "Whatever."

Ianelli dug out his phone.

The Icicle Killer.

Fucking media.

CHAPTER
21

Back in the kitchen of their Rittenhouse apartment, Conor swallowed two ibuprofen tablets. Frustration was the word for the day.

When Louisa had talked to Xander earlier, Conor had wanted to punch the dealer in the face. He'd been bouncing his own bar for a long time. He'd tossed bigger men than Xander Buch out onto their asses. The following two hours with Louisa's pompous boss had made his head ache more than the blow from the shovel.

He stretched his shoulder. Pain rolled through the joint. Thankfully, he'd seen the shadow and been able to duck. Then he'd felt almost bad for tossing the old dude on his face.

They'd stopped to pick up a few essentials for Yvonne and Tyler. Then they'd returned to their condo, fed and walked the dog, and lain down on their bed for a while. Neither of them had been able to sleep, but Conor at least wanted Louisa to rest. She'd opted for a hot shower.

She walked into the kitchen, her socks silent on the tile, the dog practically plastered to her legs. She'd dressed in jeans and a sweater. Her hair was pulled back into a simple tail, the stark style doing nothing to soften the lines of worry and exhaustion on her face.

"I wish my boss had been more help," Louisa said.

"He tried."

Desperately. The director, an archeologist wannabe, had a serious man-crush on Ward and had reviewed every paper and photo from Banks's collection. He'd been disappointed when none of the paperwork or artifacts from the Banks collection had looked familiar, and when they'd looked up the Banks's pictures on the Internet, the director hadn't recognized anyone in the family.

"I know. He's only been with the museum for seven years. The Banks's dual illnesses likely limited their social calendars primarily to doctors' appointments. I doubt they were able to attend museum functions."

She picked up the accordion file. "I'm going to go through every paper from Mr. Banks's office and see if any other ideas jump out at me."

That would take hours, and the circles under her eyes were already deep purple. "Are you sure you can't sleep?"

"Positive." She set down the file and started a pot of coffee.

Conor moved behind her and wrapped his arms around her, wishing he could insulate her from the helplessness that had to be consuming her. He rested his head against her temple. "Is there anything I can do?"

Her body relaxed, just a little. Slumped was probably a better description. "I'm beginning to think we'll never find him."

Conor wanted to tell her they would, that everything would be all right, that they could get back to living their lives and being happy together. But it wouldn't be fair to give her false hope. It was seven thirty on Thursday evening. Ward had been missing since very early the previous morning. He'd been in the hands of a killer for a day and a half. What were the odds that he was still alive?

After a brief pause, Louisa shook her head and went to the cabinet for a mug. "How are Yvonne and Tyler?"

How like her to take care of others even when she had more than enough of her own worries.

"Yvonne is asleep. I didn't wake her to find out. Tyler is in the guest shower. He's been binge-watching a show about zombies all day." From the kid's fascination with the TV programming, Conor assumed their burned apartment hadn't come with hundreds of cable channels that Louisa had but never watched.

Tyler had also eaten an entire frozen pizza. But he hadn't showered or changed out of his pajamas until Conor had pointed him in the direction of soap and water. Conor didn't remember being obsessed with personal hygiene at the age of twelve, but he suspected the kid was deep in escaping-reality mode.

"Do you think zombies are too frightening for a twelve-year-old? I'd hate to give him more nightmares."

"I think whatever distracts Tyler right now is fine. Zombies are safe. They can't be real."

"Reality is definitely more terrifying." The coffee machine beeped. Louisa filled her mug and added cream.

"Speaking of distractions, have you checked on the weather forecast?" She crossed the room, picked up the remote, and turned on the TV, lowering the volume to the bare minimum. Kirra followed.

"The last I heard, we're supposed to get freezing rain or sleet or some other frozen mess Friday night."

Louisa's next breath hitched. "Where is he, Conor? Is he inside? Is it warm?"

Heart breaking for her, Conor moved toward her just as a news flash came on the TV.

On the screen, a reporter stood in front of Fairmont Park. Floodlights brightened the dark riverbank like a night game at a football stadium. Conor recognized the spot immediately. He and his sister used to run the river trail along Kelly Drive.

A banner scrolled across the screen: The Icicle Killer Strikes Again.

Louisa's knees buckled and she dropped to the sofa. The dog rested her head on Louisa's thigh.

"Two bodies were discovered next to a jogging trail on the banks of the Schuylkill River this morning. The bodies have not yet been identified, but sources say the deaths could be linked to the work of The Icicle Killer, who also claimed two lives earlier this week. Does Philadelphia have a serial killer in its midst?"

Easing down next to her, Conor took her hand. "It's not him."

"How do you know?"

"Ianelli would have called." *Right?* Though Conor knew their relationship with the detectives was mostly a one-way street, he'd grudgingly come to accept that they were hardworking cops. Ianelli had saved Louisa's life, and Conor couldn't imagine that he wouldn't call Louisa right away if he'd found Ward.

"If the body wasn't too damaged." Panic stuttered in her voice.

"Ianelli and Jackson have met your dad," Conor said. "They'd recognize him."

Louisa's phone rang. She checked the display. "It's Detective Ianelli." She answered the call, tipping the phone so Conor could hear. "Hello."

"The victim isn't your father," Ianelli said.

Louisa exhaled. "Thank you."

"I have a question for you," the cop said. "Do you know what the letter R spelled out in icicles could mean?"

Louisa paused then said, "Nothing comes to mind, but I'll think on it."

"Let us know if you come up with anything." The cop ended the call.

"The Icicle Killer." Louisa lowered the phone. She paced in front of the sofa. "There's something nagging at me. I need to see a picture of the crime scene again. I wish I had a copy.

"Wait." She stood and went toward her office. Knocking softly, she waited for Tyler to answer before opening the door.

Conor heard her ask him how he was and if he needed anything. Tyler's answer was too quiet for him to make out the words. Louisa returned in a minute. One of her father's books and a notebook were tucked in her hand. She went back to the sofa. Then she picked up a pencil and began to sketch.

"What are you doing?" He sat next to her.

"My memory isn't eidetic like my father's, but it's very good. I'm going to sketch the scene as closely as I can and compare it to the illustration in the book. Could you find the correct page?"

Conor flipped pages until he found the picture.

She shook her head and leaned over her work. "No, don't show it to me until I'm finished. I don't want it to affect my memory."

He watched as the image took shape. He hadn't known she could draw. They had so much to learn about each other. Would it be too much to ask for a solid year of normal? Because there was nothing that appealed to him more than discovering all of Louisa's hidden talents.

Ten minutes later, she straightened. "Did I miss anything? I only saw the picture for a few seconds."

She'd captured the photograph and most of its disturbing details.

"No."

"Then let's compare." She set her drawing next to the open book. "I see it."

"What?"

"The thing that doesn't belong."

Conor enumerated the items in the two pictures. Each image depicted two bodies, a wooden pallet, food, a weapon. "The icicles."

"Yes." Her face flushed. "Ianelli asked me about the letter R spelled out in icicles. What if this isn't a letter R?"

"What do you mean?" Conor asked. "They look like a letter R."

She ripped a blank piece of paper from the back of the tablet and bookmarked the page. Then she went to the index. "I'm thinking of Viking runes." She flipped to a new page. "Do you know what they are?"

"Ancient Norse symbols." Conor had been working his way through Ward's books. "The Vikings' alphabet."

"Yes. The Vikings used them for writing, casting spells, and telling fortunes." She pointed to a chart of stick-like symbols. Next to her fingertip was a symbol that looked like a crude letter R, but the rounded portion of the letter was squared off. "This is the rune Raidho."

"What does it mean?"

"Raidho represents a person's life journey. It generally means a change is about to happen, usually for the better." She sat back. "I should tell Ianelli."

She dialed his number. When he didn't answer, she left a message asking him to call her.

Louisa rested her elbows on her knees and her chin on her balled fists. "I can't just sit here and wait. I need to do something."

"What did you have in mind?" Conor didn't love the idea he could see forming in her beautiful green eyes. Sometimes, Louisa was a little too smart.

"I need to move." She straightened. "Let's go to the gym?"

Suspicion curled in Conor's cut. "You want to box? Now?"

"I do."

Her skills were improving, but working out wasn't her favorite pastime. "Would this sudden desire to exercise have anything to do with the fact that Jordan, Mario, and Orion are all fighters?"

She blinked. "Definitely. It can't be a coincidence that three people involved in this case have boxing in common. And that two of them train at your gym."

As much as he wanted to, Conor couldn't deny her logic. "But how is Orion involved?"

"I don't know. Could he be the killer?"

The reporter on the TV piped up. "This just in. The male victim has been identified as Zach Robertson, age twenty-three, of Fishtown." A picture of a young, fit white man appeared on the screen. "A local source tells us that Robertson was an amateur boxer."

Recognition snapped Conor's spine straight. "He's a fighter too? That's four people involved with the case in boxing, two of them training at Southpaw."

The reporter continued. "One of The Icicle Killer's victims found on Monday, Mario Avana, was also an amateur boxer. Mario had recently won the welterweight division in a local tournament."

"We need to go to the gym. I'll change." Louisa disappeared into the bedroom.

Conor followed her. "Why don't you let me go alone?"

"Because this is the time we usually go together on your nights off. It will be less conspicuous if we keep to our normal routine." She stopped in front of her dresser.

But Conor didn't want her anywhere near the gym.

She pulled a sports bra, a tank top, and a pair of yoga pants from a drawer. Items in hand, she headed for the bathroom. He heard water running in the sink and clothes hitting the floor.

He changed into a pair of nylon shorts. Leaning into the bathroom, he watched Louisa tug her shirt into place. She grabbed an elastic band from the vanity and walked from the room.

In the hall, he caught her arm to stop her. "I love you, and I want to protect you."

She moved closer, resting her hand over his heart. "I love you too, but I have to find my father."

"I can go talk to the guys at the gym without you."

"We'll be together in a very public place. This is a low-risk operation."

"I know all this, but my paranoia won't listen to rational arguments." He kissed her.

"Besides, Tito likes me more than he likes you."

"This is true."

Louisa had charmed the fighters at Southpaw with enough determination to make up for her lack of coordination. Being a beautiful woman didn't hurt either. Not that the few female boxers at Southpaw weren't attractive, but even without her silk suits and pearls, Louisa's blatant femininity drew alpha males like a tractor beam.

"I'll walk the dog while you finish getting ready," Conor said. "I don't want Tyler and Yvonne tempted to go outside."

Fifteen minutes later, they were in the car driving toward South Philly. Conor parked at the curb. Getting out of the car, he checked the street in both directions. He saw nothing suspicious, but the hair on the back of his neck was waving a foam finger. Nerves or reality? So many bad things had happened to them, his senses were permanently on edge.

He kept a protective hand on the small of her back as they walked the half block to the gym. Through the window, he could see the gym was busy. Inside smelled like dirty laundry and sweat. But the crowd made him feel more secure. Fighters and trainers worked in all three rings. More men jumped rope, hit mitts, and shadowboxed.

Tonight, he didn't see another woman on the mats. Southpaw did not offer boot camp or kickboxing classes for soccer moms. It was a serious, old-school gym. Female boxers were the exception rather than the norm. But Southpaw, in an effort to be as enlightened as a large group of testosterone-fueled males could possibly be, had converted an old utility closet into a tiny women's locker room.

"Be back in a minute." Louisa headed for the back corner of the gym to lock up her coat and purse.

The men's locker room was packed with the after-work crowd. Conor shouldered his way to an empty locker and stowed his jacket.

When he emerged, Louisa had found them an empty mat. Tito was already chatting her up. The old man stretched his stooped body a quarter-inch taller as he talked to her. Was he sucking in his stomach?

Louisa set her gloves at her feet and began to loop a protective wrap around the large knuckles of her left hand.

Tito shook his head at her sloppy attempt. "Here, let me help you."

"Thank you." Louisa offered him a dainty hand.

Tito took it with exaggerated gentleness. Then he deftly wound the wrap around her hand and between her fingers, taking his sweet time in covering each knuckle with a thick layer of padding. "We can't have these pretty hands getting all bruised up."

Tito, you dog.

Stepping onto the mat, Conor slapped the trainer on the shoulder. "Hey, old man. What's happening?"

Tito grinned at him. "Hey, Sullivan. I was just helping this gorgeous lady of yours."

"Is that right?" Conor asked. "Funny, but I've seen you wrap hands a lot faster than that."

"A special lady deserves special care." Tito chuckled. When he smiled, his eyes nearly disappeared into the folds of his shoe-leather face. He reached out and gave her bicep a gentle squeeze. "Look at these."

Louisa's body was long and willowy, but she'd developed muscle tone over the past couple of months.

Conor went to the wall and selected a jump rope. Returning, he handed it to Louisa. "Why don't you warm up for a few minutes? Jump rope. Push-ups. You know the drill."

Nodding, she took the rope and moved a dozen feet away. Across the gym, a twenty-year-old featherweight champ whirred a rope at warp speed, demonstrating the coordination, footwork, and agility that developed from many hours of practice. Louisa's version was more little-girl-on-the-sidewalk.

Not that her lack of skill kept the guys from watching her.

She'd been raised in the world of yachts and ponies, and the gritty gym was about as far from her comfort zone as Mars. She'd started out injured and timid, then had gained strength and confidence as she'd improved. Conor had started her with light shadowboxing as soon as the doctor had given her the all clear. None of the athletes minded that she wasn't a serious fighter. They all knew what she'd been through, and that learning some rudimentary self-defense techniques had been vital to her recovery, as was the healthy release of exercise-induced endorphins. She'd worked hard to put her injury and innate girliness aside, though frankly, the men all loved the girliness. They also respected her sheer willpower. If there was one human quality fighters admired, it was tenacity. Most of the guys, including Tito, had grown downright protective.

Louisa was probably safer here than anywhere else. So why was Conor on edge?

Tito leaned on the painted cinder-block wall. "How did you ever land her? She's way too classy for a regular Joe like you."

"I ask myself that question every morning." Conor kept his gaze on Louisa. "Did you know Louisa's father is missing?"

"No!" Tito swore, turning pitying eyes on Louisa. "That poor thing. What is going on in this city? We got dead fighters, dead hookers, missing fathers."

"Did you know Zach or Mario?"

"I knew Zach a little. He trained with Steve Hill. Boxing is a small world."

Many of the fighting gyms had followed the trend and converted to mixed martial arts. Traditional boxing was less popular.

Tito's face crumbled. "I don't understand what's happening, Conor. What kind of sick creep is out there? I know Zach had some law trouble a few years ago, but he'd straightened out. Steve was bragging about Zach at the last tournament. He was a good one. Stayed away from the gangs. Held down a job. Helped his mamma pay the rent."

"Do you know if there was anything different in his life recently?"

"No. He had money troubles, like most everybody in this business." Tito's eyes went soft. "He wasn't even one of mine, but damn. I saw him win his weight class in the last tournament. That boy had speed and heart. He had a career ahead of him."

"Zach fought as a middleweight, right?" Conor asked.

"He did." Tito's face crunched into a mass of age spots and wrinkles.

The news report had stated that Mario won the welterweight division in a recent tournament. Was that where the killer had found them? Was he cherry-picking the winners? Conor needed a list of all the fighters from the event.

"Do you still have the card from the tournament?" Conor asked.

"I think there's a copy in the office. I'll get it for you." Tito ran a sleeve across his eyes. "Have you heard anything about what's happening with Jordan?"

"No." But Conor couldn't imagine the cops could make the murder charge stick now that two more bodies had been found.

"He seems like a good kid."

"For the most part, he is. Talented too." Conor added, "You train Orion Turner."

"Yes." Tito blew out a breath, his lips flapping like a horse. "Orion is talented, but I haven't seen any sign that he's making any attempt to go straight. He's getting his ultimatum this week. I gave him a fair shot. That's if I even see him again. He hasn't been around for weeks."

"You've been more than fair." Conor knew the decision was killing the trainer.

"If I boot him, he has nothing but the Sixes, and his life expectancy drops to a year or two, at best. On the other hand, I've given him plenty of time to come around. Orion suffers from a chronic case of I-can-have-it-all syndrome. I tell them all in the beginning. They have to make the choice to turn their lives around, but I won't tolerate any trouble. I can only afford to work with a few hard-luck cases at a time. Keeping Orion on sets a bad precedent. Plus, I have a dozen other kids just as troubled, waiting for their chance."

But booting Orion from the program could spark some sort of retribution. Gang leaders weren't known for their forgiving natures.

Conor settled a commiserative hand on Tito's shoulder. "Be careful. The Sixes might be a small gang, but they're big on violence."

Tito's head snapped around, his gaze settling on the wide windows that overlooked the street. "The cops are here again. They've been here twice this week, asking about Jordan and Orion."

Ianelli and Jackson were coming through the door. They were obviously working the case 24/7. They both looked like hell.

Louisa caught sight of the detectives. Her eyes widened. Shaking his head, Conor picked up her gloves and waved her over.

Better not to make a public declaration of their association. There were too many links between Southpaw and the murder investigation. Anyone could be watching.

And Conor's paranoia was fine-tuned enough that it felt as if a hundred pairs of eyes were focused on him and Louisa.

CHAPTER
22

He parked the van at the curb. He had a direct view through the front windows of the boxing gym across the street. In the light of his cell phone, he reviewed the fighters' publicity photos in his file and tried to match them to the men working out in the gym. But he could only see the front portion of the training area. None of the fighters that he sought were working out on the mats he could see.

From his visit last month, he knew that three rings took up the center of the large space. Behind those rings was additional training space.

How could he get a view into the back?

Going inside during the tournament had been simple. The space had been packed with spectators, fighters, and trainers. He'd wandered around in complete anonymity, admiring the fighters' skills and wondering how differently the matches would have ended without the official rules artificially imposed by the sport. Each time a match was over and a winner proclaimed, arm held high by the referee, the crowd cheering, he'd pictured himself in the ring. By the end of the day, in his mind, he'd been the champion.

But his imagination wasn't enough. He needed to actually defeat the men in a no-holds-barred fight. Only then would he truly be the superior male. And that was the moment when the plan had begun to evolve.

He shook his head, as if the motion would clear the memories and return him to the present and his current dilemma. He needed to get into the gym.

Today, he couldn't simply walk in. The only people inside were members. He'd stick out.

He couldn't sit at the curb very long either. Someone might notice his van, and that wouldn't do. He'd changed the license plates since he'd used it last, but attracting attention wasn't smart. He couldn't go in and pretend to be interested in boxing. His plan depended on him remaining completely disassociated from any of the men he killed. It was only a matter of time before the police began seeking the killer in boxing gyms. It was the one link between the two sets of deaths.

Maybe he should find someone who wasn't a boxer. Just because he'd formulated a plan didn't mean he couldn't alter it. A good battle strategy needed to be fluid to allow for unforeseen events.

His gaze landed on a shining blond head. Louisa Hancock was working out on a mat, her body clad in tight black pants and a form-fitting tank that showcased muscled shoulders. What was *she* doing here?

Watching her in a sea of masculinity, he froze, realization creeping across him like ice encroaching on a lake.

His research indicated that shield maidens, or female warriors, were part of Norse mythology. They didn't actually exist outside of legends. In the age of Vikings, men raided and fought; women raised children and ran farms. All his research had confirmed this finding. Any accounts of women participating in battles as warriors were strictly folklore.

Yet there she was.

In a large area full of rough-looking, powerful men, she stood out as refined, perfect. From her gleaming blond hair to her long, lean body, she shone like a beacon.

Dr. Louisa Hancock appeared almost mystical.

The warriors she trained among showed her respect. They handled her equipment and aided her in donning her gear. They treated her like royalty.

Before tonight, he'd thought his attraction to Louisa was based on her intelligence and beauty. She was a worthy daughter of Ward. But now he knew why he'd been so enthralled by her very presence.

He was like the fighters that trained with her. All bowed to her grace. All understood that she held a strength different from their own: a completely female power they were unable to harness.

Confidence welled inside him. He was stronger than the other men. The shield maiden should be with *him*. It was against the law of nature for her to be with an inferior male.

His mission this evening had been to find another fighter who'd competed in the boxing tournament the previous month, another challenging opponent to test his skill.

To prove his worth.

But now he changed his mind. If he wanted to win Louisa, then her boyfriend, Conor Sullivan, was the one he needed to defeat. But this man wouldn't be easy to lure. The bait would need to be the one thing that brought him to his knees: Louisa.

He opened his console and took out his camera. Using the telephoto lens, he snapped a picture of Louisa in all her splendor. Excitement coursed through his veins. She was perfect, and she was the key to his entire plan.

She was more than a female warrior. She was supernatural, and there was only one female god-like creature with battle skills and beauty.

She was the Valkyrie.

CHAPTER
23

Louisa slid her hand into the boxing glove that Conor held. Once she had one hand inside the giant, padded fist, putting on the second was like trying to tie her shoes wearing oven mitts. Conor tightened the wrist straps.

Grabbing a couple of hand targets, he ignored the detectives and started her off with some easy combinations. "Jab, jab, cross."

She fired a few distracted punches. Keeping her eyes on him, she tilted her head toward the door. "Did you see who's here?"

"I did." Conor lifted a target. "You're not turning your hand over on the cross. Do it again. We're here to work out, remember?" He leaned close to her ear. "I'd rather not advertise our relationship with the cops."

She nodded. But again, *acting casual* was not her strong suit.

Thank goodness Conor had better focus. He put her through a light workout without giving the cops a second glance and whenever her attention wavered, he changed up the drill.

"Right hook. Now block." Conor circled the mitt, catching her in the side of the head. "Hug your head and keep it tight."

He repeated the motion, and this time she was successful. The mitt struck the side of her arm.

"Now come in with a cross to my body while my arm is raised."

She plowed a fist to the center of his belly, but he tightened his abdomen against the blow. Her punch landed on a solid wall of muscles. Hitting him felt no different than hitting the heavy bag.

"Now give me a few knees." He stacked the padded targets in front of his belly. Though knee strikes weren't part of traditional boxing, Conor also taught her practical self-defense moves.

Louisa drove her knee upward into the pad three times before he nodded and straightened. "Better. Get a quick drink."

Panting, she picked up a water bottle between her mitts and took an awkward sip. Sweat soaked her workout clothes, and her head felt clearer. As she drank, her peripheral vision caught a glance of the cops exiting the office with Tito. She'd been so absorbed in following Conor's cues and blocking his moves that she'd forgotten the detectives.

That was the reason she'd become addicted to boxing. Working with Conor required one hundred percent of her focus, leaving no room for imagined threats or last night's bad dreams. Conor always said she needed to give her brain a rest, and nothing shut it down faster than a target headed toward her face. Conor would never hurt her, but if her attention wandered, he couldn't always avoid giving her a light tap to the head. Tonight, exercise gave her the first mental break she'd had all week.

Poor Tito looked miserable as he ducked away from the police. The detectives didn't look happy either. Jackson's gaze swept over the gym, landed on her and Conor, and sharpened to a laser focus. He elbowed Ianelli, who concealed his irritation better. But she could still tell by the stiffness of his posture that he was annoyed to see her and Conor at the gym.

The detectives crossed the mats. Ianelli pointed at Conor. "Funny meeting you here."

Conor lifted a casual shoulder. "You know where I work out."

"The timing is interesting, though," Ianelli shot back. "We need to talk to you both."

"Not here," Conor said under his breath. "I'll be right back." He crossed the mat. Tito was in the office doorway, waving at him.

Louisa turned away to set down her water bottle.

"You shouldn't be here." Ianelli grabbed her bicep and leaned close to her ear. "It's dangerous."

"I feel pretty safe." She pointedly glanced around at all the fighters. Then she turned her head to stare at him over her shoulder. "And my father is still missing."

The police were hindered by the law. She and Conor could skate around it, as long as they didn't get caught. Louisa would take the risk of annoying the detectives. Time was the enemy.

With his lips pressed into a frustrated line, Ianelli sighed through his nose.

Louisa tugged her arm from his grip, and he stepped back.

She used her teeth to loosen the Velcro wrist strap on a glove. Holding it between her knees, she tugged it off. With one hand free, the second glove came off easily. The detectives were probably trying their best to find her dad, but effort didn't count. The workout had burned the edge off of her nervous energy, but now fresh panic rose into her throat. She picked up her stainless steel bottle and swallowed the burning lump with another sip of water. Had her father been . . . ?

Don't go there. It won't help.

Pushing the terrible possibility from her mind, she stashed her gloves in Conor's duffel bag. "I'm going to get my coat."

There must be something else she could do, but her mind was blank. Maybe Conor had some luck getting information from Tito or the other fighters.

Carrying her water bottle, she stopped in the restroom to wash her hands. Then she headed for the short hall that led to the converted utility closet. Inside, six lockers and a padded weight bench formed a makeshift locker room. The space was empty, as usual. After removing her purse and coat from the locker, she started to tug a long-sleeve shirt over her head. The air behind her shifted, sending the hair on the back of her neck into full alert. Before she could react, an arm encircled her body, preventing her from pushing her head through the neck opening of her shirt. She drew in a deep breath for a scream, but a hand clamped over the fabric and her mouth. Her pulse reverberated in her ears. Her attacker felt like a man from the strength in his arms and the bulk of his body.

He dragged her backward. She dropped her weight, making herself as heavy as possible. She kicked at his shins with her heels, but her athletic shoes couldn't do much damage. Her breaths came faster, panic sending adrenaline rushing through her system. She fought to slow her breathing. Lightheaded and unable to see through the shirt over her head, she twisted against the thick arm encircling her waist. She managed to free her left arm and swung it over her head, striking his ear with her palm. The blow jolted him. His grip loosened, and Louisa slid toward the floor.

She used her legs to lever against him, but with an almost patient grunt, he merely stooped and corrected his grip, lifting her off the floor. She kicked wildly, twisting and bucking against his hold.

Her instincts told her that being taken by this man would mean death, and she must fight with every atom in her body.

And she knew without a doubt that this was the man who'd killed four people. The man who'd taken her father. As much as she wanted to see his face and ask him what happened to Ward, she couldn't suppress the survival instinct. Her body fought back with desperation as if it was on autopilot.

She swung her fist over her shoulder again, but he'd shifted his head out of reach. She heard the squeak of the door as he dragged her into the corridor and toward the rear exit. The gym backed to an alley. If he got her through that door, chances were that the alley would be empty. No one would see. He could take her wherever he wanted.

And do whatever he wanted.

"You belong to me," he whispered in her ear. "Stop fighting or I'll hurt you."

No!

If he'd hurt her here, in a public place, then he'd do far worse when he had her in an isolated location. Alone. At his mercy. With no one to hear her screams.

Louisa could never experience the terror of being abducted again. She'd take her chances right here and now.

She threw her legs upward. As they came down, she sent them as far to the right as possible. Her sudden weight shift caught him by surprise. His grip slipped, and she landed on one of his feet. He grunted and tried to pull her backward again, dragging her by the hand clutching her face.

In one last desperate move, she swung her free hand down and felt for his groin. *There.* She grabbed his testicles and squeezed as hard as possible. His breath whooshed in her ear as he doubled over almost on top of her. She released his balls and brought her elbow up to ram it under his chin. She heard his teeth snap together and felt his body shift backward. He let go of her.

She fell in a tailbone-jarring thud on the concrete and scrambled away. Ripping the shirt off her head, she gulped air and let loose a scream. The yell came out hoarse and weak, but the moment of silence followed by a quick thunder of footsteps told her she'd been heard. She whirled to look behind her, but all she saw was one jean-clad leg disappearing through the rear exit and the metal door banging closed.

Conor skidded into the hallway, the detectives and a small group of men close on his heels.

Still gasping for air, Louisa pointed at the door. Most of the men raced for it. A few stayed behind, standing close to her as if on guard.

Tito squatted next to her. "Take slow breaths. Do you need a paper bag?"

She shook her head. "No. I'll be—" She paused for air. "OK in a minute."

The old trainer looked her over from head to toe. He stood up to take off his zip-up and wrapped it around her shoulders. It wasn't until after the warm fabric enveloped her that she realized she was shivering.

Tito patted her arm. "Just breathe, baby. You're safe."

The rear door opened. Conor, the detectives, and a handful of boxers straggled in.

Conor crouched at her side. "You're all right?"

She nodded and extended a hand. He helped her to her feet, pulling her into his arms for a fierce hug. He didn't say anything else, but she felt the relief and tension in his grasp. Her feet weren't quite steady when he released her.

Conor held her arm. "Can you get her some water, Tito?"

"You bet." The old coach shuffled off.

Detective Jackson was on his phone at the other end of the hall. Most of the men had returned to the gym.

"What happened?" Ianelli asked.

She pointed toward the locker room. "He grabbed me in there." She gave him a rundown of the attack.

"Show me." Ianelli followed her into the converted closet.

Conor held her hand as she walked the detective through the attack.

Ianelli took notes. "You didn't see his face?"

"No. My shirt was over my face. He was taller than me. And strong. He was wearing a thick coat, so his body shape was distorted. It felt like he was wearing jeans." She closed her eyes, concentrating on the memory. "He whispered, so I couldn't hear his voice properly." Giving up, she opened her eyes. "That's all I can tell you."

You belong to me. His words echoed in her head.

The note that had accompanied the ring had read, *For my beloved.*

Somehow he'd shifted from adoration to ownership. Every drop of Louisa's blood chilled, and a hard shudder ripped through her.

He wasn't going to stop trying to get her.

The door opened and Jackson stuck his head through the opening. "Two patrol cars are here. They're canvasing the surrounding businesses. Someone must have a surveillance tape. Also, there's a traffic camera on this corner. I've already requested a copy of the video."

Conor's face was grim. "To sneak in the back door and try to kidnap someone while the gym is full of fighters was a ballsy move."

"I don't like it," Ianelli agreed.

"Me either. There's something else I need to tell you about." Louisa told him her theory about the icicles.

Jackson and Ianelli shared an excited glance.

Ianelli scrolled on his phone. "Like these?"

Louisa looked at the screen. It was a snapshot of a lined notebook. On the page, someone had scribbled letters of the rune alphabet and long paragraphs about each symbol's meaning.

Ianelli put his finger to the screen and advanced to the next picture. "There are pages and pages of these."

She took the phone from his hand and continued to move through the pictures. She stopped on a picture and enlarged part of the image. She pointed to the crude, squared-off R. "This is Raidho. Where did you get this?"

Ianelli didn't answer right away. He searched her face for a few long seconds. Then he seemed to come to a decision. "This is from a notebook we found in Jordan and Shawn Franklin's bedroom. We didn't make the connection between the drawings in the notebook and the R on the body."

Louisa felt her jaw drop open.

"Do you have any idea why Shawn or Jordan would have this?" Jackson asked.

"No." She shook her head. "They both worked with my father, but I would assume they focused on their schoolwork. You could check with the school and see if Viking runes are part of the curriculum."

Jackson shook his head. "We already did. The answer is no."

"I'm going to have a patrol car follow you home." Ianelli lifted his phone to his ear.

"Be careful, Dr. Hancock," Jackson said. "Don't forget that you're a target."

Louisa's phone vibrated. She fished it out of her purse. Excitement stirred as she read her father's cell phone number, but then her hope dimmed as she opened the text message.

Conor leaned over and read the display out loud. "I apologize. I am not yet worthy. But soon I will win your favor."

Louisa's bones went cold. Her father hadn't sent the message. It was from the killer.

CHAPTER
24

He turned the van onto Broad Street and drove slowly toward I-95. Taking the ramp, he merged into traffic. After tonight, he'd need to find another vehicle. Simply changing the license plates wasn't enough. Surely he'd been caught on a security camera.

He'd been a fool. He'd allowed his impulses to take control. Careful planning was the secret to his success so far. Tonight he'd nearly thrown everything away because he'd been overwhelmed with joy. With hope.

With her.

He shifted his position, pain shooting through his groin. She'd nailed him. He was going to need an ice pack tonight.

But why had he expected her to come easily? He hadn't shown her proper respect. He'd allowed his excitement to get the better of him. That wouldn't happen again. But he needed her like a fire required oxygen. How could he lure her to his side?

He mulled ideas in his mind for the next fifteen minutes. Then he parked and stared at his warehouse.

The answer was right before him.

The shield maiden wasn't completely of this earth. She must come to him willingly. She couldn't be forced, but maybe she could be persuaded.

How far would Louisa go to save her father?

And on that note, Conor Sullivan should be included in the summons. After all, how could *he* expect her to accept him unless he defeated her current suitor? The shield maiden would want the strongest warrior. There was no better way to prove himself worthy of Valhalla than to win the hand of a shield maiden. With a Valkyrie at his side, his ascension to the Hall of the Slain was a certainty.

Looking for his next opponent among the participants of the tournament he'd attended the month before, he'd started the evening with surveillance of the gym. But this was so much better. Tonight's revelation was a game changer in more ways than one. He opened the overhead door and drove the van into the warehouse.

He shut off the engine and climbed out of the van, then closed the overhead door. Limping into the warehouse, he grabbed an ice pack. Fifteen minutes later, walking was a bit easier. He ventured to the door of the guest room, unlocked it, and opened it.

"Hello, Ward. I saw your daughter tonight."

The scholar's face jerked up. He lunged from the cot. The manacle around his ankle stopped him just a few feet in front of the doorway. His face reddened and his mouth twisted. "Leave my daughter alone."

He almost laughed. What could this anemic academic do to stop *him*? Nothing.

"I'm sorry. I can't do that. She is meant to be mine." He cracked his neck. "Why didn't you tell me she was a shield maiden?"

Ward tilted his head. "What are you talking about?"

"You can't deny it. I saw her. She was magnificent." Anger crawled up his spine. "You've been holding out on me."

He should have expected the scholar to try to outsmart him. Ward Hancock was an intelligent man. He'd used his brains in place of brawn.

"My daughter is a scholar, like me. That's all. You know that," Ward said, his voice rising with trepidation.

"Don't lie to me!" He took a step forward. At his side, his fist curled into a tight ball. Ward was more than twenty years his senior and lived a sedentary life. One good blow would teach him a lesson he wouldn't soon forget. He used an open hand—after all he didn't want to inflict any permanent damage on the old scholar. Ward saw it coming but he couldn't move fast enough to avoid the crack. The blow knocked him to his knees.

"I thought we'd come to an agreement. You'd help me, and I wouldn't kill you."

"I never said I'd help you." Ward spit blood onto the concrete.

"I suppose I just assumed you'd be interested in something you've spent your whole life studying." He scanned the room. Some scrapes on the pipe indicated where Ward had attempted to free himself. "But I will tell you now. Either you're with me or you're against me. There is no in-between. I don't believe in gray."

Ward's face paled.

"Now we're clear. You know your options. I'll give you a day to think about it. I have a new agenda, and I'd love to share it with you as it involves your lovely daughter. But you have to agree to cooperate."

The bleak look in Ward's eyes gave him hope that the scholar would cave. He really could use his advice.

"How many kills will satisfy the Valkyrie?" he asked.

Ward didn't answer.

"Do I need to vary the method of killing?"

Nothing.

"What other qualities will the Valkyrie look for in a warrior?" He swallowed his frustration as Ward remained silent.

Soon he would have a Valkyrie at his side, so Ward would become less essential.

He closed and locked the door, leaving Ward kneeling on the slab.

There was one more element to his plan that needed completion. He turned to the pile of supplies he'd left by the back door. Most he'd picked up at the local hardware superstore: electrical tape, wire, various chemicals. He'd purchased the fireworks kit and the instructions online.

If the police came barging into his warehouse, they were going to get quite the surprise.

Even though he needed another session with the ice pack, his step was lighter as he left the warehouse. His new plan rejuvenated him.

Not only had he discovered the shield maiden, he'd found his next challenger: Conor Sullivan.

He had to act quickly. His luck couldn't hold for long. The police were stepping up their efforts. They'd find him, and it was essential he kill Conor before the warehouse was discovered. After that, his fate would be sealed. He could die knowing Louisa would lead him to Valhalla, and that she would be his forever.

CHAPTER
25

In the car, Louisa clasped her hands together to stop them from trembling, but Conor noticed.

He noticed everything.

No matter how hard she tried, she couldn't hide her emotions from him.

Reaching across the console, he took her hand and held it all the way home. "Do you think it was Xander or Shawn?"

Louisa had been asking herself that same question. "I don't know."

Both were taller than her.

Their police escort stayed with them all the way back to the Rittenhouse. Conor parked in front of the condo entrance and got out. Rounding the front of the car, he tossed the keys to the doorman. "Can you have this valet parked?"

The doorman caught the key ring. "Yes, sir."

He opened the door for Louisa. She climbed out, her shoulders and neck stiff. She hadn't expected her body to hurt this much so soon. In a way, the pain was almost a relief, as if it served as a physical outlet for her emotions.

"Being in a fight is a lot like being in a car accident," Conor said. "You feel all right for the first hour or so, then it's a steady roll downhill. By the next day, you're sore and bruised in places you didn't expect." He took her arm and led her inside. "You can lean on me."

"Conor, I'm all right. It's just a few bruises." And maybe a pulled muscle or two. She led the way into the elevator. The doors closed and the floor rose under her feet. *Two minutes.* Then she could fall apart.

"Well, I'm not." He turned her to face him. "I can't stand the thought of anything happening to you. It would kill me. Do you understand that?"

"I do." A tear rolled down her cheek. She also couldn't help thinking about all the trauma he'd endured for her. The injuries to her body were nothing compared to the pain in her heart. "I'm sorry. The effort was futile anyway. The police can't even find my father. What can I really do?"

Her eyes burned as more tears threatened.

One more minute.

The door opened and he steered her to their apartment with a hand on the small of her back. Conor unlocked and opened the door, and Louisa suppressed the flood of emotions ready to burst from her. Kirra rushed to greet them. Louisa was a half-second from dropping to her knees and burying her head in the dog's fur when she saw the people in her kitchen. For a few minutes, she'd forgotten they had company.

Tyler poured a glass of milk. Yvonne stirred a pot on the stove. A smile spread across her face. "Damian just called. They're dropping the charges against Jordan. We're hoping he'll be released tonight."

Louisa nearly lost it. How could she have forgotten they were here?

"That's great," Conor said, his enthusiasm no doubt dimmed by the events of the night. "Did he say why they're letting Jordan go?"

"The DA is unwilling to press charges since the two additional victims were discovered and Jordan was in custody when they were killed." Yvonne clasped her hands together as if she could barely contain her excitement. "Damian is going to bring him here. Is that all right? I know we can't all stay, but it's late, and we don't have anywhere else to go." Yvonne's smile evaporated as she stared at Louisa and Conor, as if just realizing something was wrong. "What happened?"

"Someone attacked Louisa at the gym." Conor took her hand and squeezed it as if he knew she was barely holding it together.

"I'm fine," Louisa said. Channeling Conor, she sucked it up, stretching taller as she lifted her chin. "Just a little shaken. Of course it's fine to bring Jordan here. The Sixes are still out there. This is the safest place for him right now. I'm out of guest beds, though. He'll have to sleep on the living room couch for tonight. Tomorrow, we'll make other arrangements."

She was sure her couch was a vast improvement over the cell he'd been in for days.

"I can't thank you enough," Yvonne said. "I found some chicken in the freezer and made stew. I hope that was all right. I wanted to do something to pay you back for all you've done. I know it isn't enough."

Louisa's smile took effort and hurt her face. "It smells wonderful, but I really need a shower first."

"I should walk the dog," Conor said.

"The doorman just took her out," Yvonne said. She and Tyler were under strict orders to stay inside. "You said I should call him if she went to the door."

"Yes. That's perfect." Louisa made a note to slip the doorman a hefty tip in the morning. "Now if you'll please excuse me." She escaped into the bedroom.

Conor followed her. Kirra's collar jingled as she raced in and jumped onto the bed. The minute the door closed, Louisa dropped onto the bed and hugged the dog. Conor headed for the bathroom and started the shower.

"I love you for taking Yvonne and Tyler in, but I really miss our privacy," he said in a low voice as he came out of the bathroom.

"So do I. Tomorrow I'm going to see about renting them their own suite, at least for a few days." Scratching Kirra's neck, Louisa stood. Her shoulder burned as she drew her T-shirt over her head. She must have pulled a muscle in her struggle to escape. "I don't have a long-term solution in mind."

"I'm not sure the city will ever be safe for them again. At least not as long as the Sixes are a force."

She dropped her T-shirt into the hamper, and lifted the elastic band of her sports bra. Wriggling, she wrestled it upward, the struggle to get it off nearly bringing tears to her eyes.

"Let me help. Raise your arms." Conor eased the bra off her rib cage and over her shoulders.

"Thanks." She let him undress her. The crying jag hovering just behind her eyes already embarrassed her, and it hadn't even happened yet. She couldn't hold it off for much longer.

"You know I'm always happy to help you with anything." His gaze skimmed the puckered scar on her rib cage before lifting to meet her gaze. His eyes were full of sympathy and anger, but all he said was, "Do you need help with your pants?"

"I think I can manage those." *Ow.* At the time of the attack, she'd been so flooded with adrenaline and focused on getting away that she hadn't realized the man had held her face so tightly. But a bruise on her cheek and a sore shoulder were the least of her worries. She wriggled out of the pants and went into the bathroom.

The bright lights highlighted red marks across her biceps and cheek. She glanced over her injuries with a detached view as she pinned up her hair. By tomorrow, bruises would mark the places her assailant had gripped her.

The fact that she'd been attacked, that someone had tried to kidnap her, couldn't compare to the fear she felt for her father. Tonight's assault might give her a lingering nightmare or two, but the reality of the here and now was that she was alive and well while her father was still missing.

What were the chances that he hadn't been killed?

Slim. None?

"Do you want company?" Conor was in the doorway. His gaze raked over her injuries, but he blinked the grimness from his eyes and moved behind her. His arms came around her body. The pressure inside her built until she could barely breathe. For a moment it felt as if he was the only thing holding her body in one piece.

Maybe he was.

"Yes." She stepped under the spray. He'd adjusted the water to the scalding temperature she loved. Hot water cascaded over sore muscles. She reached for the shower gel and squeezed some onto her loofah. She lathered her shoulders and arms, pressing hard, as if she could wash away the marks her assailant had left on her skin.

Conor stripped off his clothes and stepped into the glass enclosure. "Easy. You're going to scrub off your skin."

Taking the bottle of gel from her hands, Conor used his hands to spread the soap over her skin. With gentle pressure, he massaged her shoulders and the base of her neck. His hands slid down her arms all the way to her hands. When he washed the base of her fingers, she flinched.

She examined her hand. The third knuckle was swelling and turning dark. "I must have jammed my finger. I was trying to hit his face over my shoulder like you taught me."

"Good for you." Conor lifted it to his mouth and kissed it. The tender gesture broke her. Her resolve crumbled. A sob escaped her lips, and tears slipped from her eyes. Conor folded her against him, his embrace the tipping point for a torrent of emotions. She let loose the anger and despair she'd been containing since her father was taken.

She'd just gotten to know him. How could he be taken from her like this? It wasn't fair. Her hands balled into fists against Conor's bare shoulders. He held her as her emotions raged. She cried until her throat and eyes burned. When the water ran cool, he turned to block her from the spray with his body.

Cold water chilled her feet. She lifted her head. Her chest quivered as she drew in a shallow breath. "I'm sorry. I didn't mean to blubber all over you."

Conor's hands slid up to cradle her face. He kissed her on the mouth. "If you're going to cry on someone, I want it to be me."

She pooled some water in her hands and splashed it on her face. "I hate crying."

"I know." He reached behind his back and turned off the water.

"It solves nothing. Now my face hurts more."

"You needed to let loose some of that tension. You were wound pretty tight."

But now that her emotional reserves had bled out, she felt empty, drained, as if she'd finally exhausted the nerves that had been fueling her for days. The only feeling left inside her was sorrow. It was a decidedly less energetic emotion. Her arms fell to her sides, her muscles limp.

"It doesn't matter how much I practice boxing. I'll never be strong. I'll always be the weaker person. I can't save my father. I barely saved myself."

"That's enough of that," Conor snapped. "You fought that man off. A man who likely is the same one who beat two amateur fighters to death. That's nothing to shrug off. I wouldn't expect you to be able to defeat a full-grown man, but considering who attacked you, saving yourself tonight was a spectacular accomplishment. Would you rather have lost?"

Shocked at his uncharacteristic outburst, she shook her head.

"Frankly, I'm equally impressed and terrified about what happened tonight." Conor reached outside the shower and yanked a thick towel from its hook. He dried her first. Then wrapped her and quickly dried himself. Naked, he scooped her off her feet and carried her to the bedside. In the center of the bed, Kirra gave her a sad-eyed wag of consolation.

He set her down on her feet. "Can you stand here for a second?"

She nodded, too tired to be humiliated by her weakness.

He brought her thick robe and wrapped her in it. Tying it around her waist, he tugged the lapels together. The love in his turquoise eyes caused her tears to well all over again.

"Shh." He kissed her on the forehead. He pushed her down until she sat on the edge of the bed. "Scoot up." Then he fluffed the pillows behind her back. "I'm going to get you something to eat."

When she opened her mouth to protest, he put a fingertip on her lips. "You can't keep going without sleep or food, and you know it."

Without waiting for a response, he headed for the door. Kirra belly-crawled up the duvet and rested her head in Louisa's lap. The dog's sad eyes echoed Louisa's emotions.

"We have company," she reminded Conor as he reached for the doorknob still naked.

"That would have been quite a shock for Yvonne." He went to the closet and dressed in a pair of sweatpants and a T-shirt. "I'll be right back."

A few minutes later he returned with a bowl of steaming chicken stew. As much as Louisa had doubted her ability to eat, her stomach rumbled at the scent of food. She ate the whole bowl. Putting it aside, she sat back in the warm bed, her eyelids as heavy as bricks. The full belly and tearful purge left her feeling as if she'd been sedated. A defensive numbness had settled over her limbs.

"Is Jordan here yet?"

"He'll be here soon, but Yvonne can manage without us now that she has her boy back. She can handle anything."

"I'm glad Jordan is being released."

"Me too."

"I wish Shawn would come home too." Conor put their dishes high on the dresser, out of Kirra's reach, and tucked Louisa in. "We've been mostly awake for days. Try to close your eyes, even if it's just for a couple of hours. We'll both be more useful after some rest."

He got into bed beside her, nudging the dog to the foot of the bed. Shedding her robe, Louisa rolled and nestled close to him, resting her head against his shoulder and placing her hand above his heart. It beat against her palm like a metronome, reassuring and solid and steady. She took comfort in his simple presence: the scent of his skin, the support of his strong arms around her, the heat of his body against hers.

She spoke the words that frightened her the most. "What if they don't find him?"

He covered her hand with his. "Whatever happens, I'll be here."

But after tonight, Louisa wasn't sure she wanted to face whatever would happen next.

CHAPTER
26

Conor woke to a cold bed. The only warmth was the dog burrowed under the covers at his feet. He sat up, scanning the dark room for Louisa. He spied a glow from the floor on the other side of the bed. The light from her laptop showed her sitting on the floor in front of her computer.

"I'm sorry. Did I wake you?" she asked.

He rolled to her side of the mattress and swung his legs over the edge. "What are you doing?"

Wrapped in her thick robe, she sat cross-legged in front of her laptop. Papers were stacked in neat piles next to her. "I reviewed all the documents I copied at the Bankses' house."

"How long have you been up?" Conor glanced at the clock. Two thirty a.m. He'd slept for a couple of hours, after he'd gotten up to get help Jordan get settled. Obviously, Louisa had managed less.

"An hour or so." The shadows in her eyes said it was likely a nightmare that had woken her.

He stretched. "Why are you on the floor?"

"Jordan is asleep on the sofa. I didn't want to wake him. This is probably the first night of real sleep he's had since the police picked him up Tuesday night."

"I was hoping *you* would get some rest."

"I did. I feel better. I've been doing some online researching on Xander, Rowan Banks, and Asher Banks."

"Did you find anything?"

"A couple things." She closed the laptop. "We can talk about them in the car."

Her statement woke him up. "Where are we going?"

"I want to drive out to Xander's shop."

"It's the middle of the night. He won't be there."

"I know. That's why I want to go now." She uncurled her legs, stood, and moved toward the dresser with purpose. "He has several outbuildings on the property. If Xander is behind all this, he could be holding my father there or at his house. I thought we could check out the business property in the dark. If we don't find anything, then we could wait until he shows up at the shop and go to his house for a look around." She tugged a pair of jeans over her long legs.

"What makes you think it's him?"

"He lied to me."

"He might just have been covering up the sale of stolen artifacts."

"I know. But my choices of men connected with Viking artifacts are Shawn, Xander, Rowan, and his brother, Asher. We don't know where to find Shawn or Asher, and it's too late to knock on Vivian's door looking for Rowan. We know where Xander works and lives. Besides, it makes more sense to search a business at night."

"What about the gangs? The police haven't been able to find Orion Turner." A fact that troubled Conor. Even without evidence, he knew Turner was the one who ordered the firebombing of Yvonne's apartment. The building had been full of residents. Turner must be a cold-blooded bastard, considering how many people could have died in that fire.

Louisa shook her head. "There's no way a gang would go to all this trouble. What would be the point? What's his connection to Vikings?"

"I don't know that there is one. I wonder . . ." Conor paused, thinking. "If Xander sold the sword to Banks, how did he get it back to send it to your father?"

Louisa's lip pursed. "Maybe we've had it backward. Who said Xander sold Douglas Banks the sword? It could have been the other way around. Plus, Xander is definitely large and strong enough to pummel two amateur boxers. We saw him swinging that sword around. He looked capable."

"He's also big enough to haul a pair of bodies around with little difficulty. But why don't we present all this to Ianelli, then wait and let the police search his property?" Conor didn't like the thought of poking around a potential killer's property in the dark. Correction: he didn't like the thought of *Louisa* poking around in the dark. He'd be happy to do it alone.

But he knew better than to make the suggestion. Instead, he got out of bed and headed for the closet. Louisa's movements were fueled by determination.

"Ianelli and Jackson already talked to Xander. They don't have enough evidence to obtain a search warrant. Conor, I put the police onto Xander. If he has my father, what do you think he'll do if he thinks he's in danger of being discovered?"

He'd kill Ward and dump his body at the earliest opportunity.

"You have a point." Conor stepped into a pair of jeans and grabbed a dark blue shirt. "OK, but I'm sending Damian a text message when we get out there. That way if we disappear, someone will come looking for us."

Kirra burrowed deeper under the covers. She wasn't an early riser. They dressed and quietly sneaked out of the condo.

"We'll take the Porsche." On the way to the parking garage, Conor took his keys from his pocket. "Xander would recognize your BMW."

"All right," Louisa said. "But he won't be there at this hour."

"We hope."

Conor loved his Porsche. He'd bought the twenty-year-old 911 as a rust bucket and restored her to prime condition. But she didn't like winter and took forever to warm up. After the initial start-up, he waited a few minutes for the sound of the engine to smooth out. Then he nudged the gas pedal, and the car responded with a satisfying low rumble. Louisa rubbed her hands together as he drove out of the garage. Conor stopped for two cups of takeout coffee and a couple of egg sandwiches. Having a plan seemed to spur Louisa's appetite, and she bit into the sandwich.

"So, what did you find out about Rowan and Asher?" he asked.

"First of all, Asher isn't Douglas's son. He was three years old when Doug married Marla. She'd been widowed when Asher was an infant."

"Seriously?" Conor glanced over. "Where did you uncover that tidbit?"

"In an old interview with Douglas."

"Interesting that no one mentioned that little fact."

"It is," Louisa said. "Rowan Banks is thirty years old. He went to the University of Pennsylvania for his undergraduate studies and competed on the equestrian team there. Then he moved on to attend law school at Boston University. He passed the Pennsylvania bar, but I can't find any evidence he ever practiced law. He lives in a condo on the waterfront."

"So he has an expensive degree yet does nothing?"

"I found his bio on the website for a cancer research foundation. He's on the board. He was also the executor of his father's estate."

"Makes sense if he's a lawyer. I wonder who's in charge of the trust."

"Rowan said he and Asher were both involved with the trust management, but the terms of the trust can't be changed," Louisa said.

Conor steered the car onto the interstate. "Some charitable work and money management must leave him with plenty of free time."

"Yes, but it's not an abnormal life, considering the wealth he was born into." Louisa finished her sandwich and wiped her hands on a napkin. "I could have the same sort of life if that's what I wanted."

"But you don't."

"No." She sipped her coffee. "I would be bored."

Conor hadn't had leisure time since he was twenty. He couldn't imagine an entire life of it. "What about Asher?"

"I found his information on the website for the Boathouse Row Preservation Society, where he serves on the board. Asher is thirty-three. He went to UPenn as well and rowed on the crew team, but he never graduated."

"He dropped out?"

"That's how it appears. There are also some missing chunks of time in his bio."

"The maid told me he lives in Bala Cynwyd."

"Yes. The paid online search I utilized gave me his most recent address. When I looked on Google Earth, the house appears to have a bit of privacy. It's at the end of a street and the lot next door is empty."

Conor crumpled the fast-food wrapper and stuffed it in the paper bag. "We should definitely check out Asher's house next."

"I agree." She placed the paper bag on the floor behind her seat. "We know that Rowan is in good shape, and I also learned that Asher has competed in yacht races, so I'm assuming he's at least moderately strong."

Yachts and ponies and killers, oh my.

Conor focused on his coffee, willing the caffeine to work its magic. "Yachting is physically demanding?"

The closest Conor had come to a yacht was watching the Tall Ships sail past Penn's Landing. But Louisa, with her mother's substantial trust fund, had been born into the same world as the Banks brothers.

"At that level? You bet. Crewing a racing yacht is as tough as play-ing any competitive sport, but the field pitches under your feet and the weather can literally kill you. Hauling wet lines and cranking winches takes a great deal of upper-body strength."

Maybe Asher was tougher than his super preppy brother.

"Did you ever race a yacht?" Conor asked.

"No, but I dated a boy who did, and when I was very young, we had a boat. My mother loved to sail." Her voice turned wistful.

"So what does yachting have to do with Viking weaponry?"

"I don't know. Vikings were great sailors?" Louisa suggested. "Perhaps our aspiring Viking is embracing the whole lifestyle."

"It's possible."

They drove the remaining miles in silence.

"We're here." Conor slowed as they approached Xander's shop. Where to park? The hilltop location of Xander's little compound made sneaking up on it difficult. Plus, there weren't any other buildings close by to conceal the car. "He has plenty of room out here to hide a cargo van."

Or a kidnapping victim.

He continued past the driveway and turned at the mailbox of the vacant farm next door. He parked the car in the shadow of a tree. "We'll have to walk up the hill. But at least if we get caught, we have somewhere to run."

"OK. The shop is dark, as are all the outbuildings." Louisa tucked her bright blond hair into a dark blue knit hat. Her down coat and gloves matched. Conor pulled a pair of well-worn leather gloves from the back of the Porsche. He and Louisa had been inside the shop, but he saw no sense in leaving fresh fingerprints tonight. Removing a flashlight from the glove compartment, he stuffed it into his pocket. "Ready?"

She was already getting out of the car. They trudged up the hill, and Conor regretted their choice of attire. Dark clothes might blend in on dark city streets, but they stood out in stark relief against the snowy hillside. They crept past the store and into the rear yard. Circling the old barn, Conor did a chin-up on a sill to look through a high window. The shop was filled with machinery and drafting tables. But there was no sign of Ward. He dropped to the ground. Walking around the building, he checked each window to make sure he'd seen every interior corner of the workshop. But Xander had opened up the original floor plan to make a bright, airy work space. There didn't appear to be any hidden nooks, certainly none large enough to hide a kidnap victim.

Shaking his head, Conor said, "Let's try the garage."

They walked across the snow. The garage was a utilitarian building, square and painted white to match the barn. Overhead doors marked two bays.

"No windows," she whispered as they stared at a set of padlocked doors. "How do we get inside?"

Conor was not going home until he searched this entire property. He would not let Louisa down. If there was a chance that Ward was here, Conor was going to find him. He scanned the doorframe and spotted some dry rot. Then he stepped back and kicked the door. Wood cracked.

Next to him, Louisa jumped.

"There's no one around to hear." Conor fired another kick at the door, his boot landing right next to the rotted wood. The frame splintered. Grabbing a trim board, he pulled it away to reveal a two-inch gap between the frame and the door.

He shone the flashlight through the opening. Inside, a small motor-boat on a trailer sat in the middle of an empty garage. Shelving units lined the walls. No cargo van. No Ward.

"He's not here."

Headlights swept across the yard. Conor grabbed Louisa and yanked her into the shrubs that edged the foundation. They crouched in the shadows and waited. Conor poked his head above the foliage. A minivan pulled around the store and parked in front of the shop. The large figure that stepped out looked like Xander. He went into the barn-workshop and shut the door.

Conor slid back into the bushes. "Looks like Xander's at work early this morning. What time is it?"

Louisa checked her phone. "Four o'clock. He must have wanted to get an early start on his day."

"Let's get out of here." Conor could only hope Xander didn't look out the window.

They ran down the hill and returned to the car. He started the car and pulled out onto the road. Spotting ice, he eased off the gas and coasted. "Where to now?"

Louisa pulled out her phone. The display light trembled in her hands. "Xander's house." She rattled off an address. "It's only a few minutes from here."

The house turned out to be a small ranch-style home in a tidy development. Conor and Louisa walked around the house and looked in the windows.

Kneeling, Conor shone the flashlight in a basement window, but all he saw were stacks of boxes. "This is the type of neighborhood where people will call the police."

"Then we'd better be quick."

Conor stood. Rounding the house, he climbed on the air conditioner to look through the garage window. "There's nothing here. Just some sporting equipment."

They went back to the car, and Conor headed for home. He cranked the heater. Louisa's teeth chattered.

The back roads were slick, forcing him to keep the car at a slow speed. "If the police are watching Xander, they must think he's guilty."

"But my father isn't at Xander's home or his workshop," Louisa said, taking out her phone.

"What are you doing?"

"Getting directions to Asher's house in Bala Cynwyd."

"All right." Conor steered the car onto I-276. The drive from Holland took forty-five minutes without traffic. It was still dark as they cruised through the suburban streets. He slowed the car while Louisa read the house numbers. On the western edge of Philadelphia, Bala Cynwyd boasted good schools, large lots, and lots of families.

"There it is."

The last home on the street, the two-story Colonial wasn't anything special. The porch that spanned the front was utilitarian concrete. The front yard sported a For Sale sign.

"It's nice. Very family-oriented. But not the hip and happening locale I would expect a single guy with a trust fund to choose."

"Me either." Louisa, who actually did have a trust fund, had picked a secure, luxurious condo. "Rowan lives in that new building on the waterfront."

Conor shrugged. "To each his own. If Asher wants to live with regular people, more power to him."

"Maybe he picked it because of the privacy," Louisa said. The adjoining lot was empty.

Conor parked at the curb in front of the empty lot. "If we're going to peek in the windows, we'd better hurry. People will be up and out soon."

Louisa pointed to the For Sale sign. "If anyone asks, we'll just say we're interested in the house."

"Your lying skills have greatly improved."

"By necessity." From the sidewalk, she stared up at the house. "It doesn't look like anyone lives here."

Conor glanced up the street. "The neighbors put out their garbage cans." But not this house. Bare windows stared back at them like wide open eyes. He tried to shake off the creepy sensation sliding though his gut as they stepped past three rotting advertising circulars on the front walk. Conor checked the mailbox. "It's been a few days since he picked up his mail."

They crept up to the side window. Conor interlaced his fingers and gave her a boost.

Holding the window frame, she peered inside. "No furniture."

He lowered her to the ground, and they rounded the house. Louisa pointed to another window, and Conor boosted her up to take a look. "The kitchen is empty too."

Feeling bold, Conor walked up onto the porch. Covering his eyes, he peered through the window. Nothing. Not even a box or a lamp. They checked the remaining first floor windows and the backyard but found nothing but a skinny strip of icy grass. Yet Conor couldn't shake the feeling that they were being watched.

"I'd like to get a look in the basement, but the windows are boarded over." Louisa pointed toward the low rectangles at the base of the foundation.

A tiny sound came from the house.

Conor whispered, "Did you hear that?"

Louisa tilted her head and leaned an ear toward the house. She concentrated, listening. There. A scraping noise sounded behind the boards over the basement windows.

She stiffened. "There's someone in the basement."

The hairs on the back of Conor's neck went on full alert. "I'm going in," he said in a low voice. "Get back in the car. Lock the doors. If I don't come out in five minutes, call the police."

Louisa shook her head, returning his whisper, "I will not let you go in there alone and risk *your* neck for *my* father. You are no less valuable than I am. In reality, you're more important. You have a family that depends on you." Her chin lifted to a stubborn angle. "Besides, the girl who goes off alone in a horror movie always ends up dead. We're safer together. Always."

"Together then." He took her hand and squeezed it. "Let's see if we can get in the back door."

They walked around to the back of the house. A set of concrete steps led to a four-by-four stoop. The rear door had nine panes of glass in its upper half. Conor glanced around, but overgrown shrubbery shielded them from view. He covered the butt of the flashlight with a glove, intending to break one of the glass panes. Louisa reached around him and turned the knob. The door opened.

Tucking her behind him, he pushed the door all the way open to reveal a kitchen. Dead leaves and dirt gathered in the corners of the scuffed wooden floor, as if the door had been left open for some time. They crept inside. A board creaked underfoot, and they froze. Despite the cold, sweat broke out under Conor's leather jacket. The scratching sound grew louder.

The house was dark and felt empty. Holding his breath, Conor opened a paneled door in the back of the kitchen, but it was only an empty pantry. Leading with the beam of the flashlight, they walked through the kitchen into a dining room. Conor swept the flashlight around the room. A set of stairs led to the second floor. Through an open door tucked under the stairs, he could see wooden steps leading downward. Conor hesitated. Should he check upstairs before the basement? He stood and listened for a minute. More scratching answered his question. Basement first. Besides, the second floor was quiet. An old house like this one tended to creak and moan. He'd likely hear someone moving around upstairs.

Conor ducked his head into the front living room just to ensure that it was empty, then turned his attention to the doorway under the stairwell. Keeping Louisa behind him, he spotted a light switch on the wall and flipped it. Nothing. The flashlight revealed a narrow, crooked staircase leading into the darkness.

They went down slowly, Conor testing each old step before putting his full weight on the tread. The scratching grew louder as they descended the steps. At the bottom, Conor shone the light around the low-ceilinged basement. The light played across a furnace, a workbench, some discarded boxes, a few small pieces of furniture—and a closed door.

The door shook in its frame as something scratched against it on the other side.

Louisa rushed forward, but Conor caught her wrist, pulling her behind him and whispering, "Hold the flashlight."

She nodded, taking it and shining it in front of him. He tried the knob, but the door was locked. He went to the workbench and picked up a hammer. Using the clawed end of the tool, he returned to the door, pried the hinges loose, and pulled the door from its frame. A small body crawled out of the darkness. Louisa shone the light downward.

"Oh my God." She dropped to her knees.

A dog lay on its belly, its head lolled onto her boots. Electrical tape flapped from its swollen, bleeding muzzle.

"Someone tried to tape his mouth shut."

Conor took the flashlight and gave the second basement room a quick check, but it was empty. He turned his attention to the dog. "From the amount of feces in there, he's been in here a week at least. The puddle in the back corner probably kept him alive. If he hadn't gotten the tape loose, he wouldn't have made it."

"You poor baby," Louisa cradled the dog's head. She took off her parka and wrapped it around the shivering animal. The dog's thin tail slapped weakly on the cement.

Handing the flashlight back to Louisa, he stooped and picked up the dog. He could feel the animal's bones protruding through its flesh.

"Conor." Louisa was shining the flashlight in the opposite direction.

With the dog in his arms, Conor turned. In the center of the cracked slab was a large and fresh-looking dark red stain.

CHAPTER
27

"Is that blood?" Louisa's stomach twisted as she stared at the rusty stain. Fear for her father and her recent nightmare blended into one horrifying collage.

Conor shifted the dog in his arms. "It's possible, but it's just as possible that it's rust or paint or something else."

But his voice lacked conviction. They both knew the truth. The basement felt evil, as if her bones could sense that a terrible thing had happened in this space.

As if evil was a lingering presence.

"We have to call the police." Louisa breathed.

"We'll call Ianelli in case there's evidence that needs to be preserved. It wouldn't be good to have a random cop contaminating the scene."

"Like we just did?"

Conor snorted. "Exactly."

"What do we do?" She turned, the light passing over the poor dog's swollen face. "We have to take this dog to a vet, but with all that blood . . ." She swallowed. "Do you think it's reasonable to assume Asher is the killer?"

"Yes. He just moved to the head of my list." He glanced down at the stain. "That stain isn't going anywhere. We'll call Ianelli on the way."

Considering that they'd just broken into Asher's home, it was probably best if they made themselves scarce before the police arrived.

Had they found the place where her father had been killed?

"Are you all right?" he asked.

"Yes." She had to be.

Conor walked toward the stairs. She illuminated his path as they ascended. She opened the doors for him as he carried the dog to the car.

She was so numb; she didn't feel the rush of cold air, even without her jacket.

"I'll hold him." She slid into the passenger seat and opened her arms.

"He's not small," Conor warned.

"That's OK."

"Watch your face. He might be in pain." Conor eased the dog onto her lap.

Though emaciated, the dog was obviously a pit bull mix. He had the same heavy bones and broad forehead as Kirra. The dog curled his thin body into an impossibly small ball, resting his wedge-shaped head on Louisa's arm. Despite the horror some human had inflicted upon him, his tail wagged gently against her leg.

Not wanting to touch the wounded snout, Louisa stroked the dog's shoulder under her coat, and she wondered which one of them was comforting the other. "His mouth probably hurts too much to bite anything."

Conor climbed behind the wheel and started the car. The Porsche roared to life, and he weaved down the narrow streets back to the interstate.

"The vet won't be open yet. Should we take him to Penn?"

The University of Pennsylvania had an emergency veterinary clinic that operated twenty-four hours a day.

"I have Kirra's vet's cell number. I'll try her first." He put the phone on speaker and dialed.

The vet answered in a wide-awake voice.

"Sorry to disturb you this early." Conor gave her a rundown of the dog's condition.

"It's fine," the vet answered. "I've just arrived at the clinic. Bring him right over."

The fifteen-minute drive seemed longer. Conor parked illegally at the curb and carried the dog inside.

A vet tech in purple scrubs and cornrows ushered them into an examination room. "Where did you find him?"

"He seems to be a stray," Louisa said. "Can you help him?"

The vet rushed in, her face full of sympathy and anger. "You poor boy. Who did this to you?"

She examined the dog's muzzle. "He's going to need surgery on his mouth. It'll be expensive."

"Just do it," Conor said.

"Do you think he'll be all right?" Louisa stroked his flank. She almost didn't want to know. While it seemed silly to worry about a stray dog considering the danger to her father and the number of people who'd been killed, she couldn't help it.

"We'll do our best." The vet signaled the technician. "We'd better get started. Get an IV going." She nodded at Conor and Louisa. "We'll call you."

The tech carried the dog into the back room. Sadness welled in Louisa's throat as the door closed behind them. She retrieved her coat from the examination table and slipped into it. The smell of unwashed dog wafted to her nose.

Conor yanked a paper towel from a roll on the counter, wet it, and dabbed a stain on her shoulder.

Blood.

Though she knew the blood on her coat was from the dog's muzzle, all she could see in her mind was the giant stain on the concrete.

They went into the outer office, filled out some paperwork, and left a credit card number to cover the bill.

"Come on." Conor steered her outside. "They saved Kirra. They'll do everything they can for him."

Day had come while they were inside the vet's office, but the overcast sky blocked any warmth from its rays. Dawn felt cold and empty.

Neither of them spoke about what they'd seen at Asher Banks's house.

"What now?" Louisa asked as Conor opened the car door for her.

"Now we find a pay phone and call Ianelli." Conor shut the door, rounded the car, and slid behind the wheel.

"Do those still exist?"

"There are a few left. And I'd rather give him the option of saying the call was anonymous if that makes getting a warrant easier."

"And keeps the police from arresting us just to keep us out of their way."

"Definitely," Conor continued. "Even if he recognizes my voice, he'd have to work pretty hard to prove it's me. And his phone record will show the pay phone number." He cruised down Oregon Avenue. They passed the bar, now closed and dark. Pat wouldn't open Sullivan's for lunch until eleven o'clock. "The trick is to find one that works."

The first public phone he found had no receiver attached to the metal cord. The second had no dial tone. Conor pulled to the curb in front of the third. He got out of the car, crossed the sidewalk, and lifted the receiver. He mouthed "it works" to Louisa.

She climbed out of the sports car. Hunching against the cold, she shoved her hands into her pockets. At seven in the morning, the neighborhood was coming to life. People hurried past, hats pulled low against the icy wind.

"Who is this?" Louisa heard Ianelli's voice over the connection.

"It's an anonymous caller," Conor said.

"Oh, really?" Ianelli sounded doubtful.

Conor continued. "We found something at Asher Banks's house."

Silence.

"Are you still there?" he asked.

"I heard you," Ianelli grumbled. "What did you find?"

"A tortured stray dog and a very large stain that could be blood."

"Where?"

"In the basement."

"Should I ask what you were doing in Asher Banks's basement?"

"Remember, this is an anonymous caller," Conor said. "But ask me later. I'll come up with a reason."

The detective muttered something faint that sounded profane. Conor hung up and steered her toward the car. They slid into the Porsche and Conor drove toward Rittenhouse Square.

"He sounded very angry."

Conor navigated the sparse early-morning traffic. "Actually he took it better than I expected."

But what would the police find? Louisa shivered.

"Are you all right?" Conor asked.

"I'm trying very hard not to think about it." But her brain wouldn't let it go. Someone had suffered in that basement, likely died, considering the size of the stain. But if she let her imagination wander to the possibilities, she would remember what had happened to her last autumn. She would picture her father enduring the same horrors. Then she would break down, and that wouldn't help her father. "I need to find him, even if he's . . ."

Conor reached across the console and took her hand. "I know."

She drew a deep, shuddering breath. Her rib cage ached with more grief than fear. Was she beginning to accept that her father might not be found alive? She let her gaze drift out the passenger window and watched the city sidewalk turn a lighter shade of gray. Dawn seemed to spotlight the gap between the hope she'd been holding onto and harsh reality. Ward had gone missing very early Wednesday morning. Today was Friday. He'd been missing for more than two days. With each moment that ticked by, his chances of surviving slipped away.

"Where do you think Asher Banks is?" Louisa asked as Conor parked the car in the garage.

"I don't know." He scanned the concrete structure. "I should have let the valet park the car, but I didn't want to broadcast our coming and going this morning."

Though out of the wind, the inside of the garage felt colder than outside, as if the concrete absorbed the cold and radiated it back like an ice pack. But after the incident at Asher's house, her nerves were on alert. Even as the doorman and warm lobby greeted them, Louisa couldn't shake the feeling that they were being watched.

Conor clearly felt the same way. He kept her close, shielding her from the street with his body. But Louisa didn't breathe easily until the elevator doors closed and they were alone.

"What do we do while we wait to hear from Ianelli?" she asked.

"I don't suppose you can take a nap?"

"No." The last thing she wanted to do was close her eyes. "I'm going to call the hotel and see if I can rent a suite for Yvonne, Jordan, and Tyler. I don't mind helping them, but . . ."

"You don't need to make excuses," Conor said. "The condo is a tight fit for five people. You've done more for them than anyone could possibly expect."

"I don't want to be rude." But Louisa was terrified of the news the police would bring. If it turned out that her father . . . She couldn't even let the thought finish in her head, but she might need her privacy. "I'm glad that Shawn isn't the killer. I wish he'd come home."

"Me too."

They didn't have corroborating evidence that Asher was the killer, but the size of that stain—assuming it was blood—indicated that someone died in his basement. Louisa knew in the marrow of her bones that the stain was indeed blood. And if Asher was guilty, then Shawn was innocent.

To Louisa's surprise, Yvonne and the boys were awake when Conor opened the condo door. Yvonne was at the stove, smiling and flipping pancakes. Louisa would have expected them all to sleep in considering the exhausting few days they'd experienced.

Kirra greeted them. She pressed her nose against Louisa's coat and gave it a deep, audible sniff, no doubt smelling the wounded stray. Louisa took her coat to the laundry closet off the hall, stuffed it into the washer, and started the machine.

Jordan and Tyler sat on stools at the island. As Louisa and Conor walked into the kitchen, Jordan stared down at his plate. "Thank you for everything, Dr. Hancock."

"You're welcome." She perched on the stool next to the young man and looked him over. The sweatpants and T-shirt he was wearing looked like Conor's. "Do you need anything?"

"No. Mom said she's going to get some clothes today."

Conor shook his head. "I'll run out to the store. I think you should all stay out of sight for now. The Sixes are still out there."

Jordan's face clouded. "They're always going to be out there."

Louisa glanced at Tyler. The boy lifted a huge forkful of pancakes to his mouth and pushed his plate away. His eyes were brighter than they'd been all week. "I'm stuffed."

Yvonne took his plate. "Then go take a shower."

"Yes, ma'am." He slid off the stool.

"I swear a twelve-year-old boy cannot shower too often," Yvonne said as Tyler disappeared into the hall that led to the guest room and bath.

After the door closed behind him, Conor turned to Jordan. "We need to have a talk."

Jordan shifted on the stool.

"Why are the Sixes after you?"

He focused intently on cutting his pancakes, then set down his utensils. "They think I know where Shawn is."

"Do you? Is that why you wouldn't give the police your alibi for Sunday night?" Conor asked. "Because you spent it with Shawn?"

Jordan's mouth tightened, and he shook his head too quickly. "Of course not."

"If Jordan knew where Shawn was, he'd have told me." Yvonne searched Jordan's face. "Right?"

"Yeah." Jordan gave her a stiff nod. His lying skills were worse than Louisa's.

Louisa would bet that Jordan knew where his brother was hiding, and that he just didn't trust any of them enough to tell them.

Conor opened his mouth to push, but the way Jordan was perched on the edge of his stool told Louisa the boy was one question away from bolting. She put a hand on Conor's arm. He closed his mouth and crossed his arms over his chest.

"The police found a notebook full of notes on Vikings and runes in your room. What do you know about it?" she asked.

"That's Shawn's," Jordan said. "He was working on an extra-credit paper for his English class. Ward was helping him."

Louisa shifted forward. "Did you explain this to the police?"

Jordan shook his head. "No. I kept my mouth shut. They said the notebook tied Shawn to the murders, and I didn't want to give them any ammunition. My fingerprints were on the cover, but I knew they were lying when they said they found Shawn's on the inside. They can't prove that. He's never been arrested. They're just guessing."

The detectives had tried to bully Jordan into talking, and the ploy had backfired. Louisa was annoyed with the police but also relieved to have a plausible explanation for the notebook.

She turned to Yvonne. "I'm going to try and move you to another suite today."

"Thank you." Teary-eyed, Yvonne grabbed the sponge and began wiping the counters with vigor. "I would like to say we can take care of ourselves, but I can't. My boys' safety has to come before my pride.

For now, I'm dependent on your kindness, and I can't tell you how much I appreciate every single thing you're doing for my boys. They're everything to me."

"We know." Louisa put a hand on her shoulder.

"I will find a way to pay you back for everything." Yvonne sniffed and looked at Conor. "I'm ready to start working at the bar any time."

"As soon as I think it's safe," Conor said. "The job will be there."

Jordan turned away as his mother began to cry, and Louisa suspected his own eyes were full of tears as well. A quick wipe of his sleeve across his face confirmed it.

"Can you eat?" Yvonne asked through her tears, as if staying busy was keeping her sane.

"Maybe later." Louisa wasn't going to be able to swallow until she heard from Ianelli.

Kirra went to the door and whined.

"I'll walk her." Conor snapped the leash onto Kirra's collar.

"She just got up a little while ago. I fed her a scoop of the dog food in the pantry, and I'm pretty sure Jordan slipped her a pancake," Yvonne said. "I hope that was all right."

"It's fine." Conor took the dog out of the apartment.

Yvonne went to the guest suite to see if the shower was free. Jordan avoided eye contact with Louisa.

She filled a mug with coffee. "Conor isn't one to talk about himself, but did you know his parents both died in a car accident when he was twenty?"

Jordan lifted his gaze from his breakfast. "No."

"And that he left college to help his older brother Pat run the bar and raise their two younger siblings?"

"No." Jordan's gaze flickered to the closed door.

"Jayne and Danny were close to Tyler's age," she added. "I know sometimes it must feel like nothing is going right, but you have a mom and two brothers who love you."

"My father died, as if being in prison wasn't bad enough."

"I know. Right now I don't know if mine is alive or dead, and it hurts."

Jordan blinked. "I almost forgot Ward got snatched. I'm sorry." His gaze went back to his plate, his brow knitted as if he was thinking. "They'd be better off without me."

"Before you think about running off, consider what that would do to your mother. She isn't coping with Shawn's disappearance. It would destroy her to lose you too. Does she deserve that?"

"No." He got up and took his plate to the sink. "But I don't see a way out of this."

"We'll make a plan. The first step is to keep you alive."

"What about step two?"

"I haven't thought of it yet. Let's concentrate on step one."

"At least you're honest," Jordan said. "And thanks. I don't know what we would have done without your help."

"You can repay me by staying with your mom and out of sight. And if you hear from Shawn, try to convince him to contact your mom."

Louisa went into the bedroom, called the front desk, and rented a suite for Yvonne and the boys. She just hoped that Yvonne kept a close eye on Jordan. In Louisa's mind, the young man was a flight risk. He felt guilty for endangering his family. Plus, he was keeping a secret. He knew where his brother was hiding, but he'd never give him up while Shawn was wanted by the police.

How long would it take for Ianelli to call?

She eased her stiff muscles with a hot shower and dressed in fresh jeans, a warm sweater, and thick wool socks. Conor returned, showered, and dressed, his constant motion reflecting the nervous energy vibrating through Louisa's own veins.

By nine the hotel manager called to say that the suite was ready. Yvonne and Tyler each carried a shopping bag full of clothes, which was everything they owned. Conor bought Jordan enough clothes to get him through a few days. The hotel had supplied basic toiletries for the family, and the manager, after hearing that all of their possessions had burned with their apartment, had sent up a tray of food on the house.

An hour later, Louisa and Conor paced their empty condo and waited.

"Maybe we should have kept them here. At least they were a distraction." Louisa stopped in front of the wide window overlooking Rittenhouse Square. In the gloom, the winter-bare trees and snowy ground looked barren and lifeless, as empty of color as a pencil sketch.

Conor stopped behind her. His arms folded around her body, and he pulled her against him. "I'm sorry we haven't found him."

She rested her head back against his chest for a few seconds. Then lifted it. "I shouldn't be standing here wasting time feeling sorry for myself. I should be thinking of somewhere else to look for my father."

Conor's phone beeped. "It's Reed. He's home. He says he'll head over to the bar at lunchtime if we want to talk. Maybe he can give us some suggestions."

"I'll be glad to have his input." Louisa turned to face him, still thinking of where her father could be. "If Asher Banks was selling his house, maybe he was also buying property."

"It's worth looking into. Do you know any real estate agents?"

"We could try the agent who listed Asher's house." Moving away from him, Louisa retrieved her laptop from the bedroom. She opened the computer, turned it on, and waited for her browser to load. "Do you remember the agent's name on the sign?"

Conor shook his head. "No, you'll have to search by the address."

Louisa found the listing agent in a few minutes, but before she could make the phone call, the landline rang. They froze and exchanged glances. Conor picked up the phone. "All right. Thank you."

He set the receiver down. "The police are on the way up."

The doorbell rang a few minutes later, and Conor let Jackson and Ianelli into the condo. Neither detective looked happy, but they didn't look as if they had devastating news for her either. Louisa wanted to be angry that they hadn't found her father, but both detectives looked ragged. Their faces were haggard with lines, and their clothes bore more wrinkles than could be accumulated in a single day.

Jackson leaned against the counter and crossed his arms over his chest.

Ianelli sank onto a kitchen stool. "I want to be pissed at the pair of you, but frankly, I'm too damned tired, and your less than legal search did turn up a valuable piece of evidence."

"Can I make you some coffee?" Louisa offered.

Sliding out of his overcoat, Ianelli waved the offer away. "No thanks. We're already drowning in it."

Jackson rubbed both hands down his face. "Tell us how you ended up in Asher's basement."

"Hypothetically, if we had been at Asher Banks's house this morning, it might have gone down like this . . ." Conor told them about the stop at Asher's house and the sounds coming from the basement.

"What were you thinking?" Ianelli roared. "You couldn't call us?"

"We could have." Conor shrugged. "The need to get inside felt immediate and you might have had to wait for a warrant."

Ianelli's head dropped into his hands.

"Anyway," Conor continued. "What did you find? Is it blood?"

Ianelli lifted his head and gave Louisa a sympathetic glance. "It's human blood. We've expedited DNA testing."

The police had collected her father's toothbrush and hairbrush when he first disappeared for this very reason, but she hadn't been ready for them to need his DNA.

Louisa's knees went wobbly, and she eased onto a stool. "How long will it take?"

"I'm hoping we can get the results in a couple of days," Ianelli said.

More days of not knowing if her father was dead.

"We talked to the neighbors," Jackson said. "No one has seen Asher for a week."

"And no one missed him?" Louisa asked.

"He doesn't have a job where someone might miss him. According to the neighbors, he wasn't the friendliest guy, but no one had any complaints about him either. He kept to himself. The dog is a stray that's been hanging around the block for the last month. The homeowner across the street said he thought Asher was feeding it."

"Why would he feed the dog only to do that to it?" Louisa put a hand to the sick feeling in her stomach. Had he used food to entice the animal into his house and then tortured it?

Conor rubbed her shoulder. "Do you know if Asher had purchased any real estate lately?"

Ianelli shook his head. "We interviewed his real estate agent. He was very interested in several properties on River Road."

"Does anyone know why he lived in such an ordinary house?" Conor asked. "This guy has a lot of money, right?"

"According to the agent, Asher likes to work with his hands. He isn't much interested in the finer things."

"Unlike his brother," Conor said.

"Right," Ianelli said. "The real estate agent said Asher was looking at properties on the water, but he disappeared before he could make an offer."

"Have you found anything else?" Panic scratched at Louisa. Police procedure was too slow.

"Not yet." Ianelli got to his feet and slid his arms into his coat. "But we will."

Jackson straightened and pointed at Louisa. "You stop snooping around. You're going to get yourselves killed."

CHAPTER
28

Freezing rain hit the windshield as Conor parked the BMW in an illegal spot behind Sullivan's. There was no way he'd parade Louisa down Oregon Avenue.

"Looks like the storm is beginning." Louisa flipped up her hood and hurried to the back door.

Conor opened it for her. Walking through the kitchen, he gave the cook and dishwasher a wave. They continued down the short hall. The office door was open, and Jayne sat in their father's squeaky old chair. She looked up from her laptop as they stopped in the doorway.

"Feeling better?" Louisa asked.

"Yes. I'm perfectly fine," Jayne said. "Have you heard anything about your father?"

"No, but there's been a development." Conor took Louisa's hand.

"We need to talk to Reed," Conor said.

"He's waiting for you." Jayne gestured toward the barroom. "And I'm sorry, Louisa."

Sullivan's drew a moderate lunchtime crowd. At eleven forty-five, the bar had only been open for fifteen minutes. Business would pick up over the next half hour. Reed and Pat were behind the bar. A waitress worked the few occupied tables. A hefty regular, Tim, raised a glass of Coke in greeting. Conor waved back.

Pat rushed out from behind the bar. He folded Louisa into a bear hug. Though she was tall, Pat's size and bulk made her look tiny. He gave her a brotherly kiss on the head, just like he would do for Jayne if she were upset. "Honey, I'm so sorry."

"Thank you, Pat." Louisa straightened, but Pat held on.

"Have you heard anything?" he asked.

She tried to pull away, but Pat didn't let go. He was pushy that way with the people he cared about. He leaned back, frowned, and assessed her face. "You look done in. We'll fix you up with some soup."

"Thanks, but I'm OK." She shook her head.

"You need to eat anyway." Releasing her, Pat turned to Conor. "You don't look much better. You'll eat too." He signaled the waitress.

"Thanks, Pat." Conor leaned closer to Louisa's ear. "There's no point in arguing with him."

Pat went back to work.

"He doesn't need to go to any trouble." Louisa sighed.

Conor touched her arm. "Let him fuss. It's a compulsion. He needs to mother-hen someone."

"It must be genetic." Her mouth lifted in a sad smile.

A small spark of warmth flared in his heart. His family had taken Louisa in as one of their own, and he was grateful. No matter what, they would always look after her.

Reed shook Conor's hand and hugged Louisa. "I'm sorry you're going through this."

Conor noted that Reed's loose flannel shirt barely concealed his handgun. As a retired cop, he was entitled to carry a gun, but he didn't always. Obviously, the business with Ward had spooked him. Reed took Jayne's safety very, very seriously.

Conor steered Louisa to the family booth.

"Thanks for covering my shifts for me," he said to Reed.

"Anytime. It's a good excuse to stay close to Jayne anyway." Reed sat opposite them. "I spoke with Detective Ianelli again about five minutes ago," Reed said. "He updated me on the investigation. The second pair of bodies was partially frozen. They have to thaw before an autopsy is performed, but the forensic evidence is being processed. Hopefully, something will stand out. At the rate this killer is accelerating, he's bound to get sloppy."

Conor felt Louisa's shudder through their linked fingers.

"They've also formed a task force and requested a profiler from the FBI," Reed continued. "So I've heard about what they're doing. Tell me more about the bloodstain in Asher Banks's basement. What led you there?"

"Desperation." Conor filled him in on what had gone down at dark o'clock that morning. "Obviously the giant human bloodstain pushed Asher Banks to the top of the suspect list. The police told us they are looking for him, but no one has seen him for a week, and it looked to me like that dog had been locked up about that long."

Reed was quiet for a minute. "So this killer focused on your father because Ward is an expert on Vikings?"

"That's what we think," Louisa said. "To me, the note he sent to my father suggested he wanted Dad's approval or advice or something. But I'm just guessing."

"What about the notes he sent to you?" Reed asked.

She tugged her hand from Conor's grip and inspected a nail she must have torn when she was attacked at the gym. "I don't know what those mean."

"I do." Conor studied her profile. "He's obsessed with Louisa. It's the why I don't understand."

"If he's starstruck by Ward, that could be spilling over." Reed leaned his elbows on the table. "How long has your father been in Philadelphia?"

"Since November," she said.

"That's only three months." Reed tapped a finger on the scratched wood.

"Yes." Louisa tilted her head. "Does that mean something?"

"It's possible the killer met him recently and fixated on your dad, but the police are investigating that angle. Ward didn't use his e-mail very much. The police didn't find anything suspicious." Reed rubbed his chin.

Louisa nodded. "I went through it as well when I put the list of his e-mail contacts together for the detectives. I didn't find anything suspicious or creepy or stalker-like. Almost all his correspondence was either from the Swedish university where he used to teach or his publisher.

"The police have been in contact with the university. They found a few e-mails from students, but they all appear to still be in Sweden."

Reed's brow lowered. "Text messages?"

"The police have his phone records as well," Louisa answered.

"Did he have an e-mail address at the university?" Reed asked.

Conor sat up. "What are you thinking?"

"If this killer has been following him longer than three months, he might have corresponded with him before he came to the States," Reed said.

Louisa's hand clenched Conor's. "I don't know if Dad still has access to his university e-mail, but I can try."

Conor stood. "Let me borrow Jaynie's computer."

He hurried back to the office and retrieved it. On the way back, he opened a browser for Louisa, then set the computer in front of her as he slid into the booth.

Jayne followed him out of the office, pausing at the bar to show Pat a piece of paper. He put on his reading glasses and their red heads bowed over the page.

"Do you know his passwords?" Reed turned the computer so he could read the screen.

"I know all his current ones. They're probably the same." Louisa typed.

A scream from the street caught their attention. Through the plate glass window, Conor saw a woman with a toddler in her arms running away from three men in orange bandanas climbing out of a black Escalade. The bandana slipped from the face of the man who was standing outside the Escalade's passenger door. Ice flushed through Conor's veins.

Orion Turner.

The Sixes.

The three men lifted machine guns and pointed them at the bar.

"Get down." He pushed Louisa under the heavy table and shielded her with his body.

The room erupted in a burst of gunfire and shattering glass. Jumping to his feet, Reed crouched and ran toward Jayne. His body jerked and fell facedown on the wood floor.

Jayne reached for him, but Pat stepped between them, putting his body between the danger and his sister as he dragged her behind the bar.

Bullets zinged through the air, thudded into wood, and ricocheted off metal in a deafening barrage. Conor's back stung as debris rained down on him.

He hustled Louisa along the floorboards to get her behind a steel support post next to the table. Glass shards, bits of wood, and chunks of plaster carpeted the floor.

"You OK?" he shouted.

With her back to the post, she dug her cell phone from her pocket.

"Don't move," he yelled.

Lifting his head, he scanned the room. The next minute played out in front of him like a scene from *The Godfather*. *Rat tat tat-tat.* Bullets streamed into the back wall in a rough line. A woman screamed. She sat in the middle of the room, hands over her head, blood seeping through her pant leg.

Conor crawled across the floor and overturned a table in front of her, hoping the thick oak would provide some protection. He checked her leg; the injury didn't appear to be a bullet wound but a cut from flying glass. The bleeding was minimal. He pressed her to the floor and shouted, "Stay down."

Ten feet away, Reed belly-crawled toward the bar, leaving a trail of blood behind him. Keeping low, Conor headed for him. A spray of bullets sent a chunk of wood into his face. Flinching, he stopped and covered his head for a second. The shots moved to the right, and he resumed his path. Pat came out from behind the bar on his hands and knees. They reached Reed at the same time. They each grabbed an armpit and dragged him behind the protection of the bar as more shots reverberated through the room.

Conor searched for the source of the blood.

"Shoulder," Reed gasped. "Where's Jayne?"

"I'm here." Kneeling, she took his hand.

"Are you all right?" Reed asked.

"I'm fine." Jayne nodded, crying.

Pat pointed at a dark spot on Reed's shirt. Blood welled from both sides of his shoulder. The bullet must have gone right through him. Conor grabbed a stack of clean bar towels. Folding two, he covered the entry and exit wounds, then wrapped a third around Reed's shoulder the best he could and tied it.

The rows of liquor bottles above them exploded and more gunfire shattered the mirror behind the beer taps. Shards of glass and alcohol rained over them. Pat crouched over Jayne to shield her. Conor leaned over Reed's torso, covering the wound.

The gunfire ceased as suddenly as it had begun, and the quiet that followed was nearly as shocking. Conor's pulse thudded under the ringing in his ears. Outside, tires squealed. He peered over the top of the bar as the black Escalade peeled down the street.

"It's over." Conor snagged a random jacket from a peg and spread it over Reed. Besides slowing the bleeding and keeping him warm, there wasn't much else he could do. He stood and scanned the bar for Louisa.

The front windows were shattered. The freezing wind blew through the opening, smacking Conor in the face. Customers picked themselves up from the floor and came out from corners, their eyes glazed with shock. Glass crunched underfoot. The kitchen staff ran out. Sirens wailed.

He looked for Louisa. She was climbing to her feet exactly where he'd left her. Conor rushed to her, scanning her from head to toe. He didn't see any blood. "Are you OK?"

"Yes." She picked a small sliver of glass from her palm.

"Is anyone hurt?" Conor called to Tim, who was assessing the other customers.

"Just some minor cuts over here," Tim answered. "Watch the glass. It's everywhere."

The bar looked as if it had snowed glass.

"An ambulance is on the way. How is Reed?" Louisa crossed the room.

"The bullet went through his shoulder." Conor returned to Reed and checked the wound. The makeshift bandages were soaked through, but the bleeding seemed to be slowing. He added more towels and another wrap. "I hear sirens. Hold tight."

"I'll be fine. It didn't hit anything essential. Make sure Jayne's OK." But Reed's face was the gray-white of skim milk as blood loss and shock took their toll.

"I'm fine," Jayne said, wiping a tear from her face.

Conor checked her over anyway in case she'd been hurt and adrenaline was blocking the pain, but she looked fine except for a few tiny nicks from flying debris. "She looks good."

Reed nodded. "Thanks."

"No worries about Jayne, OK? We'll take care of her."

"I know you will."

"Oh, for heaven's sake. Reed is the one who was shot," Jayne cried.

But Conor understood his brother-in-law's request completely. Reed gave Conor a *just in case anything happens to me* look.

"Jayne, take my gun and lock it up." Reed began to tremble.

"Somebody get Reed another coat," Conor yelled as an arctic wind blew through the wide-open storefront.

"Conor," Louisa said over his shoulder.

"What?" He applied more pressure to Reed's shoulder.

"Conor!" she grabbed his arm and spun him around.

In the opening between the bar and main room, Pat swayed. His eyes rolled into the back of his head, and he keeled over. Glass on the floor rattled as he landed.

No!

CHAPTER
29

How. Dare. They.

He watched the taillights of the black Escalade fade, and he wanted to give chase, but the commotion inside the bar also commanded his attention.

What should he do now?

He wavered, his gaze drawn to the shattered windows of Sullivan's, to Louisa's shining golden hair. She was all right. But what had they been thinking? The Valkyrie couldn't be killed. She was not of this earth.

He slipped the truck into gear and set off down Oregon Avenue after the flashy SUV.

The sheer act of trying to destroy her was a sacrilege and must be punished. The SUV was several blocks ahead, but a huge, shiny Escalade wasn't difficult to follow. He hung back, driving the large vehicle just close enough to keep the SUV's turns in sight. They weaved their way through the back streets. If they noticed him behind them, they didn't show it.

His borrowed truck was dinged, dented, and otherwise non-descript. They were likely hopped up on their egos, drugs, and the natural adrenaline high thugs seemed to obtain from acts of random violence.

Except this time, there wasn't anything random about the crime. Sullivan's had been targeted.

But why? What did this gang have to do with Louisa? Did they know what she was?

No matter. They'd tried to destroy the Valkyrie. Their motivation for doing so was irrelevant. She might not even have been the main target, but they wouldn't escape the consequences of their decision.

They skipped the interstates, crossing the Schuylkill River in Gray's Ferry and slipping into West Philadelphia on the back streets. Even in daylight, the surroundings darkened. Blocks of row homes sported empty lots where random houses had been torn down, like missing teeth in a rotting smile. Of the houses still standing, more were boarded up and empty than occupied. Bars covered windows and doors, and the fronts of the red brick town houses had faded to white.

He let the Escalade get farther ahead, allowing cars to slip between them. Somewhere near the zoo, rain began to hit his windshield.

Two blocks ahead, the Escalade slowed and turned between two homes. The vehicle disappeared from sight. He cruised past. The driveway was actually a narrow vacant lot. The skinny homes on either side were boarded up. Graffiti, a mix of profanity, and multiple artistic variations of *666* decorated the bricks. The Escalade must be parked around back. It made sense for the gang to conceal the vehicle from street view. They committed their sins in broad daylight for effect then sped away before police arrived, but they knew to lay low after such a public display.

He drove around the block. Two hundred feet from the 666 house, he cruised to the curb and put the truck into park.

Now he would watch and wait. What he had in mind couldn't be accomplished in daylight. He had no idea how many men were inside the house. Only a fool would attack a complete unknown. This was the sort of neighborhood where gunshots prompted the mind-your-own-business slamming of windows and doors rather than a 911 call, but he wasn't taking any chances of being caught either. Once this detour was completed, he would return to his agenda.

But this was a calling, a clear sign put in front of him by the gods. Odin must have put this challenge before him as a trial, and he was determined to pass. The men who had attacked the shield maiden would suffer the appropriate consequences.

CHAPTER
30

Conor's heart skipped as he watched Pat fall.

"Pat!" Jayne cried.

Conor grabbed Jayne's hand and put it over the towel on Reed's shoulder. "Hold this."

A small puddle of blood spread across the uneven plank flooring. Louisa was on her knees next to Pat. She ran her hands along his sides and back. She lifted a hand and turned it. Blood coated her palm. "It's his back." She tried to roll him, but he was too heavy for her to budge.

Dropping beside his brother, Conor rolled him over and lifted the hem of his shirt. The bullet had struck Pat low on the right side, just beneath his rib cage. Dread swirled in Conor's chest as he watched the steady flow. Had it struck his kidney? "I need towels."

Louisa was ahead of him. She pressed two folded towels over the wound. Conor stacked his hands and leaned on them, but the blood kept coming, welling up and seeping between his fingers.

Louisa added another towel. "The police are here."

Uniforms rushed into the room, guns drawn. After a quick assessment and search of the premises, they holstered their guns and spoke on their radios. The paramedics came in after them. Outside, lights whirled, people shouted, and the wind blew.

"Over here." Louisa waved them toward Pat.

"Let us take care of him." A paramedic shouldered Conor aside.

He moved out of the way. Pat couldn't die. Not Pat. Never Pat. He was the glue that had held their family together for the past eighteen years. Generous, kindhearted Pat.

More sirens sounded close by, but Conor barely heard them. Red lights strobed on the bullet-riddled walls and gleamed from the carpet of shattered glass. People moved around him, but he didn't see them. All his focus was on his brother, bleeding to death on the floor.

Hands were on his biceps. Louisa. She wrapped her arms around him, but he stood numbly as a second set of medics assessed Reed and the first pair shouted for the ambulance attendants, the urgency in their voices sparking fresh terror in Conor.

He and Pat were a team. They'd saved the family business and raised two siblings together. They'd paid the bills and held family services at bay. They'd kept Danny out of jail and sheltered Jayne after she'd been brutally attacked. Neither one of them could have succeeded alone. Of all the things he'd prepared for, losing his brother was never on the list.

It took four men to hoist Pat onto the gurney.

"Conor." A hand shook his shoulder.

Terry Moran stood in front of him, in uniform. Terry must be on duty. Conor's eyes went back to Pat, lingered on the IV lines running from both arms, the bags of fluids tossed on the blankets, the medics' hyper-intense focus. They rushed him out the doors and into the waiting ambulance. The doors closed and the vehicle pulled away with a high-pitched wail.

A second ambulance pulled up, but Reed was conscious and talking, and his injury, while serious, hadn't evoked the same on-the-brink response. The ambulance attendants wheeled him out and loaded him.

"I'm following the ambulance." Jayne wiped a bloody hand on her slacks. "Someone has to call Leena."

Pat's wife would be devastated. Not the call Conor wanted to make, but he said, "I'll do it."

"Let me drive you," Tim said to Jayne.

She shook her head. "I'll need the truck. Might as well take it there now."

"I'm walking you to the lot." Tim escorted her out of the bar.

The paramedics who'd worked on Reed checked the rest of the customers for serious injuries. They bandaged the woman with the cut leg. A coworker who'd been lunching with her volunteered to take her to the ER. Unbelievably, everyone else had escaped the bullets and most of the flying debris.

"Conor." Terry shook him. "They're taking Pat to Jefferson."

Philadelphia experienced enough violence to necessitate six Level I trauma centers, but Thomas Jefferson University Hospital was the closest.

"I need to get to the hospital." Conor moved away. "And I have to call Leena."

He dialed her cell, smearing blood on his phone screen, but the call went to voice mail and he pressed end without leaving a message. She was a teacher. No doubt her phone was locked away. He'd have to call the principal and have her pulled from class. Did he have the number for the school?

"You're bleeding," Terry said.

"Let me see." Louisa shoved up his shirt. "It's a piece of glass and a bunch of small cuts. Let the paramedic put a bandage—"

"We need to go." Conor felt nothing, as if each pulse pumped lidocaine through his veins. Even his heart was numb. He took Louisa's hand and moved toward the door.

"You need to be treated," she said.

"Then we're going to the right place." He tugged on her hand, but she resisted.

"You can't sit in the car with a big piece of glass in your back." Her voice dropped to a gentle tone. "It'll take them a while to assess him. Let them put a bandage on that wound. Please?"

She was right. Rushing was pointless. Pat was still en route, and when he got to the hospital, he'd need to be evaluated and stabilized.

If he made it that far.

Adrenaline, which had been his lifeline for that last half hour, deserted him like a rat, leaving him shaking. But seeing Pat so close to death had rocked his very foundation.

God, his wife and kids . . .

Conor's gut wrenched for them all. "I have to call Leena and then pick her up. And I'll have to get someone to watch the kids when they get home from school."

"All right. Just give them two minutes to patch you up." Louisa led him to a barstool and guided him onto it.

"I'll go get her," Terry said. "I'll be able to get her to the hospital faster."

"She'll be at the school. I'll try to call the principal." Conor perched on the edge of the stool.

"Conor, I'll take care of Leena." Terry raised his hand. "I've got this."

"Thanks, Terry." The cop would be able to get Leena information from the hospital as well.

"It was the Sixes, Terry. I saw Orion Turner in the black Escalade," Conor called as Terry headed for the door.

"Damn." Terry nodded. "Do your surveillance cameras reach the street?"

"Only the area right in front of the door and the alley out back." Conor had once been jumped in the alley, and they'd added the camera on the exterior of the building.

"There are enough cameras around here." Terry scanned the street. "We'll get footage. I'll meet you at the hospital."

Louisa's grip on Conor's arm tightened, as if she could sense that he wanted to bolt out the back door.

The paramedic cut the back of his T-shirt. "They should remove this glass in the ER."

Conor had no time to sit in the ER waiting room. He reached over his shoulder and yanked it out.

The paramedic scrambled for a package of gauze. "That probably wasn't the best idea."

The gush of blood down Conor's back agreed, but he didn't care. "Just slap a Band-Aid on it."

"I'll do what I can." The paramedic irrigated the wound with something that stung, then taped down a pile of gauze. "He could use a few stitches," he said to Louisa.

Louisa nodded and touched Conor's arm. "I'll get you a clean shirt." She disappeared into the back and returned a minute later with a new T-shirt emblazoned with the Sullivan's logo.

Conor found the number of Leena's school and made the call to the principal as he and Louisa headed for the back of the bar. She grabbed their coats as they went through the kitchen. Conor looked down. His hands were red and still wet, covered in Pat's blood. Reed's too. Louisa was also wearing a fair share of it.

The Sixes had targeted his family.

Snap out of it!

He hadn't felt this terrified since Louisa had been shot. Why did people keep shooting at them? What was wrong with this world?

He wiped his hands on his jeans and dug his keys from his front pocket.

Louisa took them from him. "Does it hurt?"

"I can't feel a thing." The wound lodged deep in his heart was far worse. But underneath its chill, Conor could feel anger stirring to life.

They got into the car. Conor sat back and instantly regretted it. Pain slashed through his back. He angled his torso to avoid leaning on the bandage. "I'm getting blood all over your car."

Louisa looked down. "That makes two of us." She pulled into traffic. "If the Sixes did this, it's about Jordan."

"I assume they're unhappy with us for helping the family."

"This is my fault. The gang must have figured out we were shelter-ing them."

Anger surged in Conor's throat. "Pat would be the first one to tell you that statement is ridiculous. Who do you think suggested we hire Yvonne?"

"Pat?"

"Yes. Pat." Who lived to take care of others. Conor's hand curled into a tight fist. "Damn it. This isn't fair. Things like this shouldn't hap-pen to Pat. He's never done a bad thing in his life."

Conor looked down at his blood-streaked hands and clothes. He was no doctor, but considering the location of the wound and the size of the puddle on the floor, Conor couldn't pretend. Pat had lost a lot of blood. Enough that he might already be—

He swallowed. His brother was the best man he knew.

Was he still alive?

CHAPTER
31

Jefferson Hospital offered valet parking at the emergency department. At the covered entrance, Louisa handed the attendant the car keys, and she and Conor went inside. Few of the plastic chairs were full. A nurse with a clipboard called a name, and a woman with a towel pressed over her bloody hand got up and walked to the counter.

Conor plowed through the room and leaned over the reception desk. "They just brought my brother in with a gunshot wound."

The woman in scrubs behind the desk looked up. "By ambulance?"

"Yes." Conor gave her Pat's information.

She checked her computer screen. "Hold on. Let me find out what's happening." She got up and disappeared through a set of double doors.

Conor paced the small bit of space in front of the desk. Louisa's heart wept for him. She opened her clenched hands and stared at the dried blood on her palms. Who had bled in Asher Banks's basement? Her father? Had he lost as much blood as Pat? Poor Pat. Conor was right. Seeing Pat gunned down was like witnessing a sacrilege. He felt like the brother she'd never had. Always sweet. Always welcoming. Always trying to take care of his ever-expanding family.

She closed her eyes for one breath then opened them. Grief and worry for her father and Pat filled her to the brim until there wasn't any room for more. Emotions overloaded her until she went numb in self-defense.

They didn't know where her father was, but right now Conor needed her. She touched his forearm, stopping him midstride. He covered her hand with his, unbelievably offering *her* comfort. But wasn't that what she was doing as well? Maybe there was no give or take of support. They could suffer and help each other at the same time.

They were stronger together than apart.

But she'd brought terrible danger to his family, after all they'd done for her, and she'd have to live with the guilt.

The nurse returned in a few minutes. "He needs immediate surgery. They're stabilizing him now. You can go to the surgical waiting room and someone will update you as soon as possible."

"Then he's still alive." Conor breathed out the statement.

"Yes," the nurse said.

Conor asked for Reed's status.

"He's stable but also headed into surgery." Swiping her badge through a security slot, she ushered them through a set of doors. She pointed down the hall. "Follow the signs."

"Thank you." Conor turned away.

"Excuse me," she called out. "You're dripping."

Louisa glanced down. Red droplets dotted the floor. She tugged Conor's jacket off. The bandage had loosened, and blood soaked the back of his shirt.

The nurse gestured back through the doors. "Let's get that taken care of. You won't have any news about your brother for a while, and we're still slow. In a couple of hours, this place will be packed."

Forty-five minutes and six stitches later, Louisa and Conor followed the hallway signs to the surgical waiting room.

Leena and Jayne sat together, hands joined. On the other side of the room, Terry paced and talked on a cell phone, a Styrofoam cup in one hand.

"Is there any news?" Conor asked.

"Yes." Jayne stood and kissed him on the cheek. "Reed's surgeon was just in. He's in the recovery room. The wound was clean through. He should be fine. I'll be able to see him soon." She touched a bruise on Conor's cheek. "Are you all right?"

Louisa had texted Jayne from the ER while Conor's wound was being stitched.

"I'm fine." He turned to Pat's wife and wrapped her in his arms. "No word on Pat yet?"

Leena leaned into him. Louisa stepped back and stayed out of the way. For the thousandth time, Louisa envied the Sullivans their tight bond. She'd only been with Conor for a few months, and already she felt closer to the Sullivans than anyone in her own family. But watching the intensity of their shared grief reminded her that she was an outsider.

Stronger together than apart was a concept the Sullivan family had practiced for decades.

Leena lifted her head. "This is about that woman you're helping, isn't it?"

"Yes." Conor rubbed her back. "I'm sorry, Leena."

Leena pushed away and poked him in the chest, her tear-filled eyes fiery with anger. "I will not let you take the blame for this."

"I'm not." He shook his head, but guilt showed on his face. As much as he'd told Louisa the shooting wasn't her fault, he clearly felt responsible.

Which made two of them.

"Yes, you are." Leena wiped her eyes with her fingertips. "You always take the blame for the trouble and give Pat the credit for the work. Pat told me all about the situation. He was proud of you for keeping that boy and his family safe from the gang, and he wanted to do his share to help."

Conor's jaw tightened, and his gaze blinked away from his sister-in-law. "I know."

"Your brain gets it, but clearly, you don't believe it here." Leena tapped the center of his chest. She wasn't finished. "What were you supposed to do? Just let the gang have them? Maybe we should just give them the whole city, because that's what will happen if everyone is too afraid to get involved. Is that what you want?"

"No." He didn't sound convinced.

"Because that's exactly what the gangs want: a city full of people paralyzed with fear."

"But it was foolish of me not to have expected retaliation." Conor's mouth went flat, and Louisa learned there was no limit to the number of injuries a heart could suffer. Hers cracked for him all over again.

"Conor, Pat is going to be fine." Leena raised her chin. Her next breath hitched. "He has to be." She pressed a hand to her mouth, and Conor wrapped his arms around her and pulled her close as she cried.

Louisa eased back, not wanting to intrude on the family. She felt an arm around her shoulder.

"How are *you*?" Jayne asked, giving her a one-armed hug.

"I'm all right. Thanks to Conor, I barely got a scratch."

"He is pretty great." Jayne smiled. "But that's not what I meant. How are you holding up? You haven't heard anything about your father?"

"No." Louisa pictured the bloodstain in Asher Banks's basement but didn't mention it. Jayne had enough on her mind. "He's still missing."

"I'm sorry." Jayne rubbed Louisa's arm.

"It's been a horrible week, hasn't it?" Louisa's gaze drifted back to Conor and Leena.

"We'll get through it together." Jayne squeezed her shoulders. "We're here for you too."

Louisa felt the hot rush of tears on her cheeks. "Thank you."

"Conor loves you, so you're part of the family." Jayne released her and plucked a tissue from the box on a nearby table. Looking back at Louisa, she handed it over and snatched a second one for herself.

Louisa mopped her face.

"Hey, Conor." Terry drained his cup and dropped it into a trash can. "I already talked to Jayne. I need statements from you and Louisa."

Conor guided Leena to a chair. Jayne sat next to her.

Terry herded Conor into the hall. Then Louisa had her turn to give a statement.

"The traffic cam caught the entire shooting," Terry said. "The Escalade's plates were covered, but I'm told we have a good shot of Orion Turner's face right before he opened fire." He tucked his notebook into his pocket. "I'm going back to work, but don't leave here without calling me. I consider your whole family still in danger until Turner is off the street. I promise you. We'll get that bastard. Everybody at the precinct is pulling for Pat."

A fresh bubble of grief welled into Louisa's throat. The entire neighborhood was an extension of the Sullivan family.

"Thanks, Terry." Conor went back to Leena, taking the empty chair on her other side. Louisa sat down next to him. And the next few hours were torture. Jayne went in to see Reed in recovery, then returned while he was being transferred to a room.

Conor paced. "I have to call Danny."

"Don't you want to wait until we know more?" Jayne suggested. "He can't get here in this storm anyway."

"No. He needs to know." Conor took his phone into the hall. Ten minutes later he came back, his eyes damp. "He'll come as soon as possible."

A green-scrubbed surgeon appeared in the doorway, and Leena jumped to her feet. The doctor walked closer and perched on the low coffee table in front of her. "He's not out of the woods yet, but he made it through the surgery."

Louisa grabbed onto hope. Next to her, Conor exhaled as if he'd been holding his breath for hours.

"His heart stopped once, but we were able to get it started again. The bullet hit his kidney. Unfortunately, we couldn't save it. He can live just fine with one, though, provided we can get him through the initial trauma." The surgeon tugged his cap from his head and held it with both hands. "They're taking him into recovery. If you'd like, I'll have someone take you in to see him in a few minutes."

"Yes." Leena nodded.

Leaning forward, the doctor dropped his clasped hands between his knees. "I want you to be prepared. He's on a ventilator and various tubes and wires. There will be a lot of activity around him. You won't be able to stay more than a few minutes, but I think it's important that you go in."

The fact that the surgeon really wanted Leena to see Pat right now meant that his life was still precarious.

"Yes." Leena slumped, and she hit the back of the chair hard. "Thank you."

"If all goes well, after recovery, he'll go into intensive care. And you can spend some time with him there." With a serious and empathetic nod, the doctor left.

Movement in the doorway caught their attention. Jackson and Ianelli walked in, their faces grim.

"We're sorry about your brother," Jackson said. "He seems like a good guy."

"He's the best." Conor crossed his arms. "How's the search for Orion Turner going? We know where he was this afternoon."

"We're trying to track him on traffic cams. We have the whole shooting on film from several cameras." Jackson's head shook in frustration.

But Orion Turner had been evading the police for days. He clearly knew how to hide.

"But how long will that take?" Louisa asked.

"Any word on your brother's condition?" Ianelli changed the subject.

"He's out of surgery but still critical," Conor answered.

"We've scoured Turner's neighborhood, but he must have multiple hideouts. Unfortunately, everyone in the neighborhood is too terrified to talk to us. We're shaking down all the usual suspects. Someone will turn on him."

Louisa doubted that.

"So what happens now?" Conor asked.

"You stay here with your brother while we take care of business," Jackson said.

"My father is still out there." Louisa hated the panicky pitch of her voice, but it seemed like simultaneously hunting a killer and running down a gang leader divided police efforts. The ice storm would stretch resources even further.

Jackson opened his mouth to reply, but Ianelli put a hand on his partner's arm. "The FBI profiler is working on the case now. You should stay here. Turner is still out there. He's ballsy enough to shoot up the bar in broad daylight. I wouldn't put much past him."

"The storm started this afternoon. Side streets are slick. Wouldn't be surprised if power starts to go out. You're definitely safer here this evening," Jackson added.

Being in rooms with no windows, she hadn't even noticed that evening had come.

"You haven't had any other news?" Jackson asked. "No more messages? You haven't searched any more houses?"

"No." Louisa shook her head. "We've been here all afternoon. Have you found Asher Banks?"

"No, but we have a neighbor who says Asher has a girlfriend. We're trying to locate her, and we're trying to run down all the real estate and business investments owned by the Banks Trust." Ianelli returned his notebook to his coat pocket. "Rowan gave us a list, and we have plenty of manpower in this investigation. He must be nearby. We'll find him."

But how many people would die first?

"Please stay here." Ianelli buttoned his coat. "And let us know if you get another message."

The detectives left.

Ten minutes later, a nurse summoned Leena. Conor went with her, and Louisa waited with Jayne. When they returned a very short time later, both of their faces had gone paler.

Conor took Louisa's hand and clasped it as if he needed her to hold him together. Pat must have looked really, really bad.

"How is he?" she asked in a whisper.

Conor took a deep breath. "He's alive, but barely."

Not knowing what to say, she held tightly to his hand and tried to summon some hope.

CHAPTER
32

Ianelli drove out of the hospital parking lot. "I'll meet you back at the station in an hour. Then we can go to the morgue. Dr. Gonzalez said she should have the autopsies done by then."

In the passenger seat, Jackson grimaced. "Why don't you stop at the morgue on your way back?"

"Chicken."

"Yep," Jackson said. "I hope to hell she finds something."

The call about the shooting at Sullivan's had come in as Ianelli and Jackson were leaving a task force meeting where the captain had ordered them to take a break before the storm completely crippled the city.

Jackson rolled a shoulder. The joint cracked. "We must really look like shit for the captain to order us to go home."

"It's probably more the way we smell. I don't remember when I put on this shirt." Ianelli gave his armpit a sniff and scowled, but down deep he was grateful. His brain and body were running on empty. Frankly, he wasn't going to be very useful until he'd eaten a decent meal and showered. He'd grabbed a combat nap in the station, but he needed a break, even if it was only an hour.

And just for kicks and giggles, the storm had blown in early. Patches of black ice shone on the pavement. This was their last chance for a respite. Once the city shut down, it would be all hands on deck for the duration.

"I don't know what I'm going to do first, shower or eat. You want to come by and eat with me?" Ianelli offered.

"Nah. I don't want to impose."

"Oh, please. We're Italian. My wife does not know how to cook for less than a dozen people."

"I'll take a rain check on that offer." Jackson stretched his back. "I'm too tired to fully appreciate good food."

Ianelli patted his gut. "Not me."

Jackson's phone beeped. "Shit."

"Ignore it."

Jackson glanced down at his phone screen. "Captain wants to see me in his office."

"Oh." Ianelli paused. "You in trouble?"

He knew better than to ask why Jackson might have been called down. His partner wouldn't tell him, a fact that made Ianelli uneasy, even in his current state of exhaustion.

"If I am, it's not my first rodeo," Jackson responded. "You go ahead. See your wife, eat your lasagna, and for all that's holy, get a shower and put on some clean clothes. I'll be fine."

Jackson had been called out on the captain's carpet before, and each time, Ianelli wondered if he'd be breaking in a new partner.

Ianelli drove to the precinct and pulled around to the back of the building where his personal vehicle was parked. He left the unmarked car running for his partner.

"Thanks." Jackson got out of the car and went around to the driver's seat. Ianelli started his Chevy Malibu. He turned the defroster on high to melt the ice on his windshield. His phone pinged with a call before he'd even gotten out of the lot.

Don't look at it.

Shit.

Stupid work ethic.

He pulled it from his pocket and read the screen. Not the captain, thank God, just the CI he'd been blowing off. Not that he wanted to hear from that scumbag either.

"Yeah," he answered the call.

"Now." His CI didn't believe in texts. With a phone call, there was a record the call was made, but no proof of what was discussed.

"It's not a good time." *It would never be a good time.*

Sweat broke out under Ianelli's arms.

"The usual spot." The CI hung up.

Swearing, Ianelli headed for the expressway instead of toward his house. As much as he wanted to go home, he wanted this asshole off his back more, even if the meeting sent a wave of *ick* into the pit of his belly. The detour would only cost him ten or so minutes, then he could be on his way home to the lasagna his wife was keeping warm.

And after dealing with this CI, his need for a shower would multiply tenfold.

God, he was an idiot. How had he gotten himself into this mess?

The defroster couldn't keep ice from accumulating on his wipers. This ice storm wasn't going to help in the searches for Ward or The Icicle Killer.

Exiting onto Girard Avenue, he looped around toward East Park Reservoir. His tires slid on black ice as he drove into Fairmont Park. Discomfort prickled along his spine as he realized he wasn't that far from where the second two bodies had been dumped.

He wound his way around to the parking lot for the driving range. He backed into a space and waited. His CI would already be here, watching, and the knowledge lifted the hairs on the back of Ianelli's neck. A minute later, headlights swept into the lot and a Ford Explorer parked next to him. Even after the CI appeared, discomfort still crawled around Ianelli's gut like a cockroach in a cabinet. This couldn't be over with soon enough.

Ianelli unhooked his seat belt. Despite the cold, he didn't want to be trapped in his vehicle. He got out of the car. The CI did the same. They didn't bother with a greeting but made the agreed-upon exchange as quickly as possible. The CI opened the envelope Ianelli had passed to him, peeked inside, and nodded.

Ianelli tucked his envelope into his jacket pocket to open later. He was too exposed to linger, and he was *not* taking his eyes off the scumbag. His instincts tingled with a *get moving* vibe. Was someone else watching him? The itch on the back of his neck said yes. His CI was supposed to come alone, but he wasn't known for his integrity.

"Nice doing business with you." The CI smiled. He shoved his envelope into his coat pocket, and pulled out a gun.

Ianelli broke and ran for his car. He jumped behind the wheel as a gunshot went off and a bullet pinged into the ice near his feet. He kept moving. Closing the door, shifting into drive, and gassing the engine too hard. His tires spun on the slippery pavement.

His heart hammered against his ribs as he drove out of the lot, the CI shooting at his car from behind. Luckily, a pistol was a hell of a lot less accurate in real life than on TV, and the guy's shots missed.

Ianelli's tires hit pavement and he gulped air. He needed to get his cholesterol checked. He was one crappy case away from a heart attack. He pressed a hand to the tightness in his chest. Maybe this was the case that would push him over the edge.

The main road wasn't as icy, and he increased his speed with a nervous glance in the rearview mirror. A vehicle rushed up behind him, and the set of high beams in his rearview mirror blinded him for an instant. He adjusted the mirror, the rush of fresh sweat soaking his shirt. The height of the lights told him the pursuing vehicle was taller than his sedan—the Explorer, no doubt.

He was in trouble. Big trouble.

How could he have been so stupid? Why had he agreed to meet the CI tonight? One bad decision was going to cost him everything.

He pressed on the accelerator, putting a few yards between his sedan and his pursuer. He reached for his phone, praying there was a patrol car in the area.

The vehicle slammed into his bumper. The Malibu fishtailed, and the phone went flying. He tried to correct his direction by turning into the skid, but his car simply slid on the icy road. His vehicle careened off the road and onto the snowy grass. The nose of the car slammed into a fat tree, the airbag exploded into his face, and the world filled with dust and darkness.

He lifted his head and coughed. The windshield was spider-cracked. A tree branch had broken through the passenger window. Ianelli followed its path, right into his gut.

He'd been impaled.

CHAPTER
33

Louisa stirred, her hand rising to rub a painful crick in her neck. She'd fallen asleep sitting straight up with her head on the wall. Blurry-eyed, she glanced around, orienting herself. The hospital waiting room shifted into focus, and the day came back in a rush.

Pat!

She sat up, looking for Conor.

Was Pat still alive?

Conor wasn't in the room. She got up and went out to the hall. His cell phone was pressed to his ear. He lowered the phone and walked toward her.

"What's happening?" She pushed her hair out of her eyes.

"Pat was moved to the surgical intensive care unit. Leena is with him right now. It's still touch and go, but he's still with us." Conor rubbed her arms.

"You should have woken me."

"Why? You needed the sleep, and there wasn't anything you could do." Conor pocketed his phone. "The vet left a message earlier. I must have missed the call. The dog is better. It looks like he's going to make it."

"Some good news is better than nothing." Louisa tried to smile, but with Pat clinging to life and her father still missing, she couldn't do it. "Where's Jayne?"

"She's with Leena. Only two people can go in at a time. Visiting hours on Reed's floor were over hours ago."

"Then Reed is all right?"

"I went up to see him earlier. He's well medicated and feeling no pain."

"Thank goodness." At least someone was all right. Louisa couldn't believe she'd fallen asleep. "What time is it?"

"One a.m.," Conor said, steering her back into the waiting room. "The ice storm is going strong. Power is out in some parts of the city."

The weather report played silently on the TV mounted near the ceiling. Conor turned up the volume, and they watched a parka-clad weatherman standing on the street near city hall. Freezing rain slanted across the screen like static from bad reception.

But in the windowless waiting room, they were isolated from the time of day, the weather, the danger.

Louisa's phone buzzed. She drew it from her purse. The vibrations continued. It was a call, not a text. Her stomach balled into ice as she read her father's cell phone number. Answering, she pressed the phone to her ear.

"I left a gift for you in Mifflin Square. I hope you are pleased," a man whispered.

"Who are—?" But the call ended before Louisa could say the words.

"What's wrong?" Conor leaned over her phone.

Staring at the blank phone screen, she repeated the man's message.

"Mifflin Square? That's only a few blocks from the bar."

"Do you think he means . . . ?" Louisa didn't even want to verbalize her fear, as if saying it aloud would make it real.

"You father?" Conor completed her thought.

"I have to know. It's freezing out. If he's out there . . ." Louisa jumped to her feet. "We have to call the police, and I have to get to Mifflin Square."

"You call Ianelli," Conor said. "I'll get Terry on the phone."

No one answered. Panic scratched at Louisa's hope as she left messages for Ianelli and Jackson.

Conor ended his call. "Terry will get the closest patrol car over there right now."

Louisa lifted her jacket from a nearby chair. "I'm going."

"Hold on." Conor grabbed his coat. "The roads are covered in ice. Wait here while I get Jaynie's valet ticket. We'll borrow her vehicle. Reed always keeps chains in his truck."

Louisa paced the hall, visions of her father facedown on the ice playing through her head. Conor returned in a few minutes, but it had felt like hours.

"OK. Let's go." Conor led her down the hallway. They made their way to the exit and waited for the valet to bring Reed and Jayne's giant SUV around from the garage. Louisa zipped up her coat as freezing rain fell from the sky and pattered on the icy pavement. The truck finally arrived. They drove out of the hospital's driveway and found an empty stretch along the curb. Getting out of the vehicle, Louisa nearly went down on her butt. She caught her balance on the truck door. A thin layer of ice covered every surface.

"Maybe you should wait in the truck."

"I'm all right now." Keeping one hand on the truck for balance, she shuffled around to the back of the vehicle.

Conor opened the cargo area and dug out the chains. "See what else you can find while I put these on the tires."

The SUV was well stocked with sleeping bags, food, water, and extra winter gear. There was even a container of dog supplies. Louisa rummaged past a folding shovel. "God bless a man from Maine. Reed has two pairs of traction cleats in here." Louisa handed Conor a set and stretched the rubber-and-steel-coil cleats over the soles of her boots. She tugged on a wool hat and thick gloves, then picked up a set of chains. "I'll do this side."

Conor fastened the Velcro cleat strap over the top of his boot. "Are you sure?"

"I'm from Maine. I know how to put chains on tires. It'll be faster if we work together." Louisa skated around the truck and went to work. They put the chains into position, then Conor rolled the truck forward a few feet so they could fasten and tighten the cables. Back in the vehicle, Louisa held her hands to the heat vent. Even with gloves, her fingers ached with cold. "Have you heard from Terry?"

Conor checked his phone. "Nothing yet. Just hold tight."

The chains ground on the icy pavement as the truck crawled along 10th Street. Even in the middle of the night, it was unusual to see the city streets empty. Conor turned onto Washington Avenue. By the time they reached 6th Street, the blocks had gone dark. The absence of neon signs made the city look desolate.

"Power's out here." Conor slowed the truck by easing off the accelerator. "Can you check the glove box?"

"For what?" She pulled on the latch, but it was locked.

"You'll need Jayne's key." He took a keychain from his pocket and handed it to her. "This is the valet key." He pointed to the single, gray-handled key in the ignition.

Louisa opened the compartment. "Reed's handgun is inside."

Which explained why Jayne gave the parking attendant the valet key, which wouldn't unlock the glove compartment. She wouldn't want the valet to be able to access Reed's gun.

"That's the only place Jayne had to secure it," Conor said.

Louisa took out the weapon. She didn't love guns, but tonight she was glad to see this one. "What do you want to do with it?"

A police car turned the corner just as they approached the park. Blue lights swirled and gleamed on the ice- and snow-covered block of green space. Darkness and dread cast eerie shadows over the basketball court, playground, and picnic tables. A second cruiser approached from 5th Street.

"Looks like the cops are here," Conor said. "You should probably lock it up again."

She returned the weapon to the glove box and locked it, then put the keys in her pocket. Conor eased the truck to the curb next to a sand volleyball court. A third police car parked behind him. Louisa had her hand on the door handle before the tires stopped moving. With the power out, the square was oddly dark.

Her father could be out there.

Cold and dying.

Or already dead.

Her heart stumbled as she opened the truck door and the wind caught it, nearly ripping it from her grip. She held tight as she put her feet down. The cleats bit into the ice.

"Wait for me." Conor took a flashlight from the console and got out of the SUV.

The three policemen shuffled along the sidewalk, shining their flashlights ahead of them. The light fell on a lump on the ground. At the sight of the bloody ice around the body, Louisa rushed ahead.

Daddy?

She broke into a jog. Even with the cleats on her boots, she slid twice. Conor kept pace beside her. She skidded to a stop at the horror in front of her.

A man lay facedown, his back hacked open into a bloody mess. There was no question of whether the victim was alive or dead. No one could survive what had been done.

Louisa's vision spun, but she forced herself closer. She had to know. Her heart slammed into the back of her breastbone. She averted her eyes from the gaping wounds.

"Stop!" one of the officers called. He skated on the ice toward them.

But Louisa couldn't stop her feet. She reached the body first. Conor grabbed her shoulder and pulled her back. "Let the cop do his job."

He tried to turn her face away. "Don't look."

But she couldn't tear her eyes away. Not that it mattered. She would carry the bloody image to her grave.

The officers approached.

"Holy shit. Are those his lungs?" one asked.

Another ducked away, and Louisa could hear him retching in the bushes. Terror kept Louisa's stomach in line.

The first officer squatted a few feet from the body and spoke into the radio on his shoulder.

"Daddy?" Louisa whispered.

The cop leaned over to view the dead man's face without getting closer. "I doubt this guy is old enough to be your father."

Relief rolled through her with a wave of nausea.

Not Daddy. Not Daddy. Not Daddy.

She nearly dropped to the ground.

"Stay here." Conor released her and walked around the body, giving it a wide berth. He crouched and studied the victim, then straightened. "It's Orion Turner."

CHAPTER
34

"Why would the killer take *him*?" Louisa stared at the body of Orion Turner, her mind racing with questions. "And where is my father?"

"Jackson called. He's on his way. Let's get you inside the car where it's warm." Conor steered her toward the truck. He loaded her into the passenger seat, then climbed behind the wheel, started the engine, and turned on the heater.

"Who would do such a thing to another human being?" Still picturing the bloody sight, she shivered. Her teeth chattered as she stared at her silent cell phone. "Should I try to call *him*—?"

"No." Conor cut her off. "Wait for Jackson to get here."

Jackson arrived ten minutes later, alone. The chained tires of his unmarked car grated on the icy street. He walked out into the square to view the body and spoke with the uniformed cops before approaching Conor and Louisa in the big SUV. Conor lowered the window.

The cop shoved his hands into his coat pockets. "I hear The Icicle Killer has been in contact."

"Yes," Conor said, his tone tight and angry.

"Another message?" Jackson stamped his feet and hunched his shoulders against the rain and wind.

Conor shook his head. "No. An actual phone call."

"From Ward's number?" Jackson asked.

"Yes." Louisa leaned across the console and told the detective exactly what the killer had said, her voice sounding oddly calm.

Jackson's gaze flickered to the body in the square and back. A white van with a city emblem on the door panel pulled to the curb.

"I have to talk to the ME," Jackson said. "Then I'll have some questions for you."

"We'll wait at the bar." Conor pointed down the street. Sullivan's was just a few blocks away. "I have to check on things, and I want to get Louisa out of the open."

In case the killer was watching.

A woman got out of the city van, and Jackson conferred with her as she donned coveralls over her winter clothes. Conor turned the SUV around and drove to the bar. He parked in the alley and escorted Louisa through the back door. Inside, they both took the cleats off their boots.

"It's not that cold in here, considering." Louisa kept her hands in her pockets. The chill in her bones came from inside, not from her surroundings.

"We have a generator and someone boarded up the windows." Conor went to the coffeemaker and started a fresh pot. "I'm sure it's colder in the main room. Hopefully we can keep the temperature warm enough that the pipes don't freeze."

They wandered to the hallway and viewed the damage. Broken glass, bits of wood and wallboard, and wrappers from medical supplies littered the floor. Bullet holes dotted the walls and furniture.

"Looks like Sullivan's is getting a remodel." Unzipping his coat, Conor hooked his thumbs in his front pockets.

"I'm sorry, Conor." Louisa pressed her shoulder against his.

"None of this matters. Things can be replaced." Conor pulled out his phone. "I should check in with Jayne."

He sent Jayne a quick text. She responded immediately, and he read the message out loud. "No change. He's still hanging on."

"That's a good sign." *Right?*

He nodded, his silence uncharacteristic and filling her with unease. She had no words of comfort to offer him so she slid her hand from her pocket and grasped his. His fingers tightened around hers. They stood without speaking for a few minutes while the smell of coffee filled the kitchen. Then the coffee machine beeped, as if to tell them their time-out was over.

Conor led her back into the kitchen. He filled mugs and handed one to Louisa.

She wrapped her hands around the mug. "I suppose we can't clean up."

"No. We shouldn't touch anything out there until the insurance company has inspected the damage." Conor sipped his coffee.

As the coffee warmed them, they stripped off their outer garments and hung them to dry near the heat vents. A half hour passed before someone knocked on the back door. Conor checked the surveillance camera before opening the door to Detective Jackson.

Jackson accepted a mug of coffee from Louisa. He looked haggard, as if he'd aged ten years since Monday.

"Where's Ianelli?" Conor asked.

"I'm going to be honest with you, because you're in this as deep as I am." He took a breath. "We're not sure."

For a full minute, the only sounds were ice pattering on the windows and the hum of the commercial refrigerator.

"He ran home to shower, eat, and grab fresh clothes before the roads iced over." Jackson drank his coffee. "But he never made it."

"Can't you track police vehicles?" Conor topped off the detective's mug.

"He was in his personal car," Jackson said. "We haven't been able to locate it or his cell phone."

"Maybe he went off the road," Louisa suggested. "The roads are icy."

"We're looking. We have a water main break, widespread power outages, downed trees and power lines, people freezing from no heat, and fires from portable heaters. All public transportation is halted. The city is a mess." Jackson gripped the handle tight enough to turn his knuckles white. For all his gruffness, it was clear that he was worried about his partner.

"He's tough. He'll turn up." But Conor's voice lacked conviction.

"As you know, we've been monitoring Ward's phone number. The call you received bounced off the tower on South Columbus Boulevard." Jackson sipped more coffee.

Conor froze. "That's way too close to here."

"And close to where the first set of bodies was found." Jackson's head nodded once. "But that tower covers dozens of blocks and too many thousands of people to count. It would be impossible to find him unless we can ping his phone, and it seems he's smart enough to take the battery out of the phone after he uses it because we still can't track it."

"Damn." Conor punched his thigh.

Jackson set his empty mug on the stainless steel counter. "Now tell me what happened tonight."

Louisa relayed the details of receiving the call from the killer and finding the body.

The detective crossed his arms and stroked his chin. "I don't get why he mutilated this body and not the other four victims."

But Louisa's blood chilled as she realized that she understood completely. "Because this was an execution, and the others were burials."

"What?" Jackson turned, twin crevices appearing between his brows.

"The blood eagle," Louisa said in a voice that felt disconnected from her body. "It was a form of Viking execution. The victim was restrained facedown. His ribs were hacked out of his back in the shape of an eagle's wings. The lungs were pulled out and draped over the ribs to flutter like wings in flight. The victim died of blood loss at some point during the ceremony but not before suffering unimaginable agony."

A muscle in Jackson's cheek quivered. "That was done to him while he was alive?"

"According to legend, yes. But we don't know how much of the stories are true," she said.

"But why would he execute Turner?" Jackson asked.

"The Vikings didn't leave much in the way of written record." Louisa tried to remember the individual stories from her childhood. "The most famous account was from the late ninth or early tenth century. King Aella of Northumbria had killed the infamous Viking Ragnarr Lodbroch by tossing him into a pit of vipers. Ragnarr was legendary for his own brutality, and his son Ivarr inherited his father's savage nature. He avenged Ragnarr's death by executing Aella in a blood eagle ritual. All the accounts of the blood eagle that I can think of involve great betrayal or revenge."

"So what act did our killer feel he needed to avenge?" Conor asked.

Jackson's phone chimed. He picked it up, scrolled through a message, then turned back to Louisa. "I just got a message from our forensics team. What do you know about copper?"

She cleared her throat. "In what context?"

Jackson shrugged. "I'm not sure. Just talk."

"Humans have been smelting copper since about 4,500 B.C. Copper turns green when exposed to air and water. This oxidation process is why the copper-plated Statue of Liberty is green. It is a semiconductor. Beyond its obvious use as a metal that can be hammered and shaped, the Egyptians, Aztecs, and Romans all used copper for its medicinal properties. It is naturally antimicrobial, killing bacteria, viruses, and yeasts—"

Jackson held up a hand. "Specifically copper oxide. It was found on both of the male victims."

Louisa nodded. "Copper or cuprous oxide occurs naturally in the mineral cuprite. But for modern industrial use, it's generally manufactured using high heat and other copper salts and compounds. It's a semi-conductor and is used in photoelectric cells. It's also a natural fungicide and is used to prevent fungal diseases in plants and—" She stopped suddenly, connections clicking in her brain. "And in antifouling paints for boats."

"Asher is a sailor." Jackson stood. "Thank you, Dr. Hancock. We'll take it from here. Where will you be if we need to reach you?"

She glanced at Conor. "Back at the hospital?"

He nodded and checked his cell. "I should check on Pat."

"Be careful out there." Jackson headed for the back door. "The roads are nasty and getting worse. You might have chains, but the other guy might not."

Louisa knew he was thinking about Ianelli. If the detective had crashed his car and no one found him, it wouldn't take long for the cold to claim his life.

The detective left. Louisa helped Conor ensure the boarded windows were secure and all the faucets were open enough to drip to prevent the pipes from freezing in case the heater failed.

"Ready?" Conor asked.

"Yes." But Louisa's mind was reeling from the discussion with Jackson. Would the connection between copper oxide and boating help find her father?

Conor picked up their cleats. Louisa donned her hat, coat, and gloves. Everything was damp, but she put them on anyway. Her phone went off on the prep table, and they froze.

Louisa read the display. "It's him."

Her hand hovered over the phone for a split second, as if it were an insect she didn't want to touch. With a steadying breath, Louisa punched the Answer key.

Conor leaned toward her, and she tilted the phone so he could hear.

"Hello, Louisa." The sound of wind on the other end of the connection disguised the voice, but the caller was clearly male. "Did you get my gift?"

"Why did you kill him?" Louisa asked.

"I did it for you," was the clipped response. "I thought you'd be pleased."

Louisa trembled. "I didn't ask you to."

"He could have killed you in that drive-by." The response was matter-of-fact. "Every decision has consequences."

He'd killed Turner as retribution for shooting at Louisa.

"But torture . . ." She shuddered.

"It was an execution." The whisper was light and cold, like fog in a freezer. "And he deserved it."

"Where is my father?" Louisa asked.

"That's my second reason for calling," he said. "Ward, read that note to your daughter."

He's alive!

She'd almost given up hope. They had to find him.

The second voice sounded distant. "Stay away, Louisa. Don't do anything—"

A fleshy thud cut off her father's words. She flinched.

"As you can tell, your father isn't being very cooperative," the man said. "Put Conor Sullivan on the phone."

Conor took the phone. "What?"

"Louisa should be at my side, not yours. But I recognize why you won't give her up willingly. If I were in your shoes, I wouldn't either. Therefore, I will win her from you."

"She's not a prize," Conor said.

"She belongs with the superior male."

"Maybe she already found him," Conor challenged.

"Go to your vehicle. Take Oregon Avenue to Broad Street. I will call you again in ten minutes. If you don't follow my instructions, I will kill Ward. The only thing keeping him alive right now is my desire to please Louisa."

The line went dead. Conor lowered the phone and set it on the table again.

"What do we do now?" Louisa asked.

"We drive north on Broad Street." Conor shrugged into his jacket and called Jackson. A second later, he lowered the phone. "He must be on the line." Conor sent him a text message.

Louisa's phone buzzed again, and she jumped. "It's a text. From him."

She touched the phone with her forefinger and opened the message without picking up the device. "Oh my God." She stepped away from the table.

Conor leaned in.

`I almost forgot. I have someone else who will die if you fail.`

Below the caption was a picture of Ianelli. He lay on a cot. Blood soaked the blanket covering him. His eyes were closed, his face white as death.

CHAPTER
35

Violence had destroyed his family, and Conor was sick of it. The killer had put an end to Orion Turner, but now *he* had to be stopped. He headed for the back door.

"Conor. You can't do this." Louisa followed him.

"If I don't, your father and Ianelli are going to die." Ward was still alive. Conor was going to do everything in his power to make sure he stayed that way.

Louisa did an end-run around him and blocked his path before he could rush through the exit. "I won't sacrifice you for them."

Conor moved close and held her face in his hands for a second. "I love you, but I can't just let two men die."

He already knew she would do anything to save her father. The thought of her facing a killer held Conor by the balls. This violent nutjob wanted her, but Conor wasn't giving her up.

He gently took her by the arms and moved her aside.

"You are not going without me." Louisa held Conor's forearm. When he turned, she leaned in and kissed him. "We do this together."

He nodded.

"We'd better get moving." Conor paused, then turned and jogged to his office. He came out a few seconds later with a folding knife in his hand. He tugged up his pant leg and shoved it into his boot. "Just in case."

Louisa grabbed the traction cleats on their way out, but they didn't put them on. The car was just a few feet from the door. Gingerly skating across the ice, she opened the car door and tossed the cleats onto the floor on the passenger side of the SUV.

Conor slid behind the wheel, and they drove out of the alley. Louisa set her cell phone on the console. Conor took Oregon Avenue to Broad Street. The icy streets were empty, and the trip was silent except for the crunch of chains on ice.

Louisa's phone vibrated. She watched the message appear on the screen. "It's an address." She read it to him.

"I know where that is." He switched on the blinker and steered the SUV into the right lane. "Forward the address, message, and picture to Jackson."

"I already did." She set down the phone. "He hasn't responded."

Her phone buzzed again. Louisa read the screen. "It's the killer. We're down to five minutes."

Conor pressed on the accelerator, praying a chain didn't snap as the truck sped up.

Jackson called Conor's phone. Concentrating on driving, Conor handed the phone to Louisa. She answered and explained the situation.

"Do not let Conor go into that building," the cop roared. "I have backup units on the way. Hell, the SWAT team is suiting up."

Conor crossed to South Christopher Columbus Boulevard and went north. They traveled a few blocks and he turned right onto a narrow side street that led to the river. Even with the chains on the tires, the SUV slid into the turn as he pushed the speed. Conor glanced at the dashboard clock.

Tick-tock.

A minute later, their headlights cut through the tall shadow of a building. Conor parked in front of a two-story brick warehouse at the end of the street. Giant spools, piles of rebar, and rusting barrels cluttered the yard. Boards covered the first-floor windows, a few second-floor windows were broken, and graffiti decorated the four rolling overhead doors that fronted the street side of the warehouse.

The phone rang. Louisa picked it up, but Conor took it from her hand.

"He wants me." He turned to the window as he answered the call. "Yes."

"The door's open. You have three minutes. Clock's ticking." The call ended.

Conor put a hand on the door handle. "I love you. I want you to drive the SUV to the end of the street to wait for the cops."

"You can't go in there alone." She grabbed his shoulder. "I'll come with you."

He searched the darkness around the building. Imagining Louisa inside, Conor nearly choked. Panic crawled up his spine and circled his throat. Her father and Ianelli were in there already, but he couldn't lose her.

He took her gloved hand and kissed it. "I love you, but if you come in there with me, you'll only make me more vulnerable. He wants to fight me. It'll take some time. I only have to stall him until the police get here. Tell them I'm inside so they don't shoot me."

He didn't promise her he'd be fine. He couldn't. But nor could he allow her to be hurt. She'd already gotten lucky in one altercation with this killer.

She grabbed his arm. "He doesn't want to fight you. He wants to beat you to death."

"Yeah, well, I'm not going down without a fight." Conor had plenty of pissed-off to draw on. He leaned back and gave her a quick kiss on the mouth before reaching for the traction cleats at her feet. He slid them over his boots.

"I don't want you to do this." She nearly begged.

"I know. I love you." He kissed her again. "But this isn't only about us. There are two men in that building who are going to die if I don't go inside. I can't let that happen. I wouldn't be able to live with myself."

He opened the car door and slipped out. The cold braced him as he went up the steps and paused at the top to slip the cleats off of his boots. Then he opened the door and the darkness swallowed him.

CHAPTER
36

Ianelli awoke to pain, pain, and more pain. Agony radiated through most of his body. His left leg felt like it had swollen to eight times its normal size, and his torso was on fire. He opened his eyes. The ceiling seemed blurry and far away.

The last thing he remembered was sliding straight into a fucking tree. He blinked and his vision came into focus. The ceiling *was* far away, at least twenty feet over his head, and with the corrugated look of an industrial building. OK. Not a hospital.

Where am I?

The faint stirrings of unease slid through his pain as his instincts waved a warning flag.

Without knowing where he was, he knew he was fucked. He'd been so stupid. He deserved what he'd gotten.

Whatever that was.

He tried to turn his head but couldn't.

"Don't move." Someone leaned over him.

He squinted. Ward Hancock?

His lips formed the words *what happened*, but no sound came out of his mouth.

Ward seemed to understand him, though. He brought a wet towel to his mouth and moistened his lips. "I don't know whether I should give you water or not. Your leg is broken, you have a puncture wound in your side, and likely internal injuries. But dehydration won't help matters either." Ward's frown creased his forehead. "This is one of those times I wish I was a real doctor."

A jingling sound drew Ianelli's eyeballs sideways. Ward was tethered by a metal shackle and chain.

Oh yes. They were definitely fucked.

Ianelli's "thanks" sounded more like a grunt. A wave of cold swept over him, and he shivered hard. The movements sent pain slamming though his body. He licked his lips, but his tongue was as dry as a sheet of sandpaper.

"Do you want some water?" Ward asked, his mouth pressed flat.

Ianelli opened his mouth like a bird in answer.

"Do you have any pain in your neck or back?" Ward asked.

Ianelli moved his head left and right, slowly.

Ward supported the back of his head and tilted a water bottle to his lips. "Just a little. Trust me. You don't want to start coughing."

The tiny amount of liquid was enough to moisten his mouth. Ianelli swallowed, carefully.

"You have a few cuts on your face and forehead, but none of them look serious. Do you have pain anywhere else besides your leg and stomach?"

Ianelli assessed his body. Compared to his leg and gut, nothing else hurt enough to notice. "I don't think so," he rasped.

"I did what I could. I splinted your leg and bandaged the wound on your side." Ward lifted the covers. "Can you move your fingers?"

With great effort, Ianelli wiggled all ten. Ward tucked the blanket in and moved to his feet. "How about your toes?"

The right foot wasn't a problem, but even the tiny movement of his big toe sent unbelievable agony through his left leg. His vision dimmed, and he almost blacked out.

Ward moved the blanket again. The furrow between his brows deepened.

"What?" Ianelli asked.

"I'm going to tighten this bandage. It's probably going to hurt. But the bleeding . . ."

Yeah, he got it. The leak was serious.

Ward leaned into whatever bandage he'd rigged and split Ianelli in two.

"Holy. Fuck." He sucked wind, and his entire body erupted into a case of the shakes. Even his pinkie toe was trembling.

"We don't have any more blankets." Ward took off the coat he was wearing and spread it over him.

It didn't help much. Ianelli thought he was freezing from the inside out.

Something scraped on the other side of the wall.

"Who?" Ianelli squeaked.

"I don't know who he is." The light in Ward's eyes went out. "But I watched him kill two men. And I think he killed a woman as well, though he didn't do it here. He beat one man to death. The other . . ." The agony on Ward's face rivaled Ianelli's pain. The scholar had the dead look of a man who'd seen horrors beyond his imagination.

If Ianelli could have patted the scholar's hand, he would have. But he couldn't lift a pinkie.

A metallic clang reverberated around the space. A door closing. Was the killer coming or going?

Ianelli assessed the situation. He was slowly but surely bleeding out, certainly in no shape to defend himself or Ward, who was chained to a pipe.

"My gun?" he asked without much hope.

Ward gave his head the slightest shake. "He took it."

So they were both at the mercy of a serial killer.

CHAPTER
37

Conor stepped inside the warehouse, straining for any sound that would help him locate the killer.

"Come inside and close the door," a voice echoed from a loudspeaker. "Fasten the chains across the door handles with the padlock."

He did as instructed. Louisa couldn't follow him inside even if she wanted to. He was now locked in with a killer.

He walked by a set of dusty, cobwebbed offices. At the end of the corridor, a doorway led into the main warehouse. Through the opening, he could see concrete and a row of workbenches that lined the far wall.

"Hurry up." The voice grew irritable.

But Conor's goal was to stall until the cops arrived. He looked through the doorway. The warehouse was two stories tall. On one side, three mastless sailboats rested on jack stands. Tools cluttered the workbenches. Rolling carts, power equipment, and electrical cords around the boats suggested someone had been working on them recently. The air smelled of dust with the sharp undercurrent of varnish. Beyond the boats, Conor could see closed doors set in the wall. More offices? High windows suggested offices on the second floor as well. If Ward and Ianelli were on the premises, they must be in one of those rooms.

The other half of the warehouse space was open. Conor spied two emergency exits, one on the far wall and another on the right. Both were chained shut.

But it wasn't the chains that held Conor's attention. It was what sat in front of the doors: a barrel marked "highly flammable" with a small MacGyver-like device sitting on top. Another barrel and device blocked the second exit. Several more were spaced at regular intervals along the perimeter of the warehouse. He was no munitions expert, but he guessed the building was wired.

If the cops busted through a door, the entire warehouse would blow.

So much for stalling until the police arrived. Now Conor needed to keep them from coming entirely.

Or finish this business before they all got blown to smithereens.

In the center of the empty space, a square the size of a boxing ring had been drawn on the concrete with black paint. To one side, a workbench had been dragged into the open. A dark, rusty stain surrounded the workbench. The location of Orion Turner's execution?

Louisa's pale, pleading face slid into his mind.

Focus.

If he wanted to get back to her alive, he'd better pay attention. He blinked her away and scanned the space. Where was he?

"Come on, Asher. I don't have all day." Conor used his name, hoping it would throw him off. "Or are you afraid you've bitten off more than you can chew this time?" He paused for effect, then hammered the challenge home. "Maybe you're afraid you're not really the superior male here."

"Walk to the middle of the boxing ring," the voice over the loudspeaker commanded.

Conor moved through the doorway. His boots barely cleared the threshold before a piece of rebar whizzed toward his head. He ducked, but not fast enough to completely avoid the blow. Pain exploded through his temple, and he face-planted on the cement.

CHAPTER
38

Louisa stared at the dark building as cold seeped into the truck. Her mind couldn't fully comprehend that Conor was in there with a killer.

Her phone rang. Jackson.

She answered it. "Yes."

"I am five minutes away. Tell me he didn't go inside."

Louisa explained. "He said if Conor didn't, he would kill my father and Ianelli."

"Fuck," Jackson yelled. Behind his voice, a radio chattered. "I'll be there with two patrol cars within four minutes. SWAT is suiting up and we have a hostage negotiator on the way. We'll get him out. Sit tight."

The call ended. Louisa sat frozen in the front seat of the car as rain dotted the windshield. The messages from the killer rolled around in her head.

For my beloved.

I apologize. I am not yet worthy. But soon I will win your favor.

I left a gift for you in Mifflin Square. I hope you are pleased.

The killer's tone with Conor wasn't so subservient. No, Conor presented a challenge, almost as if the killer wanted to duel to win her hand. No, not her hand, her approval.

He wanted to prove himself the best.

And suddenly, she knew exactly what he wanted and what she needed to do. Something neither Conor nor the police could accomplish. No SWAT hostage negotiator would be able to help this time.

It had to be her.

She crawled into the back of the SUV and opened the container of emergency supplies and rooted for scissors, duct tape, and a Mylar emergency blanket. She took off her coat and slit the nylon. Compressed feathers fell to the cargo mat. Now for the tape.

Only a complete fool would try to break into a murderer's lair. But the one thing more frightening than facing a killer was losing Conor.

She hoped it was only a few minutes later when she jammed everything into her purse, crept up to the front door, and gently pulled the handle. Locked. Now how would she get inside? She eyed the broken second-floor windows. Then she turned to judge the height of the big SUV. Maybe.

She pulled the SUV up to the side of the building with the highest ground. She got out of the vehicle, climbed onto the hood, and scrambled up onto the roof. She slung her purse strap over her head and let it drape across her shoulders, then shifted the purse to her back. But the window was over her head. A narrow ledge circled the old brick building between the first and second floors, but she wasn't high enough to scramble up, especially on an ice-covered building. Conor would have been able to grab the window and haul himself up. But for all her working out, she couldn't even do a single chin-up yet.

She returned to the truck and slid to the ground. Slipping and sliding, she went around to the back of the vehicle and rummaged in the cargo area. Overturning the hard plastic container, she dragged it from the vehicle. Then she grabbed three rubber floor mats. The cleats helped on the icy ground, but made climbing on the truck harder. She took them off, and then spread two rubber floor mats on the roof. She hauled the container up to the roof, settling it onto the mats so it wouldn't slide, and climbed on top. With the extra height, the windowsill was level with her chin.

She stood on tiptoe and got her first glimpse inside. The broken window looked into a second-floor office. She used another floor mat to cover the jagged edges of broken glass. Then she put her hands on the sill and heaved herself up until her head was through the opening and her waist leaned over the floor mat. She squirmed until she fell to the floor on the other side.

A small puddle of ice covered the floor in front of the window. Louisa scooted to the edge, got her feet under her body on the solid floor, and adjusted the purse on her shoulder.

The office obviously hadn't been used in some time. Filthy windows overlooked the warehouse space. She crawled to the window and looked over. Three sailboats blocked the view of the remaining room.

Where was Conor?

Louisa went to the doorway and crept down the hall. A flight of stairs led to the first floor. She kept to the edge and stepped softly, trying to avoid squeaky treads. Hitting the first floor landing, she tiptoed down a narrow hallway. At the first doorway, she stopped to listen before peering around the doorframe into a storage area. Shelves were stocked with what appeared to be spare parts. A workbench held tools. Several four-wheeled platform carts, the type used to move heavy equipment, were lined up against the near wall. At the other end of the room sat a chest freezer. Its brazen newness shone with purpose in a room of grease and grime and well-used equipment.

She crossed the cement floor and opened the chest. At the sight of a dead body, she gasped and almost dropped the lid. Even though she'd never met him, she recognized the frozen face of Asher Banks.

CHAPTER
39

Conor shook his head and rolled to his back in the middle of the boxing ring. His jacket and shirt were missing, and his head felt like someone had used it for batting practice.

"Stand up and fight." Rowan Banks held a section of rebar with both hands.

Rowan?

What. The. Fuck? Mr. Khaki and Cashmere was the killer? Rowan didn't look tough enough to fight traffic let alone trained boxers.

"Come on. I've been waiting for this." Rowan waved the metal bar in a taunting arc.

Following its path with his eyeballs sent pain shooting through Conor's temples. Then he realized that Rowan wasn't tough enough, which was why he'd cheated.

"Is that how you defeated two professional fighters—you suckered them?" Conor let contempt color his voice.

"There are no rules in war." Rowan waved the bar.

"Still makes you a cheat. Too weak for a fair fight."

With his head still spinning, Conor didn't trust his balance. So he went for a low and hopefully unexpected attack. He rolled right into Rowan's ankles, knocking him to the floor. The rebar went flying, clanged to the concrete, and slid out of reach.

Conor scrambled across the floor. Rowan crabbed away, surprise widening his eyes.

"How's it feel?" Conor faked confidence, while his head throbbed, his stomach somersaulted, and his vision tunneled. He couldn't show any sign of weakness.

Rowan climbed to his feet and circled Conor.

"Where's your brother?" Conor wondered if the other Banks son was going to attack from a shadow. "Are you in this together?"

"Asher?" Rowan snorted. "Never. Always fucking perfect. I'm the only real son, Dad's only living blood relative. Yet Asher was the favorite son."

Was?

Pieces fell into place. The blood in Asher's basement wasn't Ward's, but the stain had to have come from someone. The boxers had been beaten, but Conor didn't remember seeing any wounds deep enough to leave a bloodstain that large. The women had been killed where they'd been dumped. That left . . .

Asher.

"You murdered your brother, didn't you?" Conor got his feet under his body and stood, praying he didn't sway or fall on his face.

"He wasn't really my brother."

"How did you do it?"

Rowan's eyes shone with the light of the crazy. "I slit his throat and let him bleed out like a pig. It was easy. Asher never suspected a thing."

"So you ambushed him too?" Conor asked, hoping for a moment to regain his balance.

Rowan ignored the jibe. "The hardest part was shutting up that mutt before someone called the police. The stupid dog went berserk."

"Dogs don't like it when someone kills their owner. They're loyal that way. Unlike brothers, who turn on their own," Conor taunted. "How did you get out without Vivian knowing? I thought she was up all night."

"Oh, please. How hard is it to slip someone a sleeping pill?" Rowan rolled his eyes.

"You drugged a sick woman? What if the drug combination killed her?"

"It would probably be doing her a favor. Her death from Parkinson's disease won't be pleasant."

"Why did you take Ward Hancock?" Conor circled and the room spun.

"He was supposed to be my mentor, but he wouldn't cooperate. The only thing he was useful for was bait."

"What about the cop?" Conor blinked hard, but his vision didn't clear. What the hell was he going to do? He needed to incapacitate Rowan before the cops took a battering ram to one of the wired doors.

"That was an impulse. Fate saw to it that I was following Turner when he met with the cop. I watched them make an exchange. After Turner ran the cop off the road, I knocked the gang leader out before he killed the cop." Rowan's eyes lit with maniacal glee. He seemed almost eager to share the details of his brilliant plan. "Then I took them both. I thought the cop might be useful in case I needed a bargaining chip. But little did I know he was a traitor too. His own kind might not even want him back." Rowan reached down to a pocket on his thigh. He drew out two envelopes. Opening one, he fanned a stack of cash. "Your cop friend had five thousand large." He lifted the flap of envelope number two. "And I found this on the gangbanger. I have to assume the chunk of hair in the police evidence bag belongs to Orion Turner." He tossed both envelopes to the floor in disgust. "What honest cop sells evidence to a wanted felon?"

None that Conor knew. Was Ianelli on the take? *Shit.* He almost liked the cop.

"But none of that matters anymore. This will be finished tonight." Rowan charged him like a bull.

Conor saw him coming and stepped out of the way. Rowan spun, swinging out with a wide right hook. Conor ducked under it. Rising, he drove an uppercut into Rowan's gut, using his legs to maximize the power of the blow.

Rowan grunted and wrapped his arms around Conor, locking him in a clinch, no doubt to give himself time to recover from the uppercut. Conor used the seconds to drag some oxygen into his own lungs. Then he pulled back an arm and hammered at Rowan's kidney with three hard punches. Rowan sagged, but Conor's vision blurred from the effort.

Pushing away, Rowan reeled backward. But he'd obviously been training because he came back for more. With his vision screwy and his balance off, Conor let twenty years of experience be his guide. He threw a jab and caught Rowan on the jaw. His head snapped back, but he didn't go down.

He came at Conor with a hard cross. Conor bobbed out of the way, parrying the strike and countering with a punch to the nose. Rowan staggered backward and covered his face with his hands. Blood streamed from his face.

"Why did you kill your brother?" Conor moved forward, driving Rowan back with his body and his words.

"He didn't deserve half of my father's estate." Rowan dropped his hands. Anger shone from his beaten face.

"You killed your brother for the money?" Conor moved in for another blow, but Rowan lunged for the floor, snatching the length of rebar.

"He wasn't really my brother, and the money should have been mine." He came at Conor, swinging hard at his head. "The Valkyrie said so."

Conor ducked. Though he'd been an amateur boxer, being a bouncer at the bar had taught him all about dirty fights. More than one drunken patron had swung a beer bottle at his head. He tackled Rowan around the knees. Conor was so unsteady, he'd be better off fighting on the ground. A whoosh of shock left the killer as they hit the concrete. The rebar slid across the floor.

Rowan flipped them over. Straddling Conor's chest, he punched at his head. The blows were close enough that they carried little force, but they were enough to dim Conor's already fuzzy vision. Blackness curled around his eyes as unconsciousness threatened.

CHAPTER
40

Shaken, Louisa eased the freezer lid down.

If Asher wasn't the killer, then who was?

It had to be Xander, who pretended to be a Viking with his reenactment group, who'd concealed his friendship with Douglas Banks. How many other secrets had he kept?

Her phone vibrated. She read the text from Jackson on the screen: `Where are you?`

She answered: `Inside.`

`Get out!`

`Can't. I have a plan.`

`NO! SWAT's hostage neg is here.`

But she was the only one the killer would talk to.

She continued her search. Stopping in front of the next room, she paused to listen at the door but heard nothing. The next door was closed and padlocked.

This must be it.

She pressed her ear to the wood and heard faint voices, recognizing her father's. But how to get them out? She ran back to the freezer and storage room. Scanning the workbench, she found bolt cutters. She raced to the door and cut the padlock. Her heart thudded and her breaths came faster as she opened the door. Her father knelt on the floor next to a body on a cot. Other than some bumps, bruises, and minor cuts, he appeared to be physically sound. But the bleakness in his eyes told a different story.

She breathed, and relief gave her a second wind.

"Daddy." She strode across the room, dropped to her knees, and hugged him. The moment didn't seem real until she touched his living and breathing body.

"Louisa," he whispered. "You found us."

"Yes." But they weren't out of danger yet.

She released him and turned to the cot. The body was Ianelli. She rested a hand on his chest. It rose and fell, and she exhaled a breath she hadn't been aware of holding.

The detective opened his eyes. "I'm still alive."

"Stay that way," she said. Turning to her father, she spied the manacle on his ankle and cut the chain with the bolt cutters.

"How are we going to get him out of here?" her father asked.

"Just go," Ianelli rasped. "Send someone back for me. Get out of here." The detective promptly passed out.

Louisa ignored him. "I have an idea."

Dropping her purse, she raced back to the storage room and returned with a wheeled cart and a screwdriver. "You're going to roll him out." She wheeled the flat surface of the cart under the cot. The gap between the two surfaces was only an inch. She handed her father the screwdriver and bolt cutters. "If you take the legs off the cot, the bed will rest on the cart, and you'll be able to roll him out of here. You'll need the bolt cutters for the front door. It's chained shut. Detective Jackson's number is in my contacts. Let him know you're coming out so they don't shoot you." She thrust her cell phone into her father's hands, then opened her purse to dig out what she'd brought from the car.

Ward didn't waste time. He pocketed the phone, then began to unscrew the legs of the cot. "Where are you going?"

Louisa headed for the door. "Conor's in here somewhere. I have to find him."

She didn't vocalize the rest of her thought.

Before it's too late.

CHAPTER
41

Conor blinked away the blurriness in his vision and grabbed the incoming punch with both hands. Yanking Rowan off balance, Conor trapped a leg and bridged over his shoulder, reversing their positions. But Rowan scrambled out from under him. Conor rolled to his hands and knees and sucked wind. Rowan wasn't in much better shape. Bloody and beaten, he picked up the rebar again and staggered to his feet. Conor lifted his pant leg, pulled the knife from his boot, and flipped it open. Two could fight dirty. There was no such thing as a clean fight outside of the ring.

Rising to a crouch, Conor kept his weapon in front of him.

"Knives it is." Tossing the rebar aside, Rowan reached into his own pocket and pulled out a long and lethal blade. He attacked, raising the knife over his head as if he were handling an ice pick. But Conor rushed forward, blocked the strike with his own blade, and sliced Rowan's bicep wide open.

Blood gushed. Rowan dropped his weapon, his arm useless with the muscle severed.

"Give it up, Rowan," Conor said. "You don't have to die today."

"There's no shame in dying, as long as the fight was good," Rowan said in a too-calm voice. He backed away from Conor, stepped behind the nearest barrel, and put his left hand on the homemade device. "But if I die, you and everyone else in this building are going with me."

A fresh burst of adrenaline shot through Conor's veins. He was going to die, and it would be for nothing because Louisa's father and Ianelli were probably in here somewhere and were going to die too.

"Why do you want to die so badly?" he asked.

"Why not?" Rowan said. "Better to die now, young and strong and healthy, than to wither away to a pile of skin and bones. My father was once a wealthy, powerful man, and he ended up wearing diapers."

"He was sick."

"He was miserable, and his afterlife will be more of the same." Rowan seemed to stretch taller, as if bolstered by beliefs. "Only the strongest warriors ascend to Valhalla. I will not wither away and spend eternity in a frigid hell. I've defeated fighters. I've proven myself worthy."

"Are you sure of that?" Conor was grateful for one thing: that Louisa wasn't here, but he'd failed her. *I'm sorry. I love you.*

Outside, a man on a bullhorn yelled, "This is the police. We want to talk to you."

Rowan ignored the request and patted the bomb. "Why don't we find out together?"

Moving away from the device, he yanked the wire connecting it to the others.

Conor held his breath and waited for the boom. The explosion was quieter than he expected, a localized pop that blew the top off the barrel. The sharp smell of gasoline flooded the air as liquid gushed across the cement. Fire whooshed across the space but stopped at the end of the puddle.

Rowan's face fell with disappointment, then lit with fury. Obviously, *he* wasn't a munitions expert either. He ran toward another container and device combo.

But a female voice yelled, "I don't think so."

Rowan skidded to a stop and whirled.

Conor's head whipped around fast enough to make him dizzy. Louisa! *No!*

Rowan's mouth gaped. Not believing what he was seeing, Conor squeezed his eyes closed and opened them again. How hard had that initial blow to the head been?

Louisa walked from one of the interior doorways across the concrete. She'd shaken her hair out so it cascaded over her shoulders. The cape that draped her was silver and . . . feathered? Yep. Unless he was hallucinating, those were feathers. In the dim light, she looked like an angel.

She halted fifteen feet away. "*I* decide who is worthy!" Her voice rose until it echoed off the hard surfaces.

Rowan looked stunned. "I knew you were the Valkyrie. You are an amazing creature. Beautiful. Strong. Intelligent. I am your servant." He bowed his head but kept his gaze on her.

"Then step away from that bomb," she commanded. "That is not how a worthy warrior behaves."

Rowan deflated. "But—"

Louisa cut him off. "*I* decide who lives and dies. *I* decide who goes to Valhalla."

Dropping to one knee, Rowan said, "I did everything you said. I killed Asher. I became a great warrior. You promised me I'd go to Valhalla. You can't change your mind now."

Louisa hesitated.

"You look so different than in my dreams." Rowan raised his head. "You sound different too." Rowan frowned. "You aren't the Valkyrie. When a Valkyrie appears on the battlefield, she always carries a sword." His eyes narrowed. "Your clothes, your hair. It's all different."

Terror gathered in Conor's chest. He was unarmed. Hell, he could barely stay on his feet. As convincing as Louisa looked and sounded, Rowan saw through her act. Rage widened his eyes. He was going to hurt her. Fear for Louisa fueled Conor's steps as he stumbled forward, determined to get between her and Rowan.

Too much white rimmed Rowan's eyes, and they shone with an insane *Here's Johnny* fervor.

"You're an imposter. You betrayed me. I'm going to kill you." Rowan picked up his knife with his left hand and raced toward Louisa.

Conor lunged to intercept them, but he knew he couldn't get there in time. Rowan was closer. He was young and strong and fast and he was going to slice her in two. "Run, Louisa!" he shouted.

But she didn't. She reached into the pocket of her coat, pulled out Reed's handgun, and shot Rowan point blank in the chest.

Holy . . .

Shock halted Conor's forward momentum. He skidded to a stop and watched Rowan crumple to the floor. Disbelief held Conor's feet in place even as blood seeped onto the cement around Rowan's body.

He blinked and shifted his gaze to Louisa. She hadn't moved a muscle since she'd fired the shot, and the shock on her face matched what was going on in Conor's head.

She'd taken the murdering bastard down with her brain. No amount of brawn could match it. The gun in her hand began to shake.

He ran to her side. He tucked her behind him and rolled Rowan to his back with the toe of his boot. Rowan stared up at the ceiling, his maniacal eyes glassed over.

"He still looks crazy, even dead." Conor backed up, pulling her with him. He wanted her far away from Rowan. "I thought he was going to kill you."

"While I'd hoped he'd surrender, I knew the chances were greater that the costume would only serve as a distraction, which is why I brought the gun with me. I should feel worse about killing a man, but I don't have the energy. Maybe later."

"No need. He deserved it. We'd better get out of here." Conor pulled her away from the fire. "He wasn't a very gifted pyromaniac, but there's gasoline everywhere."

She put the gun on the floor. "We'd better let Jackson know we're coming out."

"Good plan." Conor stumbled in a crooked line. But Rowan had been right about one thing. Louisa was the shit. And, if they didn't get blown up in the next minute or so, she was all his.

She wrapped an arm around his waist to steady him. She was stronger than she looked. *Thank God.*

"Hold on." On impulse he pulled away, staggered closer to the fire, and kicked two envelopes on the floor into the blaze. The fire crackled as it consumed the paper, and he hoped Ianelli didn't make him regret it.

Louisa ducked under his arm again and tugged him toward the door. "We'd better hurry before someone decides to use a battering ram on a back door."

"That would be bad," Conor agreed.

She steered him through the corridor, past the offices, and toward the front entrance.

"The chains are cut." He drew up, confused.

"Yes. That means my father and Ianelli are probably outside."

Conor looked at her in astonishment.

"We're coming out now," she shouted through the door, then pushed it open. They stepped out onto the stoop.

The rain had stopped. Ice gleamed in the predawn gray of first light. Police vehicles filled the lot and officers were aiming rifles at them.

"Hands in the air!" someone commanded.

They complied, but when Louisa released him, Conor nearly fell over. The wave of policemen shifted with a metallic shuffle.

"Hold your fire," Jackson yelled. He came out from behind a patrol car. A black vest covered his chest and he held a rifle. He slid across the icy lot toward them.

"It's over," Louisa said as he approached. "Rowan Banks is dead. But the whole building is rigged with explosives."

"Rowan?" Jackson asked. "Where's Asher?"

"In a freezer on the first floor." Louisa shivered as a blustery wind swept across the ice. The temperature was still frigid.

Jackson took one look at Conor, grabbed his arm, and hauled it across his shoulders. "Medic!"

Conor gazed beyond the police cars. Red lights swirled on the tops of two ambulances. Wrapped in a blanket, Ward was climbing into the back of one. A third drove away with a quick burst of its siren. No doubt the cop was inside.

"How is Ianelli?" Conor asked.

"I don't know." Jackson glanced back at the ambulance. "But without Louisa, he'd be dead. He told us she saved him."

The cop dragged Conor toward the remaining ambulance. Someone draped a blanket over Louisa's shoulders and helped her up into the back. A paramedic eased Conor onto the gurney and checked his eyes with a penlight.

Pulling the blanket around her, Louisa leaned forward and took Conor's hand. "You've looked better."

He licked blood from his lip, and his head pounded like the opening bass line of Heart's "Barracuda."

"I've felt better," he admitted. "People need to stop hitting me over the head. I thought he was going to stab you."

"I wanted him to be close so I wouldn't miss and hit something that would explode."

"Good thinking." A down feather drifted from her makeshift cape. Conor caught it in his hand. "What's with the feathers?"

Louisa set it on the bench next to her. "Valkyries wore garments made of swan feathers so they could fly and carry warriors off the battlefield to Valhalla."

Conor stared. "There is so much knowledge crammed in that big brain of yours, it's staggering. You're incredible."

She shook her head and blinked away. "I wasn't convincing enough. If I had been, I wouldn't have had to shoot him."

Conor reached for her hand, still stunned that they were alive and that Ward and Ianelli had been saved. Louisa might be feeling bad about killing Rowan, but as far as Conor was concerned, it was good riddance to a murderer.

"Hey." He caught her gaze. "You saved us all."

"Not even close." She gripped his fingers hard. "We did it together."

CHAPTER
42

Louisa walked out of the small private room where she'd given a statement to several police officers. They'd been gentle with their questions, but then she supposed they were happy to have a killer off the street. The change in attitude still felt strange. She was accustomed to Jackson's borderline rude personality.

In fact, she felt odd and disconnected inside and out, as if she were walking around in someone else's body. So much had happened in the past few hours that her emotions couldn't keep pace. Her father had been rescued. She and Conor had faced a killer and survived. She'd killed a man.

A cold shudder rippled through her bones, a hint of regret for ending a man's life.

When she'd stuffed Reed's gun into her pocket, she'd hoped she wouldn't need it. Rowan hadn't been sane. His delusions had consumed him. The act of killing him, even with all the horrors he'd committed, had changed her profoundly in way she hadn't yet processed, and she knew that pivotal moment would be playing over and over in her nightmares.

But given the choice between Rowan and her loved ones . . . Well, there really hadn't been a choice. And she'd pull that trigger again in a heartbeat.

She had a quick flashback of Conor, swaying, clenching a knife, and facing a bloody Rowan. He'd willingly walked into a killer's trap to save her father and Ianelli. Her steps quickened. Had the blow to the head been more serious than he'd admitted?

She weaved her way toward the emergency room but saw Conor and Jayne in the hallway outside the entrance. A small bandage was taped to Conor's head and his face was pale, but nothing could have made her happier than the sight of him on his feet.

Exhaustion slid through her in a greasy wave.

All she wanted to do was go home, get into bed with him, and sleep for a few days. But neither one of them would be able to rest until Pat was out of danger.

"Should you be out here?" she asked him with a nod toward the Emergency sign.

"I'm fine." Conor leaned over to kiss her. He swayed slightly.

She caught his arm. "You don't look fine."

"He has a mild concussion," Jayne said. "The doctor wanted to keep him but you know how he is." She handed Louisa a stack of stapled forms. "I'll give you his discharge papers. He won't read them."

Louisa moved to tuck them into her purse, then remembered it was back in the warehouse. She folded the sheets and slid them into her pocket.

"I'm fine," Conor insisted. "I want to see Pat."

"How is he?" Louisa slid an arm around Conor's waist to steady him.

"A little better, they think." Jayne led the way down the corridor. "His blood pressure is holding. That's a good sign."

"But he hasn't woken up?" Louisa asked.

Jayne looked at the floor. "No. Not yet."

Damn it.

Pat needed to be OK. Conor couldn't lose his brother, and the heaviness that filled her heart told her that she couldn't bear to lose him either. She'd never had a brother. Pat hadn't asked; he'd just taken on the role and pushed his way right into her heart.

In unspoken agreement, they followed the signs to the SICU.

Conor leaned on Louisa. "How did it go with the cops?"

"Fine," she said. "Easier than I expected."

"What's wrong?" he asked.

"Nothing." She shook her head. "I just thought they'd be more concerned with me shooting Rowan."

"Honey, you saved a cop and took out a serial killer." He kissed her. "Face it, you're a hero."

She flushed. Her actions hadn't felt heroic. They'd felt desperate. The whole situation had been chaotic. "There is the issue of me carrying a handgun without a permit."

Which no one seemed to care much about.

"You were always my hero, but now everybody knows how amazing you are." He kissed her again. "Is your dad all right?"

"Physically yes. He's dehydrated and stressed. They gave him a sedative, and they're going to keep him overnight just to be sure. He'll need therapy. But he's alive, and that's a good place to start." But worry nagged at her. Was her dad strong enough to get through his experience? He'd been fragile before Rowan had made him witness unspeakable horrors.

Outside the SICU, Jayne pressed the intercom button. "I'm going to get Leena and make her take a break if you'll sit with Pat."

"Good idea," Conor said.

Jayne went into the unit. Conor tightened his grip on Louisa's hand. A few minutes later, Jayne and Leena emerged. Leena looked worse than Conor. He gave her a hug and a kiss. "Please get something to eat."

She nodded and let Jayne lead her away.

Louisa and Conor went down the hall and stopped outside Pat's unit. The doctors seemed to think he was improving, but he'd lost a lot of blood. His heart had stopped. Until he regained consciousness, no one would know for sure if he'd suffered any permanent damage other than losing his kidney.

They entered the glassed-in cubicle. Louisa took a chair in the corner, trying to stay out of the way. Conor had barely scanned Pat and his monitors when Terry poked his head into the room.

"Hey, Conor. Now that you're out of the ER, we need a statement," Terry said.

"Would you sit with Pat?" Conor asked Louisa. He turned a little too quickly and wavered. Steadying himself with a hand on the bedrail, he gestured for Louisa to come closer.

"Of course." But she walked to the bedside with tentative steps. This was a place for family, not the girlfriend of family. Despite the love in her heart for Pat, she couldn't help but feel like she was intruding.

Conor nudged her toward a chair pulled up to the bed. "Just hold his hand so he knows someone is here with him. I might be a while."

He trusted her to look after Pat. The responsibility weighed on her. She glanced at his monitors and ashen face, his huge, strong body so helpless and vulnerable.

"I'll stay here. Don't worry." She turned to Terry. "You can have Conor if you promise he'll sit down."

"Scout's honor." Terry held up three fingers as they left.

IV lines led in and out of both arms, but Louisa found Pat's hand under the sheet and grasped it. The events of the night, no, the whole week, rushed back at her in a series of violent clips. Was this all her fault? She'd introduced Conor to Jordan, and it had been her and her father who had dragged the Sullivans onto a serial killer's radar. How could she ever forgive herself?

Tears spilled from her eyes as if she'd been storing them for weeks. Maybe she had. She wiped her face with her sleeve, then leaned her head back against the vinyl chair. The steady beep of the heart monitor and the whooshing of the ventilator lulled her. As long as those sounds occurred in regular rhythm, Pat was all right.

Something pulled at her hand. Startled, she looked up.

Pat!

His eyes were open, and his head was moving. His free hand was tugging on the tube taped to his face.

Louisa jumped to her feet and pressed the call button. Then she leaned over the bed so Pat could see her. Panic filled his eyes.

Louisa breathed through her own fear and forced her voice to sound soothing. "It's OK. Everything is OK."

But was it?

An alarm sounded on the ventilator.

She grabbed the hand pulling on the tube and tried to hold him. "No. Don't pull on that!"

Too late.

The ventilator tube popped out, and Pat gasped for air.

Louisa leaned closer. She put a hand on his forehead, hoping the physical contact would get through better than her words. "Pat, it's Louisa. You're OK. Try to relax. Just breathe."

His eyes fixed on hers, recognition dawned, and he calmed. His breathing steadied, and the crazy beeping of the heart monitor slowed. The ventilator continued to squeal.

Two nurses and a doctor rushed in.

"He's awake." The doctor sounded surprised.

"He pulled out the tube before I could stop him." Louisa moved to make room for the doctor.

But he shook his head and went to the opposite side of the bed. "Stay where he can see you and keep him calm."

A nurse turned off the protesting ventilator. The room fell quiet. Pat's eyes never left Louisa's.

"He seems to be breathing just fine on his own," the doctor said. "Mr. Sullivan. Can you hear me?"

Pat nodded and moved his cracked lips. The nurse gave him some water.

Louisa stroked Pat's forehead. Finally, he blinked and looked at the doctor.

"Do you know where you are?" After a nod from Pat, the doctor began to ask him about the year and month and who was president. Pat answered in a thin rasp.

Louisa exhaled, her pulse returning to normal.

Leena and Jayne returned, but when Louisa started to back away, Pat squeezed her hand before letting go. Leena kissed her husband, and Jayne cried. Ignoring the two-visitor rule, Conor rushed in next. His eyes settled on Pat and Leena and the tension seemed to drain from his body.

He crossed the room to Louisa.

Conor leaned close. "Is something wrong?"

"Nothing. Everything is wonderful." But she couldn't stop the flow of tears down her cheeks.

She could do this. If she'd had doubt about being assimilated into the Sullivan family, those doubts had evaporated when Pat had seen her face and quieted. For the very first time, she felt like part of something bigger.

Like she could give as much as she got.

Like she really was a member of a family.

CHAPTER
43

Ianelli opened his eyes.

"Oh my God." His wife was leaning over him. Gina's tears fell onto his face as she brushed the hair off his forehead.

"Hey" was what he attempted so say, but what came out of his mouth was a choked garble.

Gina ran to the door and called a nurse. Then she returned to his bedside and grabbed his hand.

A nurse and a doctor hurried in. They checked his vital signs and seemed reassured by the steady *beep beep* of the heart monitor next to his bed. The sound definitely brightened Ianelli's day. But then, so did waking up.

The doctor proclaimed him alive and left the room. The nurse stayed to fiddle with the medical paraphernalia clustered around his bed. From the sheer quantity of it—and the grateful tears in Gina's eyes—he figured he must have been pretty near dead.

The nurse poured water from a plastic pitcher into a cup and stuck a bendy straw in it. She lifted it to his lips. The cool liquid soothed his throat. She handed the cup to Gina. "Just small sips for now."

The nurse left the room.

Downside, being not dead meant facing the consequences of his actions.

Maybe it would have been better if he'd died. He was the worst. He deserved to go to jail, but Gina and the baby . . .

He'd ruined their lives too.

"What time is it?" he asked. His voice was still full of enough gravel that Gina offered him more water.

"Eight a.m."

He thought about her answer. "What *day* is it?"

"It's Sunday."

He'd been unconscious at least twenty-four hours. What happened at the warehouse? And the more selfish question: *What had happened to the envelope?*

"I love you." Gina continued to cry. "I thought you were going to die before you'd even gotten to see your baby."

"I love you too." He squeezed her hand.

Someone rapped on the wall. Jackson stood in the doorway.

Ianelli gave Gina a weak smile. "I have to talk to Jackson for a couple of minutes, OK? I'll be able to rest better if I get this out of the way. Why don't you stretch your legs?"

With a teary nod, she placed his hand gently on his chest and walked out of the room.

Jackson shoved his hands into the front pockets of his suit pants. "Looks like you're gonna live."

"That's what they said."

Jackson turned and closed the door. "We need to talk."

"I know." Ianelli stared at the ceiling tiles.

"We found your car wrapped around a tree in Fairmont Park." Jackson sauntered to the bedside. "The car that rammed it off the road was full of Orion Turner's fingerprints. Any idea what happened?"

"Yes. I have some blank spots in my memory, but I remember that." Ianelli concentrated. "Turner ran me off the road. The car slid into the tree. When I came to, Turner was pointing a gun at me. But someone cracked him over the head before he pulled the trigger. I didn't know until I woke up in the warehouse that it was Rowan Banks. He'd been following Turner, and he was really pissed off about something."

"Do you know what happened to Turner?"

"He's dead." Ianelli squeezed his eyes shut. "I didn't see it, but I heard the screaming." He opened his eyes. "Rowan made Ward watch, but Ward didn't tell me what he saw. I can only imagine . . ." He coughed, and pain slid through him like a dull blade.

Or a broken tree branch.

"I've seen a lot of nasty things, but that just might have been the worst." Jackson lifted the cup of water and put the straw in his partner's mouth.

Ianelli drank. "Is Ward all right?"

"Physically, yes. Not sure about his emotional status, though. Louisa is worried."

Ianelli glanced at the closed door then smiled. "She was awesome."

"Yes, the lady came through." Jackson chuckled. "She is tougher than she looks."

"Definitely," Ianelli agreed. "Who owned the building?"

"We found it registered under a corporation owned by the trust started for Asher to buy and build boats. The company owned the blue van. Rowan conveniently left it off the list he gave us. It didn't turn up in our initial search because of the complicated corporate structure." Jackson sobered. "Why did you do it?"

The sigh that rolled through Ianelli hurt almost as much as the truth. "How did you know?"

"You've been acting weird for weeks, and you were in the evidence room the day Orion Turner's hair disappeared. The log says you checked out evidence in the Smith case, but we both know that case is so cold it developed frost. Your car was found wrapped around a tree. The Explorer next to it had Turner's fingerprints all over it. I put the pieces together. That lock of hair was the only physical piece of evidence that tied Orion Turner to that robbery. He paid you to steal it so he couldn't be convicted."

"It's almost embarrassing how easily you figured it out."

"You aren't clever enough to be a criminal." Despite the light tone in his voice, Jackson's eyes were serious.

Ianelli stared at the ceiling. "We're gonna lose the house."

Jackson didn't rush him. He offered him more water.

Ianelli licked his lips. "Gina's been trying to get pregnant for nine years. We ran through all the insurance-covered options, and she found this private clinic. I took out a second mortgage for the first round. When that failed, I thought we were done. But Gina wanted to try one more time. I didn't have the heart to tell her we couldn't afford it. But the clinic made us a deal. Sounded a little shady to me, but I said yes. For Gina. They were trying out a new technique for hard-up cases. Like us. We wouldn't owe them any money unless she got pregnant."

"Which she did."

"Yep." Ianelli said. "When the bill came, I freaked out. I had no idea how we were going to pay it. I guess it hardly matters now. I'll be in prison, and Gina will be alone. My kid—"

"I didn't turn you in." Jackson reached for the water cup again. "No one who isn't working on all the same cases as you would figure it out."

"But the envelope was in my jacket. My fingerprints are all over it. So are Turner's." Hope was a tiny, dangerous germ in Ianelli's gut. At this point, it could do more damage than a visit from Internal Affairs.

"There was no envelope in that room you were locked up in."

"Then where is it?"

"I don't know."

"I'd feel better if we did." Ianelli digested the news. "Why are you doing this? Were you involved in that cluster at your old precinct?"

Jackson sank into the chair next to the bed. "No. But my partner was. I pulled him off of a handcuffed guy he almost beat to death. There was nothing redeemable about him. He deserved to go to jail. We've worked together long enough that I know you don't. You care, not just about the case, but about the victims and their families too. You stress about not arresting the innocent, and you keep me from steamrolling over people. But you did do something stupid."

"Supremely."

Jackson stood. "I really don't want to have to break in a new partner. Who would work with a guy whose last two partners went to jail?"

Ianelli almost laughed, but the initial rumble in his chest felt like his organs were being sliced and diced.

"Does Gina know about the debt?" Jackson asked.

"No. She isn't good with money." Ianelli's eyelids sagged. "I'll have to be straight with her, though. Before the bank forecloses on us." He wasn't out of trouble yet, but maybe, just maybe, he'd have an opportunity to make up for what he did. He was well aware that he didn't deserve it, but for Gina and the baby's sake, he'd take whatever second chance he could get.

"Look." Jackson rubbed his head. "I know I'm not the best partner."

"You don't totally suck, and I have no business judging anybody." It would take a long time for Ianelli to forgive himself for what he'd done.

"That business with my last partner fucked up my head. I didn't want to trust you. Ironically, now that I know you did something wrong, I do." Jackson shook his head.

"That makes no sense." Relief was making Ianelli sleepy.

"Well, next time you find yourself in a jam, talk to me." Jackson inhaled. "Gonzalez hit on me."

But that woke Ianelli up. "What?'"

"She asked me out for drinks. I said no. She's a little scary. Plus, I didn't want to risk our professional relationship. I'm a homicide cop. She's the ME. You know." Jackson blew out a breath. "But it turned out my rejection pissed her off. I probably didn't handle it well. I'm not exactly a diplomat."

Ianelli couldn't stop the laugh no matter how much it hurt. "You are so fucked."

Jackson smiled. "Get some rest. I'll be back."

Ianelli didn't hear his partner leave. When he opened his eyes next, Gina was in the chair next to his bed. Conor Sullivan and Louisa Hancock were knocking on his doorway.

"We just want to check on him." Sullivan sported a bandage on his temple, and the barkeep was looking rough.

Ianelli almost chuckled. Like he should talk.

Gina introduced herself, then when she realized who they were, she went into another round of waterworks thanking Louisa for saving him. The women moved out into the hallway.

While the women hugged and talked, Sullivan came closer. "How's it going? Glad to see you're not dead."

"Me too," he said.

Sullivan leaned close, his voice soft. "Are you wondering where the envelope is?"

Ianelli choked. Was Sullivan going to blackmail him? Damn, he wouldn't have expected it, but maybe Jackson was right. There weren't any more heroes. He glanced at his wife, who was totally absorbed in her conversation with Louisa.

Staring up at a water stain on the acoustic ceiling tile, he dropped his voice. "I don't know why I'm so disappointed in you. It's not like I have any room to talk, not after my epic fuck-up. But I thought you were one of the good guys." He met Sullivan's piercing gaze head-on. "If you're looking for hush money, I don't have anything to give you."

A slow smile spread across Sullivan's face. "I don't want anything, and the envelope is ashes. I wanted to make sure you're appropriately remorseful. Just don't screw up again. I'll never forget that you saved Louisa's life. So I guess we're even."

Ianelli had no words.

But Sullivan never seemed to run out of them. "You've grown on me, but your partner is still kind of an asshole."

Ianelli coughed, then recovered. "I'll tell you a secret. It's an act. Jackson is actually pretty decent."

After they left, Gina came back in and took his hand. "They're nice people."

You have no idea.

He stirred, and she fluffed his pillow for him. He stopped her fussing by taking her hand. He had one more fuck-up to fix. Well, he couldn't fix it, but at least he could come clean. "Gina. I have a confession to make. Sit down."

Her pretty brow wrinkled as she eased into the chair. She leaned her forearms on the bed so she could hold his one hand with both of hers.

"Before I say this, I want you to know how happy I am that we're having a baby. I have no regrets about it."

"Tony—"

"But now that you're pregnant, the bill is due, and we have some serious debt."

"But I thought you took out that second mortgage."

"That didn't even cover the last round." Ianelli started to sweat. "Then there's been the deductibles and copays and coinsurance that had accumulated from the conventional procedures."

"Oh." She sat back, still holding his hands. "How much is it?"

He told her. Really, the money he'd taken from Turner would have only gotten them through the next year. Then what? Had he planned on taking more bribes? He wouldn't have had a choice. Once you lay down with a dog like Turner, the fleas bred. If Turner hadn't been killed, Ianelli would have been his bitch for life.

She lifted his hand and brushed his knuckles across her face. "I wish you'd told me we couldn't afford it."

"I couldn't break your heart."

"And I love you for that." She smiled. "It's going to be all right. My parents will give us the money."

"Wha-at?"

"They offered once before, but I told them it was OK because that's what you told me."

Because he was an idiot.

"It's going to be all right, Tony." She stood, leaned over the bed, and kissed him. "Everything is going to be just fine."

When his eyes slammed closed again, Ianelli couldn't help but think he had some sort of guardian angel looking out for him. From now on, his straight and narrow was a fucking tightrope.

CHAPTER
44

Monday afternoon, Louisa rang the bell at the Banks residence. The door opened, and Vivian, leaning heavily on her cane, let her in.

"I'm so sorry for your loss." Louisa grasped one of Vivian's bony hands.

Nodding, Vivian gestured toward the living room.

They sat on the sterile white sofa. Vivian dabbed a tissue below her eyes. "It's just awful. I can't believe Rowan killed Asher. I know there was some jealousy between them. Doug really did favor Asher. But Rowan was always so sweet, and he took such good care of me."

Flowers filled the room. Louisa nearly gagged on the scent. She'd always hated lilies. They reminded her of her mother's death.

But she gave Vivian a sad, sympathetic smile. "It seems so impossible."

"I know." Vivian sniffed. "And to think he actually gave me sleeping pills so he could slip out of the house. He could have killed me."

Louisa couldn't play the game any longer. She let go. "So why did you tell him to do it?"

"What?" Vivian straightened.

"Why did you manipulate Rowan into killing Asher?" Louisa enunciated very clearly. This woman was pure, unadulterated evil.

But Vivian was also an excellent actress. She raised a shaky hand to her chest. "I have no idea what you're talking about."

"You dressed in your Viking gown and wore Doug's battle helmet. I saw the picture of you two wearing the costumes in Doug's office."

It was the photo of Vivian in her Viking noblewoman costume that had inspired Louisa to play a Valkyrie. At the time she hadn't known she'd have to compete with Vivian's interpretation of the goddess. But when she'd thought about Rowan's insistence that Louisa did not look like the part and his claims that the Valkyrie had spoken to him in the past, a new theory had taken root.

"I don't know what you're talking about." Vivian's eyes widened.

"Did you carry the replica sword too?"

Rowan's comment about Louisa not carrying her sword was the final piece that put the whole puzzle together. She should have wondered what happened to the replica sword Doug had purchased from Xander, but she'd been totally focused on the artifacts.

"Where are you hiding it?" Louisa pressed, anger heating her face. "You went into Rowan's room while he was sleeping and told him to kill his brother. How long has Rowan been mentally unstable? And more importantly, do you get the money now? Is that how the trust is structured?"

But Vivian didn't cave. "I have no idea what you mean."

Louisa pushed harder. "You deserved that money, didn't you? You were his wife for fifteen years. You took care of him. Asher was three when Doug married Asher's mother, Marla. He wasn't even a Banks and he got half the trust because Doug adopted him."

Vivian's eyes snapped. "I fed him. I wiped the drool off his chin. I listened to him moan all night long for years. Do you know what it's like to have sex with a man that much older than you? It's nasty, and thanks to Viagra, Doug was always ready to go. When he got sick, it was almost a relief. And yet, I was shut out of the trust."

"How often did you pretend to be the Valkyrie?"

"Many times." Her lips curled. "Rowan was such a mess after his father died. Really, the whole illness disgusted him. And Doug's dragged on and on. That man fought to the bitter end. He'd have sold his soul for one more breath of air. Rowan could barely stand to be in the same room with Doug once the cancer really took hold. But Doug kept asking Rowan to bring him his Viking history books and pieces of the collection. I was surprised he didn't ask to be buried with the whole lot."

Louisa was too. Maybe he'd wanted to leave the objects for his sons. The sons that Vivian destroyed.

Vivian continued. "Rowan told me over and over again that he'd rather be dead than sick. After Doug finally kicked, Rowan went right over the edge. He started spending hours in the study with Doug's Viking collection and books. Hours turned into days. Rowan became obsessed. All he could talk about was how the Vikings were right. I merely took advantage of the opportunity. I even let the live-in help go so I'd have no witnesses."

"You preyed on his grief?" Louisa couldn't contain her disgust.

"It wasn't hard. His grief was compounded by the favoritism Doug always showed to Asher. All I had to do was nurture Rowan's jealousy. He was his only real son, but Doug and Asher were more alike." And now Vivian's eyes glowed with insanity. Maybe it was a family thing. But Louisa couldn't help but notice that Vivian's hands weren't as shaky as they'd been before.

"Why not just take the money Rowan offered?"

"I've been dependent on someone else for fifteen years. I had to ask Doug for every penny. I had no money of my own. And after I put in all these years, nursing him through chemo with my own health problems, I end up with nothing." Her face went stop-sign red. "Do you think I want to spend the rest of my life begging my stepson for every nickel?" The question must have been rhetorical because Vivian kept going. "I started planting suggestions, and he started following them."

"Did you tell him to kill those other people besides Asher?"

"Not specifically. The weird burial ritual was all his. If only he had just followed my suggestions without embellishing. My plan would have worked perfectly. Rowan would have killed Asher and a few other people. Then he would have committed suicide." Vivian seemed proud, and her hands were rock-steady as she smoothed her hair.

"You're not as sick as you've been acting, are you?"

Vivian smiled. "No. But the new medication I was prescribed has a useful side effect. It causes hallucinations."

"And you gave it to Rowan."

Vivian's smile was full of pride.

Evil with a capital E.

"When you called and asked to meet me, I had a feeling you were up to something. You are too smart for your own good." Vivian shifted, her hand sliding into the couch cushions. "Now I'm afraid I'll have to kill you."

Before Vivian could level the gun at her, Louisa knocked it out of her hand. The punch was pure reflex. Louisa's fist hit Vivian right in the face. Vivian's head snapped back, and she put both hands over her face. Blood ran from her nose.

Vivian lurched for the gun on the floor, but Louisa kicked it aside and stepped on her hand. "Oh, I don't think so."

Pinned, Vivian crumpled to the floor.

Louisa pulled her phone from her pocket and spoke into it. "You can come in now."

But her instructions weren't necessary. Jackson and three uniformed officers rushed through the front door. Jackson looked panicked. He exhaled as he directed the officers toward Vivian. Louisa moved her foot, and Vivian curled into herself, cradling her hand in her lap.

In a few moments, Vivian was handcuffed and escorted out the door to a waiting squad car. Jackson laid a search warrant on the coffee table then turned back to Louisa. "Are you all right?"

"Yes." Louisa inspected her knuckles.

"Nice shot, Dr. Hancock." Jackson looked like he was working hard not to laugh.

"I can't believe I punched her in the face." Not that the woman had stood a chance. Even if Vivian's Parkinson's disease wasn't as bad as she pretended, the woman was rail-thin, and Louisa had never felt stronger. Boxing with Conor had sharpened her reflexes.

"I can't believe she pulled a gun on you. I never would have agreed to this if I thought you were in any danger. She weighs like eighty pounds." He swept a hand over his head. "This is crazy."

"What will you charge her with?" Louisa flexed her fingers. Her knuckles were sore. They'd probably be bruised tomorrow, but the sting was shamefully satisfying.

"Thankfully, that is the prosecutor's problem." Jackson turned as a uniform came down the steps.

"Detective Jackson." The uniform lifted a clear garment bag containing the Viking costume. A long sword gleamed in his other hand. Along with the drugs, a long blond wig, a sword, and a period gown had been all Vivian had needed to spark the delusions in her stepson. "We found it in her closet, just like Dr. Hancock said we would."

Louisa wished she'd been wrong.

"How did you know?"

"Rowan kept talking about what the Valkyrie had said to him in his dreams, and I remembered seeing a photo of Mr. and Mrs. Banks in Viking costumes down in the study. The incident in the warehouse was chaos. It wasn't until later, when I was thinking about everything he'd said, that I figured it out."

Jackson left the room and came back with the photo, holding it in gloved hands. "I'll be damned."

"That's where I got the idea to dress up as the Valkyrie to try and persuade Rowan to give up. I wish it had worked." Louisa still couldn't accept the fact that she'd killed a man. It seemed surreal.

"It sounds like it did, just not exactly the way you wanted." Jackson retrieved her coat.

"I suppose you're right," she said. "I wish I hadn't had to kill him. In a way, he was a victim too."

"Vivian is one greedy bitch. A four-million-dollar house wasn't enough for her. She had to have it all." Jackson shook his head. "But there wasn't anything you could have done about that. If you hadn't killed him, you, your father, Conor, and my partner might all be dead."

"I know." Her brain connected all the important dots but the picture was still ugly. "I wish none of it had happened."

"Don't we all," Jackson agreed. "Thank you for your help." He held her coat open for her. "I didn't know you had it in you."

"I'm getting much better at lying," Louisa said.

"That makes me all sorts of uncomfortable." Jackson ushered her toward the door. "I'll have an officer drive you back to the museum. Try to stay out of trouble for a little while, Dr. Hancock."

CHAPTER
45

Two days later.

Conor surveyed the barroom. Even after the broken glass had been cleaned up, Sullivan's was a disaster. His head still wasn't a hundred percent, but as long as he didn't move too quickly, he didn't fall over.

"Conor, what do you want me to do with this?" Jordan held up a bullet-riddled speaker.

"Looks like trash to me." Conor jerked a thumb toward the back door. "Toss it."

Across the room, Tyler and Yvonne sorted other broken items. Most would have to be discarded.

Next to them, Shawn lifted a broken mirror and carried it toward the back door. Yvonne could hardly keep her eyes off of him. The best surprise of the morning had been when he'd shown up at the back door of Sullivan's. Since Orion Turner was dead, Shawn had risked coming clean with the police. Orion had tried to make him execute the Big K member, but Shawn had run. He'd heard the shot and assumed Turner had killed the man. Shawn hadn't paused to look back. He'd managed to outrun Turner, and he'd been hiding since. The city still wasn't safe for him, but as long as Sullivan's windows were boarded up, no one knew he was here.

Conor crossed the bloodstained planks toward the booth where Ward sat with a stack of paperwork. Beneath the table, Kirra curled around the pit bull pup. Since they'd brought him home from the vet, she'd adopted him.

Ward looked up from the insurance forms they'd asked him to review. Conor knew exactly what was in those papers, but Ward needed to be needed. Physically, he was fine. His hand wasn't broken, just sprained, and the bumps and bruises he'd suffered would be healed in no time. But his soul had been damaged. Conor could see the wounds in his eyes.

"Have you decided what you're going to do with him?" Ward asked, reaching under the table to pet the dogs.

"It looks like Kirra wants to keep him." Conor went down on one knee and gave each dog a rub.

"Those scars on his face look like they'll be permanent." Ward frowned.

"We don't mind." Conor watched the pup's thin tail thump on the floor. "It's amazing he can be so sweet after what was done to him."

Tyler flew across the room and skidded on his knees to Conor's side. "Have you picked a name?"

"Nope. Louisa might have something in mind. She's good at picking names. Why? What do you think we should call him?"

"Lucky." Tyler stroked the pup's side. Kirra gave the boy's arm a nose flip.

"It looks like Kirra wants some attention too." Conor laughed.

"No problem. I have two hands," Tyler said in a happy voice.

"I think Lucky is a great name," Louisa said from the doorway.

Conor stood and crossed the room to kiss her on the lips.

She touched his cheek. "You're supposed to be resting."

He grinned at her. "You're sexy when you're bossy."

"You are not ready for *that* much activity yet." Louisa laughed.

"Want to make a bet?" He curled an arm around her waist, and he tugged her into the hallway for a closer embrace. She would have more nightmares. No question. But he'd be there to hold her.

"I didn't mean that you couldn't," she said, because he obviously *could*. "Only that you shouldn't."

He leaned close to her ear. "I promise to let you do all the work."

Her responding giggle made his heart do an Irish jig. She pushed off his chest. "How's the head?"

"It's fine," he lied. It was *almost* fine. "How was work?"

"Good. Normal." She was dressed in jeans and a sweatshirt. She'd obviously come to help. "How's my dad?"

"OK, considering."

"He's going to see my therapist," Louisa said. "That's a good sign, right?"

"Yes." He kissed her again. "And we'll be there for him."

They were all going to need time to recover from the horrors of the previous week.

"Hello? Is everybody decent in here?" His little brother, Danny, stood in the kitchen, one hand over his eyes.

Conor crossed the room and enveloped him in a hug. "It's damned good to see you."

"Back atcha, big brother." Danny looped an arm over Conor's shoulder. Together the three of them walked into the main room. Danny stepped away and turned in a slow circle, surveying the damage. "You really know how to throw a party."

"Sullivan's needed a remodel anyway." Conor was all for seeing the bright side these days. "Have you been to the hospital to see Pat?"

"Just came from there. He looked like shit but better than I expected." Of course Danny would see Pat the second he hit town. "I wish I could have come sooner. It sucks being so far away."

"Barring a major ice storm, a nine-hour drive isn't so bad."

"It felt really far this time," Danny said. "I don't know if I ever told you this, but you and Pat are more like my parents."

"Do not start telling people you have two dads," Conor joked.

Danny punched Conor's shoulder. "Seriously. I'm sorry for being a giant pain in your ass for so many years."

Conor gave him another hug. "I forgive you. Now get to work."

"I almost forgot. Mandy and I have finally set the date. We wanted to tell you on FaceTime over the weekend, but we've given up on waiting for things to be perfect."

"Congratulations." Louisa gave him a kiss on the cheek. "When's the big day?"

"We were going to do it in June, but now Jayne has screwed that up by being due about then. As long as it's OK with Jayne and Reed, we're doing it in August."

"Excellent." Conor patted his brother on the back. "I'd pop a bottle of champagne if I could find one. Pat stashed a bottle of scotch somewhere. I could look for it."

"Rain check," Danny said. "But you should find the bottle before Pat is up to drinking it. Scotch is not his friend."

"Amen."

Danny scanned the room and nodded toward Yvonne and her boys. "Are those the people you wanted me to meet?"

"They are." Conor waved Yvonne over. "I want you to meet my brother Danny."

Conor made the introductions.

"Conor says you need to leave town." Danny shook Yvonne's hand.

Yvonne brushed some wallboard dust off her cheek. "I don't know what we're going to do yet."

"My fiancée and I own an inn in Maine. We've expanded into a full restaurant recently. We can offer you a job."

Yvonne looked stunned, then ashamed. "How would we get there? Where would we live? We don't have any money."

"Don't sweat the details, just consider the offer. It'll be a lot of hard work, and the town isn't exciting, but I can promise you, there aren't any gangs."

"Thank you. I have to talk it over with my boys but . . ." Her eyes filled with tears. "Just thank you."

The rest of the evening passed quickly. Conor let Louisa bully him into going home early. He wouldn't admit it to her, but his ass was dragging.

Danny was staying at Pat's to spend some time with the littlest Sullivans.

Conor and Louisa went back to the condo. They fed and walked the dogs, then Kirra and Lucky curled up together on the sofa.

"Danny reminded me today that life is always changing. Waiting for something to be perfect is pointless." Conor took Louisa by the hand and tugged her into the bedroom. He pulled out the velvet jewelry box from his drawer.

A ridiculous amount of nerves jolted him as he opened the box. They loved each other. This should be simple, right? But instead it felt like the most monumental event of his life.

Which it was, he realized. This one question would change everything.

He took a moment to look into her eyes, to savor the love he saw in them, mirroring what he felt in his own heart.

"I was waiting for things to settle down, but who knows how long that will be." He dropped to one knee. "I love you more than anything in the world. I want to spend the rest of my life with you. You are the most amazing woman I have ever known. Will you marry me, Louisa Hancock?"

Louisa burst into tears.

Well, *that* wasn't what he'd expected.

He stood and wrapped his arms around her. "What's wrong?"

"Nothing," she sobbed.

"So you're crying because . . ."

"Because I'm happy." Louisa swiped a fingertip below her lashes. "Yes. I'll marry you. I don't know why you think life can never be perfect. This is pretty perfect. *You're* perfect." She took his face in both her hands. "I love you, Conor Sullivan, more than I ever thought it was possible to love another person."

He wrapped her in his arms and held her close. "You are everything to me."

Had he ever been happier? Not that he could remember. His hand dropped to her hip and he pulled her against him harder.

"*You* have a concussion." She gave him her disapproving school-teacher look, which was hotter than hell.

"I promise to lay very still." Conor put on his most serious face.

And there was that haughty eyebrow he found to be such a turn-on. "Is that so?"

Conor took her hand and led her toward the bedroom. "You'll have to do all the work."

Maybe not *all* of it.

He tugged her down onto the bed on top of him. Her long blond hair fell in a wave to brush his shoulder.

"There's nothing I wouldn't do for you." She kissed him.

And Conor's world felt pretty damned perfect.

THE END

ACKNOWLEDGMENTS

As always, credit goes to my agent Jill Marsal, and to the entire team at Montlake Romance, especially my managing editor Anh Schluep, developmental editor Charlotte Herscher, and author herder/tech goddess Jessica Poore.

Special thanks to my husband for doing everything else that needed to get done so I could write this book.

ABOUT THE AUTHOR

WSJ bestselling author Melinda Leigh abandoned her career in banking to raise her kids and never looked back. She started writing as a hobby, but soon she found her true calling creating characters and stories. Her debut novel, *She Can Run*, was a #1 Kindle bestseller in Romantic Suspense, a 2011 Best Book Finalist in *The Romance Reviews*, and a nominee for the 2012 International Thriller Award for Best First Book. She is also a RITA© nominee, a three-time Daphne du Maurier Award finalist, and the winner of the Golden Leaf Award. When she isn't writing, Melinda is an avid martial artist: she holds a second-degree black belt in Kenpo karate and teaches women's self-defense. She lives in a messy house with her husband, two teenagers, a couple of dogs, and two rescue cats.